# CHINESE FAIRY TALES

# AND

# LEGENDS

# CHINESE FAIRY TALES AND LEGENDS

Richard Wilhelm & Frederick H. Martens

BLOOMSBURY CHINA
LONDON · OXFORD · NEW YORK · NEW DELHI · SYDNEY

BLOOMSBURY CHINA
Bloomsbury Publishing Plc
50 Bedford Square, London, WC1B 3DP, UK
29 Earlsfort Terrace, Dublin 2, Ireland

BLOOMSBURY, BLOOMSBURY CHINA and the Diana logo
are trademarks of Bloomsbury Publishing Plc

First published in Great Britain 2019

A catalogue record for this book is available from the British Library

Library of Congress Cataloguing-in-Publication data has been applied for

ISBN: TPB: 978-1-9123-9215-5; eBook: 978-1-9123-9214-8

10

Typeset by Deanta Global Publishing Services, Chennai, India
Printed and bound in Great Britain by CPI Group (UK) Ltd. Croydon, CRO 4YY

To find out more about our authors and books visit www.bloomsbury.com
and sign up for our newsletter

# Contents

# Introduction

**M**any thousands of years ago, when peoples in the West looked to the night sky and saw a Milky Way, the Chinese saw a Silver River. And, on either side, they saw two stars shining brightly, the Cowherd and the Weaving Girl.

On one night of the year – the seventh day of the seventh lunar month – these two stars are at their closest in the night sky. And this is the moment when magpies flock to form a bridge across the sky so that the starry lovers may reunite. That's the way the story goes, and it's a story which was already popular when first written down 2,600 years ago, and which remains much loved to this day.

It's the inspiration for the Qixi Festival, a celebration of love that is centuries older than Valentine's Day. And just in recent years, it has been remembered in a communications satellite called *Queqiao*, or 'Magpie Bridge'.

That's the thing about folk tales and fairy tales and legends; they're not fossils, not the final traces of cultures long past. They're still with us, still part of us, accumulating new details — details that will carry across time.

Even as we wonder at the fantasies collected here in *Chinese Fairy Tales and Legends*, we will catch a glimpse of the peoples who told them, the details of their lives.

The Yellow River cradled Chinese civilisation and here are stories of the gods and spirits who sometimes turned monstrous, bursting the riverbanks and bringing floods. We read of the temples built to honour them, the plays performed.

Then come new gods, new philosophies. Buddha, Confucius, the *Tao* of Laotsze emerge, in stories that offer us legendary details while also insisting on facts. Chinese storytelling likes to ground itself in actual events, so we are told that this story took place at the time of the Emperor Ming Di, and that story took place during the first days of the Tang dynasty.

Perhaps we should expect as much: China is a culture with records dating back thousands of years. The earliest form of writing leaves us records from the second millenium BCE, so the stories we read are often stories reflecting known history. We see the scars of warfare as well as the stability that peace brings. Now there are mandarins, now magistrates, and here comes trade and contacts with foreign peoples along the Silk Road.

What is remarkable about so many of these stories is how often justice is served, even for those with no status. Snow White, that favourite of the West, is a princess, and Cinderella the daughter of a rich man. By contrast, Chinese tales give us slave girls winning their freedom; poor men earning rewards; children spared from abusive parents. In a culture that insists on the obligations owed by children to their parents, that's storytelling with a radical edge.

Setting these stories in front of a Western audience was a similar act of defiance. The year of its initial publication, 1917, was just one more year in the period the Chinese now call the century of humiliation. Between 1839 and 1949 their country fragmented under attack from foreign powers: the Austro-Hungarian Empire, the British Empire, Germany, France, Russia, Italy, the United States and Japan all imposed themselves. Fear of the 'Yellow Peril' was still a respectable philosophy and anti-Chinese sentiment still strong.

Richard Wilhelm, the editor of *Chinese Fairy Tales and Legends*, had lived in China for 25 years — and fallen in love with the people. Theirs, he insisted, was a culture worth celebrating, and he was one of the first to introduce their literature to the West.

He had travelled to the country as a missionary but was quick to recognise the value of the spiritual and philosophical traditions he encountered. In fact, in later years he would be proud to admit that he baptised not one single person into the Christian Church. He spent ten years translating the *I Ching* (*Book of Changes*), and his version, finally published in 1923, is still considered the best.

In Frederick H. Martens, Wilhelm had a sympathetic collaborator, who would go on to translate the fairy tales of other cultures. His English translation appeared in 1921, just four years after the US Immigration Act specifically barred immigration from Asia and at a time when the Chinese population in Britain was viewed with suspicion.

That a political dimension underlay Wilhelm's enthusiasm is not in doubt. In seeking to bridge the divide between East and West, he was also seeking an ally. Wilhelm was a German taking a stand against a West dominated by the English-speaking peoples.

We see this in some of his Notes to the fairy tales. He is keen to emphasise links, often spiritual links, to India. This was in line with Indo-European studies, developed during the nineteenth century, which located India as the source of a common heritage across Eurasia. Thus links between India and China were ultimately links between East and West, between cultures that were not only far more ancient than the Anglo-Saxons but also the source of universal truths — ways of thinking constant across cultures and across time.

To an extent, it's a point of view that dates Wilhelm, not the least because archaeological evidence reveals China itself to have been one of the cradles of humanity. The first peoples emerged here almost two million years ago, and along the Yellow and Yangtze rivers we find the traces of peoples from prehistory. Peoples who told their own stories about the sun and the moon and the stars, and the Silver River separating the Cowherd and the Weaving Maiden.

# Original Preface
# by Frederick H. Martens

The fairy tales and legends of olden China have in common with the 'One Thousand and One Nights' an oriental glow and glitter of precious stones and gold and multicoloured silks, an oriental wealth of fantastic and supernatural action. And yet they strike an exotic note distinct in itself. The seventy-three stories here presented after original sources, embracing Nursery Fairy Tales, Legends of the Gods, Tales of Saints and Magicians, Nature and Animal Tales, Ghost Stories, Historic Fairy Tales and Literary Fairy Tales, probably represent the most comprehensive and varied collection of oriental fairy tales ever made available for American readers. There is no child who will not enjoy their novel colour, their fantastic beauty, their infinite variety of subject. Yet, like the 'Arabian Nights', they will amply repay the attention of the older reader as well. Some are exquisitely poetic, such as 'The Flower-Elves', 'The Lady of the Moon' or 'The Cowherd and the Weaving Maiden'; others like 'How Three Heroes Came By Their Deaths Because Of Two Peaches' carry us back dramatically and powerfully to the Chinese Age of Chivalry. The summits of fantasy are scaled in the quasi-religious dramas of 'The Ape Sun Wu Kung' and 'Notscha', or the weird sorceries unfolded by 'The Kindly Magician'. Delightful ghost stories, with happy endings, such as 'A Night on the Battlefield' and 'The Ghost Who Was Foiled', are paralleled with such idyllic love-tales as that of 'Rose of Evening', or such Lilliputian fancies as 'The King of the Ants' and 'The Little Hunting Dog'. It is quite safe to say that these Chinese fairy tales will give equal pleasure to the old as well as the young. They have been retold simply, with no changes in style or expression beyond such details of presentation which differences between Eastern and Western viewpoints at times compel. It is the writer's hope that others may take as much pleasure in reading them as he did in their translation.

*Frederick H. Martens*

# NURSERY
# FAIRY TALES

# 1

# Women's Words Part Flesh and Blood

**This story, which features two brothers who have very different personalities and a mythological talking bird called a roc, is about knowing when enough is enough.**

O nce upon a time there were two brothers, who lived in the same house. The older brother listened to his wife's words, and fell out with his little brother. Summer had begun, and the time for sowing the high-growing millet had come. The little man had no grain, and asked to be loaned some, so the elder brother ordered his wife to give it to him. But she took the grain, put it in a large pot and cooked it until it was done. Then she gave it to the little fellow. Not realising what she had done, he went and sowed his field with it. Yet, since the grain had been cooked, it did not sprout. Only a single grain of seed had not been cooked; so only a single sprout shot up. The little brother was hard-working and industrious by nature, and he watered and hoed the sprout all day long. The sprout grew mightily, like a tree, and an ear of millet sprang up out of it like a canopy, large enough to shade half an acre of ground. By the autumn the ear was ripe. Then the little brother took his axe and chopped it down. No sooner had the ear fallen to the ground than an enormous roc came rushing down, took the ear in his beak and flew away. The little brother ran after him as far as the shore of the sea.

Then the bird turned and spoke to him with a human voice: 'Don't try harm to me! What is this one ear worth to you? East of the sea is the isle of gold and silver. I will carry you across. There you may take whatever you want and become very rich.'

Satisfied, the little brother climbed on the bird's back, and the latter told him to close his eyes. So he heard only the air whistling past his ears, as though he were driving through a strong wind, and beneath him the roar and surge of flood and waves. Suddenly the bird settled on a rock: 'Here we are!' he said.

The little brother opened his eyes and looked about him: and on all sides he saw nothing but the radiance and shimmer of all sorts of silver and gold objects. He took about a dozen of the little things and hid them in his breast.

'Have you enough?' asked the roc.

'Yes, I have enough,' he replied.

'That is just as well,' answered the bird. 'Moderation protects one from harm.'

With that, he once more took him up and carried him back. When the little brother reached home, he bought himself a good piece of ground in the course of time and became quite well-to-do.

His brother was jealous of him, and asked him harshly: 'Where did you manage to steal the money?'

The little man told him the whole truth. Then the elder brother went home and took counsel with his wife.

'Nothing easier,' said his wife. 'I will just cook grain again and keep back one seedling so that it is not done. Then you shall sow it, and we shall see what happens.'

No sooner said than done. And sure enough, a single sprout shot up, and sure enough, the sprout bore a single ear of millet, and when harvest time came around, the roc again appeared and carried it off in his beak. The big brother was pleased, and ran after him, and the roc said the same thing he had said before, and carried the big brother to the island. There the big brother saw gold and silver heaped up everywhere. The largest pieces were like hills, the small ones like bricks, and the real tiny ones like grains of sand. They blinded his eyes. His one regret was that he knew no way to move mountains. So he bent down and picked up as many pieces as possible.

The roc said: 'That's enough. You will overburden yourself.'

'Be patient just a little while longer,' said the elder brother. 'Don't be in such a hurry! I must get a few more pieces!'

And so time passed.

Again the roc urged him to hurry: 'The sun will appear in a moment,' said he, 'and the sun is so hot it burns humans up.'

'Wait just a little while longer,' said the elder brother. At that very moment a red disc broke through the clouds with a ferocious power. The Toc flew into the sea, stretched out both his wings, and beat the water with them in order to escape the heat. But the elder brother was shrivelled up by the sun.

# 2

# The Three Rhymesters

**A doctor and a lawyer set out to embarrass an uneducated farmer by challenging him to a rhyming game. But who can come up with the best verse and who will have to eat their words?**

Once upon a time, there were three daughters in a family. The oldest one married a physician; the second one married a magistrate; but the third, who was more than usually intelligent and a clever talker, married a farmer.

Now it chanced, one day, that their parents were celebrating a birthday. So the three daughters came, together with their husbands, to wish them long life and happiness. The parents-in-law prepared a meal for their three sons-in-law and put birthday wine on the table. But the oldest son-in-law, who knew that the third one had not attended school, wanted to embarrass him.

'It is far too boring,' said he, 'just to sit here drinking: let's have a drinking game. Each of us must invent a verse, one that rhymes and makes sense, structured around the words: "in the sky, on the earth, at the table, in the room". Whoever cannot do so, must empty three glasses as a punishment.'

All the company were satisfied. Only the third son-in-law felt embarrassed and insisted on leaving. But the guests refused to let him, obliging him to keep his seat.

The oldest son-in-law began: 'I will make a start with my verse. Here it is:

In the sky the phoenix proudly flies,
On the earth the lambkin tamely lies,
At the table through an ancient book I wade,
In the room I softly call the maid.'

The second one continued: 'And I say:

In the sky the turtle dove flies round,
On the earth the ox paws up the ground,
At the table one studies the deeds of yore,
In the room the maid she sweeps the floor.'

But the third son-in-law stuttered, and found nothing to say. And when all of them insisted, he broke out in rough tones of voice:

'In the sky – flies a leaden bullet,
On the earth – stalks a tiger beast,
On the table – lies a pair of scissors,
In the room – I call the stable boy.'

The other two sons-in-law clapped their hands and began to laugh loudly. 'Why, your four lines do not rhyme at all,' said they, 'and, besides, they do not make sense. A leaden bullet is no bird, the stable boy does his work outside, why would you call him into the room? Nonsense, nonsense! Drink!'

Yet even before they had finished, the third daughter raised the curtain of the women's room, and stepped out. Though angry, she could not suppress a smile.

'How do our lines not make sense?' said she. 'Listen a moment, and I'll explain them to you: In the sky our leaden bullet will shoot your phoenix and your turtle dove. On the earth our tiger beast will devour your sheep and your ox. On the table our pair of scissors will cut up all your old books. And finally, in the room – well, the stable boy can marry your maid!'

'Point taken!' said the oldest son-in-law. 'A fair rebuke! Sister-in-law, you know how to talk! If you were a man you would have completed your degree long ago. And, as a punishment, we will empty our three glasses.'

# 3

# How Greed for a Trifling Thing Led a Man to Lose a Great One

**Sons traditionally look after their parents when they're old. Here we meet two brothers, one who takes good care of his mother and one who doesn't. Which is which, though?**

Once upon a time there was an old woman, who had two sons. But her older son did not love his parents, and left his mother and brother. The younger one served her so faithfully, however, that all the people spoke of it.

One day, a theatrical troupe arrived to give a performance outside the village. The younger son started to carry his mother there on his back, so that she might see it. But there was a ravine before the village, and he slipped and fell. His mother was killed by the rolling stones, her blood and flesh splashed everywhere. Stroking his mother's corpse, the son wept bitterly, and was about to kill himself.

Suddenly, standing before him was a priest, who said: 'Have no fear! I can bring your mother back to life!' Gathering up her flesh and bones, he laid them together as they should be. Then he breathed upon them, and at once the mother was alive again. This made the son very happy, and he fell to his knees to thank the priest. Yet on a sharp point of rock he still saw a bit of his mother's flesh hanging, a bit about an inch long.

'That should not be left hanging there either,' he said, and hid it in his breast.

'In truth, you love your mother as a son should,' said the priest. Then he bade the son give him the bit of flesh, kneaded a manikin out of it, breathed upon it, and in a minute there it stood, a really fine-looking little boy.

'His name is Small Profit,' said he, turning to the son, 'and you may call him brother. You are poor and have not the means to nourish your mother. Now if you need something, Small Profit can get it for you.'

The son thanked him once more, took his mother on his back again and his new little brother by the hand, and went home. And when he said to Small Profit: 'Bring meat and wine!', then meat and wine were at hand at once, and steaming rice was already cooking in the pot. And when he said to Small Profit: 'Bring money and cloth!', then his purse filled itself with money, and the chests were heaped up with cloth to the brim. Whatever he asked for, he received. Thus, in the course of time, they came to be very well off indeed.

His older brother was highly envious. And when there was another theatrical performance in the village, he forced his mother onto his back and set off. And when he reached the ravine, he slipped purposely, letting his mother fall into the depths and intending only to see that she was shattered into fragments. Sure enough, his mother had such a bad fall that her limbs and trunk were strewn around in all directions. He climbed down, took his mother's head in his hands, and pretended to weep.

At once the priest was on hand again, and said: 'I can wake the dead to life again, and surround white bones with flesh and blood!'

He did as he had done before, and the mother came to life again. But the older brother had hidden one of her ribs on purpose. Pulling it out, he said to the priest: 'Here is a bone left. What shall I do with it?'

The priest took the bone, enclosed it in lime and earth, breathed upon it, as he had done the other time, and it became a little man, resembling Small Profit, but larger in stature.

'His name is Great Duty,' he told the older brother. 'If you stick to him, he will always lend you a hand.'

The son took his mother back again, and Great Duty walked beside him.

When he came to their courtyard door, he saw his younger brother coming out, holding Small Profit in his arms.

'Where are you going?' he said to him.

His brother answered: 'Small Profit is a divine being, who does not wish to dwell for all time among men. He wants to fly back to the heavens, and so I am escorting him.'

'Give Small Profit to me! Don't let him get away!' cried the older brother.

Yet, before he had ended his speech, Small Profit was rising in the air. The older brother immediately let his mother drop on the ground, and stretched out his hand to catch Small Profit. But he did not succeed, and now Great Duty, too, rose from the ground, took Small Profit's hand, and together they ascended to the clouds and disappeared.

The older brother stamped on the ground, and said with a sigh: 'Alas, I have lost my Great Duty because I was too greedy for that Small Profit!'

*Note: Traditionally, the duty of every adult son to look after his parents includes not just financial support but also the day-to-day care essential when parents are no longer able to care for themselves.*

# 4

# Who was the Sinner?

**As in many cultures, in China lightning is sometimes seen as an expression of divine wrath. In this story, a farmer finds out that when it strikes his fate hangs on what happens to his hat.**

Once upon a time there were ten farmers, who were crossing a field together. Surprised by a heavy thunderstorm, they took refuge in a half-ruined temple. But the thunder drew nearer and nearer, and so great was the tumult that the air trembled about them as the lightning circled the temple. Terrified, the farmers thought that there must be a sinner among them, and that he was the target the lightning intended to strike. To identify the sinner, they hung their straw hats up before the door – and agreed that the man whose hat was blown away would yield himself up to his fate.

No sooner were the hats outside than one of them was blown away, and the unfortunate owner was pushed out of doors without pity. As soon as he had left the temple, the lightning ceased circling and struck it with a crash.

The man thrown out by the rest had been the only righteous one among them, and for his sake the lightning had spared the temple. The other nine paid for the hard-heartedness with their lives.

The ancient Chinese worshipped many deities
and believed several different gods came together
to create a storm, including Baoshen, the Hail God.

# 5

# The Magic Cask

**In China, casks or barrels for holding liquids were made of stone, not wood, and they didn't have lids. The cask in this tale, however, also has amazing magical powers.**

Once upon a time there was a man who dug up a big, earthenware cask in his field. So he took it home with him and told his wife to clean it out. But when his wife started brushing the inside of the cask, the cask suddenly began to fill itself with brushes. No matter how many brushes she took out, others kept taking their place. So the man sold the brushes, and the family managed to live quite comfortably.

It so happened that a coin fell into the cask by mistake. At once the brushes disappeared and the cask began to fill itself with money. So now the family became rich; for they could take as much money out of the cask as ever they wished.

Now the man had an old grandfather at home, who was weak and shaky. Since there was nothing else he could do, his grandson set him to work shovelling money out of the cask, and when the old grandfather grew weary and could not keep on, the young man would fall into a rage, and shout at him angrily, telling him he was lazy and did not want to work. One day, however, the old man's strength gave out, and he fell into the cask and died. At once the money disappeared, and the cask began to fill itself with dead grandfathers. Then the man had to pull them all out and have them buried, and for this purpose he had to use up again all the money he had received. And when he was through, the cask broke, and he was just as poor as before.

# 6

# The Favourite of Fortune and the Child of Bad Luck

**Luck is very important in Chinese culture. Unfortunately, the princess in this story is cursed by being a 'child of bad luck', but fortunately she has a plan to change all that. Will she succeed?**

Once upon a time there was a proud prince who had a daughter. But the daughter was a child of bad luck. When it came time for her to marry, she had all her suitors assemble before her father's palace. Her plan was to throw down a ball of red silk among them, and whoever caught it would be her husband. Many princes and counts gathered before the castle, and among them was also a beggar. The princess could see dragons crawling into his ears and crawling out again from his nostrils, for he was a child of luck. So she threw the ball to the beggar and he caught it.

Her father asked angrily: 'Why did you throw the ball into the beggar's hands?'

'He is a favourite of fortune,' said the princess. 'I will marry him, and then, perhaps, I will share in his good luck.'

But her father would not hear of it, and since she insisted, he drove her from the castle in his rage. So the princess had to leave with the beggar. She dwelt with him in a little hut, and had to hunt for herbs and roots and cook them herself, so that they might have something to eat; and often they both went hungry. One day her husband said to her: 'I will set out and seek my fortune. And when I have found it, I will come back again and fetch you.' The princess was willing, and he went away, and was gone for eighteen years. Meanwhile the princess lived in want and affliction, for her father remained hard and merciless. If her mother had not secretly given her food and money, there is no doubt she would have starved to death.

But the beggar found his fortune, and at length became emperor. He returned and stood before his wife. She, however, no longer recognised him. She knew only that he was the powerful emperor.

He asked her how she was getting along

'Why do you ask me how I am getting along?' she replied. 'I am too far beneath your notice.'

'And who may your husband be!'

'My husband was a beggar. He went away to seek his fortune. That was eighteen years ago, and he has not yet returned.'

'And what have you done during all those long years?'

'I have been waiting for him to return.'

'Do you wish to marry someone else, seeing that he has been missing so long?'

'No, I will remain his wife until I die.'

When the emperor saw how faithful his wife was, he told her who he was, had her clothed in magnificent garments, and took her with him to his imperial palace. And there they lived in splendour and happiness.

After a few days the emperor said to his wife: 'We spend every day in festivities, as though every day were New Year.'

'And why should we not celebrate,' answered his wife, 'since we have now become emperor and empress?'

Yet his wife was a child of bad luck. She had been empress no more than eighteen days when she fell sick and died. But her husband lived for many a long year.

*Notes: The dragon is the symbol of imperial rule, and the New Year's feast, celebrated by old and young for weeks, is the greatest of Chinese festivals.*

*This story reminds us that changing your luck may not be possible.*

# 7

# The Bird with Nine Heads

**The Bird with Nine Heads probably comes from the symbol of the kingdom of Chu in central China. Here it's a monster which carries off a princess – and the king wants her back.**

Long, long ago, there lived a king and a queen who had a daughter. One day, the daughter was walking in the garden when a powerful storm suddenly came up and carried her away. Now the storm had come from the bird with nine heads, who had stolen the princess and brought her to his cave. The king, desperate to know where his daughter had disappeared, proclaimed throughout the land: 'Whoever brings back the princess may have her for his bride!'

Now, a young man had seen the bird carrying the princess to his cave. The cave, though, was in the middle of a sheer wall of rock. No one could climb up to it from below or climb down to it from above. As the young man was walking around the rock, another youth came along and asked him what he was doing there. The young man told him that the bird with nine heads had carried off the king's daughter and brought her up to his cave. The youth knew exactly what to do: he called together his friends, and they lowered him to the cave in a basket. In the cave he saw the king's daughter sitting there, washing the wound of the bird with nine heads; for the hound of heaven had bitten off his tenth head, and the wound was still bleeding. The princess motioned to the youth to hide, and he did. When the king's daughter had washed his wound and bandaged it, the bird with nine heads felt so comfortable that one after another all his nine heads fell asleep. Then the youth stepped forth from his hiding-place and cut off his nine heads with a sword. But the king's daughter said: 'It would be best if you were hauled up first, and I came after.'

'No,' said the youth. 'I will wait below here, until you are in safety.' At first the king's daughter was not willing; yet at last she allowed herself to be persuaded and climbed into the basket. But before she did so, she took a long pin from her hair and broke it into two halves, giving him one and keeping the other. She also divided her silk handkerchief with him, and told him to take good care of both her gifts. But when the young man had drawn up the king's daughter, he left with her, abandoning the youth in the cave, in spite of all his calling and pleading.

The youth now took a walk about the cave. There he saw the bodies of a number of maidens, who had all been carried off by the bird with nine heads and died there of hunger. On the wall hung a fish, attached with four nails. He touched the fish, who turned into a handsome youth and thanked him for delivering him. The two now agreed to look on each other as brothers. Soon the first youth grew very hungry. He stepped out in front of the cave to search for food, but only stones were lying there. Suddenly, he saw a great dragon, who was licking a stone. The youth imitated him, and before long his hunger had disappeared. Next he asked the dragon how to get away from the cave. The dragon nodded his head in the direction of his tail, as much as to say 'Sit yourself down.' The youth climbed up, and in the twinkling of an eye he was down on the ground, and the dragon had disappeared. He went on his way until he found a tortoise shell full of beautiful pearls. These were magic pearls: throw them into the fire, and the fire ceased to burn; throw them into the water, and the water divided, letting you walk straight through. The youth took the pearls out of the tortoise shell and put them in his pocket. Not long after, he reached the seashore. He flung a pearl into the sea, and at once the waters divided and he could see the sea dragon. The sea dragon cried: 'Who is disturbing me here in my own kingdom?' The youth answered: 'I found pearls in a tortoise shell and have flung one into the sea, and now the waters have divided for me.'

'If that is the case,' said the dragon, 'come into the sea with me and we will live there together.' Then the youth recognised him as the same dragon he had seen outside the cave. And with him was someone else he recognised: the same young man who had once been a fish and was now like a brother. This was the dragon's son.

'Since you have saved my son and become his brother, I am your father,' said the old dragon. And he entertained him hospitably with food and wine.

One day his friend said to him: 'My father is sure to want to reward you. Accept no money, nor any jewels from him, but only the little gourd flask over yonder. With it you can conjure up whatever you wish.'

Sure enough, the old dragon asked him what he wanted by way of a reward, and the youth answered: 'I want no money, nor any jewels. All I want is the little gourd flask over yonder.'

At first the dragon did not wish to give it up, but at last he did let him have it. And then the youth left the dragon's castle.

As soon as he set foot on dry land again, he felt hungry. At once standing in front of him was a table, covered with a fine and plentiful meal. He ate and drank his fill. Then he continued on his way, and after a while he felt weary. There stood an ass, waiting for him to mount. After he had ridden for a while, the ass's gait seemed too uneven to continue, but along came a wagon, and onto that he climbed. But the wagon shook him up too much, and he thought to himself: 'If I only had a litter! That would suit me better.' No more had he thought so, than the litter came along, and he seated himself in it. The bearers carried him to the city where dwelt the king, the queen and their daughter.

On the day that the young man had brought back the king's daughter, a wedding was planned. But the king's daughter refused to take part, saying: 'He is not the right man. My deliverer will come and bring with him half of the long pin for my hair, and half my silk handkerchief as a token.' But when a long time had passed and he had still not appeared, the young man pressed the king, who grew impatient and declared: 'The wedding shall take place tomorrow!' Now the king's daughter went sadly through the streets of the city, searching and searching in the hope of finding her deliverer. And on that very day the litter arrived. Seeing the youth holding the half of her silk handkerchief in his hand, she was filled with joy and led him to her father. There he showed his half of the long pin, which fitted the other exactly, convincing the king that he was the right and true deliverer. The false bridegroom was now punished, the wedding celebrated, and the two lived in peace and happiness till the end of their days.

Notes: *The long hair needle is an example of the halved jewel used as a sign of recognition by lovers.*

*Gourd flasks often occur as magic talismans in Chinese fairy tales, and spirits who serve their owners are often imprisoned in them.*

*The Bird with Nine Heads probably began as the nine-headed phoenix, the totem of the Kingdom of Chu in central China. The Chu rebelled against the Zhou dynasty during the Warring States period, and their phoenix was subsequently demonised.*

# 8

# The Cave of the Beasts

**Two young girls, on a trip to their grandmother's, find themselves alone and lost in the mountains. They seek shelter in a cave and make a rather surprising and special discovery.**

Once upon a time there was a family with seven daughters. One day, when the father went out to gather wood, he found seven wild duck eggs. He brought them home but did not think of giving any to his children, intending to eat them himself, with his wife. In the evening the oldest daughter woke up and asked her mother what she was cooking. The mother said: 'I am cooking wild duck eggs. I will give you one, but you must not let your sisters know.' And she gave her one. Then the second daughter woke up, and asked her mother what she was cooking. She said: 'Wild duck eggs. If you will not tell your sisters, I'll give you one.' And so it went. At last the daughters had eaten all the eggs, and there were none left.

In the morning the father was very angry with the children, and he now asked: 'Who wants to go along to grandmother?' His plan was to lead the children into the mountains, and let the wolves devour them there. The older daughters were suspicious and said: 'We are not going along!' But the two younger ones said: 'We will go with you.' And so they drove off with their father. After they had driven a good long way, they asked: 'Will we soon get to grandmother's house?' 'Right away,' said their father. And when they had reached the mountains, he told them: 'Wait here. I will drive into the village ahead of you and tell grandmother that you are coming.' And then he drove off with the donkey cart.

The girls waited and waited, but their father did not come. At last they realised that their father would not return, and that he had left them alone in the mountains. So they went further and further into the hills, seeking a shelter for the night. They came upon a great stone, and decided they would use it for their pillow, rolling it over to where they were going to lie down to sleep. That was when they saw that the stone was the door to a cave. There was a light in the cave, so they went inside. The light came from precious stones and jewels of every sort. These belonged to a wolf and a fox, who had filled a number of jars with precious stones and pearls that shone by night. The girls said: 'What a lovely cave this is! We will lie right down and go to bed.' For there stood two golden beds with gold-embroidered covers. They lay down and fell asleep. During the night the wolf and fox came home. And the wolf said: 'I smell human flesh!' But the fox replied: 'Nonsense! No humans can enter our cave. We lock it up too well for that.' The wolf said: 'Very well, then let us lie down in our beds and sleep.' But the fox answered: 'No, let's curl up in the kettles on the hearth. They still hold a little warmth from the fire.' The one kettle was of gold and the other of silver, and they curled up in them.

When the girls rose early in the morning, they saw the wolf and the fox lying there, and were very frightened. They put the covers on the kettles and heaped a number of big stones on them, so that the wolf and the fox could not get out again. Then they made a fire. The wolf and the fox said: 'Oh, how nice and warm it is this morning! How does that happen?' But at length it grew too hot for them. Then they noticed that the two girls had kindled a fire and they cried: 'Let us out! We will give you lots of precious stones, and lots of gold, and will do you no harm!' But the girls would not listen to them and kept on making a bigger fire. So that was the end of the wolf and the fox in the kettles.

The girls lived happily for a number of days in the cave. But their father was seized with longing for his daughters, and he went into the mountains to look for them. After some time, he needed to rest and sat right down on the stone in front of the cave, tapping his pipe against it to empty the ashes. Then the girls within called out: 'Who is knocking at our door?' The father cried out: 'Are those not my daughters' voices?' The daughters replied: 'Is that not our father's voice?', and pushed aside the stone. They saw that it was their father, and their father was glad to see them once more. He was astonished that they should have chanced on this cave full of precious stones, so they told him the whole story. Then he fetched people to help him carry home the jewels. When they all returned home, his wife wondered where he had found all these treasures. The father and daughters told her everything, and they became a very wealthy family, living happily to the end of their days.

# 9

# The Panther

**Panthers rarely appear in Chinese art or literature, but this story, which is relatively modern and has echoes of Little Red Riding Hood, features a particularly sly and cunning one.**

Once upon a time there was a widow with two daughters and a little son. One day the widow said to her daughters: 'Take good care of the house, for I am going to see Grandmother, together with your little brother!' The daughters promised her they would do so, and their mother set off. On her way she met a panther, who asked where she was going.

She replied: 'I am going with my child to see my mother.'

'Will you not rest a bit?' asked the panther.

'No,' she said, 'it is already late, and it is a long road to where my mother lives.'

But the panther kept urging her to rest, and finally she gave in and sat down by the road side.

'I will comb your hair a bit,' said the panther. And the widow let him comb her hair. But as he passed his claws through her hair, he tore off a bit of her skin and devoured it.

'Stop!' cried the widow, 'the way you comb my hair hurts!'

But the panther simply tore off a much larger piece of skin. The widow wanted to call for help, but now the panther seized and devoured her. Then he turned on her little son and killed him too, put on the woman's clothes, and laid the child's bones, which he had not yet devoured, in her basket. After that he went to the widow's home, and called in at the door: 'Open the door, daughters! Mother has come home!' But they looked out through a crack and said: 'Our mother's eyes are not so large as yours!'

The wily panther replied: 'I have been to grandmother's house, and saw her hens laying eggs. That is very pleasing, and is why my eyes have grown so large.'

'Our mother had no spots in her face such as you have.'

'Grandmother had no spare bed, so I had to sleep on the peas, and they pressed themselves into my face.'

'Our mother's feet are not so large as yours.'

'Stupid things! That comes from walking such a distance. Come, open the door quickly!'

Then the daughters said to each other: 'It must be our mother,' and they opened the door. But when the panther came in, they realised their mistake.

At evening, when the daughters were already in bed, the panther was still gnawing the bones he had brought with him.

Then the daughters asked: 'Mother, what are you eating?'

'I'm eating beets,' was the answer.

Then the daughters said: 'Oh, mother, give us some of your beets, too! We are so hungry!'

'No,' was the reply, 'I will not give you any. Now be quiet and go to sleep.'

But the daughters kept on begging until the false mother gave them a little finger. Then they saw that it was their little brother's finger, and they said to each other: 'We must escape quickly, or he will eat us as well.' They ran out of the door, climbed up into a tree in the yard, and called down to the false mother: 'Come out! We can see our neighbour's son celebrating his wedding!' But it was the middle of the night.

Then the false mother came out, and when she saw that they were sitting in the tree, she called out angrily: 'Why, I'm not able to climb!'

The daughters said: 'Get into a basket and throw us the rope and we will draw you up!'

The false mother did as they said. But when the basket was halfway up, they began to swing it back and forth, bumping it against the tree. To avoid falling, the false mother became a panther once more, leaped out of the basket and ran away.

Gradually daylight came. The daughters climbed down and seated themselves on the doorstep, crying for their mother. A needle-seller came by and asked them why they were crying. 'A panther has devoured our mother and our brother,' said the girls. 'He has gone now, but he is sure to return and devour us as well.'

The seller gave them a pair of needles, and said: 'Stick these needles in the cushion of the arm chair, with the points up.' The girls thanked him but went on crying.

Soon a scorpion catcher came by; and he asked them why they were crying. 'A panther has devoured our mother and brother,' said the girls. 'He has gone now, but he is sure to return and devour us as well.'

The man gave them a scorpion and said: 'Put it behind the hearth in the kitchen.' The girls thanked him but went on crying.

Then an egg-seller came by and asked them why they were crying. 'A panther has devoured our mother and our brother,' said the girls. 'He has gone now, but he is sure to return and devour us as well.'

So he gave them an egg and said: 'Lay it beneath the ashes in the hearth.' The girls thanked him and went on crying.

Then a dealer in turtles came by, and they told him their tale. He gave them a turtle and said: 'Put it in the water barrel in the yard.' And then a man came by who sold wooden clubs. He asked them why they were crying, and they told him the whole story. Then he gave them two wooden clubs and said: 'Hang them up over the door to the street.' The girls thanked him and at last they did as all the men had told them to do.

In the evening the panther came home, and sat down in the armchair in the room. The needles in the cushion stuck into him, so he ran into the kitchen to light the fire and see what had jabbed him so. Then it was that the scorpion hooked his sting into his hand. When at last the fire was burning, the egg burst and spurted into one of his eyes, blinding him. He ran out into the yard and dipped his hand into the water barrel to cool it, and the turtle bit it off. Running in pain through the door and into the street, the wooden clubs fell on his head – and that was the end of the panther.

*Note: The panther in this tale is effectively the same beast as the talking silver fox (49), and the fairy tale is made up of motifs found in* Little Red Riding-Hood, The Wolf and the Seven Kids *and* The Vagabonds.

# 10

# The Great Flood

**China often suffers devastating floods, particularly during monsoon season. In some ways the boy in this tale is similar to Noah, but he has a rather extraordinary ship instead of an ark.**

Once upon a time there was a widow, who had a child. He was a kind-hearted boy, and everyone was fond of him. One day he said to his mother, 'All the other children have a grandmother, but I have none. And that makes me feel very sad!'

'We will hunt up a grandmother for you,' said his mother.

Now it happened that an old beggarwoman came to the house, who was very old and feeble. When the child saw her, he said to her: 'You shall be my grandmother!' And he went to his mother and said: 'There is a beggarwoman outside, and I want her for my grandmother!' His mother was willing and invited her into the house, even though the old woman was very dirty. The boy said to his mother: 'Come, let us wash Grandmother!', and together they washed her. She had a great many burrs in her hair, so they picked them all out and put them in a jar, and they filled the whole jar. Then his new grandmother said to him: 'Don't throw them away, but bury them in the garden. And do not dig them up again before the great flood comes.'

'When is the great flood coming?' asked the boy.

'When the eyes of the two stone lions in front of the prison grow red, then the great flood will come,' said the grandmother.

So the boy went to look at the lions, but their eyes were not yet red. And the grandmother also said to him: 'Make a little wooden ship and keep it in a little box.' And this the boy did. And he ran to the prison every day and looked at the lions, much to the astonishment of the people in the street.

One day, as he passed the poultry shop, the butcher asked him why he was always running to the lions. And the boy said: 'When the lions' eyes grow red then the great flood will come.' But the butcher laughed at him. And the following morning, quite early, he took some chicken blood and rubbed it on the lions' eyes. When the boy saw that the lions' eyes were red, he ran swiftly home, and told his mother and grandmother. And then his grandmother said: 'Dig up the jar quickly, and take the little ship out of its box.' And when they dug up the jar, it was filled with the purest pearls and the little ship grew larger and larger, like a real ship. Then the grandmother said: 'Take the jar with you and get into the ship. And when the great flood comes, you may save all the animals that are driven into it; but human beings, with their black heads, you are not to save.' So they climbed into the ship, and the grandmother suddenly disappeared.

Now it began to rain, and the rain kept falling more and more heavily from the heavens. Finally there were no longer any single drops falling, but just one big sheet of water that flooded everything.

A dog came drifting along, and they saved him in their ship. Soon after came a pair of mice with their little ones, all loudly squeaking in fear. These they also saved. By now, the water was rising to the roofs of the houses, and on one roof stood a cat, arching her back and mewing pitifully. They took the cat into the ship, too. Yet still the flood waters rose, reaching the tops of the trees. In one tree sat a raven, beating his wings and cawing loudly. And him, too, they took in. Finally a swarm of bees came flying their way. The little creatures were quite wet and could hardly fly, so they took in the bees on their ship. At last a man with black hair floated by on the waves. The boy said: 'Mother, let's save him, too!' But the mother did not want to do so. 'Didn't Grandmother tell us that we must save no black-headed human beings?' The boy answered: 'We will save the man in spite of that. I feel sorry for him and cannot bear to see him drifting along in the water.' So they also saved the man.

Gradually the water subsided. Then they got out of their ship and parted from the man and the beasts. The ship grew small again and they put it away in its box.

But the man wanted the pearls for himself. He went to the judge and entered a complaint against the boy and his mother, and they were both thrown into jail. Then came the mice, and dug a hole in the wall. Through the hole came the dog to bring them meat, and the cat to bring them bread, so they did not starve in prison. And the raven flew off, high into the sky, and returned with a letter for the judge. The letter had been written by a god, and it said: 'I wandered about in the world of men disguised as a beggarwoman. And this boy and his mother took me in. The boy treated me like his own grandmother and

29

did not shrink from washing me when I was dirty. Because of this I saved them out of the great flood I sent to destroy the sinful city where they lived. Free them, Judge, or misfortune shall be your portion!'

So the judge had them brought before him, and asked what they had done and how they had made their way through the flood. They told him everything, and what they said agreed with the god's letter. So the judge punished their accuser, and set them both at liberty.

When the boy had grown up, he came to a city of many people, and it was said that the princess intended to take a husband. In order to find the right man, she had put on a veil and seated herself in a litter, and the litter was carried, along with many others, to the marketplace. In every litter sat a veiled woman, and the princess was in their midst. The man who chose the right litter would take the princess for his bride. So the youth went to the marketplace, and there he saw the bees he had saved from the great flood all swarming about a certain litter. Up he stepped to it, and sure enough, the princess was sitting in it. The two celebrated their wedding, and lived happily ever afterward.

*Notes: The Great Flood is a traditional fairy tale and has often drawn comparison with Grimms' fairy tale* The Queen of the Bees.

*The monsoon season causes hundreds of fatalities across China each year. The Yellow River overflows its banks – and about once a century these floods are catastrophic.*

# 11

# The Fox and the Tiger

**Ancient Chinese generals are known to have used the lesson from this story in battle. These two animals are frequently cast as adversaries in Chinese culture, but who triumphs here?**

Once a fox met a tiger, who bared his teeth, stretched out his claws and was about to devour him. But the fox spoke and said: 'My dear sir, you must not think that you are the only king of the beasts. Your courage does not compare with my own. Let's walk together, but make sure you stay behind me. And if men catch sight of me and do not fear me, then you may devour me.' The tiger was willing, and so the fox led him along a broad highway. And the travellers, seeing the tiger in the distance, were all frightened and ran away.

Then the fox said: 'How about it? I went ahead, and the men saw me but not you.'

Immediately the tiger drew in his tail and ran away himself.

The tiger had seen for himself that the men were afraid of the fox, but he failed to notice that the fox had simply borrowed the terror he himself inspired.

*Note: The fox exploits the tiger's might has become a well-known idiom. The first version of this story appears in Strategies of the Warring States, which describes political manipulation and warfare during the Warring States period in fifth to third centuries BCE.*

# 12

# The Tiger's Decoy

**The tiger is undoubtedly a creature to be feared, but according to this story, it is also clever and calculating, and may even have supernatural powers of deception.**

That the fox borrowed the terror inspired by the tiger is more than a saying; but that the tiger has his own decoy is something we also read about in the story books, and grandfathers talk it about a good deal, too, so there must be some truth in it.

It is said that when a tiger devours a human being, the person's spirit cannot free itself, and that the tiger then uses it for a decoy. When he goes out to seek his prey, the spirit of the person he has devoured must go before him, to hide him so that people cannot see him. And the spirit is apt to change itself into a beautiful girl, or a lump of gold or a bolt of silk. All sorts of deceptions are used to lure folk into the mountain gorges. Then the tiger comes along and devours his victim, and the new spirit must serve as his decoy. The old spirit's time of service is now over and may go free.

And so it continues, turn by turn. Probably that is why they say of people who are forced to yield themselves to cunning and powerful men, bringing harm to others: 'They are the tiger's decoys!'

*Note: This is a rare example of a fable that makes direct reference to another (The Fox and the Tiger, previous story).*

# 13

# The Fox and the Raven

**Has the cunning fox met his match in the raven? This tale may be familiar from Aesop's fables, which historians believe were known in Western China as far back as the sixth century.**

The fox knows how to flatter, and how to play many cunning tricks. Once upon a time he saw a raven, who alighted on a tree with a piece of meat in his beak. The fox seated himself beneath the tree, looked up at him, and began to praise him.

'Your colour,' he began, 'is pure black. This proves to me that you possess all the wisdom of Laotzse, who knows how to shroud his learning in darkness. The manner in which you manage to feed your mother shows that your filial affection equals the affection shown by the Master Dsong for his parents. Your voice is rough and strong. It proves that you have the courage of King Hiang, who once drove his foes to flight by the mere sound of his voice. In truth, you are the king of birds!'

The raven, hearing this, was filled with joy and said: 'I thank you! I thank you!'

And before he knew it, the meat fell to earth from his opened beak.

The fox caught it up, devoured it and then said, laughing: 'Make note of this, my dear sir: if someone praises you without occasion, he is sure to have a reason for doing so.'

*Notes: Master Dsong was King Dsi's most faithful pupil, renowned for his piety.*

*The raven is known in China as 'the bird of filial love', for it is said that the young ravens bring forth the food they have eaten from their beaks again, in order to feed the old birds.*

# 14

# Why Dog and Cat are Enemies

**The dog and the cat begin this story as firm allies, but, as the title makes clear, they end it as bitter enemies, though do spare a thought for the poor mouse and how it feels.**

Once upon a time there was a man and his wife and they had a ring of gold. It was a lucky ring, and whoever owned it always had enough to live on. But this they did not know, and they sold the ring for a small sum. No sooner was the ring gone than they began to grow poorer and poorer, until at last they did not know when they would get their next meal. They had a dog and a cat, and these had to go hungry as well. Then the two animals discussed together how they might restore their owners' good fortune. At length the dog hit upon an idea.

'They must have the ring back again,' he said to the cat.

The cat answered: 'The ring has been carefully locked up in the chest, where no one can get at it.'

'You must catch a mouse,' said the dog, 'and the mouse must gnaw a hole in the chest and fetch out the ring. And if she does not want to, say that you will bite her to death, and you will see that she will do it.'

This advice pleased the cat, and she caught a mouse. Next she set out for the house where the chest stood, and the dog followed. They came to a broad river. Since the cat could not swim, the dog took her on his back and swam across with her. Then the cat carried the mouse to the house where the chest stood. The mouse gnawed a hole in the chest, and fetched out the ring. The cat put the ring in her mouth and went back to the river, where the dog was waiting for her, and swam across with her. Then they started out together for home, to bring the lucky ring to their master and mistress. But the dog could only run along the ground; when there was a house in the way he always had to go around it. The cat, however, quickly climbed over the roof, and so she reached home long before the dog, and brought the ring to her master.

Then her master said to his wife: 'What a good creature the cat is! We will always give her enough to eat and care for her as though she were our own child!'

But when the dog came home, they beat him and scolded him, because he had not helped to bring home the ring again. And the cat sat by the fireplace, purring, and never said a word. Then the dog grew angry at the cat, because she had robbed him of his reward, and when he saw her he chased her and tried to seize her.

And ever since that day cat and dog are enemies.

*Note: This version of the fairy tale was popular when Martens and Wilhelm were preparing their collection for publication, in the years after the First World War. In another version, the tale is narrated by a mouse, who reluctantly takes a starring role.*

# LEGENDS OF
# THE GODS

# 15

# How the Five Ancients Became Men

**Although there are some similarities, this fascinating creation myth, which also explains how the Chinese philosophy of Taoism came into being, is very different to Western versions.**

Before the earth was separated from the heavens, there was only a great ball of watery vapour called chaos. And at that time the spirits of the five elemental powers took shape, and became the five Ancients. The first was called the Yellow Ancient, and he was the ruler of the earth. The second was called the Red Lord, and he was the ruler of the fire. The third was called the Dark Lord, and he was the ruler of the water. The fourth was known as the Wood Prince, and he was the ruler of the wood. The fifth was called the Mother of Metals, and ruled over them. These five Ancients set all their primal spirit into motion, so that water and earth sank down. The heavens floated upward, and the earth grew firm in the depths. Then they allowed the waters to gather into rivers and seas, and hills and plains made their appearance. So the heavens opened and the earth was divided. And there were sun, moon and all the stars, wind, clouds, rain, and dew. The Yellow Ancient set earth's purest power spinning in a circle, and added the effect of fire and water thereto. Then there came forth grasses and trees, birds and beasts, and the tribes of the serpents and insects, fishes and turtles. The Wood Prince and the Mother of Metals combined light and darkness, and thus created the human race as men and women. And thus the world gradually came to be.

At that time there was one who was known as the True Prince of the Jasper Castle. He had acquired the art of sorcery through the cultivation of magic. The five Ancients begged him to rule as the supreme god. He dwelt above the three and thirty heavens, and the Jasper Castle, of white jade with golden gates, was his. Before him stood the stewards of the eight-and-twenty houses of the moon, and the gods of the thunders and the Great Bear, and in addition a class of baneful gods whose influence was evil and deadly. They all aided the True Prince of the Jasper Castle to rule over the thousand tribes under the heavens, and to deal out life and death, fortune and misfortune. The Lord of the Jasper Castle is now known as the Great God, the White Jade Ruler.

The Five Ancients withdrew after they had done their work, and thereafter lived in quiet purity. The Red Lord dwells in the South, as the god of fire. The Dark Lord dwells in the North, as the mighty master of the sombre polar skies. He lives in a castle of liquid crystal, and in later ages he sent Confucius down upon earth as a saint. Hence this saint is known as the Son of Crystal. The Wood Prince dwells in the East. He is honoured as the Green Lord, and watches over the coming into being of all creatures. In him lives the power of spring and he is the god of love. The Mother of Metals dwells in the West, by the sea of Jasper, and is also known as the Queen Mother of the West. She leads the rounds of the fairies, and watches over change and growth. The Yellow Ancient dwells in the middle. He is always going about in the world, in order to save and to help those in distress. The first time he came to earth he was the Yellow Lord, who taught mankind all sorts of arts. In his later years he fathomed the meaning of the world on the Ethereal Mount, and flew up to the radiant sun. Under the rule of the Dschou dynasty he was born again as Li Oerl, and when he was born his hair and beard were white, for which reason he was called Laotsze, 'Old Child'. He wrote the book of *Meaning and Life* and spread his teachings through the world. He is honoured as the head of Taoism. At the beginning of the reign of the Han dynasty, he again appeared as the Old Man of the River (Ho Schang Gung). He spread the teachings of Tao abroad mightily, so that from that time on Taoism flourished greatly. These doctrines are known to this day as the teachings of the Yellow Ancient. There is also a saying: 'First Laotsze was, then the heavens were.' And that must mean that Laotsze was the very same Yellow Ancient of primal days.

*Notes: This fairy tale brings together the five elemental spirits of earth, fire, water, wood and metal to offer a creation myth.*

*The philosopher credited with establishing Taoism is Laotsze (or Lao Tzu). Tzu was born in 601 BCE and his teachings had considerable influence during the Tang Dynasty (618–907 CE).*

The God of the North Pole was believed to
set the time of someone's birth, whereas the God
of the South Pole sets their time of death.

# 16

# The Cowherd and
# the Weaving Girl

**A classic love story quite literally written in the stars, this dates
back several millennia to at least the eleventh century BCE and
is often described as one of China's 'four great folktales'.**

The Cowherd was the son of poor people. When he was twelve
years old, he went to work for a farmer, looking after his cow.
After a few years the cow had grown large and fat, and her hair
shone like yellow gold. She must have been a cow from the gods.

One day while the cow was at pasture in the mountains, she began
to speak to the Cowherd in a human voice: 'This is the Seventh Day.
Now the White Jade Ruler has nine daughters, who bathe this day in
the Sea of Heaven. The seventh daughter is beautiful and wise beyond
all measure. She is called the Weaving Maiden because she spins
cloud silk for the King and Queen of Heaven, and presides over the
weaving that maidens do on earth. And if you take her clothes while
she bathes, you may become her husband and gain immortality.'

'But she is up in heaven,' said the Cowherd. 'How can I get there?'

'I will carry you there,' answered the golden cow.

So the Cowherd climbed on the cow's back. In a moment clouds
began to stream out of her hoofs, and she rose into the air. About his
ears was a whistling like the sounds of the wind, and they flew along
swiftly as lightning. Suddenly the cow stopped: 'We are here.'

Round about him the Cowherd saw forests of chrysophrase[1] and
trees of jade. The grass was also jasper and the flowers were coral. In
the midst of all this splendour lay a great, four-sided lake, covering
some five hundred acres. Its green waves rose and fell, and fishes
with golden scales were swimming in it. In addition, countless magic
birds flew above it, singing. In the distance the Cowherd could see

---

[1] This is a gemstone variety of chalcedony, and is apple green.

the nine maidens in the water. They had all laid down their clothes on the shore.

'Take the red clothes quickly,' said the cow, 'and hide away with them in the forest. And though she ask you for them ever so sweetly, do not give them back to her until she has promised to become your wife.'

The Cowherd hastily got down from the cow's back, seized the red clothes and ran away. At the same moment the nine maidens noticed him and were very frightened.

'Where do you come from, boy, that you dare to take our clothes?' they cried. 'Put them down again quickly!'

But the Cowherd did not let what they said trouble him, and crouched down behind one of the jade trees. Eight of the maidens hastily came ashore and drew on their clothes.

'Our seventh sister,' said they, 'whom heaven has destined to be yours, has come to you. We will leave her alone with you.'

The Weaving Maiden was still crouching in the water.

But the Cowherd stood before her and laughed.

'If you will promise to be my wife,' he said, 'I will give you your clothes.'

But this did not suit the Weaving Maiden.

'I am a daughter of the Ruler of the Gods,' said she, 'and may not marry without his command. Give me back my clothes quickly, or my father will punish you!'

Then the golden cow said: 'You have been destined for each other by fate, and I will be glad to arrange your marriage, and your father, the Ruler of the Gods, will not object. Of that I am sure.'

The Weaving Maiden replied: 'You are an unreasoning animal! How could you arrange our marriage?'

The cow said: 'Do you see that old willow tree there on the shore? Ask it. If the willow tree speaks, then Heaven wishes your union.'

So the Weaving Maiden asked the willow, and the willow replied in a human voice: 'This is the Seventh Day, the Cowherd his court to the Weaver doth pay!' The Weaving Maiden was satisfied with the verdict, so the Cowherd laid down her clothes and went on ahead. Then the Weaving Maiden drew them on and followed him. And thus they became man and wife.

But after seven days she took leave of him.

'The Ruler of Heaven has ordered me to look after my weaving,' she said. 'If I delay too long, I fear that he will punish me. Yet, although we have to part now, we will meet again.'

With those words she went away. The Cowherd ran after her. But when he was quite near, she took one of the long needles from her hair and drew a line with it right across the sky, and this line turned into the Silver River. And thus they now stand, separated by the river, and watching for one another.

And since that time they meet once every year, on the eve of the Seventh Day. When that time comes, all the crows in the world of men come flying and form a bridge over which the Weaving Maiden crosses the Silver River. And on that day you will not see a single crow in the trees, from morning to night. A fine rain often falls on the evening of the Seventh Day, and then the women and old grandmothers say to one another: 'Those are the tears which the Cowherd and the Weaving Maiden shed at parting!' And for this reason the Seventh Day is a rain festival.

To the west of the Silver River is the constellation of the Weaving Maiden, consisting of three stars. Directly in front of it are three other stars in the form of a triangle. It is said that the Cowherd was angry once because the Weaving Maiden did not want to cross the Silver River, and threw his yoke at her, which fell down in front of her feet. East of the Silver River is the Cowherd's constellation, consisting of six stars. To one side of it are countless little stars forming a constellation pointed at both ends and somewhat broader in the middle. It is said that the Weaving Maiden in turn threw her spindle at the Cowherd; it did not hit him but fell to one side.

*Notes: 'The Cowherd and the Weaving Maiden' is retold after an oral source.*

*The Cowherd is a constellation in Aquila, the Weaving Maiden one in Lyra. The Silver River separating them is the Milky Way.*

*The Seventh Day of the seventh month is the festival of their reunion.*

*The Ruler of the Heavens has nine daughters in all, who dwell in the nine heavens. The oldest married Li Dsing (compare 'Notscha', 18); the second is the mother of Yang Oerlang (compare 17); the third is the mother of the planet Jupiter (compare 'Sky O'Dawn', 34); and the fourth dwelt with a pious and industrious scholar, by name of Dung Yung, whom she help to win riches and honour. The seventh is the Spinner, and the ninth had to dwell on earth as a slave in punishment for some transgression. Of the fifth, sixth and the eighth daughters nothing further is known.*

*This famous myth is referenced in the Classic of Poetry, the oldest collection of Chinese poems with works that date from the eleventh to seventh centuries BCE.*

# 17

# Yang Oerlang

**Yang Oerlang has many special skills, but when he sets out to avenge his mother he will need them all, because he's up against the might of the ten suns and the Ruler of the Heaven...**

The second daughter of the Ruler of Heaven once came down to Earth and secretly became the wife of a man named Yang. When she returned to heaven, she was blessed with a son. The Ruler of Heaven was furious, disgusted by this desecration of the heavenly halls. He banished her to Earth and covered her with the Wu-I hills. Her son, Oerlang by name, was extraordinarily gifted by nature. By the time he was full grown, he had learned magic arts and was able to control eight times nine transformations. He could make himself invisible, or he could assume the shape of birds and beasts, grasses, flowers, snakes and fishes, as he chose. He also knew how to empty the seas and move mountains from one place to another. So he went to the Wu-I hills and rescued his mother, picking her up on his back and carrying her away.

They stopped to rest on a flat ledge of rock, and his mother, the Daughter of Heaven, said: 'I am very thirsty!'

Oerlang climbed down into the valley in order to fetch her water. Some time passed before he returned, and when he did his mother was no longer there. He searched desperately, but on the rock lay only her skin and bones, and a few bloodstains. Now, you must know that at this time there were still ten suns in the heavens, glowing and burning like fire. And though it is true that the Daughter of Heaven was divine by nature, her magic powers had failed her after she was banished to Earth. What's more, she had been imprisoned for so long beneath the hills in the dark that, coming out suddenly into the sunlight, she had been devoured by its blinding radiance.

When Oerlang thought of his mother's sad end, his heart ached. He took two mountains on his shoulders and pursued the suns, determined to crush them to death, one by one, between the mountains.

And whenever he had crushed another sun disc, he picked up a fresh mountain. In this way he had already slain nine of the ten suns, and there was but one left. And as Oerlang pursued him relentlessly, the sun hid himself in his distress beneath the leaves of the portulacca plant. But there was a rainworm close by who betrayed his hiding place, repeating: 'There he is! There he is!'

Oerlang was about to seize him, when a messenger from the Ruler of the Heaven suddenly descended from the skies: 'Sky, air and earth need the sunshine. You must allow this one sun to live, so that all created beings may live. Yet, because you rescued your mother, and showed yourself to be a good son, you shall be a god, and be my bodyguard in the highest heaven, and shall rule over good and evil in the mortal world, with power over devils and demons.' Receiving this command, Oerlang ascended to heaven.

Then the sun disc came out again from beneath the portulacca leaves. Grateful that the plant had saved him, he bestowed upon it the gift of a free-blooming nature, and ordained that it never need fear the sunshine. To this very day, you may see on the lower side of the portulacca leaves quite delicate little white pearls. They are the sunshine that remained hanging to the leaves when the sun hid under them. But the sun pursues the rainworm when he ventures forth out of the ground, and dries him up as a punishment for his treachery.

Since that time Yang Oerlang has been honoured as a god. He has oblique, sharply marked eyebrows, and holds a double-bladed, three-pointed sword in his hand. Two servants stand beside him, with a falcon and a hound; for Yang Oerlang is a great hunter. The falcon is the falcon of the gods, and the hound is the hound of the gods. When brute creatures gain magic powers or demons oppress men, he subdues them by means of a falcon and hound.

*Notes: Yang Oerlang is a huntsman, as is indicated by his falcon and hound. His hound of the heavens, literally 'the divine, biting hound', recalls the hound of Indra. The myth that there were originally ten suns in the skies, of whom nine were shot down by an archer, dates from the period of the legendary ruler Yau (2356–2255 BCE). In that story the archer is named Hou I, or I (see also 19). Here, instead of the shooting down of the suns with arrows, we have the Titan motif of destruction with mountains.*

*Oerlang is a character who has become entwined in various stories. This version is the most popular, and is repeated in the classic novel Journey to the West.*

# 18

# Notscha

**This small boy is cheeky and hot-headed, and he certainly gets himself into some sticky situations, but then that's what makes the adventures of Notscha highly entertaining.**

The oldest daughter of the Ruler of Heaven married the great general Li Dsing. Her sons were named Gintscha, Mutscha and Notscha. But on conceiving Notscha, she dreamed that a Taoist priest came into her chamber and said: 'Swiftly receive the Heavenly Son!' – and straightaway a radiant pearl glowed within her. She was so frightened by her dream that she woke up. And when Notscha came into the world, it seemed as though a ball of flesh were turning in circles like a wheel, and the whole room was filled with strange fragrances and a crimson light.

Li Dsing was terrified by the sight. He struck through the circling ball with his sword, and out of it leaped a small boy. His whole body glowed with a crimson radiance, but his face was delicately shaped and white as snow. About his right arm he wore a golden armlet and around his thighs was wound a length of crimson silk, so glittering that it dazzled the eyes. When Li Dsing saw the child, he took pity on him and did not slay him, while his wife began to love the boy dearly.

When three days had passed, all his friends came to wish him joy. They were just sitting down for the festival meal when a Taoist priest entered and said: 'I am the Great One. This boy is the bright Pearl of the Beginning of Things, bestowed upon you as your son. Yet the boy is wild and unruly, and will kill many men. Therefore I will take him as my pupil to gentle his savage ways.' Li Dsing bowed his thanks and the Great One disappeared.

When Notscha was seven years old, he ran away from home. He came to the river of nine bends, whose green waters flowed along between two rows of weeping willows. The day was hot, and Notscha entered the water to cool himself. He unbound his crimson silk cloth and whisked it about in the water to wash it. But while Notscha sat there and ran his scarf in the water, it shook the castle of the Dragon King of the Eastern Sea to its very foundations. So the Dragon King sent out a Triton, a fearsome sight, to find out what was the matter. As soon as the Triton saw the boy, he began to scold him. But Notscha merely looked up and said: 'What a strange-looking beast you are! You can actually talk!' This enraged the Triton, who leaped up and struck at Notscha with his axe. Avoiding the blow, the boy threw his golden armlet at him. The armlet struck the Triton on the head and he sank down dead.

Notscha laughed and said: 'And there he has gone and made my armlet bloody!' And he sat down on the stone, to wash it. Then the crystal castle of the dragon began to tremble as though it were about to fall apart, and a watchman came to the Dragon King and reported that the Triton had been slain by a boy. So the Dragon King sent out his own son to capture the boy. The son seated himself on the beast, who divided the waters and came up with a thunder of great waves. Notscha straightened up and said: 'That is a big wave!' Suddenly he saw a creature rising out of the waves, carrying on his back an armed man, who cried in a loud voice: 'Who has slain my Triton?'

Notscha answered: 'The Triton wanted to slay me, so I killed him. What difference does it make?' The man attacked with his halberd. But Notscha said: 'Tell me who you are before we fight.' 'I am the son of the Dragon King,' was the reply. Notscha countered: 'Do not rouse my anger with your violence, or I will skin you, together with that old mudfish your father!' Then the dragon grew wild with rage, and stormed towards him in a fury. But Notscha cast his crimson cloth into the air, so that it flashed like a ball of fire, and cast the dragon-youth from his breast. Then Notscha took his golden armlet and struck him on the forehead with it, and the assailant was revealed in his true form as a golden dragon before he fell down dead.

Notscha laughed and said: 'I have heard tell that dragon sinews make good cords. I will draw one out and bring it to my father, and he can tie his armour together with it.' And with that he drew out the dragon's back sinew and took it home.

In the meantime the Dragon King, full of fury, hurried to Notscha's father Li Dsing and demanded that Notscha be surrendered to him. But Li Dsing replied: 'You must be mistaken, for my boy is only seven years old and incapable of committing such misdeeds.' While they were still quarrelling, Notscha came running up and cried: 'Father, I'm bringing along a dragon's sinew for you, so that you may bind up your armour with it!' Now the dragon broke out into tears and furious scolding. Threatening to report Li Dsing to the Ruler of the Heaven, he took himself off, snorting with rage.

Greatly distressed, Li Dsing told his wife what had happened, and the two of them began to weep. Notscha, however, came to them and said: 'Why are you crying? I will just to go my master, the Great One, and he will know what is to be done.' No sooner had he said these words than he disappeared. Coming into his master's presence, he told him the whole tale. The Great One said: 'You must get ahead of the dragon and prevent him from accusing you in heaven!' Immediately he performed some magic, and Notscha found himself seated by the gate of heaven, waiting for the dragon. It was still early in the morning; the gate of heaven had not yet been opened, nor was the watchman at his post. But the dragon was already climbing up. Notscha had been rendered invisible by his master's magic and he threw the dragon to the ground with his armlet and began to pitch into him. The dragon protested and screamed. 'There the old worm flounders about,' said Notscha, 'and does not care how hard he is beaten! I will scratch off some of his scales.' With these words he began to tear open the dragon's ceremonial robes, and rip off some of the scales beneath his left arm until red blood dripped out. The dragon could no longer stand the pain and begged for mercy. Before Notscha would let him go, he first had to promise Notscha that he would make no complaint. Then the dragon had to turn himself into a little green snake, which Notscha put into his sleeve and took back home with him. No sooner had he drawn the little snake from his sleeve than it assumed human shape, and swearing that he would punish Li Dsing in a terrible manner, he disappeared in a flash of lightning.

Li Dsing was now intensely angry with his son, so Notscha's mother sent him to the rear of the house to keep out of his father's sight. Notscha immediately disappeared, returning to his master, in order to ask him what he should do when the dragon returned. After receiving his master's advice, Notscha went back home.

There he discovered that the Dragon Kings of the four seas were assembled, and had tied up his parents to punish them. Notscha ran up and cried with a loud voice: 'I will take the punishment for whatever I have done! My parents are blameless! What is the punishment you wish to lay upon me?'

'Life for life!' said the dragons.

'Very well, then, I will destroy myself!' And he did.

The dragons went off satisfied while Notscha's mother buried him with many tears. But the spiritual part of Notscha, his soul, fluttered about in the air, and was driven by the wind to the cave of the Great One. His master took his spirit in, saying: 'You must appear to your mother! Forty miles distant from your home rises a green mountain cliff. On this cliff she must build a shrine for you. And after you have enjoyed the incense of human adoration for three years, you shall once more have a human body.' Notscha appeared to his mother in a dream, and gave her the whole message, and she awoke in tears. But Li Dsing grew angry when she told him. 'It serves the accursed boy right that he is dead! You are always thinking of him, and that's why he appears to you in dreams. Pay no attention.' The woman said no more, but thenceforward he appeared to her daily, as soon as she closed her eyes, growing more and more urgent in his demand. Finally her only course of action was to erect a temple for Notscha without Li Dsing's knowledge.

Notscha performed great miracles in the temple. All prayers made in it were granted. And from far away people streamed to it, to burn incense in his honour.

Thus six months passed. Then a great military drill took place and Li Dsing passed close to the temple, and saw the people crowding thickly about the hill like a swarm of ants. Li Dsing asked what there was to see upon the hill. 'It is a new god, who performs so many miracles that people come from far and near to honour him.' 'What sort of a god is he?' asked Li Dsing. They did not dare conceal from him who the god was. Li Dsing, now angry, spurred his horse up the hill and, sure enough, over the door of the temple was written: 'Notscha's Shrine'. And within it was the likeness of Notscha, just as he had looked while he lived. Li Dsing said: 'While you were alive, you brought misfortune to your parents. Now that you are dead, you deceive the people. It's disgusting!' With these words he drew out his whip and beat Notscha's idol to pieces. Then he had the temple burned down, and the worshippers rebuked. Finally he returned home.

Now on that day Notscha had been absent in the spirit. When he returned, he found his temple destroyed; and the spirit of the hill gave him the details. Notscha hurried to his master and in tears told him what had happened. His master was roused and said: 'It is Li Dsing's fault. After you had restored your body to your parents, you were no further concern of his. Why should he take away your enjoyment of the incense?' Then the Great One made a body of lotus plants, gave it the gift of life, and enclosed the soul of Notscha within it. This done, he called out in a loud voice: 'Arise!' The sound of an intake of breath was heard, and Notscha leaped up once more in the shape of a small boy. He flung himself down before his master and thanked him. He was given the magic of the fiery lance, and from that moment Notscha had two whirling wheels beneath his feet: the wheel of the wind and the wheel of fire. With these he could rise up and down in the air. The master also gave him a bag made of panther skin, to hold his armlet and his silken cloth.

Now Notscha had determined to punish Li Dsing. Taking advantage of a moment when he was not watched, he went away, thundering along on his rolling wheels to his father – who fled. Li Dsing was almost exhausted when his second son, Mutscha, the disciple of the holy Pu Hain, came to his aid from the Cave of the White Crane. A violent quarrel took place between the brothers; Mutscha was defeated and Notscha continued in hot pursuit of his father.

Li Dsing was at his most desperate when the holy Wen Dschu of the Hill of the Five Dragons, who was the master of his eldest son Gintscha, stepped forth and hid him in his cave. Raging, Notscha insisted that he be delivered up to him; but Wen Dschu said: 'You may indulge your wild nature to your heart's content anywhere else, but not here.'

Notscha turned his fiery lance upon him, but Wen Dschu stepped back a pace, shook the seven-petaled lotus from his sleeve, and threw it into the air. A whirlwind arose, clouds and mists obscured sight, and sand and earth were flung up from the ground. Then the whirlwind collapsed with a great crash. Notscha fainted, and when he regained consciousness found himself bound to a golden column with three thongs of gold, so that he could no longer move. Wen Dschu now called Gintscha to him and ordered him to give his unruly brother a good thrashing. Notscha had no choice but to stand it, grinding his teeth. At his most desperate, he saw the Great One floating by, and called out to him: 'Save me, O master!' But his master ignored him, instead entering the cave and thanking Wen Dschu for the severe lesson he had given Notscha.

Finally they called Notscha into them and ordered him to be reconciled to his father. Then they dismissed them both and seated themselves to play chess. But no sooner was Notscha free than he again fell into a rage and renewed his pursuit of his father. He had again overtaken Li Dsing when still another saint came forward in his defence. This time it was the old Buddha of the Radiance of the Light. Notscha attempted to do battle with him, but Radiance of Light raised his arm, and a pagoda shaped itself out of red, whirling clouds and closed around Notscha. Then Radiance of Light placed both his hands on the pagoda and a fire arose within it, burning Notscha so that he cried loudly for mercy. He had to promise to beg his father's forgiveness and always to obey him in the future – and not until he had promised all this did the Buddha let him out of the pagoda. Then he gave the pagoda to Li Dsing; and taught him a magic saying that gave him mastery over Notscha. It is for this reason that Li Dsing is called the Pagoda-bearing King of Heaven.

Later on Li Dsing and his three sons, Gintscha, Mutscha and Notscha, aided King Wu of the Dschou dynasty to destroy the tyrant Dschou-Sin.

None could withstand their might. Only once did a sorcerer succeed in wounding Notscha in the left arm. Anyone else would have died of the wound. But the Great One carried him into his cave, healed his wound and gave him three goblets of wine of the gods to drink, and three fire dates to eat. When Notscha had eaten and drunk, he suddenly heard a crash at his left side and another arm grew out from it. He could not speak and his eyes stood out from their sockets with horror. But it went on as it had begun: six more arms grew out of his body and two more heads, so that finally he had three heads and eight arms. He called out: 'What does all this mean?' But his master only laughed and said: 'All is as it should be. Equipped like this you will really be strong!' Then he taught him a magic spell that could make his arms and heads visible or invisible as he chose. When the tyrant Dschou-Sin had been destroyed, Li Dsing and his three sons were taken up into heaven and seated among the gods.

# 19

# The Lady of the Moon

**In this tale, from the time of Emperor Yau, who ruled China in the second century BCE and is often linked to myths about celestial phenomena, meet the mysterious Lady of the Moon.**

In the days of the Emperor Yau lived a prince by the name of Hou I, who was a mighty hero and a good archer. Once ten suns rose together in the sky, shining so brightly and burning so fiercely that the people on earth could not endure them. So the Emperor ordered Hou I to shoot at them. And Hou I shot nine of them down from the sky. Besides his bow, Hou I also had a horse which ran so swiftly that even the wind could not catch up with it. He mounted it to go a-hunting, and the horse ran away and could not be stopped. So Hou I came to Kunlun Mountain and met the Queen Mother of the Jasper Sea, who gave him the herb of immortality. He took it home with him and hid it in his room. His wife Tschang O ate some of it secretly when he was not at home, and immediately floated up to the clouds. When she reached the moon, she ran into the castle there, and has lived there ever since as the Lady of the Moon.

On a night in mid-autumn, an emperor of the Tang dynasty once sat at wine with two sorcerers. One of them took his bamboo staff and cast it into the air, where it turned into a heavenly bridge, and the three crossed it to the moon together. There they saw a great castle on which was inscribed: 'The Spreading Halls of Crystal Cold'. Beside it stood a cassia tree with blossoms that gave forth a fragrance filling all the air. And in the tree sat a man who was chopping off the smaller boughs with an axe. One of the sorcerers said: 'That's the man in the moon. The cassia tree grows so luxuriantly that in the course of time it would overshadow all the moon's radiance. And that's why it must be cut down once in every thousand years.' Then they entered the spreading halls. The silver storeys of the castle towered one above the other, and its walls and columns were all formed of liquid crystal. In the walls were cages and ponds, where fishes and birds moved as though alive. The whole moon world seemed made of glass. While they were still looking about them, the Lady of the Moon stepped up to them, clad in a white mantle and a rainbow-coloured gown. She smiled and said to the emperor: 'You are a prince of the mundane world of dust. Great is your fortune, since you have been able to find your way here!' And she called for her attendants, who came flying upon white birds, and sang and danced beneath the cassia tree. A pure clear music floated through the air. Beside the tree stood a mortar made of white marble, in which a jasper rabbit ground up herbs. That was the dark half of the moon. When the dance had ended, the emperor returned to earth again with the sorcerers. And he had the songs heard on the moon written down and sung to the accompaniment of flutes of jasper in his pear tree garden.

# 20

# The Morning and the Evening Star

**The ancient Chinese were great astronomers – recent archaeological work has uncovered an observatory dating to the third millennium BCE – as this short story shows.**

Once upon a time there were two stars, sons of the Golden King of the Heavens. One was named Tschen and the other Shen. One day they quarrelled, and Tschen struck Shen a terrible blow. Thereupon both stars made a vow that they would never again look upon each other. So Tschen only appears in the evening, and Shen only appears in the morning, and not until Tschen has disappeared is Shen again to be seen. And that is why people say: 'When two brothers do not live peaceably with one another they are like Tschen and Shen.'

*Note: Tschen and Shen are Hesperus and Lucifer, the morning and evening stars. The tale is told in its traditional form. Chinese records of celestial observations date back to the beginning of the Han dynasty, in the third century BCE*

# 21

# The Girl with the Horse's Head or The Silkworm Goddess

**The Chinese have been producing silk since Neolithic times, so it's no wonder the girl in this unusual tale gets rather wrapped up in it – and undergoes something of a transformation.**

In the dim ages of the past there once was an old man who went on a journey. No one remained at home save his only daughter and a white stallion. The daughter fed the horse day by day, but she was lonely and yearned for her father.

So it happened that one day she said in jest to the horse: 'If you will bring back my father to me, then I will marry you!'

No sooner had the horse heard her say this than he broke loose and ran away. He ran until he came to the place where her father was. When her father saw the horse, he was pleasantly surprised, caught him and seated himself on his back. And the horse turned back the way he had come, neighing without a pause.

'What can be the matter with the horse?' thought the father. 'Something must have surely gone wrong at home!' So he dropped the reins and rode back. And he fed the horse liberally because he had been so intelligent; but the horse ate nothing, and when he saw the girl, he struck out at her with his hoofs and tried to bite her. This surprised the father; he questioned his daughter, who told him the truth, just as it had occurred.

'You must not say a word about it to anyone,' spoke her father, 'or else people will talk about us.'

And he took down his crossbow, shot the horse and hung up his skin in the yard to dry. Then he went on his travels again.

One day his daughter went out walking with the daughter of a neighbour. When they entered the yard, she pushed the horse hide with her foot and said: 'What an unreasonable animal you were – wanting to marry a human being! What happened to you served you right!'

But before she had finished her speech, the horse hide moved, rose up, wrapped itself about the girl and ran off.

Horrified, her companion ran home to her father and told him what had happened. The neighbours looked for the girl everywhere, but she could not be found.

At last, some days afterward, they saw the girl hanging from the branches of a tree, still wrapped in the horse hide; and gradually she turned into a silkworm and wove a cocoon. The threads which she spun were strong and thick. Her girlfriend took down the cocoon and let her slip out of it; and then she spun the silk and sold it at a large profit.

But the girl's relatives longed for her. One day she appeared to them, riding in the clouds on her horse and followed by a great company. 'In heaven,' she told them, 'I have been assigned to the task of watching over the growing of silkworms. You must yearn for me no longer!' At this, they decided to build temples to her, and every year, at the silkworm season, sacrifices are offered to her, begging for her protection. And the Silkworm Goddess is also known as the Girl with the Horse's Head.

# 22

# The Queen of Heaven

**If you're a sailor in trouble on the high seas who do you turn to? Who else, but the Queen of Heaven. However, you need to be versed in the various ways of summoning her.**

The Queen of Heaven, who is also known as the Holy Mother, was in mortal life a maiden from Fukien, named Lin. She was pure, reverential and pious in her ways and died at the age of seventeen. She shows her power on the seas and for this reason sailors worship her. When they are unexpectedly attacked by wind and waves, they call on her and she is always ready to hear their pleas.

There are many sailors in Fukien, and every year people are lost at sea. This, most likely, explains why the Queen of Heaven took pity on the distress of her people during her lifetime on earth. And since her thoughts are always turned toward aiding the drowning in their distress, she now appears frequently on the seas.

In every ship that sails, a picture of the Queen of Heaven hangs in the cabin, and three paper talismans are also kept on board. On the first she is painted with crown and sceptre, on the second as a maiden in ordinary dress, and on the third she is pictured with flowing hair, barefoot, standing with a sword in her hand. When the ship is in danger, the first talisman is burnt – and help comes. But if this is of no avail, then the second and finally the third picture is burned. And if no help comes, there is nothing more to be done.

When sailors lose their course among wind and waves and darkling clouds, they pray devoutly to the Queen of Heaven. Then a red lantern appears on the face of the waters. And if they follow the lantern, they will find safety out of all danger. The Queen of Heaven may often be seen standing in the skies, dividing the wind with her sword. When she does this, the wind departs for the north and south, and the waves grow smooth.

A wooden wand is always kept before her holy picture in the cabin. It often happens that fish dragons play in the seas. These are two giant fish who spout up water against one another till the sun in the sky is obscured, and the seas are shrouded in profound darkness. Often, in the distance, a bright opening can be seen in the darkness. If the ship holds a course straight for this opening, it will win through and be suddenly floating in calm waters again. Looking back, you may see the two fishes still spouting water, and realise that the ship has passed directly beneath their jaws. But a storm is always near when the fish dragons are swimming, so it is well to burn paper or wool so that the dragons do not draw the ship down into the depths.

Or the Master of the Wand may burn incense before the wand in the cabin. Then he must take the wand and swing it over the water three times, in a circle. If he does so, the dragons will draw in their tails and disappear. When the ashes in the censer fly up into the air without any cause, and are scattered about, it is a sign that great danger is threatening.

Nearly two hundred years ago an army was fitted out to subdue the island of Formosa. The captain's banner had been dedicated with the blood of a white horse. Suddenly the Queen of Heaven appeared at the tip of the banner staff. In another moment she had disappeared, but the invasion was successful.

On another occasion, in the days of Kien Lung, the minister Dschou Ling was ordered to install a new king in the Liu-Kiu Islands. When the fleet was sailing by south of Korea, a storm arose, and his ship was driven toward the Black Whirlpool. The water had the colour of ink, both sun and moon lost their radiance, and the word was passed about that the ship had been caught in the Black Whirlpool, from which no living man had ever returned. The sailors and travellers awaited their end with lamentations. Suddenly an untold number of lights, like red lanterns, appeared on the surface of the water. Then the sailors were overjoyed and prayed in the cabins. 'Our lives are saved!' they cried, 'the Holy Mother has come to our aid!' And truly, a beautiful maiden with golden earrings appeared. She waved her hand in the air and the winds became still and the waves grew even. And it seemed as though the ship were being drawn along by a mighty hand. It moved plashing through the waves, and suddenly it was beyond the limits of the Black Whirlpool.

On his safe return, Dschou Ling explained what had happened, and begged that temples be erected in honour of the Queen of Heaven, and that she be included in the list of the gods. And the emperor granted his prayer.

Since then temples of the Queen of Heaven are to be found in all sea-port towns, and her birthday is celebrated on the eighth day of the fourth month with spectacles and sacrifices.

*Notes: 'The Queen of Heaven,' whose name is Tian Hou, or more exactly, Tian Fe Niang Niang, is a Taoist goddess of sailors, generally worshipped in all coast towns. Her story is principally made up of local legends of Fukien province, and a variation of the Indian Maritschi (who, as Dschunti with the eight arms, is the object of quite a special cult). Since the establishment of the Manchu dynasty, Tian Hou has been one of the officially recognised godheads.*

*The young woman Lin is believed to have lived in a small fishing village on Meizhou Island in the tenth century. The earliest record of her cult comes from an inscription dating to 1150.*

The Heavenly Queen, a sea goddess who protects
sailors, is known by many names, including
Celestial Empress and Holy Mother.

# 23

# The Fire God

**The Fire God is definitely not to be trifled with, but when a rich man on a long journey encounters the Fire God in disguise, will he heed the deity's warning?**

Long before the time of Fy Hi, Dschu Yung, the Magic Welder, was the ruler of men. He discovered the use of fire, and succeeding generations learned from him to cook their food. Hence his descendants were entrusted with the preservation of fire, while he himself was made the Fire God. He is a personification of the Red Lord, who showed himself at the beginning of the world as one of the Five Ancients. The Fire God is worshipped as the Lord of the Holy Southern Mountain. In the skies the Fiery Star, the southern quarter of the heavens and the Red Bird belong to his domain. When there is danger of fire, the Fiery Star glows with a peculiar radiance. When countless number of fire crows fly into a house, a fire is sure to break out in it.

In the land of the four rivers there dwelt a man who was very rich. One day he got into his wagon and set out on a long journey. And he met a girl, dressed in red, who begged him to take her with him. He allowed her to get into the wagon and drove along for half a day without even looking in her direction. Then the girl got out again and said in farewell: 'You are truly a good and honest man, and for that reason I must tell you the truth. I am the Fire God. Tomorrow a fire will break out in your house. Hurry home at once to arrange your affairs and save what you can!' Frightened, the man faced his horses about and drove home as fast as he could. All that he possessed in the way of treasures, clothes and jewels, he removed from the house. And, when he was about to lie down to sleep, a fire broke out on the hearth which could not be quenched until the whole building had collapsed in dust and ashes. Yet, thanks to the Fire God, the man had saved all his movable belongings.

*Notes: The Holy Southern Mountain is Sung-Schan in Huan.*

*The Fiery Star is Mars.*

*The constellations of the southern quarter of the heavens are grouped by the Chinese under the name of the Red Bird.*

*The 'land of the four rivers' is Setchuan, in the western part of present-day China.*

*The Sacred Mountains of China have long been important destinations for pilgrims, associated with Taoism, Buddhism and Confucianism.*

Caishen is the Chinese God of Wealth and Prosperity,
usually shown carrying a golden rod with a yuanbao
or boat-shaped ingot close to him.

# 24

# The Three Ruling Gods

**All over China there are temples built in honour of the Three Ruling Gods. They are always shown sitting together in a row, like kings, but why is the one on the right so angry?**

There are three lords: in heaven, and on the earth and in the waters, and they are known as the Three Ruling Gods. They are all brothers, and are descended from the father of the Monk of the Yangtze-kiang. When he was sailing on the river, he was cast into the water by a robber. But he did not drown, for a Triton came his way who took him along with him to the dragon castle. And when the Dragon King saw him, he realised at once that there was something extraordinary about the Monk and married him to his daughter.

From their early youth his three sons showed a preference for the hidden wisdom. Together they went to an island in the sea. There they seated themselves and began to meditate. They heard nothing, they saw nothing, they spoke not a word and they did not move. The birds came and nested in their hair; the spiders came and wove webs across their faces; worms and insects came and crawled in and out of their noses and ears. But they paid no attention to any of them.

After they had meditated thus for a number of years, they obtained the hidden wisdom and became gods. And the Lord made them the Three Ruling Gods. The heavens make things, the earth completes things, and the waters create things. The Three Ruling Gods sent out the current of their primal power to ensure that all would be aided like this. Therefore they are also known as the primal gods, and temples are erected to them all over the earth.

If you go into a temple, you will find the Three Ruling Gods all seated on one pedestal. They wear women's hats upon their heads, and hold sceptres in their hands, like kings. But he who sits on the last place, to the right, has glaring eyes and wears a look of rage. If you ask why this is, you are told: 'These three were brothers and the Lord made them the Ruling Gods. So they talked about the order in which they were to sit. And the youngest said: "Tomorrow morning, before sunrise, we will meet here. Whoever gets here first shall have the seat of honour in the middle; the second one to arrive shall have the second place, and the third the third." The two older brothers were satisfied. The next morning, very early, the youngest came first, seated himself in the middle place, and became the god of the waters. The middle brother came next, sat down on the left, and became the god of the heavens. Last of all came the oldest brother. When he saw that his brothers were already sitting in their places, he was disgusted and yet he could not say a word. His face grew red with rage, his eyeballs stood forth from their sockets like bullets, and his veins swelled like bladders. And he seated himself on the right and became god of the earth.' The artisans who make the images of the gods noticed this, so they always represent him thus.

# 25

# A Legend of Confucius

**Tsin Schi Huang was the first emperor to rule a unified China and perhaps his exploits in this story explain why he demanded his own tomb was guarded by the Terracotta Army…**

When Confucius came to the earth, the Kilin, that strange beast which is the prince of all four-footed animals and appears only when there is a great man on earth, sought the child and spat out a piece of jade. On it was written: 'Son of the Watercrystal, you are destined to become an uncrowned king!' And Confucius grew up, studied diligently, learned wisdom and came to be a saint. He did much good on earth, and ever since his death has been reverenced as the greatest of teachers and masters. He had foreknowledge of many things. And even after he had died he gave evidence of this.

Once, when the wicked Emperor Tsin Schi Huang had conquered all the other kingdoms and was travelling through the entire empire, he came to the homeland of Confucius. There he found his grave. And, finding his grave, he wished to have it opened and see what was inside. All his officials advised him not to do so, but he would not listen. So a passage was dug into the grave, and in its main chamber they found a coffin made of wood that seemed to be quite fresh. When struck, it sounded like metal. To the left of the coffin was a door leading into an inner chamber. In this chamber stood a bed, and a table with books and clothing, all as though meant for the use of a living person. Tsin Schi Huang seated himself on the bed and looked down. And there on the floor stood two shoes of red silk, whose tips were adorned with a woven pattern of clouds. A bamboo staff leaned against the wall. The Emperor, in jest, put on the shoes, took the staff and left the grave. But as he did so a tablet suddenly appeared before his eyes on which were carved the following lines:

O'er kingdoms six Tsin Schi Huang his army led,
To ope my grave and find my humble bed;
He steals my shoes and takes my staff away
To reach Schakiu – and his last earthly day!

Tsin Schi Huang was much alarmed, and had the grave closed again. But when he reached Schakiu he fell ill of a hasty fever of which he died.

*Notes: The Kilin is an okapi-like legendary beast of the most perfected kindness, prince of all the four-footed animals.*

*The Watercrystal is the dark Lord of the North, whose element is water and wisdom, for which last reason Confucius is termed his son.*

*Tsin Schi Huang (B.C. 200) is the burner of books and reorganiser of China, famed in history.*

*Schakiu (Sandhill) was a city in the western part of the China of that day.*

Confucius, the highly influential Chinese philosopher,
lived from 551 to 479 BCE and established the set
of beliefs known as Confucianism.

# 26

# The God of War

**This story chronicles the life of Guan Yu, a brave and loyal general who served the warlord Liu Bei. Guan Yu was executed in 220 CE, but his legend lives on.**

The God of War, Guan Di, was really named Guan Yu. When the rebellion of the Yellow Turbans was raging throughout the empire, he met two others by the wayside and, discovering that they shared the same love of country he felt, made a pact of friendship. One of the men was Liu Be, afterward emperor; the other was named Dschang Fe. The three met in a peach orchard and swore to be brothers one to the other, although they were of different families. Sacrificing a white steed, they vowed to be true to each other to the death.

Guan Yu was faithful, honest, upright and brave beyond all measure. He loved to read Confucius's *Annals of Lu*, which tell of the rise and fall of empires. He helped his friend Liu Be to subdue the Yellow Turbans and to conquer the land of the four rivers. The horse he rode was known as the Red Hare and could run a thousand miles in a day. Guan Yu had a knife called the Green Dragon and shaped like a half moon. His eyebrows were beautiful like those of the silk butterflies, and his eyes were long-slitted like the eyes of the phoenix. His face was scarlet red in colour; and his beard so long that it hung down over his stomach. Once, when he appeared before the emperor, the latter called him Duke Fairbeard, and presented him with a silken pocket to hold his beard. He also wore a garment of green brocade. Whenever he went into battle, he showed invincible bravery. Whether he were opposed by a thousand armies or by ten thousand horsemen – he attacked them as though they were merely air.

Once, the evil Tsau Tsau incited the enemies of his master, the emperor, to take the city by treachery. When Guan Yu heard of it, he hurried with an army to relieve the town. But he fell into an ambush, and, together with his son, was brought captive to the capital of the enemy's land. The prince of that country would have been glad to have him come over to his side; but Guan Yu swore that he would not, preferring to yield to death himself. Thereupon father and son were slain. His horse Red Hare ceased to eat and died. A faithful captain of his, by name of Dschou Dsang, who was black of face and wore a great knife, had just invested a fortress when the news of the sad end of the duke reached him. Neither he, or his other faithful followers, wished to survive their master, and perished.

At the time a monk, who was an old compatriot and acquaintance of Duke Guan, was living in the Hills of the Jade Fountains. He used to walk at night in the moonlight.

Suddenly he heard a loud voice cry down out of the air: 'I want my head back again!'

The monk looked up and saw Duke Guan, sword in hand, seated on his horse, just as he had appeared in life. At his right and left hand, shadowy figures in the clouds, stood his son Guan Ping and his captain, Dschou Dsang.

The monk folded his hands and said: 'While you lived you were upright and faithful, and in death you have become a wise god; and yet you do not understand fate! Many thousands of your enemies lost their lives through you, and if you insist on having your head back again, they too will insist that life be restored to them – but to whom should they appeal?'

When he heard this the Duke Guan bowed and disappeared. Since that time, he has been spiritually active. Whenever a new dynasty is founded, his holy form may be seen. For this reason, temples and sacrifices have been established for him, and he has been made one of the gods of the empire. Like Confucius, he received the great sacrifice of oxen, sheep and pigs. His rank increases with the passing of centuries. First he was worshipped as Prince Guan, later as King Guan, and then as the great god who conquers the demons. The last dynasty, finally, worships him as the great, divine helper of the Heavens. He is also called the God of War, and is a strong deliverer in all need, when men are plagued by devils and foxes. Together with Confucius, the Master of Peace, he is often worshipped as the Master of War.

*Notes: The Chinese God of War is a historical personality from the epoch of the three empires, which later joined the Han dynasty, about 250 CE. Liu Be founded the Little Han dynasty in Setchuan, with the help of Guan Yu and Dschang Fe. Guan Yu or Guan Di – i.e., 'God Yuan' – has become one of the most popular figures in Chinese legend, both God of War and deliverer in one and the same person.*

*The argument made by the monk is based on the Buddhist law of karma. Because Guan Di had slain other men – even though his motives were good – he must endure similar treatment at their hands, despite being a god.*

Guan Di, the God of War, was originally a
bean curd seller, but became such a famous general
that he ultimately achieved the status of deity.

# TALES OF SAINTS
# AND MAGICIANS

# 27

# The Halos of the Saints

**What's in a halo? Quite a lot it seems, particularly if it's red. According to this story, halos can be quite dazzling, so take care if you enter the presence of someone entitled to wear one.**

True gods all have halos around their heads. When lesser gods and demons see these halos, they hide and dare not move. The Master of the Heavens on the Dragon-Tiger Mountain meets the gods at all times. One day Guan Di, the God of War, came down to the mountain while the mandarin of the neighbouring district was visiting the Master of the Heavens. The latter advised the mandarin to withdraw and hide himself in an inner chamber. Then he went out to receive the God of War. But the mandarin peeped through a slit in the door, and he saw the red face and green garment of the God of War as he stood there, terrible and awe-inspiring. Suddenly a red halo flashed up above his head, whose beams penetrated into the inner chamber so that the mandarin grew blind in one eye. After a time the God of War went away again, and the Master of the Heavens accompanied him. Suddenly Guan Di said, with alarm: 'Confucius is coming! The halo he wears illumines the whole world. I cannot endure its radiance even a thousand miles away, so I must hurry and get out of the way!' With that he stepped into a cloud and disappeared. The Master of the Heavens then told the mandarin what had happened, and added: 'Fortunately you did not see the God of War face to face! Whoever does not possess the greatest virtue and the greatest wisdom, would be melted by the red glow of his halo.' So saying he gave him a pill of the elixir of life to eat, and his blind eye gradually regained its sight.

It is also said that scholars wear a red halo around their heads which devils, foxes and ghosts fear when they see it.

There was once a scholar who had a fox for a friend. The fox came to see him at night, and went walking with him in the villages. They could enter the houses, and see all that was going on, without people being any the wiser. But when at a distance the fox saw a red halo hanging above a house he would not enter it. The scholar asked him why not.

'Those are all celebrated scholars,' answered the fox. 'The greater the halo, the more extensive is their knowledge. I dread them and do not dare enter their houses.'

Then the scholar said: 'But I am a scholar, too! Have I no halo that makes you fear me, instead of going walking with me?'

'There is only a black mist about your head,' answered the fox. 'I have never yet seen it surrounded by a halo.'

The scholar was mortified and began to scold him; but the fox disappeared with a laugh.

*Notes: The Master of the Heavens, Tian Schi, who dwells on the Lung Hu Schan, is the so-called Taoist pope.*

*Halos are associated with scholars to suggest that they have received divine enlightenment.*

Zhurong, the Fire God, whose domain is the
southern quarter of Heaven, is said to have
discovered fire and taught humans to use it.

# 28

# Laotsze

**Laotsze founded Taoism and is an important figure in Chinese culture. However, as the servant in this story discovers to his cost, he may not always have been an ideal employer.**

Laotsze is really older than heaven and earth put together. He is the Yellow Lord or Ancient, who created this world together with the other four. At various times he has appeared on earth, under various names. His most celebrated incarnation, however, is that of Laotsze, 'The Old Child', which name he was given because he made his appearance on earth with white hair.

He acquired all sorts of magic powers and thereby extended his lifespan. Once he hired a servant to do his bidding. He agreed to give him a hundred pieces of copper daily; yet he did not pay him, and finally he owed him seven million, two hundred thousand pieces of copper. Then he mounted a black steer and rode to the West. He took his servant along, but when they reached the Han-Gu pass, the servant refused to go further, and insisted on being paid. Laotsze gave him nothing.

When they came to the house of the Guardian of the Pass, red clouds appeared in the sky. The Guardian understood that a holy man was drawing near, and went out to meet him, taking him into his house. He questioned him with regard to hidden knowledge, but Laotsze only stuck out his tongue at him and would not say a word. Nevertheless, the Guardian of the Pass treated him with the greatest respect in his home.

Laotsze's servant told the Guardian's servant that his master owed him a great deal of money, begging him to put in a good word. Hearing just how large a sum it was, the Guardian's servant was tempted to win so wealthy a man for a son-in-law, and he married him to his daughter. Finally the Guardian heard of the matter and came to Laotsze and the servant. Then Laotsze said to his servant: 'You rascally man. You should have died long ago. I hired you, and since I was poor and could give you no money, I gave you a life-giving talisman to eat. That is why you still happen to be alive. I said to you: "If you will follow me into the West, the land of Blessed Repose, I will pay you your wages in yellow gold. But you did not wish to do this.'" With that, he patted his servant's neck. Thereupon the servant opened his mouth and spat out the life-giving talisman. The magic signs written on it with cinnabar, quite fresh and well-preserved, were still visible, but the servant suddenly collapsed and turned into a heap of dry bones.

Instantly the Guardian of the Pass cast himself to earth and pleaded for him, promising to pay the debt for Laotsze and begging he be restored to life. So Laotsze placed the talisman among the bones and at once the servant came to life again. The Guardian of the Pass then paid him his wages and dismissed him. Then he venerated Laotsze as his master, and was taught the art of eternal life, and received his teachings, in five thousand words, writing them down. The book which thus came into being is the *Tao Teh King, The Book of the Way and Life*. Laotsze then disappeared from the eyes of men. The Guardian of the Pass, however, followed his teachings, and was given a place among the immortals.

*Notes: Taoists insist that Laotsze's journey to the West was undertaken before the birth of Buddha, who, according to many, is only a reincarnation of Laotsze.*

*The Guardian of the Han-Gu Pass is mentioned by the name of Guan Yin Hi, in the* Lia Dsi *and the* Dschuang Dsi.

*'Laotsze' simply means 'Old Master'. Long considered as the author of the Tao Te Ching, he is the founder of Taoism and is worshipped as the 'Supreme Old Lord'.*

# 29

# The Ancient Man

**In Chinese folklore, Fu Hi is described as 'the original human' and he was said to have lived for 197 years. Judge for yourself whether being extremely old meant he was also incredibly wise.**

O nce upon a time there was a man named Huang An. He must have been well over eighty and yet he looked like a youth. He lived on cinnabar and wore no clothing. Even in winter he went about without garments. He sat on a tortoise three feet long. Once he was asked: 'About how old might this tortoise be?' He answered: 'When Fu Hi first invented fishnets and eel pots, he caught this tortoise and gave it to me. And since then I have worn its shield quite flat sitting on it. The creature dreads the radiance of the sun and moon, so it only sticks its head out of its shell once in two thousand years. Since I have had the beast, it has already stuck its head out five times.' With these words he took his tortoise on his back and went off. And the legend arose that this man was ten thousand years old.

*Notes: Cinnabar is frequently used in the preparation of the elixir of life (compare 30).*
  *Tortoises live to a great age.*

Laotsze, the philosopher and teacher,
was probably born in 601 BCE and is generally
considered to have founded the religion of Taoism.

# 30

# The Eight Immortals (I)

**Meet the Eight Immortals. Some of them are real historical characters, while others are purely mythical, but there's no denying they all have an impressive set of superpowers.**

There is a legend which declares that Eight Immortals dwell in the heavens. The first is named Dschung Li Kuan. He lived in the time of the Han dynasty, and discovered the wonderful magic of golden cinnabar, the philosopher's stone. He could melt quicksilver and burn lead and turn them into yellow gold and white silver. And he could fly through the air in his human form. He is the chief of the Eight Immortals.

The second is named Dschang Go. In primal times he gained hidden knowledge. It is said that he was really a white bat, who turned into a man. In the first days of the Tang dynasty, an ancient with a white beard and a bamboo drum on his back was seen riding backward on a black ass in the town of Tschang An. He beat the drum and sang, and called himself old Dschang Go. Another legend says that he always had a white mule with him, which could cover a thousand miles in a single day. When he had reached his destination, he would fold up the animal and put it in his trunk. When he needed it again, he would sprinkle water on it with his mouth, and the beast would regain its first shape.

The third is named Lu Yuan or Lu Dung Bin (the Mountain Guest). His real name was Li, and he belonged to the ruling Tang dynasty. But when the Empress Wu seized the throne and destroyed the Li family to almost the last man, he fled with his wife into the heart of the mountains. They changed their names to Lu and, since they lived in hiding in the caverns in the rocks, he called himself the Mountain Guest or the Guest of the Rocks. He lived on air and ate no bread. Yet he was fond of flowers. And in the course of time he acquired the hidden wisdom.

In Lo Yang, the capital city, the peonies bloomed luxuriantly. And there dwelt a flower fairy, who changed herself into a lovely maiden.

Whenever Guest of the Rocks came to Lo Yang, he liked to converse with her. Suddenly along came the Yellow Dragon in the form of a handsome youth. He mocked the flower fairy. Guest of the Rocks grew furious and cast his flying sword at him, cutting off his head. From that time onward he fell back again into the world of mundane pleasure and death. He sank down into the dust of daily life, and was no longer able to wing his way to the upper regions. Later he met Dschung Li Kuan, who delivered him, and then he was taken up in the ranks of the Immortals.

Willowelf was his disciple. This was an old willow tree, which had drawn into itself the most ethereal powers of the sunrays and the moonbeams, and had thus been able to assume the shape of a human being. His face is blue and he has red hair. Guest of the Rocks received him as a disciple. Emperors and kings of future times honour Guest of the Rocks as the ancestor and master of the pure sun. The people call him Grandfather Lu. He is very wise and powerful, so people still stream into his temples to obtain oracles and pray for good luck. If you want to know whether you will be successful or not in an undertaking, go to the temple, light incense and bow your head to earth. On the altar is a bamboo goblet, in which are some dozens of little lottery sticks. Shake them while kneeling, until one of the sticks flies out. On the lottery stick is inscribed a number. Look up this number in the *Book of Oracles*, where it is accompanied by a four-line stanza. It is said that fortune and misfortune occur just as foretold by the oracle.

The fourth Immortal is Tsau Guo Gui (Tsau, the Uncle of the State). He was the younger brother of the Empress Tsau, who ruled the land for a time, and for this reason he was called the Uncle of the State. From his earliest youth he had been a lover of the hidden wisdom. Riches and honours were no more to him than dust. It was Dschung Li Kuan who helped him become immortal.

The fifth is called Lan Tsai Ho. Nothing is known of his true name, his time nor his family. He was often seen in the marketplace, clad in a torn blue robe and wearing only a single shoe, beating a block of wood and singing about the nothingness of life.

The sixth Immortal is known as Li Tia Guai (Li with the Iron Crutch). He lost his parents in early youth and was brought up in his older brother's home. His sister-in-law treated him badly and never gave him enough to eat. Because of this he fled into the hills, and there learned the hidden wisdom.

Once he returned in order to see his brother, and said to his sister-in-law: 'Give me something to eat!' She answered: 'There is no kindling wood on hand!' He replied: 'You need only to prepare the rice. I can use my leg for kindling wood. Just make sure not to say that the fire might injure me – and if you do not, no harm will be done.'

Wanting to see his skill, his sister-in-law poured the rice into the pot. Li stretched one of his legs out under it and lit it. The flames leaped high and the leg burned like coal.

When the rice was nearly boiled, his sister-in-law said: 'Won't your leg be injured?'

And Li replied angrily: 'Did I not warn you not to say anything! Then no harm would have been done. Now one of my legs is lame.' With these words he took an iron poker and fashioned it into a crutch for himself. Then he hung a bottle-gourd on his back and went into the hills to gather medicinal herbs. And that is why he is known as Li with the Iron Crutch.

It is also told of him that he was in the habit of ascending into the heavens in the spirit to visit his master Laotsze. Before he left, he would order a disciple to watch his body and the soul within it, so that his soul did not escape. Should seven days have gone by without his spirit returning, then he would allow his soul to leave the empty room. Unfortunately, after six days had passed, the disciple was called to the deathbed of his mother, and when the master's spirit returned on the evening of the seventh day, the life had gone out of its body. Since there was no place for his spirit in his own body, he seized in his despair upon the first handy body from which the vital spark was not yet extinguished. It was the body of a neighbour, a lame cripple, who had just died, so that from that time on the master appeared in his form.

The seventh Immortal is called Hang Siang Dsi. He was the nephew of the famous Confucian scholar Han Yu, of the Tang dynasty. From his earliest youth he cultivated the arts of the deathless gods, left his home and became a Taoist. Grandfather Lu awakened him and raised him to the heavenly world. Once he saved his uncle's life. His uncle had been driven from court after objecting when the emperor sent for a bone of the Buddha with great pomp. Reaching the Blue Pass in his flight, he discovered that a deep snowfall had made the road impassable. His horse floundered in a snowdrift, and he himself was well-nigh frozen. Suddenly Hang Siang Dsi appeared, helped him and his horse out of the drift, and brought them safely to the nearest inn along the Blue Pass. Han Yu sang a verse, including the following lines:

Tsin Ling Hill 'mid clouds doth lie,
And home is far, beyond my sight!
Round the Blue Pass snow towers high,
And who will lead the horse aright?

Suddenly it occurred to him that several years before, Hang Siang Dsi had come to his house to congratulate him on his birthday. Before leaving, he had written these words on a slip of paper, and his uncle had read them, without grasping their meaning. Now he was unconsciously singing the very lines of that song that his nephew had written. So he said to Hang Siang Dsi, with a sigh: 'You must be one of the Immortals, since you were able to tell the future!'

Three times Hang Siang Dsi sought to deliver his wife from the bonds of earth. When he had left his home to seek the hidden wisdom, she sat all day long yearning for his presence. Hang Siang Dsi wished to release her into immortality, but he feared she was not capable of the transition. He appeared to her in various forms, in order to test her, once as a beggar, another time as a wandering monk. But his wife did not grasp these opportunities. At last he took the shape of a lame Taoist, who sat on a mat, beat a block of wood and read sutras before the house.

His wife said: 'My husband is not at home. I can give you nothing.'

The Taoist answered: 'I do not want your gold and silver, I want you. Sit down beside me on the mat, and we will fly up into the air and you shall find your husband again!'

Hereupon the woman grew angry and struck at him with a cudgel.

Then Hang Siang Dsi changed himself into his true form, stepped on a shining cloud and was carried aloft. His wife looked after him and wept loudly; but he had disappeared and was not seen again.

The eighth Immortal is a girl called Ho Sian Gu. She was a peasant's daughter, and though her stepmother treated her harshly she remained respectful and industrious. She loved to give alms, though her stepmother tried to prevent her. And she was never angry, even when her stepmother beat her. She had sworn not to marry, and at last her stepmother did not know what to do with her. One day, while she was cooking rice, Grandfather Du came and delivered her. She was still holding the rice spoon in her hand as she ascended into the air. In the heavens she was appointed to sweep up the fallen flowers at the Southern Gate of Heaven.

*Notes: Some of the Immortals, like Han Siang Dsi, are historic personages, others purely mythical. In the present day they play an important part in art and crafts. Their emblems also occur frequently:*

- *Dschung Li Kuan is represented with a fan.*
- *Dschang Go has a bamboo drum with two drumsticks (and his donkey).*
- *Lu Dung Bin has a sword and a flower basket on his back.*
- *Tsau Guo Gui has two small boards (Yin Yang Ban), which he can throw into the air.*
- *Li Tia Guai carries the bottle-gourd, out of which emerges a bat, the emblem of good fortune.*
- *Lan Tsai Ho, who is also pictured as a woman, has a flute.*
- *Han Siang Dsi has a flower basket and a dibble.*
- *Ho Sian Gu has a spoon, usually formed in the shape of a lotus flower.*

# 31

# The Eight Immortals (II)

**In this tale a man who is starving and homeless meets the Eight Immortals and asks them for help, but does he come out of the encounter ahead? Make your own mind up.**

Once upon a time there was a poor man, who at last had no roof to shelter him and not a bite to eat. Weary and worn, he lay down beside a little temple of the field god standing by the roadside and fell asleep. And he dreamed that the old, white-bearded field god came out of his little shrine and said to him: 'I know of a way to help you! Tomorrow the Eight Immortals will pass along this road. Cast yourself down before them and plead to them!'

When the man awoke, he seated himself beneath the great tree beside the field god's little temple and waited all day long for his dream to come true. At last, when the sun had nearly sunk, eight figures came down the road, which the beggar clearly recognised as those of the Eight Immortals. Seven of them were hurrying as fast as they could, but one, who had a lame leg, limped along after the rest. Before him – it was Li Tia Guai – the man cast himself down to earth. But the lame Immortal did not want to bother with him, and told him to go away. Yet the poor man would not give over pleading with him, begging that he might go with them and be one of the Immortals, too. That would be impossible, said the cripple. Yet, as the poor man did not cease his prayers and would not leave him, he at last said: 'Very well, then, take hold of my coat!' This the man did and off they went in flying haste over paths and fields, on and on, and even further on. Suddenly they stood together high up on the tower of Pong-lai-schan, the ghost mountain by the Eastern Sea. And, lo, there stood the rest of the Immortals as well! But they were very displeased by the companion whom Li Tia Guai had brought along. Yet since the poor man pleaded so earnestly, they too allowed themselves to be moved, and said to him: 'Very well! We will now leap down into the sea. If you follow us, you may also become an Immortal!' And one after another the seven leaped down into the sea. But when it came to the man's turn, he was frightened and would not dare the leap. Then the cripple said to him: 'If you are afraid, you cannot become an Immortal!'

'What shall I do now?' wailed the man, 'I am far from my home and have no money!' The cripple broke off a fragment of the battlement of the tower and thrust it into the man's hand; then he also leaped from the tower and disappeared into the sea like his seven companions.

When the man examined the stone in his hand more closely, he saw that it was the purest silver. This provided him with travelling money during the many weeks it took him to reach his home. But by that time the silver was completely used up, and he found himself just as poor as he had been before.

*Note: Little field god temples, Tu Di Miau, are miniature stone chapels that stand before every village.*

Dshung Li Kuan, the First of the Eight Immortals
and their chief, can fly through the air in his human
form and is often represented by a fan.

# 32

# The Two Scholars

**Peach blossom represents love and peaches mean long life, so the peach tree is a symbol of immortality. Here two scholars meet two maids, but will it be happy ever after for the couples?**

O nce upon a time there were two scholars, one named Liu Tschen and the other Yuan Dschau. Both were young and handsome. One spring day they went together into the hills of Tian Tai to gather healing herbs. There they came to a little valley where peach trees blossomed luxuriantly on either side. In the middle of the valley was a cave, where two maidens stood under the blossoming trees, one of them clad in red garments, the other in green. And they were beautiful beyond all telling. They beckoned to the scholars with their hands.

'Have you come?' they asked. 'We have been waiting for you overlong!'

Then they led them into the cave and served them with tea and wine.

'I have been destined for the lord Liu,' said the maiden in the red gown; 'and my sister is for the lord Yuan!'

And so they were married. Every day the two scholars gazed at the flowers or played chess so that they forgot the mundane world completely. They noticed only that at times the peach blossoms on the trees before the cave opened, and at others that they fell from the boughs. And, at times, unexpectedly, they felt cold or warm, and had to change the clothing they were wearing. And they marvelled within themselves that it should be so.

Then, one day, they were suddenly overcome by homesickness. Both maidens were already aware.

'When our lords have once been seized with homesickness, then we may hold them no longer,' said they.

On the following day they prepared a farewell banquet, gave the scholars magic wine to take along with them and said: 'We will see one another again. Now go your way!'

And the scholars bade them farewell with tears.

When they reached home, the gates and doors had long since vanished. The people of the village were all strangers to them, crowding about and asking who they might be.

'We are Liu Tschen and Yuan Dschau. Only a few days ago we went into the hills to pick herbs!'

With that a servant came hastening up and looked at them. At last he fell at Liu Tschen's feet with great joy and cried: 'Yes, you are really my master! Since you went away, we have had no news of any kind regarding you. Some seventy years or more have passed.'

Thereupon he drew the scholar Liu through a high gateway, ornamented with bosses and a ring in a lion's mouth, as is the custom in the dwellings of those of high estate.

And when he entered the hall, an old lady with white hair and bent back, leaning on a cane, came forward and asked: 'Who is this?'

'Our master has returned again,' replied the servant. Turning to Liu, he added: 'Here is our mistress. She is nearly a hundred years old, but fortunately she is still strong and in good health.'

Tears of joy and sadness filled the old lady's eyes.

'Since you went away among the immortals, I had thought that we should never see each other again in this life,' said she. 'What great good fortune that you should have returned after all!'

And before she had ended, the whole family, men and women, came streaming up and welcomed him in a great throng outside the hall.

His wife pointed out this one and then that and said: 'That is so and so, and this is so and so!'

At the time the scholar had disappeared, there had been only a tiny boy in his home, but a few years old. And now he was an old man of eighty. He had served the empire in a high office, and had retired to enjoy his old age in the ancestral gardens. There were three grandchildren, all celebrated ministers; there were more than ten great-grandchildren, of whom five had already passed their examinations for the doctorate; there were some twenty great-great-grandchildren, of whom the oldest had just returned home after having passed his induction examinations for the magistracy with honour. And the little ones, who were carried in their parents' arms, were not to be counted. Those grandchildren who were away, busy with their duties, all asked for leave and returned home when they heard that their ancestor had returned. And the granddaughters, who had married into other families, also came. This filled Liu with joy, and he had a family banquet prepared in the hall, and all his descendants, with their wives and husbands sat about him in a circle. He and his wife, a white-haired, wrinkled old lady, sat in their midst at the upper end. The scholar himself still looked like a youth of twenty years, so that all the young people in the circle looked around and laughed.

Then the scholar said: 'I have a means of driving away old age!'

And he drew out his magic wine and gave his wife some of it to drink. And when she had taken three glasses, her white hair gradually turned black again, her wrinkles disappeared, and she sat beside her husband, a handsome young woman. Then his son and the older grandchildren came up and all asked for a drink of the wine. And whichever of them drank only so much as a drop of it was turned from old age back to youth. The tale spread quickly abroad and came to the emperor's ears. The emperor wanted to call Liu to his court, but Liu declined with many thanks. Nonetheless he sent the emperor some of his magic wine as a gift. This pleased the emperor greatly, and he gave Liu a tablet of honour, inscribed: 'The Common Home of Five Generations'.

Besides this he sent him three signs, written with his own imperial brush, signifying:

'Joy in longevity'.

As to the other of the two scholars, Yuan Dschau, he was not so fortunate. When he came home, he found that his wife and child had long since died, and his grandchildren and great-grandchildren were mostly useless people. So he did not remain long but returned to the hills. Yet Liu Tschen remained for some years with his family, and then, taking his wife with him, he went again to the Tai Hills and was seen no more.

*Note: This tale is placed in the reign of the Emperor Ming Di (58–75 CE). Its motif is that of the legend of* The Seven Sleepers – *who hid in a cave to escape religious persecution – and is often found in Chinese fairy tales.*

Dshang Go, the Second of the Eight Immortals,
is known for riding a white donkey, which he folds
up and packs into a trunk at the end of the day.

# 33

# The Miserly Farmer

**A stubborn farmer, a bonze (or Buddhist monk), and a cart full of pears feature in this story. In China, a gift of pears is never welcome, because it implies a wish for separation or even death.**

Once upon a time there was a farmer who had carted pears to market. Since they were very sweet and fragrant, he hoped to get a good price for them. A bonze, wearing a torn cap and tattered robe stepped up to his cart and asked for one. The farmer refused, but the bonze did not go. Then the farmer grew angry and began to call him names. The bonze said: 'You have pears by the hundred in your cart. I ask for only one. Surely that does you no great injury. Why suddenly grow so angry about it?'

The bystanders told the farmer that he ought to give the bonze one of the smaller pears and let him go. But the farmer would not and did not. An artisan saw the whole affair from his shop, and since the noise annoyed him, he took some money, bought a pear and gave it to the bonze.

The bonze thanked him and said: 'One like myself, who has given up the world, must not be miserly. I have beautiful pears myself, and I invite you all to eat them with me.' Then someone asked: 'If you have pears, then why do you not eat your own?' He answered: 'I first must have a seed to plant.'

And with that he began to eat the pear with gusto. When he had finished, he held the pit in his hand, took his pickaxe from his shoulder and dug a hole a couple of inches deep. Into this he thrust the pit, and covered it with earth. Then he asked the folk in the marketplace for water. A pair of curious onlookers brought him hot water from the hostelry in the street, and with it the bonze watered the pit. Thousands of eyes were turned on the spot. And the pit could already be seen to sprout. The sprout grew, and in a moment it had turned into a tree. Branches and leaves burgeoned out from it. It began to blossom and soon the fruit had ripened: large, fragrant pears, which hung in thick clusters from the boughs. The bonze climbed into the tree and handed down the pears to the bystanders. In a moment all the pears had been eaten up. Then the bonze took his pickaxe and cut down the tree. Crash, crash! so it went for a while, and the tree was felled. Then he took the tree on his shoulder and walked away at an easy gait.

When the bonze had begun performing his magic, the farmer had mingled with the crowd. With neck outstretched and staring eyes, he had stood there and had entirely forgotten the business he hoped to do with his pears. When the bonze walked off, he turned around to look after his cart. His pears had all disappeared. Then he realised that the pears the bonze had divided had been his own. He looked more closely, and saw that the axle of his cart had disappeared. It was plainly evident that it had been chopped off quite recently. The farmer fell into a rage and hastened after the bonze as fast as ever he could. And when he turned the corner, there lay the missing piece from the axle by the city wall. And then he realised that the pear tree which the bonze had chopped down must have been his axle. The bonze, however, was nowhere to be found. And the whole crowd in the market burst out into loud laughter.

*Note: The axle in China is really a handle, for the little Chinese carts are one-wheel push-carts with two handles or shafts.*

# 34

## Sky O'Dawn

**Whistling was a form of meditation for Taoists and the most skilful whistlers were said to be able to control the weather. Whistling is one of Sky O'Dawn's talents, but he has many...**

Once upon a time there was a man who took a child to a woman in a certain village and told her to take care of him. Then he disappeared. And because the dawn was just breaking in the sky when the woman took the child into her home, she called him Sky O'Dawn. When the child was three years old, he would often look up to the heavens and talk with the stars. One day he ran away and many months passed before he came home again. The woman gave him a whipping. But he ran away again, and did not return for a year. His foster mother was frightened, and asked: 'Where have you been all year long?' The boy answered: 'I only made a quick trip to the Purple Sea. There the water stained my clothes red. So I went to the spring at which the sun turns in, and washed them. I went away in the morning and came back at noon. Why do you speak about my having been gone a year?'

Then the woman asked: 'And where did you pass on your way?'

The boy answered: 'When I had washed my clothes, I rested for a while in the City of the Dead and fell asleep. And the King Father of the East gave me red chestnuts and rosy dawn-juice to eat, and my hunger was stilled. Then I went to the dark skies and drank the yellow dew, and my thirst was quenched. And I met a black tiger and wanted to ride home on his back. But I whipped him too hard, and he bit me in the leg. And so I came back to tell you about it.'

Once more the boy ran away from home, thousands of miles, until he came to the swamp where dwelt the Primal Mist. There he met an old man with yellow eyebrows and asked him how old he might be. The old man said: 'I have given up the habit of eating, and live on air. The pupils of my eyes have gradually acquired a green glow, which enables me to see all hidden things. Whenever a thousand years have passed, I turn around my bones and wash the marrow. And every two thousand years, I scrape my skin to get rid of the hair. I have already washed my bones thrice and scraped my skin five times.'

Afterwards Sky O'Dawn served the Emperor Wu of the Han dynasty. The emperor, who was fond of the magic arts, was much attached to him. One day he said to him: 'I wish that the empress might not grow old. Can you prevent it?'

Sky O'Dawn answered: 'I know of only one means to keep from growing old.'

The emperor asked what were the herbs to eat. Sky O'Dawn replied: 'In the North-East grow the mushrooms of life. There is a three-legged crow in the sun who always wants to get down and eat them. But the Sun God holds his eyes shut and does not let him get away. If human beings eat them, they become immortal, but when animals eat them, they grow stupefied.'

'And how do you know this?' asked the emperor.

'When I was a boy I once fell into a deep well, from which I could not get out for many decades. And down there was an immortal who led me to this herb. But one has to pass through a red river with water so light that not even a feather can swim on it. Everything that touches its surface sinks to the depths. But the man pulled off one of his shoes and gave it to me. And I crossed the water on the shoe, picked the herb and ate it. Those who dwell in that place weave mats of pearls and precious stones. They led me to a spot where hung a curtain of delicate, coloured skin. And they gave me a pillow carved of black jade, on which were graven sun and moon, clouds and thunder. They covered me with a dainty coverlet spun of the hair of a hundred gnats. A cover of that kind is very cool and refreshing in summer. I felt of it with my hands, and it seemed to be formed of water; but when I looked at it more closely, it was pure light.'

One time, it so happened that the emperor called together all his magicians in order to talk with them about the fields of the blessed spirits. Sky O'Dawn was there, too, and said: 'Once I was wandering about the North Pole and I came to the Fire-Mirror Mountain. There neither sun nor moon shines. But there is a dragon who holds a fiery mirror in his jaws to light up the darkness. On the mountain is a park, and in the park is a lake. By the lake grows the glimmer-stalk grass, which shines like a lamp of gold. If you pluck it and use it for a candle, you can see all things visible, and the shapes of the spirits as well. It even illuminates the interior of a human being.'

One time Sky O'Dawn went to the East, into the country of the fortunate clouds. And he brought back with him from that land a steed of the gods, nine feet high. The emperor asked him how he had come to find it.

So he told him: 'The Queen Mother of the West had him harnessed to her wagon when she went to visit the King Father of the East. The steed was staked out in the field of the mushrooms of life. But he trampled down several hundred of them. This made the King Father angry, and he drove the steed away to the heavenly river. There I found him and rode him home. I rode three times around the sun, because I had fallen asleep on the steed's back. And then, before I knew it, I was here. This steed can catch up with the sun's shadow. When I found him, he was quite thin and as sad as an aged donkey. So I mowed the grass of the country of the fortunate clouds, which grows once every two thousand years on the Mountain of the Nine Springs, and fed it to the horse; and that made him lively again.'

The emperor asked what sort of a place the country of the fortunate clouds might be. Sky O'Dawn answered: 'There is a great swamp there. The people prophesy fortune and misfortune by the air and the clouds. If good fortune is to befall a house, clouds of five colours form in the rooms, which alight on the grass and trees and turn into a coloured dew. This dew tastes as sweet as cider.'

The emperor asked whether he could obtain any of this dew. Sky O'Dawn replied: 'My steed could take me to the place where it falls four times in the course of a single day!'

And sure enough he came back by evening, and brought along dew of every colour in a crystal flask. The emperor drank it and his hair grew black again. He gave it to his highest officials to drink, and the old grew young again and the sick became well.

One time a comet appeared in the heavens, so Sky O'Dawn gave the emperor the astrologer's wand. The emperor pointed it at the comet and the comet was quenched.

Sky O'Dawn was an excellent whistler. And whenever he whistled in full tones, long drawn out, the motes in the sunbeams danced to his music.

Once he said to a friend: 'There is not a soul on earth who knows who I am with the exception of the astrologer!'

When Sky O'Dawn had died, the emperor called the astrologer to him and asked: 'Did you know Sky O'Dawn?'

He replied: 'No!'

The emperor said: 'What do you know?'

The astrologer answered: 'I know how to gaze on the stars.'

'Are all the stars in their places?' asked the emperor.

'Yes, but for eighteen years I have not seen the Star of the Great Year. Now it is visible once more.'

Then the emperor looked up towards the skies and sighed: 'For eighteen years Sky O'Dawn kept me company, and I did not know that he was the Star of the Great Year!'

*Notes: Dung Fang So, the mother of Sky O'Dawn, is, according to one tradition, the third daughter of the Lord of the Heavens (compare Note to 16). Dung Fang So is an incarnation of the Wood Star or Star of the Great Year (Jupiter).*

*The King Father of the East, one of the Five Ancients, is the representative of wood (compare 15).*

*Red chestnuts, like fire-dates, are fruits of the gods, and bestow immortality.*

*The Emperor Wu of the Han dynasty was a prince reputed to have devoted much attention to the magic arts. He reigned from 140 to 86 BCE.*

*The three-legged crow in the sun is the counterpart of the three-legged ram-toad in the moon.*

*The Red River recalls the Weak River by the Castle of the Queen Mother of the West.*

Dung Bin, the Third of the Eight Immortals,
has a magic sword that makes him invisible and
often carries a flower basket on his back.

# 35

# King Mu of Dschou

**King Mu dreams of achieving immortality, so when a magician with rather expensive tastes arrives from the west, Mu wonders whether this magician can make his dreams come true.**

In the days of King Mu of Dschou, a magician came out of the uttermost west, who could walk through water and fire, and pass through metal and stone. He could make mountains and rivers change place, shift about cities and castles, rise into emptiness without falling, strike against solid matter without finding it an obstruction; and he knew a thousand transformations in all their inexhaustible variety. And not only could he change the shape of things; he could also change men's thoughts. The King honoured him like a god, and served him as he would a master. He resigned his own apartments that the magician might lodge in them, ordered that beasts of sacrifice be offered to him, and selected sweet singers to give him pleasure.

But the rooms in the King's palace were too humble – the magician could not dwell in them; nor were the King's singers musical enough to be allowed to be near him. So King Mu had a new palace built for him. The work of the bricklayers and carpenters, the painters and stainers was unsurpassed in terms of skill, and the King's treasury was empty by the time the tower had reached its full height. A thousand fathoms high, it rose above the top of the mountain before the capital.

The King selected maidens, the loveliest and most dainty, and they were given fragrant essences, their eyebrows were groomed into beautiful curves, and their hair and ears were adorned with jewels. He dressed them in fine cloth, and white silks fluttered about them, while their faces were painted white and their eyebrows stained black. He had them put on armlets of precious stones and mix sweet-smelling herbs. They filled the palace and sang the songs of the ancient kings in order to please the magician. Every month, the most costly garments were brought him, and every morning the most delicate food. The magician allowed them to do so, and since he had no choice, he made the best of it.

Not long afterwards, the magician invited the King to go travelling with him. The King grasped the magician's sleeve, and thus they flew up through the air to the middle of the skies. When they stopped, they found they had reached the palace of the magician. Built of gold and silver, it was adorned with pearls and precious stones. It towered high over the clouds and rain; and where it stood no one could say. Layer upon layer of clouds, it seemed. All that the palace offered the senses was different from the things of the world of men. It seemed to the King as though he were in the midst of the purple depths of the city of the air, of the divine harmony of the spheres, where the Great God dwells. He looked down, and his castles and pleasure-houses looked like hills of earth and heaps of straw. And there he remained for some decades, thinking no more of his kingdom.

Then the magician again invited the King to go travelling with him once more. And in the place to which they came there was to be seen neither sun nor moon above, nor rivers or sea below. The King's eyes were so dazzled he could not see the radiant shapes that showed themselves; his ears so dulled he could not hear the sounds playing about them. His body seemed to be dissolving in confusion; his thoughts began to stray, and consciousness threatened to leave him. So he begged the magician to return. The magician put a spell on him, and the King felt that he was falling into empty space.

When he regained consciousness, he was sitting exactly where he had been sitting when the magician had asked him to travel with him for the first time. The servants waiting on him were the same, and when he looked down, his goblet was not yet empty, and his food had not yet grown cold.

The King asked what had happened. The servants answered: 'The King sat for a space in silence.' At this, the King lost all reason, and it was three months before he regained his right mind. Then he questioned the magician. The magician said: 'I was travelling with you in the spirit, O King! What need was there for the body to go along? The place where we stayed at that time was no less real than your own castle and your own gardens. But you are used only to permanent conditions, so visions that dissolve so suddenly seem strange to you.'

The King was content with the explanation. He gave no further thought to the business of government and took no more interest in his servants, resolving instead to travel afar. He had his eight famous steeds harnessed, and accompanied by a few faithful retainers, he drove a thousand miles away. There he came to the country of the great hunters. The great hunters brought the King the blood of the white brant to drink, and washed his feet in the milk of mares and cows. When the King and his followers had quenched their thirst, they drove on and camped for the night on the slope of the Kunlun Mountain, south of the Red River. The next day they climbed to the peak of Kunlun Mountain and gazed at the castle of the Lord of the Yellow Earth. Then they travelled on to the Queen Mother of the West. Before they reached her, they had to pass the Weak River. This is a river whose waters will bear neither floats nor ships: all that attempts to float will sink into its depths. When the King reached the shore, fish and turtles, crabs and salamanders came swimming up and formed a bridge, so that he could drive across with the wagon.

It is said of the Queen Mother of the West that she goes about with hair unkempt, with a bird's beak and tiger's teeth, and that she is skilled in playing the flute. Yet this is not her true figure, but that of a spirit who serves her and rules over the Western sky. The Queen Mother entertained King Mu in her castle by the Springs of Jade. She gave him rock-marrow to drink and fed him with the fruit of the jade trees. Then she sang him a song and taught him a magic formula that guaranteed a long life. The Queen Mother of the West gathers the immortals around her, and gives them to eat of the peaches of long life; and then they come to her with wagons with purple canopies, drawn by flying dragons. Ordinary mortals sink in the Weak River when they try to cross. But she was kindly disposed to King Mu.

When he took leave of her, he went on to the spot where the sun turns in after running three thousand miles a day. Then he returned again to his kingdom.

When King Mu was a hundred years old, the Queen Mother of the West drew near his palace and led him away with her into the clouds.

And from that day on he was seen no more.

*Notes: King Mu of Dschou reigned from 1001 to 946 BCE. With his name are associated the stories of the marvellous travels into the land of the far West, and especially to the Queen Mother (who is identified by some with Juno).*

*The peaches of immortality suggest the apples of the Hesperides (compare with the story of 'The Ape Sun Wu Kung', 74).*

# 36

# The King of Huai Nan

**Eight elderly gentlemen call on Lui An, King of Huai Nan, who is desperate to live for ever... Although a legend, this tale does bear some resemblance to the events of Lui An's life.**

The King of Huai Nan was a learned man of the Han dynasty. Since he was of the blood royal, the emperor had given him a kingdom in fee. He cultivated the society of scholars, could interpret signs and foretell the future. Together with his scholars he had compiled the book that bears his name.

One day, eight aged men came to see him. They all had white beards and white hair. The gatekeeper announced them to the King. The King wished to test them, so he sent back the gatekeeper to put difficulties in the way of their entrance. He said to them: 'Our King is striving to learn the art of immortal life. You gentlemen are old and feeble. How can you help him? There is no reason for you to pay him a visit.'

The eight old men smiled and said: 'Oh, and are we too old to suit you? Well, then, we will make ourselves young!' And before they had even finished speaking they had turned themselves into boys of fourteen and fifteen, with hair-knots as black as silk and faces like peach blossoms. The gatekeeper was frightened, and at once told the

King what had happened. When the King heard, he did not even take the time to slip into his shoes but hurried out barefoot to receive them. Leading them into his palace, he ordered rugs of brocade to be spread for them, and beds of ivory set up, fragrant herbs burned and tables of gold and precious stones set in front of them. Bowing before them as pupils do before a teacher, he told them how glad he was that they had come.

The eight boys changed into old men again and said: 'Do you wish to go to school with us, Your Majesty? Each one of us is master of a particular art. One of us can call up wind and rain, cause clouds and mists to gather, rivers to flow and mountains to heave themselves up, if he wills it. The second can cause high mountains to split asunder and check great streams in their course. He can tame tigers and panthers and soothe serpents and dragons. Spirits and gods do his bidding. The third can send out doubles, transform himself into other shapes, make himself invisible, cause whole armies to disappear, and turn day into night. The fourth can walk through the air and clouds, can stroll on the surface of the waves, pass through walls and rocks and cover a thousand miles in a single breath. The fifth can enter fire without burning, and water without drowning. The winter frost cannot chill him, nor the summer heat burn him. The sixth can create and transform living creatures if he feels inclined. He can form birds and beasts, grasses and trees. He can move houses and castles. The seventh can bake lime so that it turns to gold, and cook lead so that it turns to silver; he can mingle water and stone so that the bubbles effervesce and turn into pearls. The eighth can ride on dragons and cranes to the eight poles of the world, converse with the immortals, and stand in the presence of the Great Pure One.'

The King kept them beside him from morning to night, entertained them and had them show him what they could do. And, true enough, they could do everything just as they had said. And now the King began to distil the elixir of life with their help. He had finished, but not yet drunk it when a misfortune overtook his family. His son had been playing with a courtier, who had carelessly wounded him. Fearing that the prince might punish him, the courtier joined other malcontents and excited a revolt. Hearing of this, the emperor sent one of his captains to judge between the King and the rebels.

The eight aged men spoke: 'It is now time to go. This misfortune has been sent you from heaven, Your Majesty! Had it not befallen you, you would not have been able to resolve to leave the splendours and glories of this world!'

They led him to a mountain. There they offered sacrifices to heaven and buried gold in the earth. Then they ascended into the skies in bright daylight. The footprints of the eight aged men and the king were imprinted in the mountain rock, and may be seen there to this very day. Before they had left the castle, however, they had set what was left of the elixir of life out in the courtyard. Hens and hounds picked and licked it up, and all flew up into the skies. In Huai Nan to this very day the crowing of cocks and the barking of hounds may be heard in the skies, and it is said that these are the creatures who followed the King at the time.

One of the King's servants, however, followed him to an island in the sea, from where he was sent back. He explained that the King himself had not yet ascended to the skies but had only become immortal and was wandering about the world. When the emperor heard this, he was filled with regret that he had sent soldiers into the King's land and driven him out. He called magicians to help him, in hope of meeting the eight old men himself. Yet, for all that he spent great sums, he was not successful. The magicians only cheated him.

*Note: The King of Huai Nan was named Liu An. He belonged to the Han dynasty. He dabbled largely in magic and drew to his court many magicians whose labours are collected in the philosophical work bearing his name: Huainanzi. Living at the time of the Emperor Wu (see 34), who had no heirs, Liu An entered into a conspiracy which, however, was discovered. As a consequence he killed himself, in 122 BCE.*

# 37

# Old Dschang

**In a Chinese tradition that continues to this day, before a marriage takes place the groom gives the bride's family a dowry. The groom in this story, though, isn't quite what he seems.**

O nce upon a time there was a man who went by the name of Old Dschang. He lived in the country, near Yangdschou, as a gardener. His neighbour, named Sir We, held an official position in Yangdschou. Sir We had decided that it was time for his daughter to marry, so he sent for a matchmaker and commissioned her to find a suitable husband. Old Dschang heard this and was pleased. He prepared food and drink, entertained the matchmaker, and told her to recommend him as a husband. But the old matchmaker left immediately, scolding him as she went.

The next day he invited her to dinner again and gave her money. Then the old matchmaker said: 'You do not know what you wish! Why should a gentleman's beautiful daughter condescend to marry a poor old gardener like yourself? Even though you had money to burn, your white hair would not match her black locks. Such a marriage is out of the question!'

But Old Dschang did not cease to entreat her: 'Make an attempt, just one attempt, to mention me! If they will not listen to you, then I must resign myself to my fate!'

The old matchmaker had taken his money, so she could not well refuse, and though she feared being scolded, she mentioned him to Sir We. He grew angry and wanted to throw her out of the house.

'I knew you would not thank me,' said she, 'but the old man urged it so that I could not refuse to mention his intention.'

'Tell the old man that if this very day he brings me two white jade stones, and four hundred ounces of yellow gold, then I will give him my daughter's hand in marriage.'

With this command, he wished only to mock the old man's folly, for he knew that his neighbour could not give him anything of the kind.

The matchmaker delivered the message to Old Dschang – who made no objection but at once brought the exact quantity of gold and jewels to Sir We's house. Sir We was terrified, and when his wife heard, she began to weep and wail loudly. But the girl encouraged her mother: 'My father has given his word now and cannot break it. I will know how to bear my fate.'

So the wedding took place. But even after the wedding Old Dschang did not give up his work as a gardener. He dug the field and sold vegetables as usual, and his wife had to fetch water and build the kitchen fire herself. But she did her work without false shame and, though her relatives reproached her, she continued to do so.

Once an aristocratic relative visited Sir We and said: 'If you had really been poor, were there not enough young gentlemen in the neighbourhood for your daughter? Why did you have to marry her to such a wrinkled old gardener? Now that you have thrown her away, so to speak, it would be better if both of them left this part of the country.'

Then Sir We prepared a banquet and invited his daughter and Old Dschang to visit him. When they had had sufficient to eat and drink, he allowed them to get an inkling of what was in his mind.

Said Old Dschang: 'I have remained here because I thought you would long for your daughter. But since you are tired of us, I will be glad to go. I have a little country house back in the hills, and we will set out for it early tomorrow morning.'

The following morning, at break of dawn, Old Dschang came with his wife to say farewell. Sir We said: 'Should we long to see you at some later time, my son can make inquiries.' Old Dschang placed his wife on a donkey and gave her a straw hat to wear. He himself took his staff and walked after.

A few years passed without any news from either of them. Then Sir We and his wife felt quite a longing to see their daughter and sent their son to make inquiries. When he reached the hills, he met a plough boy who was ploughing with two yellow steers. He asked him: 'Where is Old Dschang's country house?' The plough boy left the plough in the harrow, bowed and answered: 'You have been a long time coming, sir! The village is not far from here: I will show you the way.'

They crossed a hill. At the foot of the hill flowed a brook, and when they had crossed the brook they had to climb another hill. Gradually the landscape changed. From the top of the hill could be seen a valley, level in the middle, surrounded by abrupt crags and shaded by green trees, among which houses and towers peeped forth. This was the country house of Old Dschang. Before the village flowed a deep brook full of clear, blue water. They passed over a stone bridge and reached the gate. Here flowers and trees grew in luxurious profusion, and peacocks and cranes flew about. From the distance could be heard the sound of flutes and stringed instruments. Crystal-clear tones rose to the clouds. A messenger in a purple robe received the guest at the gate and led him into a hall of surpassing splendour. Strange fragrances filled the air, and there was a ringing of little bells made from pearl. Two maidservants came forth to greet him, followed by two rows of beautiful girls in a long procession. After them a man in a flowing turban, clad in scarlet silk, with red slippers, came floating along. The guest saluted him. He was serious and dignified, and at the same time seemed youthfully fresh. At first We's son did not recognise him, but then he looked more closely, and why, it was Old Dschang! The latter said with a smile: 'I am pleased that the long journey has not prevented your coming. Your sister is just combing her hair. She will welcome you in a moment.' Then he invited him to sit down and drink tea.

After a short time a maidservant came and led him to the inner rooms, to his sister. The beams of her room were of sandalwood, the doors of tortoiseshell and the windows inlaid with blue jade; her curtains were formed of strings of pearls and the steps leading into the room of green nephrite. His sister was magnificently gowned, and far more beautiful than before. She asked him carelessly how he was getting along, and what her parents were doing; but was not very cordial. After a splendid meal she had an apartment prepared for him.

'My sister wishes to make an excursion to the Mountain of the Fairies,' said Old Dschang. 'We will be back about sunset, and you can rest until we return.'

Then many-coloured clouds rose in the courtyard, and dulcet music sounded on the air. Old Dschang mounted a dragon, while his wife and sister rode on phoenixes and their attendants on cranes. So they rose into the air and disappeared in an easterly direction. They did not return until after sunset.

Old Dschang and his wife then said to him: 'This is an abode of the blessed. You cannot remain here overlong. Tomorrow we will escort you back.'

On the following day, when the young man was taking his leave, Old Dschang gave him eighty ounces of gold and an old straw hat. 'Should you need money,' said he, 'go to Yangdschou and inquire in the northern suburb for Old Wang's pharmacy. There you can collect ten million pieces of copper. This hat is the order for them.' Then he ordered his plough boy to take him home again.

Quite a few of the folks at home, to whom he described his adventures, thought that Old Dschang must be a holy man, while others assumed the whole thing was a magic vision.

After five or six years, Sir We's money came to an end. So his son took the straw hat to Yangdschou and there asked for Old Wang. The latter just happened to be standing in his pharmacy, mixing herbs. When the son explained his errand he said: 'The money is ready. But is your hat genuine?' He took the hat and was examining it when a young girl came from an inner room and said: 'I wove the hat for Old Dschang myself. There must be a red thread in it.' And sure enough, there was. Then Old Wang gave Young We the ten million pieces of copper, and the latter now believed that Old Dschang was really a saint. So he once more went over the hills to look for him. He asked the forest-keepers, but they could tell him naught. Sadly he retraced his steps and decided to inquire of Old Wang, but he too had disappeared.

When several years had passed he once more came to Yangdschou, and was walking in the meadow before the city gate. There he met Old Dschang's plough boy, who cried out: 'How are you? How are you?' and drew out ten pounds of gold. This he gave to him, saying: 'My mistress told me to give you this. My master is this very moment drinking tea with Old Wang in the inn.' Young We followed the plough boy, intending to greet his brother-in-law. But when he reached the inn there was no one in sight. And when he turned around the plough boy had disappeared as well. And since that time no one has ever heard from Old Dschang again.

*Note: According to Chinese custom – and the custom of other peoples across Asia – the matchmaker is an essential mediator between the two families. There are old women who make their living at this profession.*

# 38

# The Kindly Magician

**This curious tale concerns an idle, undeserving man who wastes all his money on having a good time. However, his ultimate fate is not necessarily what you might expect...**

Once upon a time there was a man named Du Dsi Tschun. In his youth he was a spendthrift and paid no heed to his property. He was given to drink and idling, and when he had run through all his money, his relatives cast him out. One winter day he was walking barefoot about the city, with an empty stomach and torn clothes. Evening came on and still he had not found any food. Without end or aim he wandered about the marketplace. He was hungry, and the cold seemed well-nigh unendurable. Turning his eyes upwards, he began to lament aloud.

Suddenly an ancient man stood before him, leaning on a staff, who said: 'What do you lack since you complain so?'

'I am dying of hunger,' replied Du Dsi Tschun, 'and not a soul will take pity on me!'

The ancient man said: 'How much money would you need in order to live in all comfort?'

'If I had fifty thousand pieces of copper, it would answer my purpose,' replied Du Dsi Tschun.

The ancient said: 'That would not answer.'

'Well, then, a million!'

'That is still too little!'

'Well, then, three million!'

The ancient man said: 'That is well spoken!' He fetched a thousand pieces of copper out of his sleeve and said: 'That is for this evening. Expect me tomorrow by noon, at the Persian bazaar!'

At the time set, Du Dsi Tschun went to the Persian bazaar and there, sure enough, was the ancient, who gave him three million pieces of copper. Then he disappeared, without giving his name.

When Du Dsi Tschun held the money in his hand, his old extravagance returned. He rode pampered steeds, clothed himself in the finest furs, went back to his wine, and led such an extravagant life that the money gradually came to an end. Instead of wearing brocade he had to wear cotton, and instead of riding horseback he went to the dogs. Finally he was again running about barefoot and in rags as before, and did not know how to satisfy his hunger. Once more he stood in the marketplace and sighed. But the ancient was already there and, taking him by the hand, said: 'Are you back already to where you were? That's strange! However, I will help you once more!'

But Du Dsi Tschun was ashamed and did not want to accept his help. The ancient insisted, and led him along to the Persian bazaar. This time he gave him ten million pieces of copper, and Du Dsi Tschun thanked him with shame in his heart.

With money in hand, he tried to give time to adding to it and saving in order to gain great wealth. But, as is always the case, it is hard to overcome ingrown faults. Gradually he began to fling his money away again, and gave free rein to all his desires. Once more his purse grew empty. In a couple of years he was as poor as ever he had been.

Then he met the ancient the third time, but was now so ashamed that he hid his face when he passed him.

The ancient seized his arm and said: 'Where are you going? I will help you once more. I will give you thirty million. But if then you do not improve, you are past all help!'

Full of gratitude, Du Dsi Tschun bowed before him and said: 'In the days of my poverty, my wealthy relatives did not seek me out. You alone have helped me three times. The money you give me today shall not be squandered, that I swear; but I will devote it to good works in order to repay your great kindness. And when I have done this, I will follow you – through fire and through water if needs be.'

The ancient replied: 'That is right! When you have ordered these things, ask for me in the temple of Laotsze beneath the two mulberry trees!'

Du Dsi Tschun took the money and went to Yangdschou. There he bought a hundred acres of the best land, and built a lofty house with many hundreds of rooms on the highway. And there he allowed widows and orphans to live. Then he bought a burial place for his ancestors, and supported his needy relations. Countless people were indebted to him for their livelihood.

When all was finished, he went to inquire after the ancient in the temple of Laotsze. The ancient was sitting in the shade of the mulberry trees blowing the flute. He took Du Dsi Tschun along with him to the cloudy peaks of the holy mountains of the West. When they had gone some forty miles into the mountains, they came to a dwelling, fair and clean. It was surrounded by many-coloured clouds, and peacocks and cranes were flying about it. Within the house was a herb oven nine feet high. The fire burned with a purple flame, and its glow leaped along the walls. Nine fairies stood at the oven, and a green dragon and a white tiger crouched beside it. Evening came. The ancient was no longer clad like an ordinary man but instead wore a yellow cap and wide, flowing garments. Taking three pellets of the White Stone, he put them into a flagon of wine and gave them to Du Dsi Tschun to drink. He spread out a tiger skin against the western wall of the inner chamber, and bade Du Dsi Tschun sit down on it, with his face turned toward the East. Then he said to him: 'Now beware! No matter what happens to you – whether you encounter powerful gods or terrible demons, wild beasts or ogres, or all the tortures of the underworld, or even if you see your own relatives suffer – do not speak a single word for all these things are only deceitful images! They cannot harm you. Think only of what I have said, and let your soul be at rest!' No sooner had he said this than the ancient disappeared.

Then Du Dsi Tschun saw only a large stone jug full of clear water standing before him. The fairies, dragon and tiger had all vanished. Suddenly he heard a tremendous crash, which made heaven and earth tremble. A man towering more than ten feet in height appeared. He called himself the great captain, and he and his horse were covered with golden armour. He was surrounded by more than a hundred soldiers, who drew their bows and swung their swords, and halted in the courtyard.

The giant called out harshly: 'Who are you? Get out of my way!'

Du Dsi Tschun did not move. And made no answer to his questions.

The giant flew into a passion and cried with a thundering voice: 'Chop off his head!'

But Du Dsi Tschun remained unmoved, so the giant went off raging.

Then a furious tiger and a poisonous serpent came up roaring and hissing. They made as though to bite him and leaped over him. But Du Dsi Tschun remained unperturbed, and after a time they dissolved and vanished.

Suddenly a great rain began to fall in streams. It thundered and lightninged incessantly, so that his ears rang and his eyes were blinded. It seemed as though the house would fall. The water rose to a flood in a few moments' time, and streamed up to the place where he was sitting. But Du Dsi Tschun remained motionless and paid no attention to it. After a time, the water receded.

Then came a great demon with the head of an ox. He set up a kettle in the middle of the courtyard, bubbling with boiling oil. He caught Du Dsi Tschun by the neck with an iron fork and said: 'If you will tell me who you are, I will let you go!'

Du Dsi Tschun shut his eyes and kept silent. Then the demon picked him up with the fork and flung him into the kettle. He withstood the pain, and the boiling oil did not harm him. Finally the demon dragged him out again, and drew him down the steps of the house before a man with red hair and a blue face, who looked like the Prince of the Underworld. The Prince cried: 'Drag in his wife!'

After a time Du Dsi Tschun's wife was brought on in chains. Her hair was torn and she wept bitterly.

The demon pointed to Du Dsi Tschun and said: 'If you will speak your name, we will let her go!'

But he answered not a word.

Then the Prince of Evil ordered the woman to be tormented in all sorts of ways. And she pleaded with Du Dsi Tschun: 'I have been your wife now for ten years. Will you not speak one little word to save me? I can endure no more!' And the tears ran in streams from her eyes. She screamed and scolded. Yet he spoke not a word.

Thereupon the Prince of Evil shouted: 'Chop her into bits!' And there, before his eyes, it seemed as though she were being chopped to pieces. But Du Dsi Tschun did not move.

'The scoundrel's measure is full!' cried the Prince of Evil. 'He shall dwell no longer among the living! Off with his head!' And so they killed him, and it seemed to him that his soul fled his body. The ox-headed demon dragged him down into the lower regions, where he tasted all the tortures in turn. But Du Dsi Tschun remembered the words of the ancient. And the tortures, too, seemed bearable. So he did not scream and he said not a word.

Now he was dragged once more before the Prince of Evil. The latter said: 'As punishment for his obstinacy, this man shall come to earth again in the shape of a woman!'

The demon dragged him to the Wheel of Life and he returned to earth in the shape of a girl. He was often ill, had to take medicine continually, and was pricked and burned with hot needles. Yet he never uttered a sound. Gradually he grew into a beautiful maiden. But since he never spoke, he was known as the dumb maid. A scholar finally took him for his bride, and they lived in peace and good fellowship. And a son came to them who, in the course of two years was already beyond measure wise and intelligent. One day the father was carrying the son on his arm. He spoke jestingly to his wife and said: 'When I look at you it seems to me that you are not really dumb. Won't you say one little word to me? How delightful it would be if you were to become my speaking rose!'

The woman remained silent. No matter how he might coax and try to make her smile, she would return no answer.

Then his features changed: 'If you will not speak to me, it is a sign that you scorn me; and in that case your son is nothing to me, either!' With that, he seized the boy and flung him against the wall.

And since Du Dsi Tschun loved this little boy so dearly, he forgot the ancient's warning, and cried out.

Before his cry had died away, Du Dsi Tschun awoke as though from a dream and found himself seated in his former place. The ancient was there as well. It must have been about the fifth hour of the night. Purple flames rose wildly from the oven, flaring up to the sky. The whole house caught fire and burned like a torch.

'You have deceived me!' cried the ancient, seizing him by the hair and thrusting him into the jug of water. In a minute the fire went out. The ancient spoke: 'You overcame joy and rage, grief and fear, hate and desire, it is true; but love you had not driven from your soul. Had you not cried out when the child was flung against the wall, my elixir would have taken shape and you would have attained immortality. But in the last moment you failed me. Now it is too late. Now I can begin brewing my elixir of life once more from the beginning and you will remain a mere mortal man!'

Du Dsi Tschun saw that the oven had burst, and that instead of the philosopher's stone it held only a lump of iron. The ancient man cast aside his garments and chopped it up with a magic knife. Du Dsi Tschun took leave of him and returned to Yangdschou, where he lived in great affluence. In his old age he regretted that he had not completed his task. He once more went to the mountain to look for the ancient. But the ancient had vanished without leaving a trace.

*Notes: The 'pieces of copper' are the ancient Chinese copper coins, with a hole in the middle, usually hung on strings to the number of 500 or 1,000.*

*Evidence suggests that the earliest bazaars were established about five thousand years ago. They seem to have developed to service the needs of travellers along the old Silk Road.*

*The Persian bazaar: During the reign of the Tang dynasty China maintained active dealings with the West. At that time Persian bazaars were no novelty in the city of Si-An-Fu, then the capital.*

*'Herb-oven': a tripod kettle used for brewing the elixir of life, with which the fairies, dragon and tiger are connected. In order to prepare the elixir, the master must have absolute endurance. It is for this reason that he placed Du Dsi Tschun in his debt.*

*The yellow cap which the master wears is connected with the teachings of the Yellow Ancient (compare to 15).*

*The 'prince of the underworld,' Yan Wang, or Yan Lo Wang, is the Indian god Yama. There are in all ten princes of the underworld, of whom the fifth is the highest and most feared.*

*'Obstinacy,' literally; his real offence, however, is reticence, or the keeping secret of a thing. This quality belongs to the Yin, the dark or feminine principle, and determines Du Dsi Tschun's reappearance on earth as a woman.*

*'Purple flames rose wildly from the oven': though Du Dsi Tschun had overcome his other emotions, so that fear and terror did not affect him, love, and love in its highest form, mother love, still remained in him. This love created the flames that threatened to destroy the building. The highest point in Taoism – as in Buddhism – is, however, the absolute negation of all feeling.*

Tsau Guo Gui, the Fourth of the Eight Immortals,
has no interest in worldly possessions or accolades,
but carries two small boards for throwing.

# NATURE AND
# ANIMAL TALES

# 39

# The Flower Elves

**To unlock the heavy symbolism of this fable, it might help to know that the willow and peach both represent immortality, the plum means renewal and the pomegranate promises prosperity.**

Once upon a time there was a scholar who lived retired from the world in order to gain hidden wisdom. He lived alone and in a secret place. And all about the little house in which he dwelt he had planted every kind of flower, and bamboos and other trees. There his house lay, quite concealed in its thick grove of flowers. With him he had only a boy servant, who dwelt in a separate hut, and who carried out his orders. He was not allowed to appear before his master unless summoned. The scholar loved his flowers as he did himself. Never did he set his foot beyond the boundaries of his garden.

It chanced that once there came a lovely spring evening. Flowers and trees stood in full bloom, a fresh breeze was blowing, the moon shone clearly. The scholar sat over his goblet, grateful for the gift of life.

Suddenly he saw a maiden in dark garments come tripping up in the moonlight. She made a deep curtsy, greeted him and said: 'I am your neighbour. We are a company of young maids who are on our way to visit the eighteen aunts. We should like to rest in this court for a while, and ask your permission to do so.'

The scholar saw that this was something quite out of the common, and gladly gave his consent. The maiden thanked him and went away.

In a short time she brought back a whole crowd of maids carrying flowers and willow branches. All greeted the scholar. They were charming, with delicate features, and slender, graceful figures. When they moved, their sleeves exhaled a delightful fragrance. There is no fragrance known to the human world to compare with it.

The scholar invited them to sit down for a time in his room. Then he asked them: 'Whom have I really the honour of entertaining? Have you come from the castle of the Lady in the Moon, or the Jade Spring of the Queen Mother of the West?'

'How could we claim such high descent?' said a maiden in a green gown, with a smile. 'My name is Salix.' Then she presented another, clad in white, and said: 'This is Mistress Prunophora'; then one in rose, 'and this is Persica'; and finally one in a dark-red gown, 'and this is Punica. We are all sisters and we want to visit the eighteen zephyr aunts today. The moon shines so beautifully this evening and it is so charming here in the garden. We are most grateful to you for taking pity on us.'

'Yes, yes,' said the scholar, embarrassed.

Suddenly the sober-clad servant announced: 'The zephyr aunts have already arrived!'

At once the girls rose and went to the door to meet them.

'We were just about to visit you, aunts,' they said, smiling. 'This gentleman here had just invited us to sit for a moment. What a pleasant coincidence that you aunts have come here, too. This is such a lovely night that we must drink a goblet of nectar in honour of you!'

They ordered the servant to bring what was needed.

'May we sit down here?' asked the aunts.

'The master of the house is most kind,' replied the maids, 'and the spot is quiet and hidden.'

Then they presented the aunts to the scholar. He spoke a few kindly words to the eighteen aunts. They had a somewhat careless, airy manner. Their words fairly gushed out, and from them came a frosty chill.

Meanwhile the servant had already brought in table and chairs. The eighteen aunts sat at the upper end of the board, the maids followed, and the scholar sat down with them at the lowest place. Soon the entire table was covered with delicious foods and magnificent fruits, and the goblets were filled with a fragrant nectar. These were delights such as the world of men does not know! The moon shone brightly and the flowers exhaled intoxicating fragrances. After they had shared food and drink, the maids rose, danced and sung. The sound of their singing echoed sweetly through the falling gloam, and their dance was like butterflies fluttering about the flowers. The scholar no longer knew whether he was in heaven or on earth.

When the dance had ended, the girls sat down again at the table, and drank the health of the aunts in flowing nectar. The scholar, too, was remembered with a toast, to which he replied with well-turned phrases.

But the eighteen aunts were somewhat careless. One of them, raising her goblet, accidentally poured some nectar on Punica's dress. Punica was young and fiery, and very neat, and seeing the spot on her red dress she stood up angrily.

'You are really very careless. My other sisters may be afraid of you, but I am not!'

This angered the aunts too, who said: 'How dare this young chit insult us in such a manner!'

With that they gathered up their garments and rose.

All the maids crowded about them and said: 'Punica is so young and inexperienced! You must not bear her any ill will! Tomorrow she shall go to you switch in hand, and receive her punishment!'

But the eighteen aunts would not listen and left. Thereupon the maids also said farewell, scattered among the flower beds and disappeared. The scholar sat for a long time lost in dreams and longing.

On the following evening the maids returned.

'We all live in your garden,' they told him. 'Every year we are tormented by naughty winds, so we have always asked the eighteen aunts to protect us. But yesterday Punica insulted them, and now we fear they will help us no more. We know that you have always been well disposed toward us, and are heartily grateful. And now we have a great favour to ask, that every New Year's Day you make a small scarlet flag, paint the sun, moon and five planets on it, and set it up in the eastern part of the garden. Then we sisters will be left in peace and will be protected from all evil. But since New Year's Day has passed for this year, we beg you to set up the flag on the twenty-first of this month. For the East Wind is coming and the flag will protect us against him!'

The scholar readily promised to do as they wished, and the maids all said with a single voice: 'We thank you for your great kindness and will repay it!' Then they departed and a sweet fragrance filled the entire garden.

The scholar made a red flag, and early in the morning of the day in question, the East Wind really did begin to blow and he quickly set it up in the garden.

Suddenly a wild storm broke out, one that caused the forests to bend and broke the trees. Only the flowers in the garden did not move.

Then the scholar noticed that Salix was the willow; Prunophora the plum; Persica the peach, and the saucy Punica the Pomegranate, whose powerful blossoms the wind cannot tear. The eighteen zephyr aunts, however, were the spirits of the winds.

In the evening the flower elves all came and brought the scholar radiant flowers as a gift of thanks.

'You have saved us,' they said, 'and we have nothing else we can give you. If you eat these flowers, you will live long and avoid old age. And if you, in turn, will protect us every year, then we sisters, too, will live long.'

The scholar did as they told him and ate the flowers. And his figure changed and he grew young again like a youth of twenty. And in the course of time he attained the hidden wisdom and was placed among the Immortals.

*Notes. Salix: the names of the 'Flower Elves' are given in the Chinese as family names, whose sound suggests the flower names without exactly using them. In the translation the play on words is indicated by the Latin names.*

*'Zephyr aunts': In Chinese the name given the aunt is 'Fong', which in another stylisation means 'wind.'*

# 40

# The Spirit of the Wu-Lian Mountain

**Scholars were expected to set a good example to others and live a moral life. The scholar in this story encounters a terrifying monster, but will his upstanding record save him?**

To the west of the gulf of Kiautschou is the Wu-Lian Mountain, where there are many spirits. Once upon a time a scholar who lived there was sitting up late at night, reading. Then he stepped out before the house, and a storm rose up suddenly.

A monster stretched out his claws and seized him by the hair, lifting him up in the air and carrying him away. They passed by the tower that looks out to sea, a Buddhist temple in the hills. And in the distance, in the clouds, the scholar saw the figure of a god in golden armour. The figure looked exactly like the image in the tower of Weto. In its right hand it held an iron mace, while its left pointed toward the monster, looking at it with anger. Then the monster let the scholar fall, right on top of the tower, and disappeared. No doubt the saint in the tower came to the scholar's aid because his whole family worshipped Buddha dutifully.

When the sun rose, the priest came and saw the scholar on his tower. He piled up hay and straw on the ground so that he could jump down without hurting himself. Then he took the scholar home, yet there where the monster had seized his hair, the hair remained stiff and unyielding. It did not improve until half a year had gone by.

*Notes: This legend comes from Dschungschong, west of the gulf of Kiautschou.*

*'The tower which looks out to sea' is a celebrated tower that gives a view of the ocean.*

*Weto (Sanskrit, Veda) was a legendary Boddhisatva, leader of the hosts of the four kings of heaven. His picture, with drawn sword, may be found at the entrance of every Buddhist temple. In China, he is often represented with a mace (symbolising a thunderbolt) instead of a sword. When this is the case, he has probably been confused with Vaisramana.*

Lan Tsai Ho, the Fifth of the Eight Immortals,
disguises himself in ordinary clothes, sometimes
as a woman, and plays the flute.

# 41

# The King of the Ants

**The miniature knights who invade the home of the educated but poor scholar in this tale create a marvellous spectacle, but who on earth are they – and are they friend or foe?**

O nce upon a time there was a scholar, who wandered away from his home and went to Emmet village. There stood a house that was said to be haunted. Yet it was beautifully situated and surrounded by a lovely garden. So the scholar hired it. One evening he was sitting over his books, when suddenly came several hundred knights galloping into the room. They were quite tiny, and their horses were about the size of flies. They had hunting falcons and dogs about as large as gnats and fleas.

They came to his bed in the corner of the room, and there they held a great hunt, with bows and arrows: one could see it all quite plainly. They caught a tremendous quantity of birds and game, and all this game was no larger than little grains of rice.

When the hunt was over, in came a long procession with banners and standards. They wore swords at their side and bore spears in their hands, and came to a halt in the north-west corner of the room. They were followed by several hundred serving men, who brought with them curtains and covers, tents and tent poles, pots and kettles, cups and plates, tables and chairs. And after them some hundreds of other servants carried in all sorts of fine dishes, the best that land and water had to offer. Several hundred more ran to and fro without stopping, to guard the roads and carry messages.

The scholar gradually accustomed himself to the sight. Although the men were so very small, he could distinguish everything quite clearly.

Before long, a bright-coloured banner appeared. Behind it rode a personage wearing a scarlet hat and garments of purple. He was surrounded by an escort of several thousands, and before him went runners with whips and rods to clear the way.

Then a man wearing an iron helmet and with a golden axe in his hand cried out in a loud voice: 'His Highness is graciously pleased to look at the fish in the Purple Lake!' Whereupon the one who wore the scarlet hat got down from his horse, and, followed by a retinue of several hundred men, approached the saucer used by the scholar for his writing ink. Tents were put up on the edge of the saucer and a banquet was prepared. A great number of guests sat down to the table. Musicians and dancers stood ready. There was a bright confusion of mingled garments of purple and scarlet, crimson and green. Pipes and flutes, fiddles and cymbals sounded, and the dancers moved in the dance. The music was very faint, yet its melodies could be clearly distinguished. All that was said, too, the table talk and orders, questions and calls, could be quite distinctly heard.

After three courses, he who wore the scarlet hat said: 'Quick! Make ready the nets and lines for fishing!'

And at once nets were thrown out into the saucer holding the water in which the scholar dipped his brush. And they caught hundreds of thousands of fishes. The one with the scarlet hat contented himself with casting a line in the shallow waters of the saucer, and caught a baker's dozen of red carp.

Then he ordered the head cook to cook the fish, and the most varied dishes were prepared with them. The odour of roasting fat and spices filled the whole room.

And then the wearer of the scarlet hat, in his arrogance, decided to amuse himself at the scholar's expense. Pointing to him, he said: 'I know nothing at all about the writings and customs of the saints and wise men, and still I am a king who is highly honoured! Yonder scholar spends his whole life toiling over his books and yet he remains poor and gets nowhere. If he could make up his mind to serve me faithfully as one of my officials, I might allow him to partake of our meal.'

This angered the scholar, who picked up his book and struck at them. And they all scattered, wriggling and crawling out of the door. He followed them and dug up the earth where they had disappeared. And there he found an ants' nest as large as a barrel, in which countless green ants were wriggling around. So he built a large fire and smoked them out.

# 42

# The Little Hunting Dog

**In this tale, a scholar is entranced by the appearance of tiny knights on horseback accompanied by falcons and hunting dogs. They do him a great service, but how does he repay them?**

Once upon a time, in the city of Shansi, there lived a scholar who found the company of others too noisy for him. So he made his home in a Buddhist temple. Yet here too he suffered because there were always so many gnats and fleas in his room that he could not sleep at night.

Once, while he was resting on his bed after dinner, two little knights with plumes in their helmets rode into the room. Perhaps two inches high, they rode horses about the size of grasshoppers, and on their gauntleted hands they held hunting falcons as large as flies. They raced about the room with remarkable speed. The scholar had no more than set eyes on them when a third entered, clad like the others but carrying a bow and arrows and leading a little hunting dog the size of an ant with him. After him came a great throng of footmen and horsemen, several hundred in all. And they had hunting falcons and hunting dogs by the hundred, too. The fleas and gnats began to rise in the air; but all were slain by the falcons. And the hunting dogs climbed on the bed, sniffed along the walls trailing the fleas, and ate them up. They followed the trace of whatever hid in the cracks, and nosed it out, so that in a short space of time they had killed nearly all the vermin.

The scholar pretended to be asleep as he watched them. And the falcons settled down on him, and the dogs crawled along his body. Shortly after came a man clad in yellow, wearing a king's crown, who climbed on an empty couch and seated himself there. At once all the horsemen rode up, climbed down from their horses and brought him all the birds and game. Then they gathered beside him in a great throng, and spoke with him in a strange tongue.

Shortly afterwards, the king got into a small chariot and his bodyguards saddled their horses as quickly as they could. Then they galloped out, raising loud cries of homage, till it looked as though someone were scattering beans. A heavy cloud of dust rose behind them.

The scholar's eyes were fixed on them, full of terror and astonishment, and he could not imagine where they came from. They had nearly all of them disappeared when he slipped on his shoes and set out to follow them; but they had vanished without a trace. Then he returned and looked all about his room; but there was nothing to be seen. Only, on a brick against the wall, a little hunting dog, which they had forgotten. The scholar quickly caught it and found it quite tame. He put it in his paintbox and examined it closely. It had a very smooth, fine coat, and wore a little collar around its neck. He tried to feed it a few breadcrumbs, but the little dog only sniffed at them and let them lie. Then it leaped into the bed and hunted up some nits and gnats in the folds of the linen, which it devoured. Then it returned and lay down. When he woke up the next morning, the scholar feared it might have run away; but there it lay, curled up as before. Whenever the scholar went to bed, the dog climbed into it and bit to death any vermin it could find. Not a fly or gnat dared alight while it was around. The scholar loved it like a precious jewel.

But once he took a nap in the daytime, and the little dog crawled into bed beside him. The scholar woke and turned around, supporting himself on his side. As he did so he felt something, and feared it might be his little dog. He quickly rose and looked, but it was already dead – pressed flat, as though cut out of paper!

But at any rate none of the vermin had survived it.

*Notes: This is a parallel to the preceding story and shows how the same material returns in a different version.*

*This tale is taken from the* Liao Chai Chih I *(Strange Tales from a Chinese Studio) of P'u Sung Lang (b. 1622). These were first published in China in 1740, and by the nineteenth century translations had reached Europe. Franz Kafka admired the 'exquisite' tales.*

# 43

# The Dragon after
# his Winter Sleep

**The Chinese believe dragons sleep during the winter and wake up when the first spring storm comes. The scholar in this story is quietly reading. What is it that interrupts him?**

O nce there was a scholar who was reading in the upper storey of his house. It was a rainy, cloudy day and the weather was gloomy. Suddenly he saw a little thing that shone like a fire-fly. It crawled upon the table, and wherever it went it left traces of burns, curved like the tracks of a rainworm. Gradually it wound itself about the scholar's book, and the book, too, grew black. Then it occurred to him that it might be a dragon, so he carried it out of doors on the book. There he stood for quite some time; but it sat uncurled, without moving in the least.

Then the scholar said: 'It shall not be said of me that I was lacking in respect.' With these words he carried back the book and once more laid it on the table. Then he put on his ceremonial robes, made a deep bow and escorted the dragon out on it again.

No sooner had he left the door than he noticed that the dragon raised his head and stretched himself. Then he flew up from the book with a hissing sound, like a radiant streak. Once more he turned around toward the scholar, who saw that his head had already grown to the size of a barrel while his body must have been a full fathom in length. The dragon gave one more snaky twist, then there was a terrible crash of thunder and the creature went sailing through the air.

The scholar went back inside and looked to see which way the little creature had come. And he could follow his tracks hither and thither, to his chest of books.

Li Tia Guai, the Sixth of the Eight Immortals,
usually carries a gourd containing medicine
and can be identified by his iron crutch.

# 44

# The Spirits of the Yellow River

**Don't doubt the power of the river gods, because they can unleash devastating floods. In fact, in the last two centuries the Yellow River has flooded more than 1,500 times...**

The spirits of the Yellow River are called Dai Wang – Great King. For many hundreds of years past the river inspectors continued to report that all sorts of monsters show themselves in the waves of the stream, at times in the shape of dragons, at times in the shape of cattle and horses. Whenever such a creature makes an appearance, a great flood follows. Hence temples are built along the riverbanks. The higher spirits of the river are honoured as kings, the lower ones as captains, and hardly a day goes by without their being honoured with sacrifices or theatrical performances. Whenever a dam has been broken and then the leak closed again, the emperor sends officials with sacrifices and ten great bars of Tibetan incense. This incense is burned in a large sacrificial censer in the temple court, and the river inspectors and their subordinates all go to the temple to thank the gods for their help. These river gods, it is said, are the good and faithful servants of former rulers, who died toiling to keep the dams unbroken. After they died, their spirits became river kings; in their physical bodies, they appear as lizards, snakes and frogs.

The mightiest of all the river kings is the Golden Dragon King. He frequently appears in the shape of a small golden snake with a square head, low forehead and four red dots over his eyes. He can make himself large or small at will, causing the waters to rise and fall. He appears and vanishes unexpectedly, and lives in the mouths of the Yellow River and the Imperial Canal. But in addition to the Golden Dragon King there are dozens of river kings and captains, who each has his own place. The sailors of the Yellow River all have exact lists in which the lives and deeds of the river spirits are described in detail.

The river spirits love to see theatrical performances. Opposite every temple is a stage. In the hall stands the little spirit tablet of the river king, and on the altar in front of it a small bowl of golden lacquer filled with clean sand. When a little snake appears in it, the river king has arrived. Then the priests strike the gong and beat the drum and read from the holy books. The official is at once informed and he sends for a company of actors. Before they begin to perform, the actors go up to the temple, kneel and beg the king to let them know which play they are to give. And the river god picks one out and points to it with his head; or else he writes signs in the sand with his tail. The actors then immediately perform the chosen play.

The river god cares nothing for the fortunes or misfortunes of human beings. He appears suddenly and disappears in the same way, as best suits him.

Between the outer and the inner dam of the Yellow River are a number of settlements. Now it often happens that the yellow water moves to the very edge of the inner walls. Rising perpendicularly, like a wall, it gradually advances. When people see it coming, they hastily burn incense, bow in prayer before the waters, and promise the river god a theatrical performance. Then the water retires and the word goes round: 'The river god has asked for a play again!'

In a village in that section there once dwelt a wealthy man. Around the village, he built a stone wall, twenty feet high, to keep away the water. He did not believe in the spirits of the river, but trusted in his strong wall and was quite unconcerned.

One evening the yellow water suddenly rose and towered in a straight line before the village. The rich man had them shoot cannon at it. Then the water grew stormy, and surrounded the wall to such a height that it reached the openings in the battlements. The water foamed and hissed, and seemed about to pour over the wall. Everyone in the village was terrified and they dragged up the rich man, who had to kneel and beg for pardon. They promised the river god a theatrical performance, but in vain; only when they promised to build him a temple in the middle of the village and give regular performances did the water sink bit by bit, gradually returning to its bed. And the village fields suffered no damage, for the earth, fertilised by the yellow slime, yielded a double crop.

Once a scholar was crossing the fields with a friend to visit a relative. On their way they passed a temple of the river god, where a new play was just being performed. The friend asked the scholar to go in with him and look on. When they entered the temple court, they saw two great snakes upon the front pillars, who had wound themselves about the columns and were thrusting out their heads as though watching the performance. In the hall of the temple stood the altar with the bowl of sand. In it lay a small snake with a golden body, a green head and red dots above his eyes. His neck was thrust up and his glittering little eyes never left the stage. The friend bowed and the scholar followed his example.

Softly he said to his friend: 'What are the three river gods called?'

'The one in the temple,' was the reply, 'is the Golden Dragon King. The two on the columns are two captains. They do not dare to sit in the temple with the king.'

This surprised the scholar, and in his heart he thought: 'Such a tiny snake! How can it possess a god's power? It would have to show me its might before I would worship it.'

He had not yet expressed these secret thoughts before the little snake stretched forth his head from the bowl, above the altar. In front of the altar burned two enormous candles. They weighed more than ten pounds and were as thick as small trees. Their flame burned like the flare of a torch. The snake now thrust his head into the middle of the candle flame, which must have been at least an inch broad and was burning red. Suddenly its radiance turned blue, and was split into two tongues. The candle was so enormous and its fire so hot that even copper and iron would have melted in it; but it did not harm the snake.

Then the snake crawled into the censer. The censer was made of iron, and was so large that it could not be clasped in both arms. Its cover showed a dragon design in openwork. The snake crawled in and out of the holes in this cover, winding his way through all of them until he looked like an embroidery made of threads of gold. All the openings of the cover, large and small, were filled by the snake, who must have made himself several dozen feet long. Then he stretched out his head at the top of the censer and began once more to watch the play.

At this the scholar was frightened. Bowing twice, he prayed: 'Great King, you have taken this trouble on my account! I honour you from my heart!'

No sooner had he spoken these words than, in a moment, the little snake was back in his bowl, just as small as he had been before.

In Dsiningdschou they were celebrating the river god's birthday in his temple, offering him a theatrical performance for a present. The spectators were crowded around as thick as a wall, when who should pass but a simple peasant from the country, who said in a loud voice: 'Why, that is nothing but a tiny worm! It is a great piece of folly to honour it like a king!'

Before ever he had finished speaking, the snake flew out of the temple. He grew larger and larger, winding himself three times around the stage. He swelled to the thickness of a small pail, and his head seemed like that of a dragon: his eyes sparkled like golden lamps, and he spat out red flame with his tongue. When he coiled and uncoiled himself, the whole stage trembled and it seemed as though it would collapsed. The actors stopped their music and fell down on the stage in prayer. The whole crowd was seized with terror and bowed to the ground. Some of the older men came along, grabbed the peasant and threw him on the ground to give him a good thrashing. He could do nothing else but fall to his knees before the snake and worship him. Then all the crowd heard a noise as though a great many firecrackers were exploding. This lasted for some time, and then the snake disappeared.

East of Shantung lies the city of Dongschou. There rises an observation tower with a great temple. At its feet lies the water city, with a sea gate at the North, through which the flood tide rises up to the city. A camp of the boundary guard is established at this gate.

Once upon a time there was an officer who had been transferred to this camp as captain. He had formerly belonged to the land forces, and had not yet been long at his new post. He gave some friends a banquet, and before the pavilion where they feasted lay a great stone shaped like a table. Suddenly a little snake was seen crawling on this stone. It was spotted with green, and had red dots on its square head. The soldiers were about to kill the little creature when the captain went to look into the matter. He laughed and said: 'You must not harm him! He is the river king of Dsiningdschou. When I was stationed in Dsiningdschou, he sometimes visited me, and then I always gave sacrifices and performances in his honour. Now he has come here expressly in order to wish his old friend luck, and to see him once more.'

There was a band in camp; the bandsmen could dance and play like a real theatrical troupe. The captain quickly had them begin a performance, ordered another banquet to be prepared with wine and dainty foods, and invited the river god to sit down to the table.

Gradually evening came and yet the river god made no move to go.

So the captain stepped up to him with a bow and said: 'Here we are far removed from the Yellow River, and these people have never yet heard your name spoken. Your visit has been a great honour for me. But the women and fools who have crowded together chattering outside are afraid of hearing about you. Now you have visited your old friend, and I am sure you wish to get back home again.'

With these words he had a litter brought up; cymbals were beaten and fireworks set off, and finally a salute of nine guns was fired to escort him on his way. Then the little snake crawled into the litter, and the captain followed after. In this order they reached the port, and just when it was about time to say farewell, the snake was already swimming in the water. Now grown much larger, he nodded to the captain with his head, and disappeared.

Then came doubts from the people and questions: 'But the river god lives a thousand miles away from here, how does he get to this place?'

Said the captain: 'He is so powerful that he can get to any place, and besides, from where he dwells a waterway leads to the sea. To come down that way and swim to sea is something he can do in a moment!'

# 45

# The Dragon-Princess

**There is much to be learned about how to deal with dragons from this entrancing tale of three brothers who are sent to the dragon's castle by the emperor on a quest for pearls.**

In the Sea of Dungting there is a hill, and in that hill there is a hole, and this hole is so deep that it has no bottom.

Once a fisherman was passing there and he slipped and fell into the hole. He came to a country full of winding ways that led over hill and dale for several miles. Finally he reached a dragon castle lying in a great plain. There grew a green slime which reached to his knees. He went to the gate of the castle. It was guarded by a dragon who spouted water that dispersed in a fine mist. Within the gate lay a small hornless dragon who raised his head, showed his claws, and would not let him in.

The fisherman spent several days in the cave, satisfying his hunger with the green slime, which tasted like rice-mush. At last he found a way out again. He told the district mandarin what had happened to him, and the matter was reported to the emperor. The emperor sent for a wise man to question him.

The wise man said: 'There are four paths in this cave. One path leads to the south-west shore of the Sea of Dungting, the second path leads to a valley in the land of the four rivers, the third path ends in a cave on the mountain of Lo-Fu and the fourth in an island of the Eastern Sea. In this cave dwells the seventh daughter of the Dragon King of the Eastern Sea, who guards his pearls and his treasure. It happened once in the ancient days, that a fisher boy dived into the water and brought up a pearl from beneath the chin of a black dragon. The dragon was asleep, which was the only reason the fisher boy could bring the pearl to the surface without being harmed. The treasure which the daughter of the Dragon King has in her charge is made up of thousands and millions of such jewels. Several thousands of small dragons watch over them in her service. Dragons have the peculiarity of fighting shy of wax. But they are fond of beautiful jade stones, and kung-tsing, the hollowgreen wood, and like to eat swallows. If you were to send a messenger with a letter, it would be possible to obtain precious pearls.'

The emperor was greatly pleased, and announced a large reward for the man who was competent to go to the dragon castle as his messenger.

The first man to come forward was named So Pi-Lo. But the wise man said: 'A great-great-great-great-grandfather of yours once slew more than a hundred of the dragons of the Eastern Sea, and was finally himself slain by the dragons. The dragons are your family's enemies and you cannot go.'

Then came a man from Canton, Lo-Dsi-Tschun, with his two brothers, who said that his ancestors had been related to the Dragon King. Hence they were well liked by the dragons and well known to them. They begged to be entrusted with the message.

The wise man asked: 'And have you still in your possession the stone that compels the dragons to do your will?'

'Yes,' said they, 'we have brought it along with us.'

The wise man had them show him the stone. Then he spoke: 'This stone is only obeyed by the dragons who make clouds and send down the rain. It will not do for the dragons who guard the pearls of the sea king.' Then he questioned them further: 'Do you have dragon-brain vapour?'

When they admitted that they had not, the wise man said: 'How then will you compel the dragons to yield their treasure?'

And the emperor said: 'What shall we do?'

The wise man replied: 'On the Western Ocean sail foreign merchants who deal in dragon-brain vapour. Someone must go to them and seek it from them. I also know a holy man who is an adept in the art of taming dragons, and who has prepared ten pounds of the dragonstone. Someone should be sent for that as well.'

The emperor sent out his messengers. They met one of the holy man's disciples and obtained two fragments of dragonstone from him.

Said the wise man: 'That is what we want!'

Several more months went by, and at last a pill of dragon-brain vapour had also been secured. The emperor felt much pleased and had his jewellers carve two little boxes of the finest jade. These were polished with the ashes of the Wutung-tree. And he had an essence prepared of the very best hollowgreen wood, pasted with sea-fish lime, and hardened in the fire. Of this, two vases were made. Then the bodies and the clothing of the messengers were rubbed with tree wax, and they were given five hundred roasted swallows to take along with them.

They went into the cave. When they reached the dragon castle, the little dragon who guarded the gate smelled the tree wax, so he crouched down and did them no harm. They gave him a hundred roasted swallows as a bribe to announce them to the daughter of the Dragon King. They were admitted to her presence and offered her the jade caskets, the vases and the four hundred roasted swallows as gifts. The dragon's daughter received them graciously, and they unfolded the emperor's letter.

In the castle was a dragon more than a thousand years old. He could turn himself into a human being, and could interpret the language of humans. Through him the dragon's daughter learned that the emperor was sending her the gifts, and she returned them with a gift of three great pearls, seven smaller pearls and a whole bushel of ordinary pearls. The messengers took leave, rode off with their pearls on a dragon's back, and in a moment they had reached the banks of the Yangtze-kiang. They made their way to Nanking, the imperial capital, and there handed over their treasure of gems.

The emperor was much pleased and showed them to the wise man. He said: 'Of the three great pearls, one is a divine wishing-pearl of the third class, and two are black dragon-pearls of medium quality. Of the seven smaller pearls, two are serpent-pearls, and five are mussel-pearls. The remaining pearls are in part sea-crane pearls, in part snail-and oyster-pearls. They do not approach the great pearls in value, and yet few will be found to equal them on earth.'

The emperor showed them to all his servants, who thought the wise man's words all talk, and did not believe what he said.

Then the wise man said: 'The radiance of wishing-pearls of first-class quality is visible for forty miles; of second class for twenty miles; and of third class for ten miles. As far as their radiance carries, neither wind nor rain, thunder nor lightning, water, fire nor weapons may reach. The pearls of the black dragon are nine-coloured and glow by night. Within the circle of their light, the poison of serpents and worms is powerless. The serpent pearls are seven-coloured, the mussel-pearls five-coloured. Both shine by night. Those most free from spots are the best. They grow within the mussel, and increase and decrease in size as the moon waxes and wanes.'

Someone asked how the serpent and sea-crane pearls could be told apart, and the wise man answered: 'The animals themselves recognise them.'

Then the emperor selected a serpent-pearl and a sea crane-pearl, put them together with a whole bushel of ordinary pearls, and poured the lot out in the courtyard. A large yellow serpent and a black crane were fetched and placed among the pearls. At once the crane took up a sea-crane pearl in his bill and began to dance and sing and flutter around. But the serpent snatched at the serpent-pearl, and wound himself about it in many coils. And when the people saw this, they acknowledged the truth of the wise man's words. As for the radiance of the larger and smaller pearls, it turned out, too, just as the wise man had said.

In the dragon castle the messengers had enjoyed dainty fare, which tasted like flowers, herbs, ointment and sugar. They brought a remnant of it with them to the capital, but exposed to the air it became as hard as stone. The emperor commanded that these fragments be preserved in the treasury. Then he bestowed high rank and titles on the three brothers, and made each one of them a present of a thousand rolls of fine silk stuff. He also ordered an investigation to explain why it was that the fisherman, when he chanced upon the cave, had not been destroyed by the dragons. It turned out that his fishing clothes had been soaked in oil and tree wax. The dragons had dreaded the odour.

# 46

# Help in Need

**When a dragon princess asks for his help, the mandarin in this story can hardly refuse. He sends his best general to fight for the princess, but is this a battle a mere mortal can win?**

Some twenty miles east of Gingdschou lies the Lake of the Maidens. It is several miles square and surrounded on all sides by thick green thickets and tall forests. Its waters are clear and dark blue. All kinds of wondrous creatures often show themselves in the lake. Local people have erected a temple there for the Dragon Princess. And in times of drought all make a pilgrimage there to offer up prayers.

West of Gingdschou, two hundred miles away, is another lake, whose god is named Tschauna, and who performs many miracles. During the time of the Tang dynasty, there lived in Gingdschou a mandarin by name of Dschou Bau. While he was in office it chanced that in the fifth month clouds suddenly arose in the sky, piling themselves up like mountains, and between them wriggled dragons and serpents, rolling up and down between the two seas. Tempest and rain, thunder and lightning arose so that houses fell to pieces, trees were torn up by the roots, and the crops were badly damaged. Dschou Bau took the blame upon himself, and prayed to the heavens that his people might be pardoned.

On the fifth day of the sixth month, he sat in his hall of audience giving judgment when suddenly he felt quite weary and sleepy. Taking off his hat, he laid down on the cushions. No sooner had he closed his eyes than he saw a warrior in helmet and armour, with a halberd in his hand, standing on the steps leading to the hall. The warrior announced: 'A lady is waiting outside who wishes to enter!' Dschou Bau asked him: 'Who are you?' The answer came: 'I am your doorkeeper. In the invisible world I have already been performing this duty for many years.'

Meanwhile two figures clad in green came up the steps, knelt before him and said: 'Our mistress has come to visit you!' Dschou Bau rose. He saw lovely clouds, from which fell a fine rain, and strange fragrances enchanted him. Suddenly floating down from on high came a lady clad in a simple gown but of surpassing beauty, attended by a retinue of many female servants. Neat and clean in appearance, they waited upon the lady as though she were a princess. When she entered the hall, she raised her arms in greeting. Dschou Bau came forward to meet her and invited her to be seated. From all sides bright-coloured clouds came floating in, and the courtyard was filled with a purple ether. Dschou Bau ordered wine and food to be brought and entertained them all in the most splendid way. But the goddess sat staring straight before her with wrinkled brows, and seemed to feel very sad. Then she rose and said with a blush: 'I have been living in this neighbourhood for many years. A wrong has been done to me, which allows me to pass beyond what is fitting and encourages me to ask a favour of you. Yet I do not know whether you will want to save me!'

'May I hear what it is all about?' answered Dschou Bau. 'If I can help, I will be glad to place myself at your disposal.'

The goddess said: 'For hundreds of years my family has been living in the depth of the Eastern Sea. But we were unfortunate in that our treasures excited the jealousy of men. The ancestor of Pi-Lo nearly destroyed our entire clan by fire. My ancestors had to fly and hide themselves. And not long ago, our enemy Pi-Lo himself wanted to deliver an imperial letter to the cave of the Sea of Dungting. Under the pretext of begging for pearls and treasures, he wished to enter the dragon castle and destroy our family. Fortunately a wise man saw through his treachery, and Lo-Dsi-Tschun and his brothers were sent in his place. Yet still my people did not feel safe from future attacks, and for this reason they withdrew to the distant West. My father has done much good to mankind and is highly honoured there. I am his ninth daughter. When I was sixteen I was wedded to the youngest son of the Rock Dragon. But my good husband had a fiery temper, which often caused him to offend against the laws of courtesy, and in less than a year's time the punishment of heaven was his portion. I was left alone and returned to the home of my parents. My father wished me to marry again; but I had promised to remain true to the memory of my husband, and vowed not to comply with my father's wish. My parents grew angry, and I was obliged to retire to this place. That was three years ago. How could I have imagined that the contemptible dragon Tschauna would seek a wife for his youngest brother and try to force a wedding gift on me? I refused to accept it; but Tschauna knew how to argue his case with my father. And regardless of my wishes, my father promised me to him. Then the dragon Tschauna appeared with his youngest brother and wanted to carry me off by sheer force of arms. I encountered him with fifty faithful followers, and we fought on the meadow before the city. We were defeated, and I am more than ever afraid that Tschauna will attempt to drag me off. That's why I have plucked up courage to beg you to lend me your mercenaries so that I may beat off my foes and remain as I am. If you help me, I will be grateful till the end of my days.'

Dschou Bau answered: 'You come from a noble family. Have you no kinsfolk who will hasten to help you in your need? Why are you compelled to turn to a mortal man?'

'It is true that my kinsfolk are famous far and wide, and numerous too. If I were to send out letters and they came to my aid, they would rub out that scaly scoundrel Tschauna as easily as rubbing garlic. But my deceased husband offended the high heavens and he has not yet been pardoned. And my parents' will, too, is opposed to mine, so that I dare not call upon my kinsfolk for help. You will understand my need.' At this, Dschou Bau promised to help her, and the princess thanked him and departed.

When he awoke, he sighed long, thinking over his strange experience. The following day he sent fifteen hundred soldiers to stand guard by the Lake of the Maidens.

On the seventh day of the sixth month, Dschou Bau rose early. Darkness still lay before the windows, yet it seemed to him as though he could glimpse a man before the curtain. He asked who it might be. The man said: 'I am the princess's adviser. Yesterday you were kind enough to send soldiers to aid us in our distress. But they were all living men, and cannot fight against invisible spirits. If you wish to help, you will have to send us soldiers of yours who have died.'

Reflecting on this for some time, Dschou Bau finally understood that such indeed must be the case. He had his field secretary examine the roster to see how many of his soldiers had fallen in battle. The secretary counted some two thousand foot soldiers and five hundred horsemen. Dschou Bau appointed his deceased officer Mong Yuan as their leader, and wrote his commands on a paper that he burned, thus placing them at the princess's disposal. The living soldiers he recalled.

When they were all being reviewed in the courtyard after their return, one soldier suddenly fell unconscious. Not until early the following morning did he come to his senses again. On being questioned, he replied: 'I saw a man clad in red, who approached me and said: "Our princess is grateful for the help your master has so kindly given her. Yet she still has a request to make and has asked me to call you." I followed him to the temple. The princess bade me come forward and said to me: "I thank your master from my heart for sending me the ghost soldiers, but Mong Yuan, their leader is incapable. Yesterday the robbers came with three thousand men, and Mong Yuan was beaten by them. When you return and again see your master, say that I earnestly beg him to send me a good general. Perhaps that will save me in my need." Then she had me led back again and I regained consciousness.'

When Dschou Bau heard these words, which seemed to fit strangely well with what he himself had dreamed, he decided to test the matter himself. So he chose his victorious general Dschong Tschong-Fu to take the place of Mong Yuan. That evening he burned incense, offered wine and handed over to the princess this captain's soul.

On the twenty-sixth of the month news came from the camp that the general had died suddenly at midnight on the thirteenth. Frightened, Dschou Bau sent a man to bring him a report. This informed him that the general's heart had hardly ceased to beat, and that, in spite of the hot summer weather, his body was free from any trace of decay. The order was therefore given not to bury him.

One night an icy, spectral wind arose, whirling up sand and stones, breaking trees and tearing down houses. The storm lasted all day, and the standing corn in the fields was blown down. Finally came the crash of a terrific thunderbolt, clearing the skies and scattering the clouds. That very hour the dead general began to breathe painfully on his couch, and when his attendants came to him, he had returned to life.

They questioned him and he told them: 'First I saw a man in a purple gown riding a black horse, who came up with a great retinue. He dismounted before the door. In his hand he held a decree of appointment which he gave me, saying: "Our princess begs you most respectfully to become her general. I hope that you will not refuse." Then he brought forth gifts and heaped them up before the steps. Jade stones, brocades, and silken garments, saddles, horses, helmets and suits of mail – he heaped them all up in the courtyard. I wanted to refuse, but this he would not allow, and he urged me to enter his chariot with him. We drove a hundred miles and met a train of three hundred armoured horsemen who had ridden out to escort me. They led me to a great city, and before the city a tent had been erected, and a band of musicians played inside. A high official welcomed me.'

'When I entered the city, the onlookers were crowded together like walls. Servants ran to and fro bearing orders. We passed through more than a dozen gates before we reached the princess. There I was requested to dismount and change my clothes before entering her presence, for she wished to receive me as her guest. But I thought this too great an honour and greeted her below, on the steps. She, however, invited me to seat myself near her in the hall. She sat upright in all her incomparable beauty, surrounded by female attendants adorned with the richest jewels. They plucked lute strings and played flutes. A throng of servitors stood about in golden girdles with purple tassels, ready to carry out her commands. Countless crowds were assembled before the palace. Five or six visitors sat in a circle about the princess, and a general led me to my place. The princess said to me: "I have begged you to come here in order to entrust the command of my army to you. If you will break the power of my enemy, I will reward you richly." I promised to obey her. Then wine was brought in, and the banquet was served to the sound of music.'

'While we were at table, a messenger entered: "The robber Tschauna has invaded our land with ten thousand footmen and horsemen, and is approaching our city by various roads. His way is marked by columns of fire and smoke!" The guests all grew pale with terror when they heard the news. And the princess said: "This is the enemy who has made me seek your aid. Save me in my hour of need!" Then she gave me two chargers, a suit of golden armour, and the insignia of a commander-in-chief, and bowed to me. I thanked her and went, called together the captains, had the army mustered and rode out before the city. At several decisive points I placed troops in ambush. The enemy was already approaching in great force, careless and unconcerned, intoxicated by his former victories. I sent out my most untrustworthy soldiers in advance, who allowed themselves to be beaten in order to lure him on. Light-armed men then went out against him, and retreated in skirmish order. And thus he fell into my ambush. Drums and kettledrums sounded together, the ring closed around them on all sides and the robber army suffered a grievous defeat. The dead lay about like stalks of hemp, but little Tschauna succeeded in breaking through the circle. I sent out the light horsemen after him, and they seized him before the tent of the enemy's commanding general.'

'Hastily I sent word to the princess, and she reviewed the prisoners before the palace. All the people, high and low, streamed together, to acclaim her. Little Tschauna was about to be executed in the marketplace when a messenger came spurring up with a command from the princess's father to pardon him. The princess did not dare to disobey. He was dismissed to his home after he had sworn to give up all thought of realising his traitorous plans. I was loaded with benefits as a reward for my victory. I was invested with an estate with three thousand peasants, and given a palace, horses and wagons, all sorts of jewels, menservants and womenservants, gardens and forests, banners and suits of mail. And my subordinate officers, too, were duly rewarded.'

'On the following day a banquet was held, and the princess herself filled a goblet, sent it to me by one of her attendants, and said: "Widowed early in life, I opposed the wishes of my stern father and fled to this spot. Here the infamous Tschauna harassed me and well-nigh put me to shame. Had not your master's great kindness and your own courage come to my assistance, my lot would have been hard!" She began to thank me, and her tears flowed like a stream. I bowed and begged her to grant me leave of absence, so that I might look after my family. I was given a month's leave and the following day she dismissed me with a splendid retinue. Before the city a pavilion had been erected in which I drank the stirrup cup[2]. Then I rode away and when I arrived before our own gate a peal of thunder crashed and I awoke.'

Thereupon the general wrote an account of what had happened to Dschou Bau, and conveyed the princess's thanks. After that, he paid no further heed to worldly matters, but set his house in order and turned it over to his wife and son. When a month had passed, he died without any sign of illness.

That same day one of his officers was out walking. Suddenly he saw a heavy cloud of dust rising along the highway, while flags and banners darkened the sun. A thousand knights were escorting a man who sat on his horse proudly and like a hero. When the officer looked at his face, it was the general Dschong Tschong-Fu. Hastily he stepped to the edge of the road, to allow the cavalcade to pass, and he watched it ride by. The horsemen took the way to the Lake of the Maidens, where they disappeared.

*Notes: The expression 'Dschou Bau took the blame upon himself' is explained by the fact that the territorial mandarin is responsible for his district, just as the emperor is for the whole empire. Since extraordinary natural phenomena are the punishment of heaven, their occurrence presupposes the guilt of humans. This train of thought is in accord with the idea that differences occurring among the spirits of the air lead to misfortune, because when virtue is in the ascendant in the mortal world, the spirits are prevented from giving way to such demonstrations.*

*'Drums and kettledrums sounded together': the kettledrums sounded the attack, and the drums the retreat. The simultaneous sounding of both signals was intended to throw the enemy's army into disorder.*

*Central to Confucian ethics is the belief that children are obliged to respect their parents. Defiance is never acceptable, so a child making an argument that fails to persuade must be obedient, and thereby avoid dishonouring the family name.*

---

[2] An alcoholic drink served to guests who have already saddled up and are on horseback, preparing to leave.

Han Siang Dsi, the Seventh of the Eight Immortals,
can see into the future and can be recognised by
his flower basket and dibble.

# 47

# The Disowned Princess

**It's never a good idea to get involved in someone else's family feud, but when the families in question are those of dragon kings, it's probably a doubly bad idea...**

At the time that the Tang dynasty was reigning there lived a man named Liu I, who had failed to pass his examinations for the doctorate. So he was travelling home again. He had gone six or seven miles when a bird flew up in a field, and his horse shied and ran ten miles before he could stop him. There he saw a woman who was herding sheep on a hillside. He looked at her and she was lovely to look upon, yet her face bore traces of hidden grief. Astonished, he asked her what was the matter.

The woman began to sob and said: 'Fortune has forsaken me, and I am in need and ashamed. Since you are kind enough to ask, I will tell you all. I am the youngest daughter of the Dragon King of the Sea of Dungting, and was married to the second son of the Dragon King of Ging Dschou. My husband treated me badly and disowned me. I complained to my step-parents, but they loved their son blindly and did nothing. And when I grew insistent, they both became angry, and I was sent out here to herd sheep.' When she had done, the woman burst into tears and lost all control of herself. Then she continued: 'The Sea of Dungting is far from here; yet I know that you will have to pass it on your homeward journey. I should like to give you a letter to my father, but I do not know whether you would take it.'

Liu I answered: 'Your words have moved my heart. Would that I had wings and could fly away with you. I will be glad to deliver the letter to your father. Yet the Sea of Dungting is long and broad, so how am I to find him?'

'On the southern shore of the Sea stands an orange tree,' answered the woman, 'which people call the Tree of Sacrifice. When you get there, you must loosen your girdle and strike the tree with it three times in succession. Then someone will appear whom you must follow. When you see my father, tell him in what need you found me, and that I long greatly for his help.'

Then she fetched out a letter from her breast and gave it to Liu I. She bowed to him, looked toward the east and sighed, and, unexpectedly, tears rolled from the eyes of Liu I as well. He took the letter and thrust it in his bag.

Then he asked her: 'I cannot understand why you have to herd sheep. Do the gods slaughter cattle like men?'

'These are not ordinary sheep,' answered the woman; 'these are rain sheep.'

'But what are rain sheep?'

'They are the thunder rams,' replied the woman.

And when he looked more closely he noticed that these sheep walked around in proud, savage fashion, quite different from ordinary sheep.

Liu I added: 'But if I deliver the letter for you, and you succeed in getting back to the Sea of Dungting in safety, you must not treat me like a stranger.'

The woman answered: 'How could I treat you like a stranger? You shall be my dearest friend.'

And with these words they parted.

In course of a month Liu I reached the Sea of Dungting, asked for the orange tree and, sure enough, he found it. Loosening his girdle, he struck the tree with it three times. At once a warrior emerged from the waves of the sea, and asked: 'Where do you come from, honoured guest?'

Liu I said: 'I have come on an important mission and want to see the King.'

The warrior made a gesture in the direction of the water, and the waves turned into a solid street along which he led Liu I. The dragon castle rose before them with its thousand gates, and magic flowers and rare grasses bloomed in luxurious profusion. The warrior bade him wait at the side of a great hall.

Liu I asked: 'What is this place called?'

'It is the Hall of the Spirits,' was the reply.

Liu I looked about him: all the jewels known to earth were there in abundance. The columns were of white quartz, inlaid with green jade;

the seats were made of coral, the curtains of mountain crystal as clear as water, the windows of burnished glass, adorned with rich lattice work. The beams of the ceiling, ornamented with amber, rose in wide arches. An exotic fragrance filled the hall, whose outlines were lost in darkness.

Liu I waited for the king a long time. To all his questions the warrior replied: 'Our master is pleased at this moment to talk with the priest of the sun up on the coral tower about the sacred book of the fire. He will, no doubt, soon be through.'

Liu I went on to ask: 'Why is he interested in the sacred book of the fire?'

The reply was: 'Our master is a dragon. The dragons are powerful through the power of water. They can cover hill and dale with a single wave. The priest is a human being. Human beings are powerful through fire. They can burn the greatest palaces by means of a torch. Fire and water fight each other, being different in their nature. For that reason our master is now talking with the priest, to find a way in which fire and water may complete each other.'

Before they had quite finished there appeared a man in a purple robe, bearing a sceptre of jade in his hand.

The warrior said: 'This is my master!'

Liu I bowed before him.

The king asked: 'Are you not a living human being? What has brought you here?'

Giving his name, Liu I explained: 'I have been to the capital and there failed to pass my examination. When I was passing by the Ging Dschou River, I saw your daughter, whom you love, herding sheep in the wilderness. The winds tousled her hair, and the rain drenched her. I could not bear to see her trouble and spoke to her. She complained that her husband had cast her out and wept bitterly. Then she gave me a letter for you. And that is why I have come to visit you, O King!'

With these words, he fetched out his letter and handed it over. When the king had read it, he hid his face in his sleeve and said with a sigh: 'It is my own fault. I picked out a worthless husband for her. Instead of securing her happiness, I have brought her to shame in a distant land. You are a stranger and yet you have been willing to help her in her distress, for which I am very grateful.' Once more he began to sob, and all those about him also shed tears. Then the monarch gave the letter to a servant who took it into the interior of the palace; and soon the sound of loud lamentations rose from the inner rooms.

The king was alarmed and turned to an official: 'Go and tell them within not to weep so loudly! I am afraid that Tsian Tang may hear them.'

'Who is Tsian Tang?' asked Liu I.

'He is my beloved brother,' answered the king. 'Formerly he was the ruler of the Tsian Tang River, but now he has been deposed.'

Liu I asked: 'Why should the matter be kept from him?'

'He is so wild and uncontrollable,' was the reply, 'that I fear he would cause great damage. The deluge that covered the earth for nine long years in the time of the Emperor Yau was the work of his anger. He fell out with one of the kings of heaven, and caused a great deluge that rose and covered the tops of five high mountains. Then the king of heaven grew angry with him, and gave him to me to guard. I had to chain him to a column in my palace.'

Before he had finished speaking a tremendous turmoil arose, splitting the skies and making the earth tremble. The whole palace began to rock, and smoke and clouds rose, hissing and puffing. A red dragon, a thousand feet long, with flashing eyes, blood-red tongue, scarlet scales and a fiery beard came surging up, dragging through the air the column to which he had been bound, together with its chain. Thunders and lightnings roared and darted around his body; sleet and snow, rain and hailstones whirled about him in confusion. There was a crash of thunder, and he flew up to the skies and disappeared.

Liu I fell to earth in terror. The king helped him up with his own hand and said: 'Do not be afraid! That is my brother, who is hastening to Ging Dschou in his rage. We will soon have good news!'

Then he had food and drink brought in for his guest. When the goblet had made the rounds three times, a gentle breeze began to murmur and a fine rain fell. A youth clad in a purple gown and wearing a lofty hat entered. A sword hung at his side. His appearance was manly and heroic. Behind him walked a girl radiantly beautiful, wearing a robe of misty fragrance. And when Liu I looked at her, lo, it was the dragon princess he had met on his way! A throng of maidens in rosy garments received her, laughing and giggling, and led her into the interior of the palace. The king, however, presented Liu I to the youth and said: 'This is Tsian Tang, my brother!'

Tsian Tang thanked him for having brought the message. Then he turned to his brother and said: 'I have fought against the accursed dragons and have utterly defeated them!'

'How many did you slay?'

'Six hundred thousand.'

'Were any fields damaged?'

'The fields were damaged for eight hundred miles around.'

'And where is the heartless husband?'

'I ate him alive!'

Then the king was alarmed and said: 'What that boy did was not to be endured, it is true. But even so that was too much. You must never again do anything like it.' Tsian Tang gave his word.

That evening Liu I was feasted at the castle. There was music and dancing. A thousand warriors with banners and spears in their hands stood at attention. Trombones and trumpets resounded, drums and kettledrums thundered and rattled as the warriors danced a war dance. The music described how Tsian Tang had broken through the ranks of the enemy, and as the guest Liu I listened, the hair on his head rose in terror. Then, again, came the music of strings, flutes and little golden bells. A thousand maidens in crimson and green silk danced around, while the music described the return of the princess. This was a song of sadness and plaining, and all who heard it were moved to tears. The King of the Sea of Dungting was filled with joy. Raising his goblet, he drank to the health of his guest, and all their sorrows left. Both rulers thanked Liu I in verses, and Liu I answered them in a rhymed toast. The crowd of courtiers in the palace hall applauded. Then the King of the Sea of Dungting drew forth a blue cloud-casket, and in it lay the horn of a rhinoceros, which divides the water. Tsian Tang brought out a platter of red amber, and on it lay a garnet. These they presented to their guest, and the other inmates of the palace also heaped up embroideries, brocades and pearls by his side. Surrounded by shimmer and light, Liu I sat there, smiling, and bowed his thanks to all sides. When the banquet was ended, he slept in the Palace of Frozen Radiance.

On the following day another banquet was held. Tsian Tang, who was not quite himself, sat carelessly on his seat and said: 'The Princess of the Dungting Sea is handsome and delicately fashioned. She has had the misfortune to be disowned by her husband, and today her marriage is annulled. I should like to find another husband for her.

If you are agreeable, it would be to your advantage. But if you are not willing to marry her, you may go on your way, and should we ever meet again we will not know each other.'

Liu I was angered by the careless way in which Tsian Tang spoke. The blood rose to his head and he replied: 'I served as a messenger because I felt sorry for the princess, not to gain an advantage for myself. To kill a husband and carry off a wife is something an honest man does not do. And since I am only an ordinary man, I prefer to die rather than do as you say.'

Tsian Tang rose, apologised and said: 'My words were overhasty. I hope you will not take them badly!' The King of the Dungting Sea also spoke kindly to him, and censured Tsian Tang. So no more was said about marriage.

On the following day Liu I took his leave, and the Queen of the Dungting Sea gave a farewell banquet in his honour.

With tears the queen said to Liu I: 'My daughter owes you a great debt of gratitude, and we have not had an opportunity to make it up to you. Now you are going away and we see you go with heavy hearts!' Then she ordered the princess to thank Liu I.

The princess stood there, blushing, bowed to him and said: 'We will probably never see each other again!' Tears choked her voice.

It is true that Liu I had resisted the stormy urging of her uncle, but when he saw the princess standing before him in all the charm of her loveliness, he felt sad at heart; yet he controlled himself and went his way. He took with him treasures beyond value, and the king and his brother themselves escorted him as far as the river.

On his return home, he sold no more than a hundredth part of what he had received, and even so his fortune already ran into the millions, making him wealthier than all his neighbours. He decided to take a wife, and heard of a widow who lived in the North with her daughter. Her father had become a Taoist in his later years and had vanished in the clouds without ever returning. The mother lived in poverty with the daughter; yet she was hoping for a distinguished husband for her since the girl was beautiful beyond measure.

Liu I was content to take her, and the day of the wedding was set. And when he saw his bride unveiled on the evening of her wedding day, she looked just like the dragon princess. He questioned her, but she merely smiled and said nothing.

After a time, heaven sent them a son. Then she told her husband: 'Today I will confess to you that I am truly the Princess of Dungting Sea. When you rejected my uncle's proposal and went away, I fell ill of longing, and was near death. My parents wanted to send for you, but they feared you might take exception to my family. So it was that I married you disguised as a human maiden. I did not dare tell you until now, but since heaven has sent us a son, I hope that you will love his mother as well.'

At this, Liu I awoke as though from a deep sleep, and from that time on both were very fond of each other.

One day his wife said: 'If you wish to stay with me for all time, we cannot continue to dwell in the world of men. We dragons live ten thousand years, and you shall share our longevity. Come back with me to the Sea of Dungting!'

Ten years passed and no one knew where Liu I might be. Then, by chance, a relative went sailing across the Sea of Dungting. Suddenly a blue mountain rose up out of the water.

The sailors cried in alarm: 'There is no mountain on this spot! It must be a water demon!'

While they were still pointing to it and talking, the mountain drew near the ship, and a gaily coloured boat slid from its summit into the water. A man sat in the middle, and fairies stood on either side. It was Liu I. He beckoned to his cousin, who picked up his robes and stepped into the boat with him. No sooner had he entered the boat than it turned into a mountain. On the mountain stood a splendid castle, and in the castle stood Liu I, surrounded by radiance, and with the music of stringed instruments floating about him.

They greeted each other, and Liu I said to his cousin: 'We have been parted no more than a moment, and your hair is already grey!'

His cousin answered: 'You are a god and blessed: I have only a mortal body. Thus fate has decreed.'

Liu I gave him fifty pills and said: 'Each pill will extend your life for the space of a year. When you have lived the tale of these years, come to me and dwell no longer in the earthly world of dust, where there is nothing but toil and trouble.'

Then he took him back across the sea and disappeared.

His cousin retired from the world, and fifty years later, when he had taken all the pills, he disappeared and was never seen again.

*Notes: The outcast princess is represented as 'herding sheep'. In Chinese the word sheep is often used as an image for clouds. (Sheep and goats are designated by the same word in Chinese.)*

*Tsian Tang is the name of a place used for the name of the god of that place.*

*The deluge is the flood which the great Yu oversaw as minister of the Emperor Yau. It is here represented as a deluge. There is archaeological evidence of a devastating flood, perhaps even a megaflood, that took place around 1920 BCE.*

*Imperial examinations were first held during the Han dynasty (206 BCE – 220 CE ), but by the mid-Tang dynasty (618 – 907 CE these had become the major way to office. Success rates were low: in some years, only between 1 and 2 per cent of examinees passed.*

# 48

# Fox Fire

**Is that a dog? Or maybe it's a fox? And it appears to be breathing fire. A farmer on his way home decides to stop and take a look. Perhaps he'll see something to his advantage?**

Once upon a time there was a strong young farmer who came home late one evening from market. His way led him past the gardens of a wealthy gentleman, in which stood a number of tall buildings. Suddenly he saw something floating in the air inside the gardens, glowing like a ball of crystal. Astonished, he climbed the wall around the gardens, but there was not a human being in sight; all he could see, at a distance, was something that seemed to be a dog, looking up at the moon. Whenever it blew its breath out, a ball of fire came out of its mouth and rose to the moon. Whenever it drew its breath in, the ball sank down again, and the creature caught it in its jaws. And so it went on without a stop. Then the farmer realised that it was a fox, who was preparing the elixir of life. He hid in the grass and waited until the ball of fire came down again, at about the height of his own head. Then he stepped hastily from his hiding place, took it away and at once swallowed it. He could feel it glowing as it passed down his throat into his stomach. When the fox saw what had happened, he grew angry. He looked furiously at the farmer, but fearing his strength he did not dare attack and went angrily on his way.

From that time on the farmer could make himself invisible, was able to see ghosts and devils, and had dealings with the spirit world. In cases of sickness, when people lay unconscious, he could call back their souls, and he could also plead for a sinner. These gifts let him earn a lot of money.

On reaching his fiftieth year, he retired and would no longer exercise his arts. One summer evening he was sitting in his courtyard, enjoying the cool air. While there he drank a number of goblets of wine, and by midnight had fallen fast asleep. Suddenly he awoke, feeling ill. He felt as if someone were patting him on the back, and before he knew it, the ball of fire had leaped out from his throat. At once a hand reached for it and a voice said: 'For thirty long years you kept my treasure from me, and from being a poor farmer lad you have grown to be a wealthy man. Now you have enough, and I would like to have my fire ball back again!'

Then the man knew what had happened, but the fox was gone.

*Notes: The thought underlying the story is the belief that the fox prepares the elixir of life from his own breath, which he allows to rise to the moon. Anyone who robs him of the elixir will gain supernatural powers.*

*Foxes feature in Chinese storytelling throughout the centuries, the first appearance being in 1100 BCE in the* Classic of Poetry.

# GHOST STORIES

# 49

# The Talking Silver Foxes

**Silver foxes are special, because they can talk. They tend to be very sure of themselves and love taunting humans, but they may have met their match in the farmer in this story.**

Silver foxes resemble other foxes but are yellow, fire red or white in colour. They know how to influence human beings, too. There is a kind of silver fox that can learn to speak like a man in the space of one year. These foxes are called Talking Foxes.

South-west of the bay of Kaiutschou is a mountain by the edge of the sea. Shaped like a tower, it is known as Tower Mountain. On the mountain stands an old temple with the image of a goddess, known as the Old Mother of Tower Mountain. When children fall ill in the surrounding villages, the magicians often give orders that paper figures of them be burned at her altar, or little lime images of them be placed around it. For this reason, the altar and its surroundings are covered with hundreds of figures of children made in lime. Paper flowers, shoes and clothing are also brought to the Old Mother, and lie in a confusion of colours.

Pilgrimage festivals take place on the third day of the third month, and the ninth day of the ninth month, and then there are theatrical performances, and the holy writings are read. There is also an annual fair. The girls and women of the neighbourhood burn incense and pray to the goddess. Parents who have no children go there and pick out one of the little children made of lime, and tie a red thread around its neck, or even secretly break off a small bit of its body, dissolve it in water and drink it. Then they pray quietly that a child may be sent them.

Behind the temple is a great cave where, in former times, some talking foxes used to live. They would even come out and seat themselves on the point of a steep rock by the wayside. When a wanderer came by, they would talk to him in this fashion: 'Wait a bit, neighbour, and smoke a pipe!' The traveller would look around in astonishment and fear, to see where the voice came from. Unless he were exceptionally brave, he would break out in a sweat and run away in terror. Then the foxes would laugh: 'Hi, hi!'

It so happened one day that a farmer was ploughing on the side of the mountain. When he looked up, he saw a man with a straw hat, wearing a mantle of woven grass and carrying a pick across his shoulder coming along the way.

'Neighbour Wang,' said the stranger, 'first smoke a pipeful and take a little rest! Then I will help you plough.' Then he called out 'Hu!', the way farmers do when they talk to their cattle.

The farmer looked at him more closely and saw then that he was a Talking Fox. He waited for his chance, and when it came gave him a lusty blow with his ox whip. This struck home, for the fox screamed, leaped into the air and ran away. His straw hat, his mantle of woven grass and the rest he left lying on the ground. Then the farmer saw that the straw hat was just woven out of potato leaves; he had cut it in two with his whip. The mantle was made of oak leaves, tied together with little blades of grass. And the pick was only the stem of a kau-ling plant, to which a bit of brick had been fastened.

Not long after, a woman in a neighbouring village became possessed. A picture of the head priest of the Taoists was hung up in her room, but the evil spirit did not depart. Since there were none who could exorcise devils in the neighbourhood, and the trouble she gave was unendurable, the woman's relatives decided to send to the temple of the God of War and beg for help.

But when the fox heard, he said: 'I am not afraid of your Taoist high priest nor of your God of War; the only person I fear is your neighbour Wang in the Eastern village, who once struck me cruelly with his whip.'

The people immediately sent to the village, and found out who Wang was. And Wang took his ox whip and entered the house of the possessed woman.

Then he said in a deep voice: 'Where are you? Where are you? I have been on your trail for a long time. And now, at last, I have caught you!'

With that he snapped his whip.

The fox hissed and spat and flew out of the window.

For more than a hundred years afterwards, they told stories about the Talking Fox of Tower Mountain. One fine day, a skilful archer came to that part of the country. He saw a creature like a fox, with a fiery red pelt and a back striped with grey, lying under a tree. The archer aimed and shot off its hind foot.

At once it said in a human voice: 'I brought myself into this danger because of my love for sleep; but none may escape their fate! If you capture me, you will get at the most no more than five thousand pieces of copper for my pelt. Why not let me go instead? I will reward you richly, so that all your poverty will come to an end.'

But the archer would not listen to him. He killed him, skinned him and sold his pelt; and, sure enough, he received five thousand pieces of copper for it.

From that time on the fox spirit ceased to show itself.

*Notes: The silver fox is known in Chinese as 'Pi', the same word also used for 'panthers', since this legendary beast shares the nature of both animals.*

*'The Old Mother' is really the mother-goddess of the Taischan. But in other localities she is chiefly honoured as a child-giving goddess.*

*'A picture of the head priest of the Taoists': talismans painted by the head priest of the Taoists or the Taoist pope, the so-called 'Master of the Heavens' (Tian Schi), have special virtues against all kinds of sorcery and enchantment.*

*Traditionally, the festival on the third day of the third month is a day to pray for fertility and ward off disaster; while the festival on the ninth day of the ninth month was a day for climbing mountains to prevent disease.*

Ho Sian Gu, the Eighth of the Eight Immortals and the only woman among them, is usually represented by a lotus flower.

# 50

# The Constable

**This relatively modern cautionary tale about corruption centres on the rather surprising relationship between two police men, one of whom is not quite what he seems.**

In a city in the neighbourhood of Kaiutschou there once lived a constable by the name of Dung. One day, twilight was falling even as he was returning from searching for thieves. So before he waded through the stream that flowed through the city he sat down on the bank, lit a pipe and took off his shoes. When he looked up, he saw a man in a red hat dressed as a constable crouching beside him.

Astonished, he inquired: 'Who are you? Your clothes indicate that you are a member of our profession, but I have never yet seen you among the men of our local force. Tell me, pray, where you come from?'

The other answered: 'I am weary, having come a long journey, and would like to enjoy a pipeful of tobacco in your company. I am sure you will not object to that.'

Dung handed him a pipe and tobacco.

But the other constable said: 'I don't need them. Just keep on smoking. It's enough for me to enjoy the odour.'

They chatted awhile, and then waded together through the stream. They began to trust each other and the stranger said: 'I will be frank with you. I am the head constable of the Underworld, and am subject to the Lord of the Great Mountain. You are a constable of reputation here in the upper world. And I have standing in the world below. Since we are so well suited to each other, I should like to enter into a bond of brotherhood with you.'

Dung was willing and asked: 'But what really brings you here?'

Said the other: 'In your district lives a certain Wang, who was once superintendent of the granaries, and at that time caused the death of an officer. This man has now accused him in the Underworld. The King

161

of the Underworld cannot reach a decision in the case, and has asked the Lord of the Great Mountain to settle it. The Lord of the Great Mountain has ordered that Wang's property and life be shortened. First his property is to be sequestered here in the upper world, and then his soul is to be dragged to the lower one. I have been sent out by the Judge of the Dead to fetch him. Yet there is a precedent to follow: when someone is sent for, the constable must first report to the god of the city. The god of the city then issues a summons, and sends one of his own spirit constables to seize the soul and deliver it to me. Only then may I take it away with me.'

Dung asked him further particulars; but the other merely said: 'Later on you will see it all for yourself.'

When they reached the city, Dung invited his colleague to stay at his home, and offered him wine and food. But the other only talked and touched neither the goblet nor the chopsticks.

Said Dung: 'In my haste I could not find any better meal for you. I am afraid it is not good enough.'

But his guest replied: 'Oh no, I am already full and satisfied! We spirits feed only on odours; in that respect we differ from men.'

It was late at night before he set out to visit the temple of the city god.

No sooner did morning dawn than he reappeared to take his farewell and said: 'Now all is in order, I am off! In two years' time you will go to Taianfu, the city near the Great Mountain, and there we will meet again.'

Dung began to feel ill at ease. A few days later, in fact, came the news that Wang had died. The district mandarin journeyed to the dead man's birth village to express his sympathy. The innkeeper there was a tenant of Wang's.

Dung asked him: 'Did anything out of the ordinary happen when Sir Wang died?'

'Yes. It was all very strange,' answered the innkeeper. 'My mother, who had been very busy in his house, came home and fell into a violent fever. She was unconscious for a day and a night, and could hardly breathe. She came to on the very day when the news of Sir Wang's death was made public, and said: "I have been to the Underworld and I met him there. He had chains about his neck and several devils were dragging him along. I asked him what he had done, but he said: 'I have no time to tell you now. When you return, ask my wife and she will tell you all!'" And yesterday my mother went there and asked her. And Wang's wife told her with tears: "My master was an official, but for a long time he did not make any headway. He was superintendent of the granaries in Nanking, and in the same city was a high officer, with whom my master became very friendly. He always came to visit at our house and he and my master would talk and drink together. One day my master said to him: 'We administrative mandarins have a large salary and a good income besides. You are an officer, and have even reached the second step in rank, yet your salary is so small that you cannot possibly make it do. Have you any other income?' The officer replied: 'We are such good friends that I know I can speak openly. We officers must find additional sources of revenue so that our pockets may not be altogether empty. When we pay our men, we make a small percentage of gains on the exchange; and we also carry more soldiers on our rosters than there actually are. If we had to live on our salaries, we would die of hunger!'

"When my husband heard this, he could not rid himself of the idea that revealing these criminal proceedings would make the State indebted to him, surely helping his plans for promotion. On the other hand, he reflected that it would not be right to abuse his friend's trust. Wrestling with these ideas, he retired to his inner sanctum. In his courtyard stood a round pavilion, and for a long time he walked round and round it, lost in thought, his hands crossed behind his back. Finally he concluded with a sigh: 'Charity begins at home; I will sacrifice my friend!' Then he drew up his report, indicting the officer. An imperial order was issued, the matter was investigated, and the officer was condemned to death. My husband was immediately promoted, and from that time on advanced rapidly. And with the exception of myself no one ever knew anything of the matter." When my mother told them of her encounter with Wang in the Underworld, the whole family burst into noisy tears. Four tents full of Buddhist and Taoist priests were sent for, who fasted and read masses for thirty-five days in order that Wang might be delivered. Whole mountains of paper money, silk and straw figures were burned, and the ceremonies have not as yet come to an end.'

When Dung heard this, he was very much afraid.

Two years later he was ordered to journey to Taianfu, to arrest some robbers. He thought to himself: 'My friend, the spirit, must be very powerful indeed, to have known about this trip so far in advance. I must inquire for him. Perhaps I will see him again.'

When he reached Taianfu, he sought out an inn.

The innkeeper received him with the words: 'Are you Master Dung, and have you come from the bay of Kaiutschou?'

'I am the man,' answered Dung, alarmed, 'how do you happen to know me?'

The innkeeper replied: 'The constable of the temple of the Great Mountain appeared to me last night and said: 'Tomorrow a man by the name of Dung who is a good friend of mine is coming from the bay of Kaiutschou!' And then he described your appearance and your clothes to me exactly, and told me to make careful note, and to treat you with the greatest consideration and to take no pay from you, since he would repay me lavishly. So when I saw you coming everything was exactly as my dreams had foretold, and I knew you at once. I have already prepared a quiet room for you, and beg you to make yourself at ease.'

Joyfully Dung followed him, and the innkeeper waited on him with the utmost care, and saw that he had plenty to eat and to drink.

At midnight the spirit arrived. Without opening the door, he stood by Dung's bedside, gave him his hand, and asked how things had gone with him since he had last seen him.

Dung answered all his questions and thanked him into the bargain for appearing to the innkeeper in a dream.

He continued to live for some days at the inn. During the day he went walking on the Great Mountain and at night his friend came to visit him and talked with him, asking at the same time what had happened to Sir Wang.

'His sentence has already been spoken,' came the reply. 'This man pretended to be conscientious, but his betrayal brought about the death of his friend. Of all sins there is no greater sin than this. As a punishment he will be sent forth again into the world as an animal.' Then he added: 'When you reach home, you must take constant care of your health. Fate has allowed you seventy-eight years of mortal life. When your time is up, I will come to fetch you myself. Then I will see that you obtain a place as constable in the Underworld, where we can always be together.'

When he had said this, he disappeared.

*Note: The Lord of the Great Mountain (Taischan) is even greater than Yan Wang, the God of Death. His Temple of the Easterly Holy Mountain (Dung Yuo Miau) is to be found in every district capital. These temples play an important part in the care of the dead before burial.*

# 51

# The Dangerous Reward

**If the Lord of the Great Mountains asks a favour it's difficult to refuse – and anyway he might grant you a favour in return. Perhaps the man in this story wishes he'd said no, though.**

Once upon a time a man named Hu-Wu-Bau, who lived near the Great Mountain, went out walking. Under a tree, he met a messenger in a red robe who called out to him: 'The Lord of the Great Mountain would like to see you!' The man was very frightened but dared not object. The messenger bade him shut his eyes, and when he was allowed to open them again after a short time, he found himself standing before a lofty palace. He entered it to see the god, who had a meal prepared for him and then said: 'I only sent for you today because I had heard you intended travelling to the West and I should like to give you a letter to take to my daughter.'

'But where is your daughter?' asked the man.

'She is married to the river god,' was the reply. 'All you need to do is to take along the letter lying there. When you reach the middle of the Yellow River, beat against the side of the ship and call out: "Greencoat!" Then someone will appear and take the letter from you.'

With these words he handed over the letter, and was taken back again to the upper world.

When Hu-Wu-Bau came to the Yellow River on his journey, he did what the Lord of the Great Mountain had told him and cried: 'Greencoat!' Sure enough, a girl in green garments rose from the water, took him by the hand and told him to close his eyes. Then she led him into the palace of the river god and he delivered the letter. The river god entertained him splendidly, and thanked him as best he knew how. At parting he said: 'I am grateful that you have made this long journey to see me. I have nothing to give you, however, save this pair of green silk shoes. While you are wearing them, you can walk as long as you like and will never grow weary. They will also give you second sight, so that you will be able to see the spirits and gods.'

The man thanked him for the gift and returned to his ship. He continued on his journey to the West, and after a year had passed, returned. When he reached the Great Mountain, he thought it would be fit and proper to report to the god. So he knocked once more against the tree and gave his name. In a moment the red-clad messenger appeared and led him to the Lord of the Mountain. He reported that he had delivered the letter to the river god, and explained how things were there, and the Lord of the Mountain thanked him. During the meal which the god had prepared for him, he withdrew for a few moments to a quiet place. Suddenly he saw his dead father, bound and loaded with chains, doing menial labour along with several hundred other criminals.

Moved to tears, he asked: 'Father, why are you here?'

His father replied: 'During my life on earth I happened to tread on bread, so I was condemned to hard labour at this spot. I have passed two years in this manner, and their bitterness has been unspeakable. Since you are acquainted with the Lord of the Mountain, you might plead for me. Beg him to excuse me from this task and make me the field god in our village.'

Promising to do so, his son went back and pleaded with the Lord of the Mountain. The latter seemed inclined to listen to his prayer, but added this warning: 'The quick and the dead tread different paths. It is not well for the dead and the living to live near one another permanently.'

The man returned home – and in about a year's time nearly all his children had died. With terror in his heart he turned to the Lord of the Great Mountain. He beat on the tree; the red coat came and led him into the palace. There he told of his misfortune and begged the god to protect him. The Lord of the Mountain smiled: 'Did I not tell you at the start that the quick and the dead tread different paths, and that it is not well if they abide near each other permanently? Now you see what has happened!' Even so, he sent his messenger to fetch the man's father. The father came and the god spoke to him as follows: 'I forgave you your offence and sent you back to your home as a field god. It was your duty to bring happiness to your family. Instead, nearly all of your grandchildren have died off. Why?'

And the father said: 'I had been away from home so long that I was overjoyed to return. Besides I had meat and drink in overflowing measure. So I thought of my little grandchildren and called them to me.'

Then the Lord of the Great Mountain appointed another field god for that village, and also gave the father another place. And from that time no further misfortune happened to the family of Hu-Wu-Bau.

*Note: The Lord of the Great Mountain was originally Huang Fe-Hu, a faithful servant of the tyrant Dschou-Sin. Insulted, he joined King Wu, who later overcame the tyrant. After this, he was made Lord of the Mountain, and overlord of the ten princes of the underworld.*

# 52

# Retribution

**Does the time come when we must atone for our sins? The mysterious figure of the water carrier haunts this memorable story about murder, secrets, and the circle of life and death.**

Once upon a time there was a boy named Ma, whose father taught him himself, at home. The window of the upper storey looked out at the back upon a terrace belonging to Old Wang, who had a garden of chrysanthemums there. One day Ma rose early, and stood leaning against the window, watching the day dawn. Out came Old Wang from his terrace and watered his chrysanthemums. When he had just finished and was going in again, along came a water carrier, bearing two pails on his shoulders, who seemed to want to help him. But the old man grew annoyed and motioned him off. Yet the water carrier insisted on mounting the terrace. So they jostled each other about on the edge of the terrace. It had been raining, the terrace was slippery, its border high and narrow, and when the old man thrust back the water carrier with his hand, the latter lost his balance, slipped and tumbled down the slope. Then the old man hastened down to pick him up; but the two pails had fallen on his chest and he lay there with feet outstretched. The old man was extremely frightened. Without uttering a sound, he took hold of the water carrier's feet, and dragged him through the back door to the bank of the stream which flowed by the garden. Then he fetched the pails and set them down beside the corpse. After that he went home, locked the door and went to bed again.

Little Ma thought it would be better to say nothing about a case like this, involving a human life. So shutting the window, he withdrew inside. The sun rose higher, and soon he heard a clamour from outside: 'A dead man is lying on the riverbank!' The constable gave notice, and in the afternoon the judge came up to the beating of gongs, and the inspector of the dead knelt down and uncovered the corpse; yet the body showed no wound. The general consensus was: 'He slipped and fell to his death!' The judge questioned the neighbours, but the neighbours all insisted that they knew nothing of the matter. The judge immediately had the body placed in a coffin, sealed it with his seal, and ordered that the relatives of the deceased be found. And then he went his way.

Nine years passed by, and young Ma had reached the age of twenty-one and passed the baccalaureate. His father had died, and the family was poor. So it came about that in the same room in which he had once studied his own lessons, he now gathered a few pupils about him to teach them.

The time for examinations drew near. Ma rose early, in order to work. He opened the window and there, in the distant alley, he saw a man with two pails gradually drawing nearer. When he looked more closely, it was the water carrier. Terrified, he thought that the carrier had returned to repay Old Wang. Yet he passed the old man's door without entering it. Then he went a few steps further to the house of the Lis; and there went in. The Lis were wealthy people, but since they were near neighbours the Mas were on visiting terms. And so, because the whole thing puzzled Ma, he got up and followed the water carrier.

At the door of the Li house, he met an old servant who was just coming out and who said: 'Heaven is about to send a child to our mistress! I must go buy incense to burn to the gods in order to show our gratitude!'

Ma asked: 'Did not a man with two pails of water on his shoulder just go in?'

The servant said there had not, but before he had finished speaking a maid came from the house and said: 'You need not go to buy incense, for I have found some. And, through the favour of heaven, the child has already come to us.' Then Ma began to realise that the water carrier had returned to be born again into the life of earth, and not to exact retribution. He did wonder, though, what merit of the former water carrier had earned him rebirth into so wealthy a family. So he kept the matter in mind, and from time to time inquired as to the child's wellbeing.

Seven more years went by, and the boy gradually grew up. He did not show much taste for learning, but he loved to keep birds. Old Wang was still strong and healthy. And though he was by this time more than eighty years old, his love for his chrysanthemums had only increased with age.

One day Ma once more rose early, and stood leaning against his window. And he saw Old Wang come out upon his terrace and begin to water his chrysanthemums. Little Li sat in the upper storey of his house flying his pigeons. Suddenly some of the pigeons flew down on the railing of the flower garden. The boy was afraid they might fly off and called them, but the pigeons did not move. The boy did not know what to do: he picked up stones and threw them at the birds. By mistake one of them struck Old Wang. The old man started, slipped and fell down over the terrace. Time passed and he did not rise. He lay there with his feet outstretched. The boy was very much frightened. Without uttering a sound, he softly closed his window and went away. The sun gradually rose higher, and the old man's sons and grandsons all came out to look for him. They found him and said: 'He slipped and fell to his death!' And they buried him as was the custom.

# 53

# The Ghost who was Foiled

**In this ghoulish tale, a ghost is intent on persuading a young woman to kill herself by hanging, which was considered to be an acceptable form of suicide in ancient China.**

There are ghosts of many kinds, but the ghosts of those who have hung themselves are the worst. Such ghosts are always coaxing other living people to hang themselves from the beams of the roof. If they succeed in persuading someone to hang himself, then the road to the Underworld is open to them, and they can once more enter into the cycle of life, and the Wheel of Transformation. The following story of such a ghost is told by people worth believing.

Once upon a time there lived a man in Tsing Tschoufu who had passed his military examination and had been ordered to Tsinanfu to report for duty. It was at the season of rains. So it happened that evening came on before he could reach the town where he had intended to pass the night. Just as the sun was setting, he reached a small village and asked for a night's lodging. But there were only poor families in the village and they had no room for him in their huts. So they directed him to an old temple standing outside the village, and said he could spend the night there.

The images of the gods in the temple were all decayed, and it was impossible to distinguish one from the other. Thick spiderwebs covered the entrance, and the dust lay inches high everywhere. So the soldier went out into the open, where he found an old flight of steps. He spread out his knapsack on a stone step, tied his horse to an old tree, took his flask from his pocket and drank – for it had been a hot day. A heavy rain had just cleared. The new moon was on the decline. The soldier closed his eyes and tried to sleep.

Suddenly he heard a rustling sound in the temple, and a cool wind passed over his face, making him shudder. He saw a woman come out of the temple, dressed in an old dirty red gown, and with a face as white as a chalk wall. She stole past quietly as though she were afraid of being seen. The soldier knew no fear. Pretending to be asleep, he did not move, but watched her with half-shut eyes. He saw her draw a rope from her sleeve and disappear. Then he knew that she was the ghost of someone who had hung herself. He got up softly and followed her, and, sure enough, she went into the village.

When she came to a certain house, she slipped into the court through a crack in the door. The soldier leaped over the wall after her. It was a house with three rooms. In the rear room a lamp was burning dimly. The soldier looked through the window into the room, and there was a young woman of about twenty sitting on the bed, sighing deeply, and her handkerchief was wet through with tears. Beside her lay a little child, asleep. The woman looked up towards the beam of the ceiling. One moment she was weeping and the next she was stroking the child. When the soldier looked more closely, he saw the ghost sitting up on the beam. She had passed the rope around her neck and was hanging herself in dumb show. And whenever she beckoned with her hand, the woman looked up towards her. This went on for some time.

Finally the woman said: 'You say it would be best for me to die. Very well, then, I will die; but I cannot part from my child!'

And once more she burst into tears. But the ghost merely laughed and coaxed her again.

So the woman said with determination: 'It is enough. I will die!'

With these words she opened her chest of clothes, put on new garments, and painted her face before the mirror. Then she drew up a bench and climbed up on it. She undid her girdle and knotted it to the beam. She had already stretched forth her neck and was about to leap from the bench, when the child suddenly awoke and began to cry. The woman climbed down again and soothed and quieted her child, and while she was petting it she wept, so that the tears fell from her eyes like a string of pearls. The ghost frowned and hissed, fearful of losing its prey. In a short time the child had fallen asleep again, and the woman once more began to look upwards. Once more she rose and climbed on the bench, and she was about to lay the noose about her neck when the soldier began to call out loudly and drum on the windowpane. Then he broke the glass and climbed into the room. The woman fell to the ground and the ghost disappeared. The soldier recalled the woman to consciousness, and then he saw something hanging down from the beam, like a cord without an end. Knowing that it belonged to the ghost of the hanged woman, he took and kept it.

Then he said to the woman: 'Take good care of your child! You have but one life to lose in this world!'

With that, he left.

Remembering that his horse and his baggage were still in the temple, he went there to get them. And when he came out of the village, there was the ghost, waiting for him in the road.

The ghost bowed and said: 'I have been looking for a substitute for many years, and today, when it seemed as though I should actually get one, you came along and spoiled my chances. There is nothing more for me to do. Yet there is something that I left behind me in my hurry. You must have found it, and I ask you to return it to me. If I have only this one thing, my not having found a substitute will not worry me.'

Then the soldier showed her the rope and said with a laugh: 'Is this the thing you mean? Why, if I were to give it back to you, someone is sure to hang themselves. And that I could not allow.'

With these words he wound the rope around his arm, drove her off and said: 'Now be off with you!'

The ghost grew angry. Her face turned greenish-black, her hair fell in disorder down her neck, her eyes grew bloodshot, and her tongue hung far out of her mouth. She stretched forth both hands and tried to seize the soldier, but he struck out at her with his clenched fist. By mistake he hit himself in the nose and it began to bleed. He sprinkled a few drops of blood in her direction. Since ghosts cannot endure human blood, she stopped her attack, moving off a few paces and beginning to abuse him. This she did for some time, until the cock in the village began to crow. Then the ghost disappeared.

In the meantime the farmers of the village had come to thank the soldier. For after he had left the woman, her husband had come home, and asked his wife what had happened. And then for the first time he had learned what had occurred. So they all set out together along the road to look for the soldier outside the village. When they found him, he was still beating the air with his fists and talking wildly. They called out to him and he told them what had taken place. The rope could still be seen on his bare arm; it had grown fast to it, and surrounded it with a red ring of flesh.

The day was just dawning, so the soldier swung himself into his saddle and rode away.

# 54

# The Punishment of Greed

**Grave-robbing is the subject here. However, don't let that put you off. Granted, there are some rather gruesome moments, but it's also a dramatic and engaging story.**

Once upon a time there lived a man south of the Yangtze-kiang. He had taken a position as a teacher in Sutschoufu, on the border of Shantung. But when he got there, he found that the schoolhouse had not yet been completed. In the meantime, a two-storey building in the neighbourhood had been rented, and this was where the teacher was to live and hold school. The house stood outside the village, not far from the riverbank. A broad plain, overgrown with tangled brush, stretched out from it on every side, and the teacher was pleased with the view.

Well, one evening he was standing in the door of his house watching the sun go down. The smoke that rose from the village chimneys gradually merged with the twilight shadows. All the noises of the day had died away. Suddenly, off in the distance, along the riverbank, he noticed a fiery gleam. He hurried to see what it might be. And there, on the bank, he found a wooden coffin radiating light. Thought the teacher to himself: 'The jewels with which they adorn the dead on their journey shine by night. Perhaps there are gems in the coffin!' Overcome by greed, he forgot that a coffin is the resting-place for the dead and should be respected. Taking up a large stone, he broke the cover of the coffin and bent over to look more closely. There in the coffin lay a youth. His face was as white as paper, he wore a mourning turban on his head, his body was wrapped in hempen garments, and he wore straw sandals on his feet. The teacher was terrified and turned to go away. But the corpse had already raised itself to a sitting posture. The teacher's fear got the better of him, and he began to run. The corpse climbed out of its coffin and ran after him.

Fortunately the house was not far away. The teacher ran as fast as he could, flew up the steps and locked the door after him. Gradually he caught his breath again. Outside there was not a sound to be heard, and he thought that perhaps the corpse had not followed him all the way. He opened the window and peered down. The corpse was leaning against the wall of the house. Suddenly it saw that the window had been opened, and with one leap it bounded up and through it. Overcome by terror, the teacher fell down the stairs of the house, and rolled unconscious to the bottom of the flight. And the corpse fell down on the floor of the room above.

At the time the school children had all long since gone home, and the landlord himself lived in another house, so no one knew what had happened. On the following morning the children came to school as usual. They found the door locked, and when they called no one answered. Breaking down the door, they found their teacher lying unconscious on the ground. They sprinkled him with ginger, but it took a long time before he woke from his coma. When they asked, he told them all that had happened. Then they all went upstairs and took away the corpse. It was taken outside the village limits and burned, and the bones that remained were once more laid in the coffin. But the teacher said, with a sigh: 'Because of a moment's greed, I nearly lost my life!' He resigned his position, returned home and never, through all the days of his life, did he speak of gain again.

Notes: The tale is taken from the Su Tsi Hia.

The corpse wears a mourning turban and is dressed in mourning clothes. Young people who die before their parents are traditionally laid in their coffins in mourning dress, so that even in death they may do their duty and be able to mourn when their own parents have died.

The City God, or Cheng Huang Shen, protects
the inhabitants of a village, town or city, and the
souls of the dead from that place.

# 55

# The Night on the Battlefield

**There are more ghostly goings on in this story. This time a merchant spends a night at an inn and, well, let's just say he has some very strange and disturbing dreams.**

O nce upon a time there was a merchant, who was wandering towards Shantung with his wares, along the road from the South. At about the second watch of the night, a heavy storm blew up from the North. He chanced to see an inn at one side of the road, where the lights were just being lit. He went in to get something to drink and order lodgings for the night, but most of the people at the inn objected. Only an old man among them took pity on his unhappy situation and said: 'We have just prepared a meal for warriors who have come a long distance, and we have no wine left to serve you. But there is a little side room here which is still free, and there you may stay overnight.' With these words he led him into it. But the merchant could not sleep because he was so hungry and thirsty. Outside he could hear the noise of men and horses. And since all these proceedings did not seem quite natural to him, he got up and looked through a crack in the door. He saw that the whole inn was filled with soldiers, who were sitting on the ground, eating and drinking, and talking about campaigns of which he had never heard. After a time they began calling to each other: 'The general is coming!' From far in the distance came the cries of his bodyguard. All the soldiers hurried out to receive him. Then the merchant saw a procession with many paper lanterns, and riding in their midst a man of martial appearance with a long beard. He dismounted, entered the inn, and took his place at the head of the board. The soldiers mounted guard at the door, awaiting his commands, while the innkeeper served food and drink – and to this the general did full justice.

When he had finished his officer entered, and he said to them: 'You have now been underway for some time. Go back to your men. I shall rest a little myself. It will be time enough to beat the assembly when the order to advance is given.'

The officers received his commands and withdrew. Then the general called out: 'Send Asti in!' and a young officer entered from the left side of the house. The people of the inn locked the gates and withdrew for the night, while Asti conducted the long-haired general to a door at the left, through a crack of which shone the light of a lamp. The merchant stole from his room and looked through the crack in the door. Within the room was a bed of bamboo, without covers or pillows. The lamp stood on the ground. The long-bearded general first took hold of his head. Off it came, and he placed it on the bed. Then Asti took hold of his arms. Off these also came, and were carefully placed beside the head. Then the old general threw himself down on the bed crosswise, and Asti took hold of his body, which came apart below the thighs, and the two legs fell to the ground. Then the lamp went out. Overcome by terror the merchant hurried back to his room as fast as he could, holding his sleeves before his eyes. Lying down on his bed, he tossed about sleepless all night.

At last he heard a cock crow in the distance. Shivering, he took his sleeves from his face and saw that dawn was stealing along the sky. And when he looked about him, he saw he was lying in the middle of a thick clump of brush. Round about him was a wilderness, and not a house, not even a grave was to be seen anywhere. He was chilled to the bone, but even so he ran about three miles till he came to the nearest inn. The innkeeper opened the door and asked him where on earth he came from at that early hour. The merchant told him his experiences and asked him what sort of place it was where he had spent the night. The innkeeper shook his head: 'The whole neighbourhood is covered with old battlefields,' was his reply, 'and all sorts of supernatural things take place on them after dark.'

*Notes: This tale is taken from the* Sin Tsi Hia.

*It's probably no coincidence that Shandong (Shantung) was an area fought over repeatedly throughout its history, especially following the era of the Three Kingdoms.*

# 56

# The Kingdom of the Ogres

**This is a family saga, but one with a difference, because the family in question are ogres. Yes, of course they're terrifying, but in many ways they're actually frighteningly normal.**

In the land of Annam, there once dwelt a man named Su, who sailed the seas as a merchant. Once his ship was suddenly driven onto a distant shore by a great storm. This was a land of hills broken by ravines and green with luxuriant foliage, yet he could see something along the hills which looked like human dwellings. So he took some food with him and went ashore. No sooner had he entered the hills than he could see at either hand the entrances to caves, one close beside the other, like a row of beehives. He stopped and looked into one of the openings. There sat two ogres, with teeth like spears and eyes like fiery lamps, and they were devouring a deer. The merchant was terrified and turned to flee, but the ogres had noticed him and they caught him and dragged him into their cave. Then they talked to each other with animal sounds, and were about to tear his clothes from his body and devour him. But the merchant quickly took out a bag of bread and dried meat and offered it to them.

They divided it, ate it up and it seemed to taste good to them. Then they rifled through the bag again; but he gestured with his hand to show them that he had no more. 'Let me go!' he said. 'Aboard my ship I have frying pans and cooking pots, vinegar and spices. With these I could prepare your food.'

But the ogres did not understand what he was saying, and were still ferocious. He used gestures and signs to try to make them understand, and finally they seemed to get some idea of his meaning. So they went to the ship with him, and he brought his cooking gear to the cave, collected brushwood, made a fire and cooked the remains of the deer. When it was done to a turn, he gave them some of it to eat, and the two creatures devoured it with the greatest satisfaction. Then they left the cave and closed the opening with a great rock. In a short space of time they returned with another deer they had caught. The merchant skinned it, fetched fresh water, washed the meat and cooked several kettles full of it. Suddenly in came a whole herd of ogres, who devoured all he had cooked, and became quite animated over their eating. They all kept pointing to the kettle, which seemed too small to them. When three or four days had passed, one of the ogres dragged in an enormous cooking pot on his back, and after that this was used exclusively.

Now the ogres crowded about the merchant, bringing him wolves and deer and antelopes, which he had to cook for them, and when the meat was done they would call him to eat it with them.

Thus a few weeks passed and gradually they came to have such confidence in him that they let him run about freely. The merchant listened to the sounds they uttered, and learned to understand them. In fact, before very long he was able to speak the language of the ogres. This pleased them greatly, and they brought him a young ogre girl and made her his wife. She gave him valuables and fruit to win his confidence, and in course of time they grew much attached to each other.

One day the ogres all rose very early, and each one of them hung a string of radiant pearls about his own neck. They ordered the merchant to be sure and cook a great quantity of meat. The merchant asked his wife what it all meant.

'This will be a day of high festival,' answered she, 'for we have invited the great king to a banquet.'

But to the other ogres she said: 'The merchant has no string of pearls!'

Then each of the ogres gave him five pearls and his wife added ten, so that he had fifty pearls in all. These his wife threaded and hung the pearl necklace about his neck, and there was not one of the pearls which was not worth at least several hundred ounces of silver.

Then the merchant cooked the meat, and afterwards left the cave with the whole herd to receive the great king. They came to a broad cave, in the middle of which stood a huge block of stone, as smooth and even as a table. Round it were stone seats. The place of honour was covered with a leopard skin, and the rest of the seats with deerskins. Several dozen ogres were sitting around the cave in rank and file.

Suddenly a tremendous storm blew up, whirling around the dust in columns, and a monster appeared who had the figure of an ogre.

The ogres all crowded out of the cave in a high state of excitement to receive him. The great king ran into the cave, sat down with his legs outstretched, and glanced about him with eyes as round as an eagle's. The whole herd followed him into the cave, and stood at either side of him, looking up to him and folding their arms across their breasts in the form of a cross in order to do him honour.

The great king nodded, looked around and asked: 'Are all the folk of the Wo-Me hills present?'

The entire herd declared that they were.

Then he saw the merchant and asked: 'From where does he hail?'

His wife answered for him, and all spoke with praise of his art as a cook. A couple of ogres brought in the cooked meat and spread it out on the table. Then the great king ate of it till he could eat no more, praised it with his mouth full, and said that in the future they were always to furnish him with food of this kind.

Then he looked at the merchant and asked: 'Why is your necklace so short?'

With these words he took ten pearls from his own necklace, pearls as large and round as the bullets of a blunderbuss. The merchant's wife quickly took them on his behalf and hung them around his neck; and the merchant crossed his arms like the ogres and spoke his thanks. Then the great king went off again, flying away like lightning on the storm.

In the course of time, heaven sent the merchant children, two boys and a girl. They all had human form and did not resemble their mother. Gradually the children learned to speak and their father taught them the language of humans. They grew up and were soon so strong that they could run across the hills as though on level ground.

One day the merchant's wife had gone out with one of the boys and the girl. She had been gone for half a day, and the north wind was blowing briskly, and in the merchant's heart there awoke a longing for his old home. He took his son by the hand and went down to the seashore. There his old ship was still lying, so he climbed into it with his boy, and in a day and a night he was back in Annam again.

When he reached home, he loosened two of his pearls from his chain, and sold them for a great quantity of gold so that he could keep house in handsome style. He gave his son the name of Panther, and when the boy was fourteen years of age he could lift thirty hundred weight with ease. Yet he was rough by nature and fond of fighting. The general of

Annam, astonished at his bravery, appointed him a colonel, and in putting down a revolt his services were so praiseworthy that he had become a general of the second rank by the time he was eighteen.

At about this time another merchant was also driven ashore by a storm on the island of Wo-Me. When he reached land, he saw a youth who asked him with astonishment: 'Are you not from the Middle Kingdom?'

The merchant told him how he had come to be driven ashore on the island, and the youth led him to a little cave in a secret valley. Then he brought deer flesh for him to eat, and talked with him. He told him that his father had also come from Annam, and it turned out that his father was an old acquaintance of the man.

'We will have to wait until the wind blows from the North,' said the youth, 'then I will come and escort you. And I will give you a message of greeting to take to my father and brother.'

'Why do you not go along yourself and hunt up your father?' asked the merchant.

'My mother does not come from the Middle Kingdom,' replied the youth. 'She is different in speech and appearance, so it cannot go well.'

One day the wind began blowing strongly from the North. The youth escorted the merchant to his ship, ordering him, when they parted, not to forget a single one of his words.

When the merchant returned to Annam, he went to the palace of Panther, the general, and told him all that had happened. When Panther heard him talking of his brother, he sobbed with bitter grief. Securing a leave of absence, he sailed out to sea with two soldiers. Suddenly a typhoon arose, lashing the waves until they spurted sky-high. The ship turned turtle, and Panther fell into the sea. He was seized by a creature and flung up on a strand where there seemed to be dwellings. The creature looked like an ogre, so Panther addressed him in the ogre tongue. The ogre was surprised and asked him who he was. Panther told him the whole story.

The ogre was pleased and said: 'Wo-Me is my old home, but it lies about eight thousand miles away from here. This is the kingdom of the poison dragons.'

Then the ogre fetched a ship and had Panther seat himself in it, while he himself pushed the ship before him through the water so that it struck through the waves like an arrow. It took a whole night, but in the morning a shoreline appeared to the North, and there on the strand stood a youth on lookout. Panther recognised his brother. He stepped ashore and they clasped hands and wept. Then Panther turned around to thank the ogre, who had already disappeared.

Panther now asked after his mother and sister, and was told that both were well and happy. He wanted to go to them, but his brother told him to wait and went off alone. Not long after, his brother came back with their mother and sister. And when they saw Panther, both wept with emotion. Panther now begged them to return with him to Annam.

But his mother replied: 'I fear that if I went, people would mock me because of my figure.'

'I am a high officer,' replied Panther, 'and people would not dare to insult you.'

So they all went down to the ship together with him. A favourable wind filled their sails and they sped home swiftly as an arrow flies. On the third day they reached land. But all the people that they met were seized with terror and ran away. Then Panther took off his mantle and divided it among the three so that they could dress themselves.

When they reached home and the mother saw her husband again, she at once began to scold him violently because he had said not a word to her before going away. The members of his family all came to greet the wife of the master of the house, but did so with fear and trembling. Panther advised his mother to learn the language of the Middle Kingdom, dress in silks, and accustom herself to human food. This she agreed to do, though initially she and her daughter dressed in men's clothing. The brother and sister gradually grew more fair of complexion, and looked like the people of the Middle Kingdom. Panther's brother was named Leopard, and his sister Ogrechild. Both possessed great bodily strength.

Panther was not pleased to think that his brother was so uneducated, so he made him study. Leopard was highly gifted – he understood a book at first reading – but he felt no inclination to become a man of learning. To shoot and to ride was what he best loved to do. So he rose to high rank as a professional soldier, and finally married the daughter of a distinguished official.

It was long before Ogrechild found a husband, because all suitors were afraid of their potential mother-in-law. Finally Ogrechild married one of her brother's subordinates. She could draw the strongest bow, and strike the tiniest bird at a distance of a hundred paces. Her arrow never fell to earth without having scored a hit. When her husband went out to battle, she always accompanied him, and that he finally became a general was largely due to her. Leopard was a field marshal by the age of thirty, and his mother accompanied him on his campaigns. When a dangerous enemy drew near, she buckled on armour and took a knife in her hand to meet him in place of her son. And among the enemies who encountered her there was not a single one who did not flee in terror. In recognition of her courage, the emperor bestowed upon her the title 'The Superwoman'.

# 57

# The Maiden who was Stolen Away

**The young man is all you could want in a suitor – charming, handsome and certainly persistent – but is he almost too good to be true? Could he be hiding his true nature from the maiden?**

In the western portion of the old capital city of Lo Yang there was a ruined cloister, in which stood an enormous pagoda, several hundred stories high. Three or four people could still find room to stand on its very top.

Not far from it there lived a beautiful maiden, and one very hot summer's day she was sitting in the courtyard of her home, trying to keep cool. A cyclone arose suddenly and carried her off. When she opened her eyes, there she was, on top of the pagoda, and beside her stood a young man in the dress of a student.

He was very polite and affable, and said to her: 'It seems as though heaven meant to bring us together, and if you promise to marry me, we will be very happy.' But to this the maiden would not agree. So the student said that she would have to remain on the pagoda-top until she changed her mind. He produced bread and wine for her to satisfy her hunger and thirst, and disappeared.

Thereafter he appeared each day and asked her whether she had changed her mind, and each day she told him she had not. When he went away, he always carefully closed the openings in the pagoda-top with stones, and he also removed some of the steps of the stairs, so that she could not climb down. And when he came to the pagoda-top he always brought her food and drink, and he also presented her with rouge and powder, dresses and mandarin coats and all sorts of jewellery. He told her he had bought them in the marketplace. And he also hung up a great garnet so that the pagoda-top was bright by night as well as by day. The maiden had all that her heart could wish, and yet she was not happy.

One day when he went away, he forgot to lock the window. The maiden spied on him without him realising, and saw that he turned himself into an ogre, with hair as red as madder and a face as black as coal. His eyeballs bulged out of their sockets, and his mouth looked like a dish full of blood. Crooked white fangs thrust themselves from his lips, and two wings grew from his shoulders. Spreading them, he flew down to earth and at once turned into a man again.

The maiden was seized with terror and burst into tears. Looking down from her pagoda, she saw a wanderer passing below. She called out, but the pagoda was so high that her voice did not carry down to him. She beckoned with her hand, but the wanderer did not look up. Then she could think of nothing else to do but to throw down the old clothes she had formerly worn. They fluttered through the air to the ground.

The wanderer picked up the clothes. Then he looked up at the pagoda, and quite up at the very top he saw a tiny figure that looked like a girl; yet he could not make out her features. For a long time he wondered who it might be, but in vain. Then he saw a light.

'My neighbour's daughter,' said he to himself, 'was carried away by a magic storm. Is it possible that she may be up there?'

Taking the clothes with him, he showed them to the maiden's parents, and when they saw them they burst into tears.

But the maiden had a brother, who was stronger and braver than anyone for miles around. Taking a heavy axe, he went straight to the pagoda. There he hid himself in the tall grass and waited for what would happen. When the sun was just going down, along came a youth, tramping the hill. Suddenly he turned into an ogre, spread his wings and was about to fly. But the brother flung his axe at him and struck him on the arm. Roaring loudly, the ogre fled to the western hills. But when the brother saw that it was impossible to climb the pagoda, he went back and enlisted the aid of several neighbours. With them he returned the following morning and they climbed up into the pagoda. Most of the steps of the stairway were in good condition, for the ogre had destroyed only those at the top. They were able to get up with a ladder, and then the brother fetched down his sister and brought her safely home again.

And that was the end of the enchantment.

# 58

# The Flying Ogre

**A monk encounters a girl who is being chased by a man on horseback. The monk's natural impulse is to protect her, but this time could it be the girl who is not all she seems?**

There once lived in Sianfu an old Buddhist monk, who loved to wander in lonely places. In the course of his wanderings he once came to the Kuku-Nor, and there he saw a tree that was a thousand feet high and many cords in breadth. It was hollow inside and one could see the sky shining down into it from above.

When he had gone on a few miles, he saw in the distance a girl in a red coat, barefoot, and with unbound hair, who was running as fast as the wind. In a moment she stood before him. 'Take pity on me and save my life!' she pleaded.

When the monk asked her what was the trouble, she replied: 'A man is pursuing me. If you tell him you have not seen me, I will be grateful to you all my life long!'

With that, she ran up to the hollow tree and crawled into it.

When the monk had gone a little further, he met a man riding an armoured steed. He wore a garment of gold, a bow was slung across his shoulders, and a sword hung at his side. His horse ran with the speed of lightning, and covered a couple of miles with every step. Whether it ran in the air or on the ground, its speed was the same.

'Have you seen the girl in the red coat?' asked the stranger. And when the monk replied that he had seen nothing, the other continued: 'Teacher, you should not lie! This girl is not a human being, but a flying ogre. Of flying ogres there are thousands of varieties, who bring ruin to people everywhere. I have already slain countless numbers, and have pretty well done away with them. But this one is the worst of all. Last night the Lord of the Heavens gave me a triple command, and that is the reason I have hurried down from the skies. There are eight thousand of us under way in all directions to catch this monster. If you do not tell the truth, monk, then you are sinning against heaven itself!'

Upon that the monk did not dare deceive him but pointed to the hollow tree. The messenger of the skies dismounted, stepped into the tree and looked about him. Then he once more mounted his horse, which carried him up the hollow trunk and out at the end of the tree. The monk looked up and could see a small, red flame come out of the treetop. It was followed by the messenger of the skies. Both rose up to the clouds and disappeared. After a time there fell a rain of blood. The ogre had probably been hit by an arrow or captured.

Afterwards the monk told the tale to the scholar, who wrote it down.

# 59

# Black Arts

**Delicious as they are, the young man in this story may have bitten off more than he can chew when he ignores his wife's advice and samples his mother-in-law's birthday noodles.**

The wild people who dwell in the South-West are masters of many black arts. They often lure men of the Middle Kingdom to their country by promising them their daughters in marriage, but their promises are not to be trusted. Once there was the son of a poor family, who agreed to labour for three years for one of the wild men in order to become his son-in-law. At the end of that time the wedding was celebrated, and the couple were given a little house for a home. But no sooner had they entered it than the wife warned her husband to be on his guard, since her parents did not like him and would seek to do him harm. In accordance with custom she entered the house first with a lighted lantern, but when the bridegroom followed her she had disappeared. And so it went, day by day: during the daytime she was there, but when evening came she disappeared.

And one day, not long after they had been married, his wife said to him: 'Tomorrow morning my mother celebrates her birthday, and you must go to congratulate her. They will offer you tea and food. The tea you may drink, but be sure not to touch any of the food. Keep this in mind!'

The following day the wife and husband went to her mother's home and offered their congratulations. Her parents seemed highly pleased, and served them tea and sweets. The son-in-law drank, but ate nothing, though his wife's parents, with kind words and friendly gestures, kept urging him to help himself. At last the son-in-law did not know what to do, and thought that surely they could mean him no ill. And seeing the fresh caught eels and crabs on the plate before him, he ate a little. His wife gave him a reproachful glance, so he now offered an excuse for taking his leave.

But his mother-in-law said: 'This is my birthday. You simply must taste my birthday noodles!'

With that she placed a great dish before him, filled with noodles that looked like threads of silver, mingled with fat meat and spiced with fragrant mushrooms. During all the time he had been living in the country the son-in-law had never yet seen such an appetising dish. Its pleasant odour rose temptingly to his nostrils, and he could not resist raising his chopsticks. His wife glanced over at him, but he pretended not to see her. She coughed significantly, but he pretended not to hear. Finally she trod on his foot under the table; and then he regained control of himself.

Though he had not as yet eaten half of the food, he said: 'My hunger is satisfied.'

Then he took his leave and left with his wife.

'This is a serious matter,' she told him. 'You would not listen to my words, and now surely you will have to die!'

But still he did not believe her. Suddenly he felt terrible pains, and these soon became so unbearable that he fell to the ground unconscious. At once, his wife hung him up by the feet from the roof beam. Then she put a panful of glowing charcoal under his body, and directly below his mouth she placed a great jar of water, into which she had poured sesame oil. When the fire had heated him thoroughly, he suddenly opened his mouth – and can you imagine what came out? A squirming, crawling mass of poisonous worms, centipedes, toads and tadpoles, who all fell into the water. Then his wife untied him, carried him to bed, and gave him wine mingled with realgar to drink – and he recovered.

'What you ate believing that they were eels and crabs,' said his wife, 'were nothing but toads and tadpoles, and the noodles were poisonous worms and centipedes. But you must continue to be careful. My parents know that you have not died, and they will think up other evil plans.'

A few days later his father-in-law said to him: 'There is a large tree growing on the precipice jutting over the cave. In it is the nest of the phoenix. You are still young and able to climb, so go there quickly and fetch me the eggs!'

His son-in-law went home and told his wife.

'Take long bamboo poles,' said she, 'and tie them together, and fasten a curved sword at the top. And take these nine loaves of bread and these hens' eggs; there are seven times seven of them. Carry them along with you in a basket. When you come to the spot, you will see a large nest up in the branches. Do not climb the tree, but chop it down with the curved sword. Then throw away your poles, and run for dear life. Should a monster appear and follow you, throw him the loaves of bread, three loaves at a time, and finally throw down the eggs on the ground and make for home as quickly as you can. In this way you may escape the danger threatening you.'

The man noted all she said exactly and set off. Sure enough, he saw the bird's nest – as large as a round pavilion. Then he tied his curved sword to the poles, chopped at the tree with all his strength, laid down his poles on the ground and never looked around but ran for dear life. Suddenly he heard the roaring of a thunderstorm rising above him. When he looked up, he saw a great dragon, many fathoms long and some ten feet across. His eyes gleamed like two lamps and he was spitting fire and flame from his maw. With two feelers stretched out, he was feeling along the ground. Then the man swiftly flung the loaves into the air. The dragon caught them, and it took a little time before he had devoured them. But no sooner had the man gained a few steps than the dragon once more came flying after him. He flung him more loaves, and when the loaves came to an end, he turned over his basket so that the eggs rolled over the ground. The dragon had not yet satisfied his hunger and opened his greedy jaws wide. When he suddenly caught sight of the eggs, he descended from the air, and since the eggs were scattered round about, it took some time before he had sucked them all. In the meantime the man succeeded in escaping to his home.

When he entered the door and saw his wife, he said to her, amid sobs: 'It was all I could do to escape, and I am lucky not to be in the dragon's stomach! If this sort of thing keeps up much longer, I am bound to die!'

Kneeling in front of his wife, he begged her pitifully to save his life.

'Where is your home?' asked his wife.

'My home is about a hundred miles away from here, in the Middle Kingdom, and my old mother is still living. The only thing that worries me is that we are so poor.'

His wife said: 'I will flee with you, and we will find your mother. Waste no regrets on your poverty.'

With that she gathered up all that the house held in the way of pearls and precious stones, put them in a bag and had her husband tie it around his waist. She also gave him an umbrella, and in the middle of the night they climbed the wall with the aid of a ladder and stole away.

His wife said to him: 'Take the umbrella on your back and run as fast as ever you can! Do not open it, and do not look around! I will follow you in secret.'

So he turned North and ran with all his might and main. He had been running for a day and a night, covering nearly a hundred miles and passing the boundaries of the wild people's country, when his legs gave out and he grew hungry. Before him lay a mountain village. He stopped at the village gate to rest, drew some food from his pocket and began to eat. Looking around, he could not see his wife.

Said he to himself: 'Perhaps she has deceived me after all, and is not coming with me!'

After he had finished eating, he took a drink from a spring and despite his pain dragged himself further. The heat of the day was at its greatest when a violent mountain rain suddenly began to fall.

Forgetting what his wife had told him, he opened his umbrella. And out fell his wife upon the ground.

She reproached him: 'Once more you have not listened to my advice. Now the damage has been done!'

Quickly she gave him instructions to go to the village, and there to buy a white cock, seven black teacups and half a length of red nettlecloth. As he set off, she cried after him: 'Do not spare the silver pieces in your pocket!'

He went to the village, bought what he had been told and came back. The woman tore the cloth apart, made a coat of it and put it on. No sooner had they walked a few miles before they could see a red cloud rising up in the South, like a flying bird.

'That is my mother,' said the woman.

In a moment the cloud was overhead. Then the woman took the black teacups and threw them at it. Seven she threw and seven fell to earth again. They could hear the mother in the cloud weeping and scolding, and thereupon the cloud disappeared.

They continued on their way for about four hours. They heard a sound like the noise of silk being torn, and could see a cloud as black as ink, rushing up against the wind.

'Alas, that is my father!' said the woman. 'This is a matter of life and death, for he will not let us be! My love for you means that I will now have to disobey the holiest of laws!'

With these words she seized the white cock, separated its head from its body, and flung the head into the air. At once the black cloud dissolved, and her father's body, the head severed from the trunk, fell down by the edge of the road. Then the woman wept bitterly, and when she had wept her fill they buried the corpse. Thereupon they went together to her husband's home, where they found his old mother still living. They undid the bag of pearls and jewels, bought a piece of good ground, built a fine house, and became wealthy and respected members of the community.

*Notes: The Chinese believe that realgar is both a tonic and a mithridate – a universal antidote against poison and disease.*

*Traditionally noodles are eaten at birthdays, to symbolise long life. Ideally an unbroken noodle should fill an entire bowl and be eaten in one strand.*

# HISTORIC LEGENDS

# 60

# The Sorcerer of the
# White Lotus Lodge

**The moral of this story is probably don't give in to temptation and always do what your teacher tells you, especially if he happens to be a sorcerer with a novel line in punishments.**

O nce upon a time there was a sorcerer who belonged to the White Lotus Lodge. He knew how to deceive the multitude with his black arts, and many who wished to learn the secret of his enchantments became his pupils.

One day the sorcerer wished to go out. In the hall of his house, he placed a bowl, which he covered with another bowl, and he ordered his pupils to watch it. But he warned them against uncovering the bowl to see what might be in it.

No sooner had he gone than the pupils uncovered the bowl and saw that it was filled with clear water. And floating on the water was a little ship made of straw, with real masts and sails. Surprised, they pushed it with their fingers till it capsized. Quickly they righted it again and once more covered the bowl. By that time the sorcerer was already standing among them. He was angry and scolded them, saying: 'Why did you disobey my command?'

His pupils rose and denied that they had done so.

But the sorcerer answered: 'Did not my ship turn turtle at sea, and yet you try to deceive me?'

On another evening he lit a giant candle in his room, and ordered his pupils to watch it lest it be blown out by the wind. It must have been at the second watch of the night and the sorcerer had not yet come back. The pupils grew tired and sleepy, so they went to bed and gradually fell asleep. When they woke up again the candle had gone out. They rose quickly and relit it. But the sorcerer was already in the room, and again he scolded them.

'Truly we did not sleep! How could the light have gone out?'

Angrily the sorcerer replied: 'You let me walk fifteen miles in the dark, and still you can talk such nonsense!'

Then his pupils were very frightened.

In the course of time one of his pupils insulted the sorcerer, who made a note of the insult but said nothing. Soon after he told the pupil to feed the swine, and no sooner had he entered the sty than his master turned him into a pig. The sorcerer then at once called in a butcher and sold the pig, who went the way of all pigs that go to the butcher.

One day this pupil's father turned up to ask after his son, for he had not come back to his home for a long time. The sorcerer told him that his son had left him long ago. The father returned home and inquired everywhere for his son without success. But one of his son's fellow pupils, who knew what had happened, informed the father. The father complained to the district mandarin, who feared, however, that the sorcerer might make himself invisible. Not daring to have him arrested, he informed his superior and begged for a thousand well-armed soldiers. They surrounded the sorcerer's home and seized him, together with his wife and child. All three were put into wooden cages to be transported to the capital.

The road wound through the mountains, and in the midst of the hills up came a giant as large as a tree, with eyes like saucers, a mouth like a plate and teeth a foot long. The soldiers stood there trembling and did not dare to move.

Said the sorcerer: 'That is a mountain spirit. My wife will be able to drive him off.'

They did as he suggested, unchained the woman, and she took a spear and went to meet the giant. Angered, he swallowed her, tooth and nail. This frightened the rest all the more.

The sorcerer said: 'Well, if he has done away with my wife, then it is my son's turn!'

So they let the son out of his cage. But the giant swallowed him in the same way. The rest all looked on without knowing what to do.

The sorcerer wept with rage. 'First he destroys my wife, and then my son. If only he might be punished for it! But I am the only one who can punish him!'

Sure enough, they took him out of his cage, too, gave him a sword, and sent him out against the giant. The sorcerer and the giant fought with each other for a time, and at last the giant seized the sorcerer, thrust him into his maw, stretched his neck and swallowed him. Then he went his way contentedly.

And now when it was too late, the soldiers realised that the sorcerer had tricked them.

# 61

# The Three Evils

**This is a lively story of derring-do with an engaging hero who is given a challenge to accomplish, but at the heart of it is an intriguing philosophical question – what is the root of evil?**

Once upon a time, in the old days, there lived a young man by the name of Dschou Tschu. He was of more than ordinary strength, and no one could withstand him. He was also wild and undisciplined, and wherever he was, quarrels and brawls arose. Yet the village elders never ventured to punish him seriously. He wore a high hat on his head, adorned with two pheasants' wings. His garments were woven of embroidered silk, and at his side hung the Dragonspring sword. He was given to play and to drinking, and his hand was inclined to take what belonged to others. Whoever offended him had reason to dread the consequences, and he always involved himself in other people's disputes. Thus he behaved for years, and he was a pest throughout the neighbourhood.

Then a new mandarin came to that district. When he arrived, he first went quietly about the country, listening to the people's complaints. And they told him that there were three great evils in that district.

Clothing himself in coarse garments, the mandarin wept before Dschou Tschu's door. Dschou Tschu was just coming from the tavern, where he had been drinking. He was slapping his sword and singing in a loud voice.

When he reached his house, he asked: 'Who is weeping here so pitifully?'

And the mandarin replied: 'I am weeping because of the people's distress.'

Then Dschou Tschu saw him and broke out into loud laughter.

'You are mistaken, my friend,' said he. 'Revolt is seething round about us like boiling water in a kettle. But here, in our little corner of the land, all is quiet and peaceful. The harvest has been abundant, corn is plentiful, and all go happily about their work. When you talk to me about distress, I think of the man who groans without being sick. And tell me, who are you that instead of grieving for yourself, you grieve for others? And what are you doing before my door?'

'I am the new mandarin,' replied the other. 'Since I left my litter, I have been looking about in the neighbourhood. I find the people are honest and simple in their way of life, and everyone has sufficient to wear and to eat. This is all just as you state. Yet, strange to say, when the elders come together, they always sigh and complain. And if they are asked why, they answer: 'There are three great evils in our district!' I have come to ask you to do away with two of them. As to the third, perhaps I had better remain silent. And this is the reason I weep before your door.'

'Well, what are these evils?' answered Dschou Tschu. 'Speak freely and tell me openly all that you know!'

'The first evil,' said the mandarin, 'is the evil dragon at the long bridge, who causes the water to rise so that man and beast are drowned in the river. The second evil is the tiger with the white forehead, who dwells in the hills. And the third evil, Dschou Tschu – is yourself!'

A blush of shame rose to the man's cheek. Bowing, he said: 'You have come here from afar to be the mandarin of this district, and yet you feel such sympathy for the people? I was born in this place and yet I have only made our elders grieve. What sort of a creature must I be? I beg you to return home again – and I will see to it that matters improve!'

He ran without stopping to the hills, and hunted the tiger out of his cave. The tiger leaped into the air and the whole forest was shaken as though by a storm. Rushing up he came roaring and stretching out his claws savagely to seize his enemy. Dschou Tschu stepped back a pace, and the tiger landed directly in front of him. He thrust the tiger's neck to the ground with his left hand, and beat him without stopping with his right, until he lay dead on the earth. Then he loaded the tiger on his back and went home.

Next he went to the long bridge. He undressed, took his sword in his hand, and dived into the water. No sooner had he disappeared than there was a boiling and hissing, and the waves began to foam and billow. It sounded like the mad beating of thousands of hoofs. After a time, a stream of blood shot up from the depths, and the water turned red. Dschou Tschu, holding the dragon in his hand, rose out of the waves.

He went to the mandarin and reported, with a bow: 'I have cut off the dragon's head and have done away with the tiger. I have happily carried out your orders. And now I shall wander away so that you may be rid of the third evil as well. Lord, watch over my country, and tell the elders that they need sorrow no more!'

He now enlisted as a soldier. In combat against the robbers he gained a great reputation and there came a time when they were pressing him hard and he saw that he could not save himself, so he bowed to the East and said: 'The day has come at last when I can atone for my sins with my life!' Then he offered his neck to the sword and died.

# 62

# How Three Heroes Came By Their Deaths Because of Two Peaches

**Yes, the title of this story does rather give away the plot, but it's a colourful tale of heroism and honour, and what's interesting is not so much what happens as how it happens.**

At the beginning of his reign, Duke Ging of Tsi loved to draw heroes about him. Among these were three of quite extraordinary bravery. The first was named Gung Sun Dsia, the second Tian Kai Giang, the third Gu I Dsi. All three were highly regarded by the prince, but this honour made them presumptuous; their behaviour reduced the court to a turmoil, and they ignored the boundaries that lie between a prince and his servants.

At the time Yan Dsi was chancellor of Tsi. The duke sought his advice, and the chancellor suggested giving a great court banquet and inviting all his courtiers. On the table stood a platter holding four magnificent peaches – the choicest dish of all.

In accordance with his chancellor's advice, the Duke rose and said: 'Here are some magnificent peaches, but I cannot give one to each of you. Only those most worthy may eat of them. I myself reign over the land, and am the first among the princes of the empire. I have been successful in holding my possessions and power, and that is my distinction. Hence one of the peaches falls to me. Yan Dsi sits here as my chancellor. He regulates communications with foreign lands and keeps the peace among the people. He has made my kingdom powerful among the kingdoms of the earth. That is his distinction, and hence the second peach falls to him. Now there are but two peaches left; yet I cannot tell which ones among you are the worthiest. You may rise yourselves and tell us of your distinctions. But whoever has performed no great deeds, let him hold his tongue!'

Gung Sun Dsia beat upon his sword, rose up and said: 'I am the prince's captain general. In the South I besieged the kingdom of Lu, in the West I conquered the kingdom of Dsin, in the North I captured the army of Yan. All the princes of the East come to the Duke's court and acknowledge the overlordship of Tsi. That is my distinction. I do not know whether it deserves a peach.'

The Duke replied: 'Great is your merit! A peach is your just due!'

Then Tian Kai Giang rose, beat on the table, and cried: 'I have fought a hundred battles in the army of the prince. I have slain the enemy's general-in-chief, and captured the enemy's flag. I have extended the borders of the Duke's land till the size of his realm has been increased by a thousand miles. What do you think of my distinction?'

The Duke said: 'Great is your distinciton! A peach is your just due!'

Then Gu I Dsi arose; his eyes started from their sockets, and he shouted with a loud voice: 'Once, when the Duke was crossing the Yellow River, wind and waters rose. A river dragon snapped up one of the steeds of the chariot and tore it away. The ferryboat rocked like a sieve and was about to capsize. Then I took my sword and leaped into the stream. I fought with the dragon in the midst of the foaming waves. And by my strength I managed to kill him, though my eyes stood out of my head with my exertions. Then I came to the surface with the dragon's head in one hand and the rein of the rescued horse in the other, and I had saved my prince from drowning. Whenever our country was at war with neighbouring states, I refused no service. I commanded the van, I fought in single combat. Never did I turn my back on the foe. Once the prince's chariot stuck fast in the swamp, and the enemy hurried up on all sides. I pulled the chariot out and drove off the hostile mercenaries. Since I have been in the prince's service, I have saved his life more than once. I grant that my distinction is not to be compared with the prince or the chancellor, yet it is greater than that of my two companions. Both have received peaches, while I must do without. This means that real distinction is not rewarded, and that the Duke looks on me with disfavour. And in such case how may I ever show myself at court again!'

With these words he drew his sword and killed himself.

Then Gung Sun Dsia rose, bowed twice, and said with a sigh: 'Neither my distinction nor Tian Kai Giang's compares with Gu I Dsi's and yet the peaches were given us. We have been rewarded beyond our deserts, and such reward is shameful. It is better to die than to live dishonoured!'

With that he took his sword and swung it, and his own head rolled on the sand.

Tian Kai Giang looked up and uttered a groan of disgust. He blew the breath from his mouth in front of him like a rainbow, and his hair rose on end with rage. Then he took sword in hand and said: 'We three have always served our prince bravely. We were like the same flesh and blood. The others are dead, and it is my duty not to survive them!'

He thrust his sword into his throat and died.

The Duke sighed incessantly, and commanded that they be given a splendid burial. A brave hero values his honour more than his life. The chancellor knew this and that was why he purposely arranged to incite the three heroes to kill themselves by means of the two peaches.

Note: Duke Ging of Tsi (Eastern Shantung) was an older contemporary of Confucius. The chancellor Yan Dsi, who is the reputed author of a work on philosophy, is the man who prevented the appointment of Confucius to the court of Tsi.

# 63

## How the River God's Wedding was Broken Off

**Here a local politician attempts to end what you might describe as an extreme version of arranged marriage. His approach is somewhat unusual – and is no guarantee of success.**

At the time of the seven empires, there lived a man by the name of Si-Men Bau, who was a governor on the Yellow River. In this district the river god was held in high honour. The sorcerers and witches who dwelt there said: 'Every year the river god looks for a bride, who must be selected from among the people. If she is not found, the wind and rain will not come at the proper seasons, and there will be a poor harvest and floods!' Whenever a girl came of age in some wealthy family, the sorcerers would suggest that she be selected. Her parents, desperate to protect their daughter, would bribe them with large sums of money to look for someone else, until the sorcerers would give in and order the rich folk to share the expense of buying some poor girl to be cast into the river. The remainder of the money they would keep for themselves as their profit on the transaction. But whoever would not pay, their daughter was chosen to be the bride of the river god, and was forced to accept the wedding gifts brought to her by the sorcerers. The people of the district chafed grievously under this custom.

Now when Si-Men entered office, he heard of this evil custom. He had the sorcerers come before him and said: 'See to it that you let me know when the day of the river god's wedding comes, for I myself wish to be present to honour the god! This will please him, and in return he will shower blessings on my people.' With that he dismissed them. And the sorcerers were full of praise for his piety.

Accordingly, when the day arrived, they gave him notice. Si-Men dressed himself in his robes of ceremony, entered his chariot and drove to the river in festival procession. The elders, as well as the sorcerers and the witches, were all present. Men, women and children had flocked together from near and far to see the show. The sorcerers placed the river bride on a couch, having adorned her with her bridal jewels, and kettledrums, snare drums and merry airs vied with each other in joyful sound.

Just as they were about to thrust the couch into the stream, the girl's parents saying farewell amid their tears, Si-Men ordered them to wait: 'Do not be in such a hurry! I have appeared in person to escort the bride, so everything must be done solemnly and in order. First someone must go to the river god's castle, and let him know that he may come himself and fetch his bride.'

With these words, he looked at a witch and said: 'You may go!' The witch hesitated, but he ordered his servants to seize her and thrust her into the stream. About an hour went by.

'That woman did not understand her business,' said Si-Men, 'or else she would have been back long ago!' With that he looked at one of the sorcerers and added: 'Do you go and do better!' The sorcerer paled with fear, but Si-Men had him seized and cast into the river. Half an hour went by.

Then Si-Men pretended to be uneasy. 'Both of them have made a botch of their errand,' said he, 'and are causing the bride to wait in vain!' Once more he looked at a sorcerer and said: 'Do you go and hunt them up!' But the sorcerer flung himself on the ground and begged for mercy. And all the rest of the sorcerers and witches knelt to him in a row, pleading for grace. And they took an oath that they would never again seek a bride for the river god.

Then Si-Men held his hand, and sent the girl back to her home, and the evil custom was at an end forever.

*Notes: Si-Men Bau was an historical personage, who lived five centuries before Christ. He was the first engineer in China to create a canal irrigation system and was also a famous philosopher.*

The Lord of the Great Mountain is associated with
Mountain Tai in Shandong, a sacred place and one
of the five Great Mountains of China.

# 64

# Dschang Liang

**This is a classic Chinese folk tale, in which the hero meets an enigmatic old man, and a traditional moral message is wrapped up in a series of tasks and a hefty dose of mysticism.**

Dschang Liang was a native of one of those states destroyed by the Emperor Tsin Schi Huang. He determined to do a deed for his dead king's sake, and to that end gathered followers in order to slay Tsin Schi Huang.

It so happened that Tsin Schi Huang was making a progress through the country. When he came to the plain of Bo Lang, Dschang Liang armed his people with iron maces in order to kill him. But Tsin Schi Huang always had two travelling coaches that were identical. In one of them he sat himself, while in the other was seated someone else. Dschang Liang and his followers met the decoy wagon, and Dschang Liang was forced to flee from the Emperor's rage.

He came to a ruined bridge. An icy wind was blowing, and the snowflakes were whirling through the air. There he met an old, old man wearing a black turban and a yellow gown. The old man let one of his shoes fall into the water, looked at Dschang Liang and said: 'Fetch it out, little one!'

Dschang Liang controlled himself and fetched out the shoe. He brought it to the old man, who stretched out his foot to allow Dschang Liang to put it on. This the younger man did in a respectful manner, which pleased the old man, who said: 'Little one, something may be made of you! Come here tomorrow morning early, and I will have something for you.'

The following morning at the break of dawn, Dschang Liang appeared. But the old man was already there and reproached him: 'You are too late. Today I will tell you nothing. Tomorrow you must come earlier.'

So it went on for three days, and Dschang Liang's patience was not exhausted. Then the old man was satisfied, brought forth the *Book of Hidden Complements*, and gave it to him. 'You must read it,' said he, 'and then you will be able to rule like a great emperor. When your task is completed, seek me at the foot of the Gu Tschong Mountain. There you will find a yellow stone, and I will be by that yellow stone.'

Dschang Liang took the book and helped the ancestor of the Han dynasty to conquer the empire. For this service, the emperor made him a count. From that time forward Dschang Liang ate no human food and concentrated in spirit. He kept company with the four whitebeards of the Shang Mountain, and with them shared the sunset roses in the clouds. Once he met two boys who were singing and dancing:

> Green the garments you should wear,
> If to heaven's gate you'd fare;
> There the Golden Mother greet,
> Bow before the Wood Lord's feet!

When Dschang Liang heard this, he bowed before the youths and said to his friends: 'Those are angel children of the King Father of the East. The Golden Mother is the Queen of the West. The Lord of Wood is the King Father of the East. They are the two primal powers, the parents of all that is male and female, the root and fountain of heaven and earth, to whom all that has life is indebted for its creation and nourishment. The Lord of Wood is the master of all the male saints, the Golden Mother is the mistress of all the female saints. Whoever would gain immortality, must first greet the Golden Mother and then bow before the King Father. Then he may rise up to the three Pure Ones and stand in the presence of the Highest. The song of the angel children shows the manner in which the hidden knowledge may be acquired.'

At about that time the emperor was persuaded to have some of his faithful servants slain. Then Dschang Liang left his service and went to the Gu Tschong Mountain. There he found the old man by the yellow stone, gained the hidden knowledge, returned home and, feigning illness, released his soul from his body and disappeared.

Later, when the rebellion of the Red Eyebrows broke out, his tomb was opened. But all that was found within it was a yellow stone. Dschang Liang was wandering with Laotsze in the invisible world.

Once his grandson Dschang Dau Ling went to Kunlun Mountain, to visit the Queen Mother of the West. There he met Dschang Liang. Dschang Dau Ling now gained power over demons and spirits, and became the first Taoist pope. And the secret of his power has been handed down in his family from generation to generation.

# 65

# Old Dragonbeard

**As well as a wise old man, the cast of colourful characters in this legend includes a brave hero and a feisty heroine, but can they help bring peace to the empire and establish a dynasty?**

At the time of the last emperor of the Sui dynasty, power lay in the hands of the emperor's uncle, Yang Su. He was proud and extravagant. In his halls stood choruses of singers and bands of dancing girls, and serving maids stood ready to obey his least sign. When the great lords of the empire came to visit him, he received them while remaining comfortably seated on his couch.

In those days there lived a bold hero named Li Dsing. He came to see Yang Su dressed in humble clothes and bringing him a plan for quieting the empire.

Making a low bow, which Yang Su ignored, he said: 'The empire is about to be troubled by dissension and heroes are everywhere taking up arms. You are the highest servant of the imperial house. It should be your duty to gather the bravest around the throne. And you should not rebuff people by your haughtiness!'

When Yang Su heard this he collected himself, rose from his place, and spoke to him in a friendly manner.

Li Dsing handed him a memorial, and Yang Su now began talking with him about all manner of things. A serving maid of extraordinary beauty stood beside them. She held a red fan in her hand, and kept her eyes fixed on Li Dsing. Finally he took his leave and returned to his inn.

Later in the day someone knocked at his door. He looked out, and there, before the door, stood a person turbaned and gowned in purple, and carrying a bag slung from a stick across his shoulder.

Asking who it was, Li Dsing received the answer: 'I am the fan bearer of Yang Su!'

With that she entered the room, threw back her mantle and took off her turban. Li Dsing saw that she was a maiden of eighteen or nineteen.

She bowed to him, and when he had replied to her greeting she began: 'I have dwelt in the house of Yang Su for a long time and have seen many famous people, but none who could equal you. I will serve you wherever you go!'

Li Dsing answered: 'The minister is powerful. I am afraid that we will plunge ourselves into misfortune.'

'He is a living corpse, in whom the breath of life grows scant,' said the fan bearer, 'and we need not fear him.'

He asked her name, and she said it was Dschang, and that she was the oldest of her brothers and sisters.

When he looked at her, and considered her courageous behaviour and her sensible words, he realised that she was a girl cast from the heroic mould. They agreed to marry and make their escape from the city in secret. The fan bearer put on men's clothes, and they mounted horses and rode away, determined to go to Taiyuanfu.

On the following day they stopped at an inn. They had their room put in order and made a fire on the hearth to cook their meal. The fan bearer was combing her hair. It was so long that it swept the ground, and so shining that you could see your face in it. Li Dsing had just left the room to groom the horses. Suddenly a man with a long curling moustache like a dragon made his appearance. He came along riding on a lame mule, threw down his leather bag on the ground in front of the hearth, took a pillow, made himself comfortable on a couch and watched the fan bearer as she combed her hair. Li Dsing saw him and grew angry; but the fan bearer had seen through the stranger instantly. She gestured Li Dsing to control himself, quickly finished combing her hair and tied it in a knot.

Then she greeted the guest and asked his name.

He told her that he was named Dschang.

'Why, my name is also Dschang,' said she, 'so we must be relatives!' And she bowed to him as if he were her elder brother.

'How many are there of you brothers?' she then inquired.

'I am the third,' he answered, 'and you?'

'I am the oldest sister.'

'How fortunate that I should have found a sister today,' said the stranger, highly pleased.

Then the fan bearer called to Li Dsing through the door and said: 'Come in! I wish to present my third brother to you!'

Li Dsing came in and greeted him.

They sat down beside each other and the stranger asked: 'What have you to eat?'

'A leg of mutton,' was the answer.

'I am quite hungry,' said the stranger.

So Li Dsing went to the market and brought bread and wine. The stranger drew out his dagger, cut the meat, and they all ate together. When they had finished, he fed the rest of the meat to his mule.

Then he said: 'Sir Li, you seem to be a penniless knight. How did you happen to meet my sister?'

Li Dsing told him what had happened.

'And where do you wish to go now?'

'To Taiyuanfu,' was the answer.

Said the stranger: 'You do not seem to be an ordinary fellow. Have you heard anything about a hero who is supposed to be in this neighbourhood?'

Li Dsing answered: 'Yes, indeed, I know of one, whom heaven seems destined to rule.'

'And who might he be?' inquired the other.

'He is the son of Duke Li Yuan of Tang, and he is no more than twenty years of age.'

'Could you present him to me some time?' asked the stranger. And when Li Dsing had assured him he could, he continued: 'The astrologers say that a special sign has been noticed in the air above Taiyuanfu. Perhaps it is caused by the very man. Tomorrow you may await me at the Fenyang Bridge!'

With these words he mounted his mule and rode away, and he rode so swiftly that he seemed to be flying.

The fan bearer said to him: 'He is not a pleasant customer to deal with. I noticed that at first he had no good intentions. That is why I united him to us by bonds of relationship.'

Then they set out together for Taiyuanfu, and at the appointed place, sure enough, they met Dragonbeard. Li Dsing had an old friend, a companion of the Prince of Tang.

He presented the stranger to this friend, named Liu Wendsing, saying: 'This stranger is able to foretell the future from the lines of the face, and would like to see the prince.'

Thereupon Liu Wendsing took him in to the prince. The prince was clothed in a simple indoor robe, but there was something impressive about him, which made him remarked among all others. When the stranger saw him, he fell into a profound silence and his face turned ashen. After he had drunk a few flagons of wine, he took his leave.

'That man is a true ruler,' he told Li Dsing. 'I am almost certain of the fact, but to be sure my friend must also see him.'

Then he arranged to meet Li Dsing on a certain day at a certain inn. 'When you see this mule before the door, together with a very lean jackass, you may be certain I am there with my friend.'

On the day set Li Dsing went there and, sure enough he saw the mule and the jackass before the door. He gathered up his robe and descended to the upper storey of the inn. There sat Old Dragonbeard and a Taoist priest over their wine. When Old Dragonbeard saw Li Dsing, he was much pleased, bade him sit down and offered him wine. After they had pledged each other, all three returned to Liu Wendsing. He was playing a game of chess with the prince, who rose with respect and asked them to be seated.

As soon as the Taoist priest saw his radiant and heroic countenance, he was disconcerted, and greeted him with a low bow, saying: 'The game is up!'

When they took their leave, Dragonbeard said to Li Dsing: 'Go on to Sianfu, and when the time has come, ask for me at such and such a place.'

And with that he went away, snorting.

Li Dsing and the fan bearer packed up their belongings, left Taiyuanfu and travelled on toward the West. At that time Yang Su died, and great disturbance arose throughout the empire.

In the course of a few days Li Dsing and his wife reached the meeting-place appointed by Dragonbeard. They knocked at a little wooden door, and out came a servant, who led them through long passages. When they emerged, magnificent buildings arose before them, and standing in front was a crowd of slave girls. They entered a hall in which the most valuable dowry that could be imagined had been piled up: mirrors, clothes, jewellery, all more beautiful than is usually seen on Earth. Handsome slave girls led them to bathe, and when they had changed their garments their friend was announced. He stepped in clad in silks and fox pelts, looking almost like a dragon or a tiger. He greeted his guests with pleasure and also called in his wife, an exceptional beauty. A festive banquet was served, and all four sat down to it. The table was covered with the most expensive foods, so rare that no one even knew their names. The flagons and dishes and all the utensils were made of gold and jade, and ornamented with pearls and precious stones. Two companies of girl musicians alternately blew flutes and chalameaus. They sang and danced, and it seemed to the visitors that they had been transported to the palace of the Lady of the Moon. Rainbow garments fluttered, and the dancing girls were beautiful beyond all the beauty of earth.

After they had banqueted, Dragonbeard commanded couches to be brought, which had been spread with embroidered silken covers. After they had seen everything worth seeing, he presented them with a book and a key.

Then he said: 'In this book are listed the valuables and the riches I possess. They are my wedding present to you. Nothing great may be undertaken without wealth, and it is my duty to endow my sister properly. My original intention had been to take the Middle Kingdom in hand and do something with it. But since a ruler has already arisen to reign over it, what is there to keep me in this country? For Prince Tang of Taiyuanfu is a real hero, and will have restored order within a few years' time. You must both of you help him, and you will be certain to rise to high honours. You, my sister, are not merely beautiful, but you have also the right way of looking at things. No one other than yourself would have been able to recognise the true worth of Li Dsing, and no one other than Li Dsing would have had the good fortune to encounter you. You will share the honours destined for your husband, and your name will be recorded in history. Use the treasures I bestow upon you to help the true ruler. Bear this in mind! And in ten years' time a glow will rise far away to the south-east, and it shall be a sign that I have reached my goal. Then you may pour a libation of wine in the direction of the south-east, to wish me good fortune!'

Then, one after another, he had his servants and slave girls greet Li Dsing and the fan bearer, and said to them: 'This is your master and your mistress!'

When he had spoken these words, Dragonbeard took his wife's hand and they mounted three steeds held ready for them, and rode away.

Li Dsing and his wife now established themselves in the house, and found themselves possessed of untold wealth. They followed Prince Tang, who restored order to the empire, and helped him with their money. Thus the great work was accomplished, and after peace had been restored throughout the empire, Li Dsing was made Duke of We, and the fan bearer became a duchess.

Some ten years later the duke was informed that in the empire beyond the sea a thousand ships had landed an army of a hundred thousand armoured soldiers. They had conquered the country, killed its prince, and set up their leader as its king. And order now reigned in that empire.

Then the duke knew that Dragonbeard had accomplished his aim. He told his wife, and they dressed themselves in ceremonial robes and offered wine to wish him good fortune. They saw a radiant crimson ray flash up on the south-eastern horizon. No doubt Dragonbeard had sent it in answer. And both of them were very happy.

*Notes: The Li Dsing of this tale has nothing in common with Li Dsing, the father of Notscha (18). He was a historical personage, 571–649 CE.*

*Li Yuan was the founder of the Tang dynasty, 565–635 CE. His famous son, called the Prince of Tang and to whom he owed the throne, was named Li Schi Min. His father abdicated in 618 in his favour. This tale is not, of course, historical, but legendary. Compare with the beginning of the following story.*

# 66

# How Molo Stole the Lovely Rose-Red

**This love story involves a daring act of rescue. Can the hero pull it off? Fortunately, he can rely on the help of his wily servant Molo, who is not just an expert swordsman.**

At the time when the Tang dynasty reigned over the Middle Kingdom, there were master swordsmen of various kinds. Those who came first were the saints of the sword. They were able to take different shapes at will, and their swords were like strokes of lightning. Before their opponents even knew that they had been struck, their heads had already fallen. Yet these master swordsmen were men of high ideals, and did not lightly mingle in the quarrels of the world. The second kind of master swordsmen were the sword heroes. It was their custom to slay the unjust, and to come to the aid of the oppressed. They wore a hidden dagger at their side and carried a leather bag at their belt. By means of magic, they were able to turn human heads into flowing water. They could fly over roofs and walk up and down walls, and they came and went and left no trace. The swordsmen of the lowest sort were the mere hired killers. They hired themselves out to those who wished to do away with their enemies. And death was an everyday matter to them.

Old Dragonbeard must have been a master swordsman standing midway between those of the first and of the second order. By contrast, Molo, of whom this story tells, was a sword hero.

At that time there lived a young man named Tsui, whose father was a high official and the friend of the prince. The father once sent his son to visit his friend, who was ill. The son was young, handsome and gifted. When he entered the prince's palace, there stood three beautiful slave girls, who piled rosy peaches into a golden bowl, poured sugar over them and presented them to him. After he had eaten he took his leave, and his host ordered one of the slave girls, Rose-Red by name, to escort him to the gate. As they went along, the young man kept looking back at her. She smiled at him and made signs with her fingers. First she stretched out three fingers, then she turned her hand around three times, and finally she pointed to a little mirror that she wore on her breast. When they parted, she whispered to him: 'Do not forget me!'

When the young man reached home, his thoughts were all in confusion. He sat down absent-mindedly, like a wooden rooster. Now it happened that he had an old servant named Molo, who was an extraordinary being.

'What is the trouble, master,' said he. 'Why are you so sad? Do you want to tell your old slave about it?'

The boy told him what had occurred, and also mentioned the signs the girl had made to him in secret.

Said Molo: 'When she stretched out three fingers, it meant that she is quartered in the third court of the palace. When she turned round her hand three times, it meant the sum of three times five fingers, which is fifteen. When she pointed at the little mirror, she meant to say that on the fifteenth, when the moon is round as a mirror, at midnight, you are to go for her.'

Then the young man was released from his confusion, and was so happy he could hardly control himself. But soon he grew sad again and said: 'The prince's palace is shut off as though by an ocean. How would it be possible to win my way into it?'

'Nothing easier,' said Molo. 'On the fifteenth we will take two pieces of dark silk and wrap ourselves up in them, and thus I will carry you there. There is a wild dog on guard at the slave girl's court, who is strong as a tiger and watchful as a god. No one can pass by him, so he must be killed.'

When the appointed day came, the servant said: 'There is no one else in the world who can kill this dog but myself!'

Full of joy the youth gave him meat and wine, and the old man took a chain hammer and disappeared.

And after no more time had elapsed than it takes to eat a meal he was back again and said: 'The dog is dead, and there is nothing further to hinder us!'

At midnight they wrapped themselves in dark silk, and the old man carried the youth over the tenfold walls surrounding the palace. They reached the third gateway, where the gate stood ajar, and saw the glow of a little lamp and heard Rose-Red sighing deeply. The entire court was otherwise silent and deserted. The youth raised the curtain and stepped into the room. For a long time, Rose-Red looked at him searchingly, and then she seized his hand.

'I knew that you were intelligent and would understand my sign language. But what magic power have you at your disposal, that you were able to get here?'

The youth told her in detail how Molo had helped him.

'And where is Molo?' she asked.

'Outside, before the curtain,' was his answer.

Straightaway she called him in and gave him wine to drink from a jade goblet. 'I am of good family,' she told him 'and have come here from far away. Force alone has made me a slave in this palace. I long to leave. For though I eat with jasper chopsticks, and drink my wine from golden flagons, though silk and satin rustle around me and jewels of every kind are at my disposal, all these are but so many chains and fetters to hold me here. Dear Molo, you are endowed with magic powers. I beg you to save me in my distress! If you do, I will be glad to serve your master as a slave, and will never forget the favour you have done me.'

The youth looked at Molo, who was quite willing – but asked first for permission to carry away Rose-Red's gear and jewels in sacks and bags. Three times he went away and returned until he had taken all. Then he took his master and Rose-Red upon his back, and flew away with them over the steep walls. None of the watchmen of the prince's palace noticed anything. At home the youth hid Rose-Red in a distant room.

When the prince discovered that one of his slave girls was missing, and that one of his wild dogs had been killed, he said: 'That must have been some powerful sword hero!' He gave strict orders that the matter should not be mentioned and insisted that investigations be carried out in secret.

Two years passed, and the youth thought that any danger had passed. So when the flowers began to bloom in the spring, Rose-Red went driving in a small wagon outside the city, near the river. One of the prince's servants saw her, and informed his master. He sent for the youth, who knew he could not conceal the matter and told him the whole story exactly as it had happened.

Said the prince: 'The whole blame rests on Rose-Red. I do not reproach you. Since she is now your wife, I will let the whole matter rest. But Molo will have to suffer!'

He ordered a hundred armoured soldiers, with bows and swords, to surround the youth's house and, no matter what, take Molo captive. But Molo drew his dagger and flew up the high wall, where he looked about him like a hawk. Though the arrows flew as thick as rain, not one hit him. In a moment he had disappeared, no one knew where.

Ten years later one of his former master's servants ran across him in the South, where he was selling medicine. And he looked exactly as he had looked ten years before.

*Notes: This fairy tale has many features in common with the fairy tales of India, noticeably the use of sign language, which is understood not by the hero himself but only by his companion.*

*The dao, or sword, is one of the four traditional weapons of China. A single-handed 'belt' dao was the most common weapon during the Tang dynasty, often carried as a side arm.*

*A chain hammer – two weights on a long chain – is an ancient weapon and a skilled handler could use it to strike, ensnare or strangle.*

# 67

# The Golden Canister

**A rather extraordinary slave girl is the central character in this tale, which involves the audacious theft of the golden canister of the title and a mission apparently doomed to failure.**

In the days of the Tang dynasty there lived a certain count in the camp at Ludschou. He had a slave who could play the lute admirably, and was also so well versed in reading and writing that the count employed her to compose his confidential letters.

Once a great feast was held in the camp. Said the slave girl: 'The large kettledrum sounds so sad today; some misfortune must surely have happened to the kettledrummer!'

The count sent for the kettledrummer and questioned him.

'My wife has died,' he replied, 'but I did not dare ask for leave of absence. That is why, in spite of me, my kettledrum sounded so sad.'

The count allowed him to go home.

At that time there was much strife and jealousy among the counts along the Yellow River. The emperor wished to put an end to this discord by allying them to each other by marriage. Thus the daughter of the Count of Ludschou married the son of the old Count of Webo – but this did not much improve matters. The old Count of Webo had lung trouble, which always grew worse when the hot season came, and he would say: 'Yes, if I only had Ludschou! It is cooler and I might feel better there!'

Finally he gathered three thousand warriors around him, gave them good pay, questioned the oracle to a choose lucky day, and set out to take Ludschou by force.

The Count of Ludschou heard of these plans. He worried day and night but could see no way out of his difficulties. One night, when the water clock had already been set up and the gate of the camp locked, he walked about the courtyard, leaning on his staff. Only his slave girl followed him.

'Lord,' said she, 'it is now more than a month since sleep and appetite have abandoned you! You live sad and lonely, wrapped up in your grief. Unless I am greatly mistaken, this is on account of Webo.'

'It is a matter of life and death,' answered the count, 'of which you women understand nothing.'

'I am no more than a slave girl,' said she, 'and yet I have been able to guess the cause of your grief.'

The count realised that there was meaning in her words and replied: 'You are in truth an extraordinary girl. The fact is, I am quietly reflecting on some way of escape.'

The slave girl said: 'That is easily done! Do not give it a thought, master! I will go to Webo and see how things are. This is the first watch of the night. If I go now, I can be back by the fifth watch.'

'If you do not succeed,' said the count, 'you will merely bring misfortune upon me the more quickly.'

'Failure is out of the question,' answered the slave girl.

Then she went to her room and prepared for her journey. Combing her raven hair, she tied it in a knot on the top of her head and fastened it with a golden pin. Then she put on a short garment embroidered with purple, and shoes woven of dark silk. In her breast she hid a dagger with dragon-lines graved on it, and upon her forehead she wrote the name of the Great God. Then she bowed before the count and disappeared.

Pouring wine for himself, the count waited for her, and when the morning horn was blown, the slave girl floated down before him as light as a leaf.

'Did all go well?' asked the count.

'I have done no discredit to my mission,' replied the girl.

'Did you kill anyone?'

'No, I did not have to go to such lengths. Yet I took the golden canister at the head of Webo's couch along as a pledge.'

The count asked what had happened, and she began to tell her story:

'I set out when the drums were beating their first tattoo and reached Webo three hours before midnight. When I stepped through the gate, I could see the sentries asleep in their guard rooms. Their snoring sounded like thunder. The camp sentinels were pacing their beats, and I went in through the left entrance to the room where the count was sleeping. There lay your relative on his back behind the curtain, plunged in sweet slumber. A costly sword showed from beneath his pillow; and beside it stood an open canister of gold. In the canister were various slips. On one of them was set down his age and the day of his birth, on another the name of the Great Bear God. Grains of incense and pearls were scattered over it. The candles in the room were burning dimly, and the incense in the censers was paling to ash. The slave girls lay all round about, huddled up and asleep. I could have drawn out their hairpins and raised their robes and they would not have awakened. Your relative's life was in my hand, but I could not bring myself to kill him. So I took the golden canister and returned. The water clock marked the third hour when I had finished my journey. Now you must have a swift horse saddled quickly, and send a man to Webo with the golden canister. Then he will come to his senses, and abandon his plans.'

The Count of Ludschou at once ordered an officer to ride to Webo as swiftly as possible. All day long he rode and half the night and finally he arrived. In Webo everyone was excited by the loss of the golden canister, and they were searching the whole camp rigorously. The messenger knocked at the gate with his whip, and insisted on seeing the Lord of Webo. Since he had come at so unusual an hour, the Lord of Webo guessed that he had brought important information and left his room to receive the messenger. He was handed a letter, which said: 'Last night a stranger from Webo came to us. He informed us that he had taken with his own hands a golden canister from beside your bed. I have not ventured to keep it and hence am sending it back to you by messenger.' When the Lord of Webo saw the golden canister, he was very frightened. He took the messenger into his own room, treated him to a splendid meal, and rewarded him generously.

On the following day he sent the messenger back again, giving him thirty thousand bales of silk and a team of four horses along as a present for his master. He also wrote a letter to the Count of Ludschou:

'My life was in your hands. I thank you for having spared me, regret my evil intentions and will improve. From this time forward peace and friendship shall ever unite us, and I will let no thought to the contrary enter my mind. The citizen soldiery I have gathered I will use only as a protection against robbers. I have already disarmed the men and sent them back to their work in the fields.'

And from that very moment the heartiest friendship existed between the two relatives North and South of the Yellow River.

One day the slave girl came and wished to take leave of her master.

'In my former life,' said the slave girl, 'I was a man. I was a physician and helped the sick. Once, however, I gave a little child a poison to drink by mistake instead of a healing draught, and the child died. This led the Lord of Death to punish me and I came to earth again in the shape of a slave girl. I remembered my former life, though, and tried to do well in my new surroundings, even finding a rare teacher who taught me the swordsman's art. Already I have served you for nineteen years. I went to Webo for you to repay your kindness. And I have succeeded in shaping matters so that you are living at peace with your relatives again, and the lives of thousands of people have been saved. For a weak woman this is a real service, enough to absolve me of my original fault. Now I shall retire from the world and dwell among the silent hills, to labour for sanctity with a clean heart. Perhaps I may thus succeed in returning to my former life. So I beg of you to let me depart!'

The count saw that it would not be right to detain her any longer. Preparing a great banquet, he invited a number of guests to the farewell meal and many a famous knight sat down to the board. All present honoured her with toasts and poems.

The count could no longer hide his emotion, and the slave girl also bowed before him and wept. Then she secretly left the banquet hall, and no human being ever discovered where she had gone.

*Note: During the Tang dynasty, slavery was a profitable enterprise, and young slave girls were the most valuable on the market. Only foreigners and criminals could be enslaved, and Turkish, Persian and Korean slaves were an important commodity traded on the Silk Road.*

# 68

# Yang Gui Fe

**In this affecting tale of enduring love, an emperor, who has lost his beautiful wife in rather tragic circumstances, enlists the services of a magician whom he hopes will help him find her.**

The favourite wife of the emperor Ming Huang of the Tang dynasty was the celebrated Yang Gui Fe. She so enchanted him by her beauty that he did whatever she wished him to do. But she brought her cousin to the court, a gambler and a drinker, and the people began to murmur against the emperor. Finally a revolt broke out, and the emperor was obliged to flee. He fled with his entire court to the land of the four rivers.

But when they reached a certain pass, his own soldiers mutinied. They shouted that Yang Gui Fe's cousin was to blame for everything, and that he must die or they would go no further. The emperor did not know what to do. At last the cousin was delivered up to the soldiers and was slain. But still they were not satisfied.

'As long as Yang Gui Fe is alive, she will do all in her power to punish us for the death of her cousin, so she must die as well!'

Sobbing, she fled to the emperor. He wept bitterly and endeavoured to protect her, but the soldiers grew more and more violent, and finally she was hung from a pear tree by a eunuch.

The emperor longed so greatly for her that he stopped eating and could no longer sleep. Then one of his eunuchs told him of a man named Yang Shi Wu, who was able to call up the spirits of the departed. The emperor sent for him and Yang Shi Wu appeared.

That very evening he recited his magic incantations, and his soul left its body to go in search of Yang Gui Fe. First he went to the Underworld, where the shades of the departed dwell. Yet no matter how much he looked and how many questions he asked, he could find no trace of her. Then he ascended to the highest heaven, where the sun, moon and stars make their rounds, and he looked for her in empty space. Yet she was not to be found there, either. So he came back and told the emperor of his experience. The emperor was dissatisfied and said: 'Yang Gui Fe's beauty was divine. How can it be possible that she had no soul!'

The magician answered: 'Between hill and valley and amid the silent ravines dwell the blessed. I will go back once more and search for her there.'

So he wandered about on the five holy hills, by the four great rivers and through the islands of the sea. He went everywhere, and finally he came to Fairyland.

The fairy said: 'Yang Gui Fe has become a blessed spirit and dwells in the great south palace!'

The magician went there and knocked on the door. A maiden came out and asked what he wanted, and he told her that the emperor had sent him to look for her mistress. She let him in. The way led through broad gardens filled with flowers of jade and trees of coral, giving forth the sweetest of odours. Finally they reached a high tower, and the maiden raised the curtain hanging before a door. The magician kneeled and looked up. There he saw Yang Gui Fe sitting on a throne, adorned with an emerald headdress and furs of yellow swans' down. Her face glowed with rosy colour, yet her forehead was wrinkled with care.

She said: 'Well do I know the emperor longs for me! But for me there is no path leading back to the world of men! Before my birth I was a blessed sky fairy, and the emperor was a blessed spirit as well. Even then we loved each other dearly. When the emperor was sent down to earth by the Lord of the Heavens, I, too, descended to earth and found him there among men. In twelve years' time, we will meet again. Once, on the evening of the seventh day, when we stood looking up at the Weaving Maiden and the Cowherd, we swore eternal love. The emperor had a ring, and he broke it in two. One half he gave to me, the other he kept himself. Take this half of mine, bring it to the emperor, and tell him not to forget the words we said to each other in secret that evening. Tell him also not to grieve too greatly because of me!'

With that she gave him the ring, suppressing her sobs with difficulty. The magician brought back the ring with him. At sight of it the emperor's grief broke out anew.

He said: 'What we said to each other that evening no one else has ever learned! And now you bring me back her ring! By that sign I know that your words are true and that my beloved has really become a blessed spirit.'

Then he kept the ring and rewarded the magician lavishly.

*Notes: The emperor Ming Huang of the Tang dynasty ruled 713–756 CE.*

*The introduction to the tale is historical.*

*The 'land of the four rivers' is Setchuan.*

*Yang Gui Fe is one of the Four Great Beauties, said to have a face that put all flowers to shame. The An Lushan Rebellion was blamed on her family, and her cousin Yang Guozhong in particular – and what followed, as described in this story, is a matter of fact.*

# 69

# The Monk of the Yangtze-kiang

**Although at one level a discussion of faith, this engaging tale features a boy who is destined to become an important religious leader, a terrible drought and some unruly dragons.**

Buddhism arose in southern India, on the island of Ceylon. It was there that the son of a Brahminic king lived, who had left his home in his youth and had renounced all desire and all sensation. With the greatest renunciation of self, he did penance so that all living creatures might be saved. In the course of time he gained the hidden knowledge and was called Buddha.

In the days of the Emperor Ming Di, of the dynasty of the Eastern Hans, a golden glow was seen in the West, a glow that flashed and shone without interruption.

One night the emperor dreamed that a golden saint, twenty feet in height, barefoot, with shaven head and Indian dress, entered his room and said to him: 'I am the saint from the West! My gospel must be spread in the East!'

When the ruler awoke, he wondered about this dream, and sent out messengers to the lands of the West to discover what it meant.

So it was that the gospel of Buddha came to China, and continued to gain in influence up to the time of the Tang dynasty. At that time, from emperors and kings down to the peasants in the villages, the wise and the ignorant alike were filled with reverence for Buddha. But under the last two dynasties his gospel came to be more and more neglected. Now, in these days, the Buddhist monks run to the houses of the rich, read their sutras and pray for pay. And one hears nothing of the great saints of the days gone by.

At the time of the Emperor Tai Dsung, of the Tang dynasty, it once happened that a great drought reigned in the land, so that the emperor and all his officials erected altars everywhere in a plea for rain.

Then the Dragon King of the Eastern Sea talked with the Dragon of the Milky Way and said: 'Today they are praying for rain on earth below. The Lord of the Heavens has granted the prayer of the King of Tang. Tomorrow you must let three inches of rain fall!'

'No, I must let only two inches of rain fall,' said the old dragon.

So the two dragons made a wager, and the one who lost promised as a punishment to turn into a mud salamander.

The following day the Highest Lord issued an order saying that the Dragon of the Milky Way was to instruct the wind and cloud spirits to send down three inches of rain upon the earth. To contradict this command was out of the question.

But the old dragon thought to himself: 'It seems that the Dragon King had a better idea of what was going to happen than I had, yet it is altogether too humiliating to have to turn into a mud salamander!' So he let only two inches of rain fall, and reported back to the heavenly court that the command had been carried out.

Yet the Emperor Tai Dsung then offered a prayer of thanks to heaven: 'The precious fluid was bestowed upon us to the extent of two inches of depth. We beg submissively that more may be sent down, so that the parched crops may recover!'

When the Lord of the Heavens read this prayer, he was very angry and said: 'The criminal Dragon of the Milky Way has dared diminish the rain I ordered. He cannot be suffered to continue his guilty life. So We Dschong, who is a general among men on earth, shall behead him, as an example for all living beings.'

In the evening the Emperor Tai Dsung had a dream. He saw a giant enter his room, who pleaded with barely restrained tears: 'Save me,

O Emperor! Because I diminished the rainfall on my own account, the Lord of the Heavens, in his anger, has commanded that We Dschong behead me tomorrow at noon. If you will only ensure that We Dschong falls asleep at that time, and pray that I may be saved, misfortune once more may pass me by!'

The emperor promised, and the other bowed and left him.

The following day the emperor sent for We Dschong. They drank tea together and played chess.

Towards noon We Dschong suddenly grew tired and sleepy; but he did not dare take his leave. The emperor fixed his gaze for a moment on the chessboard, since one of his pawns had been taken, and pondered, and before he knew it We Dschong was snoring with a sound like distant thunder. The emperor was frightened, and hastily called out to him; but he did not awake. Then he had two eunuchs shake him, but a long time passed before he could be aroused.

'How did you come to fall asleep so suddenly!' asked the emperor.

'I dreamed,' replied We Dschong, 'that the Highest God had commanded me to behead the old dragon. I have just hewn off his head, and my arm still aches from the exertion.'

And before he had even finished speaking a dragon's head, as large as a bushel, suddenly fell down out of the air. The emperor was terribly frightened and rose.

'I have sinned against the old dragon,' said he. Then he retired to the inner chambers of his palace and was confused in mind. He remained lying on his couch, closed his eyes, said not a word, and breathed but faintly.

Suddenly he saw two persons in purple robes who had a summons in their hands. They spoke to him as follows: 'The old Dragon of the Milky Way has complained against the emperor in the Underworld. We beg that you will have the chariot harnessed!'

Instinctively the emperor followed them, and in the courtyard stood his chariot before the castle, ready and waiting. The emperor entered it, and off they went flying through the air. In a moment they had reached the City of the Dead. When he entered he saw the Lord of the High Mountain sitting in the midst of the city, with the ten princes of the Underworld in rows at his right and left. They all rose, bowed to him and bade him be seated.

Then the Lord of the High Mountain said: 'The old Dragon of the Milky Way has committed a deed that deserved punishment. Yet Your

Majesty has promised to beg the Highest God to spare him, which prayer would probably have saved the old dragon's life. That this matter was neglected over the chessboard might well be considered a mistake. Now the old dragon complains to me over and over without end. When I think of how he has striven to gain sainthood for more than a thousand years, and must now fall back into the Cycle of Transformations, I am really depressed. For this reason I have called together the princes of the ten pits of the Underworld, to find a way out of the difficulty, and have invited Your Majesty to come here to discuss the matter. In heaven, on earth and in the Underworld, only the gospel of Buddha has no limits. Hence, when you return to Earth, great sacrifices should be made to the three and thirty lords of the heavens. Three thousand six hundred holy priests of Buddha must read the sutras to deliver the old dragon so that he may rise again to the skies and keep his original form. But the writings and readings of men will not be enough to ensure this. You must go to the Western Heavens and from this bring words of truth.'

The emperor agreed, and the Lord of the Great Mountain and the ten princes of the Underworld rose, saying as they bowed to him: 'We beg that you will now return!'

Suddenly Tai Dsung opened his eyes again, and there he was lying on his imperial couch. Then he admitted publicly that he was at fault, and ordered the holiest among the priests of Buddha to be sent to fetch the sutras from the Western Heavens. And it was Huan Dschuang, the Monk of the Yangtze-kiang, who appeared at court.

Huan Dschuang had originally been called Tschen. His father had passed the highest examinations during the reign of the preceding emperor, and had been entrusted with the office of district mandarin on the Yangtze-kiang. He set out with his wife for this new district, but when their ship reached the Yellow River it fell in with a band of robbers. Their captain killed the whole retinue, threw father Tschen into the river, took his wife and the document appointing him mandarin, went to the district capital under an assumed name and himself took charge. All the serving men accompanying him were members of his robber band. As for Tschen's wife and her little boy, he imprisoned them in a tower room. And all the servants attending her were in the confidence of the robbers.

Now below the tower was a little pond, and in this pond rose a spring that flowed beneath the walls to the Yellow River. One day,

Tschen's wife took a little basket of bamboo, pasted up the cracks and laid her little boy in the basket. Then she cut her finger, wrote down the day and hour of the boy's birth on a strip of silk paper with the blood, and added that the boy must come and rescue her when he had reached the age of twelve. She placed the strip of silk paper beside the boy in the basket, and at night, when no one was about, she put the basket in the pond. The current carried it away to the Yangtze-kiang, and from there it drifted on as far as the monastery on the Golden Hill, an island lying in the middle of the river. A priest, who had come to draw water, found it, fished it out and took it to the monastery.

When the abbot saw what had been written in blood, he ordered his priests and novices to say nothing to anyone. And he brought up the boy in the monastery.

When the boy had reached the age of five, he was taught to read the holy books. More intelligent than any of his fellow students, he soon grasped the meaning of the sacred writings, and entered more and more deeply into their secrets. So he was allowed to take his vows, and when his head had been shaven was named the Monk of the Yangtze-kiang.

By the time he was twelve, he was as large and strong as a grown man. The abbot, who knew of the duty he still had to perform, called him to a quiet room. There he drew forth the letter written in blood and gave it to him.

When the monk had read it, he flung himself down on the ground and wept bitterly. Thereupon he thanked the abbot for all he had done for him. He set out for the city in which his mother dwelt, ran around the yamen of the mandarin, beat upon the wooden fish and cried: 'Deliverance from all suffering! Deliverance from all suffering!'

In the intervening years, the robber who had killed his father and slipped into the post by false pretences, had taken care to strengthen his position by making powerful friends. By this point, he even allowed Tschen's wife, who had now been a prisoner for some ten years, a little more liberty.

On that day, official business kept him abroad. The woman was sitting at home, and when she heard the wooden fish beaten so insistently before the door and heard the words of deliverance, the voice of her heart cried out. She sent out the serving maid to call in the priest. He came in by the back door, and when she saw that he resembled his father in every feature, she could no longer restrain herself but burst into tears. Then the monk of the Yangtze-kiang, realising that this was his mother, took out the bloody writing and returned it to her.

She stroked it, saying amid sobs: 'My father is a high official, who has retired from affairs and dwells in the capital. But I have been unable to write to him, because this robber guarded me so closely. I kept alive as well as I could, waiting for you to come. Now hurry to the capital for the sake of your father's memory, and if his honour is made clear, I can die in peace. But you must hurry so that no one finds out.'

The monk set off quickly. First he went back to his cloister to bid farewell to his abbot; and then he set out for Sianfu, the capital.

By that time his grandfather had already died. But one of his uncles, who was known at court, was still living. Mustering a band of soldiers, he soon made an end of the robbers. But by then the monk's mother had died.

From that time on, the Monk of the Yangtze-kiang lived in a pagoda in Sianfu and was known as Huan Dschuang. When the emperor issued the order calling the priests of Buddha to court, he was some twenty years of age. He came into the presence of the emperor, who honoured him as a great teacher. Then he set out for India.

He was absent for seventeen years. When he returned, he brought three collections of books with him, and each collection comprised five-hundred and forty rolls of manuscript. With these he once more entered the presence of the emperor. The emperor was overjoyed, and with his own hand wrote a preface to the holy teachings, recording all that had happened. Then a great sacrifice was held to deliver the old Dragon of the Milky Way.

*Notes: It was the responsibility of the Emperor to provide assistance to areas hit by the famine that inevitably followed when the rains failed. An emperor who could not prevent a famine was said to have lost the Mandate of Heaven – the divine right to be emperor.*

*The emperor Tai Dsung is Li Schi Min, the Prince of Tang mentioned in 65. He was the most glorious and splendid of all Chinese rulers.*

*The 'Dragon-King of the Eastern Sea' has appeared frequently in these fairy tales.*

*In regard to the 'Lord of the High Mountain,' and the ten princes of the Underworld, compare 38 and 50. The Highest Lord is Yu Huang, the Lord of Jade or of Nephrite.*

*Huan Dschuang was originally known as Tschen. Regarding his father's fate subsequent to his being drowned, and that of his sons in the spirit world, see 24.*

*The 'bamboo basket' is a Moses motif that occurs in other Chinese fairy tales.*

*'The Monk of the Yangtze-kiang' (in Chinese, Giang Liu Ho Schang) is, literally: 'The monk washed ashore by the stream'.*

*'Wooden fish': a hollow piece of wood in the form of a fish, beaten by the Buddhists as sign of watchfulness.*

# VII

# LITERARY
# FAIRY TALES

# 70

# The Heartless Husband

**Heartlessness is probably the least of the catalogue of crimes which the husband in this story is guilty of, but does it end with forgiveness and redemption?**

In olden times, Hanchow was the capital of Southern China, and a great number of beggars had gathered there. These beggars were in the habit of electing a leader, who was officially entrusted with supervising all begging in the town. It was his duty to see that the beggars did not molest the townsfolk, and he received a tenth of their income from all his beggar subjects. When it snowed or rained, and the beggars could not go out to beg, he saw to it that they had something to eat. He was also expected to conduct their weddings and funerals. The beggars obeyed him in all things.

Well, it happened that there was a beggar king of this sort in Hanchow by the name of Gin, in whose family the office had been handed down from father to son for seven generations. What they had taken in by way of beggars' pence they had lent out on interest, and so the family had gradually become well-to-do and finally even rich.

The old beggar king had lost his wife at the age of fifty. But he had an only child, a girl who was called Little Golden Daughter. She had a face of rare beauty and was the jewel of his eye. From childhood, she had been versed in the lore of books, and could write, improvise poems and compose essays. She was also experienced in needlework, a skilled dancer and singer, and could play the flute and zither. The old beggar king wanted her to have, above all else, a scholar for a husband. Yet because he was a beggar king the distinguished families avoided him, while he refused to have anything to do with families of less standing than himself. So it came about that Little Golden Daughter had reached the age of eighteen without being betrothed.

Now at that time there dwelt in Hanchow, near the Bridge of Peace, a scholar by the name of Mosu. He was twenty years of age, and universally popular thanks to his handsome looks and talent. His parents were both dead, and he was so poor that he could hardly manage to keep alive. His house and lot had long since been mortgaged or sold, and he lived in an abandoned temple, and many a day passed which ended with him going hungry to bed.

A neighbour took pity on him and said to him one day: 'The beggar king has a child named Little Golden Daughter, who is beautiful beyond all telling. And the beggar king is rich and has money but no son to inherit. If you marry into his family, his whole fortune would in the end come to you. Is that not better than dying of hunger as a poor scholar?'

At that time Mosu was in dire extremity and these words offered a lifeline. He begged the neighbour to act as a go-between.

So the latter visited the old beggar king and talked with him, and the beggar king talked over the matter with Little Golden Daughter, and since Mosu came from a good family and was, in addition, talented and learned, and had no objection to marrying into their family, they were both much pleased with the prospect. So they agreed to the proposal, and the two were married.

So Mosu became a member of the beggar king's family. He was happy in his wife's beauty, always had enough to eat and good clothes to wear. He thought himself lucky beyond his deserts, and lived with his wife in peace and happiness.

The beggar king and his daughter, to whom their low estate was a thorn in the flesh, admonished Mosu to study hard. They hoped that he would make a name for himself and so bring glory to their family as well. They bought books for him, old and new, at the highest prices, and they supplied him liberally with money so that he could move in aristocratic circles. They also paid his examination expenses. As a result, his learning increased day by day, and the fame of it spread through the entire district. He passed one examination after another in rapid succession, and at the age of twenty-three was appointed mandarin of the district of Wu We. He returned from his audience with the emperor in ceremonial robes, high on horseback.

Mosu had been born in Hanchow, and the whole town soon knew that he had passed his examination successfully. The townsfolk crowded together on both sides of the street to look at him as he rode to his father-in-law's house. Old and young, women and children gathered to enjoy the show, and some idle loafer called out in a loud voice: 'The old beggar's son-in-law has become a mandarin!'

Mosu blushed with shame when he heard these words. Speechless and out of sorts, he seated himself in his room. The old beggar king did not notice his ill humour, so delighted was he. He ordered a great festival banquet to be prepared, inviting all his neighbours and good friends. Most of the guests were beggars and poor folk, and he insisted that Mosu eat with them. Only with great difficulty was Mosu persuaded to leave his room – and when he saw the guests gathered around the table, as ragged and dirty as a horde of hungry devils, he retired again with disdain. Little Golden Daughter, who realised how he felt, tried to cheer him up again in a hundred and one ways, but all in vain.

A few days later Mosu, together with his wife and servants, set out for the new district he was to govern. The journey from Hanchow to Wu We is by water, so they boarded a ship and sailed out to the Yangtze-kiang. At the end of the first day they reached a city where they anchored. The night was clear and the moon's rays glittered on the water, and Mosu sat in the front part of the ship enjoying the moonlight. Suddenly he chanced to think of the old beggar king. It was true that his wife was wise and good, but should heaven happen to bless them with children, these children would always be the beggar king's nephews and nieces; there was no way of avoiding the disgrace. And so a plan occurred to him. He called Little Golden Daughter out of the cabin to come and enjoy the moonlight, and she came out to him happily. Menservants and maidservants and all the sailors had long since gone to sleep. He looked about him on all sides, but there was no one to be seen. Little Golden Daughter was standing at the front of the ship, in her innocence, when a hand suddenly thrust her into the water. Feigning fear, Mosu began to call out: 'My wife made a misstep and has fallen into the water!'

And when they heard his words, the servants hurried up and wanted to fish her out.

But Mosu said: 'She has already been carried away by the current, it is pointless to trouble yourselves!' And he gave orders to set sail again as soon as possible.

By chance – who would have thought it? – Sir Hu, the mandarin appointed to oversee transport for the province, was also about to take charge of his department, and had anchored in the same place. He was sitting with his wife at the open window of the ship's cabin, enjoying the moonlight and the cool breeze.

Suddenly he heard someone crying on the shore; it sounded like a girl's voice. He quickly sent people to assist her, and they brought her aboard. It was Little Golden Daughter.

When she fell into the water, something beneath her feet held her up so that she did not sink. And she had been carried along by the current to the riverbank, where she crept out of the water. It was then she realised that her husband had forgotten how poor he had been – and for all that she had not been drowned, she felt very lonely and abandoned, and her tears began to flow. When Sir Hu asked her what was the matter, she told him the whole story.

Sir Hu comforted her. 'You must not shed another tear. If you care to become my adopted daughter, we will look after you.'

Little Golden Daughter bowed in thanks. Hu's wife ordered her maids to bring clothes to take the place of the wet ones, and to prepare a bed for her. The servants were strictly bidden to call her 'Miss,' and to say nothing of what had occurred.

So the journey continued and in a few days' time Sir Hu entered upon his official duties. Wu We, where Mosu was district mandarin, was subject to his rule, so Mosu visited to pay his respects. When Sir Hu saw him, he thought to himself: 'What a pity that so highly gifted a man should be so heartless!'

After a few months had passed, Sir Hu said to his subordinates: 'I have a daughter who is very pretty and good, and I would like to find a son-in-law to marry into my family. Do you know of anyone who might answer?'

His subordinates all knew that Mosu was young and had lost his wife, so they unanimously suggested him.

Sir Hu replied: 'I have also thought of that gentleman, but he is young and has risen very rapidly. I am afraid he has higher ambitions, and would not care to marry into my family and become my son-in-law.'

'He was originally poor,' answered his people, 'and he is your subordinate. Should you care to show him a kindness of this sort, he will be sure to accept it joyfully, and will not object to marrying into your family.'

'Well, if you all believe it can be done,' said Sir Hu, 'pay him a visit and find out what he thinks. But you must not say that I have sent you.'

Mosu, who was reflecting at that moment on how he might win Sir Hu's favour, took up the suggestion with pleasure, and urgently begged them to act as his go-between, promising them a rich reward once the connection was established.

They reported as much to Sir Hu.

He said: 'I am very pleased that the gentleman in question does not disdain this marriage. But my wife and I are extremely fond of this daughter of ours, and we can hardly resign ourselves to giving her up. Sir Mosu is young and aristocratic, and our little daughter has been spoiled. If he were to ill treat her, or at some future time regret having married into our family, my wife and I would be inconsolable. For this reason, everything must be clearly understood in advance. Only if he positively agrees to my terms will I be able to receive him into my family.'

Mosu was informed of all the conditions, and declared himself ready to accept. Then he brought gold and pearls and coloured silks to Sir Hu's daughter as wedding gifts, and a lucky day was chosen for the wedding. Sir Hu charged his wife to talk to Little Golden Daughter.

'Your adopted father,' said she, 'feels sorry for you, because you are lonely, so he has picked out a young scholar for you to marry.'

But Little Golden Daughter replied: 'It is true that I am of humble birth, yet I know what is fitting. It chances that I agreed to cast my lot with Mosu for better or for worse. And though he has shown me but little kindness, I will marry no other man so long as he lives. I cannot bring myself to form another union and break my vows.' And the tears poured from her eyes.

When Sir Hu's wife saw that nothing would alter her resolve, she told her how matters really stood.

'Your adopted father,' said she, 'is disgusted by Mosu's heartlessness. And although he will see to it that you meet again, he has said nothing which would lead Mosu to believe that you are not our own daughter. Mosu was delighted to marry you. But when the wedding is celebrated this evening, you must do as I tell you, for he must taste your righteous anger.'

When she had heard all this, Little Golden Daughter dried her tears, and thanked her adopted parents. Then she adorned herself for the wedding.

The same day, late at evening, Mosu came to the house wearing golden flowers on his hat and a red scarf across his breast, riding on a gaily trapped horse, and followed by a great retinue. All his friends and acquaintances came with him, to be present at the festival celebration.

Sir Hu's house had been adorned with coloured cloths and lanterns. Mosu dismounted from his horse at the entrance of the hall. Here Sir Hu had spread a festival banquet to which Mosu and his friends were led. And when the goblet had made the rounds three times, serving maids came and invited Mosu to follow them to the inner rooms. The bride, veiled in a red veil, was led in by two maidservants. Following the injunctions of the master of the ceremony, they worshipped heaven and earth together, and then the parents-in-law. Thereupon they went into another apartment. Here brightly coloured candles were burning, and a wedding dinner had been prepared. Mosu felt as happy as though he had been raised to the seventh heaven.

But when he wanted to leave the room, seven or eight maids with bamboo canes in their hands appeared at each side of the door, and began to beat him without mercy. They knocked his bridal hat from his head, and the blows rained down upon his back and shoulders. When Mosu cried for help he heard a delicate voice say: 'There is no reason to kill that heartless bridegroom of mine! Ask him to come in and greet me!'

The maids stopped beating him, and gathered about the bride, who removed her bridal veil.

Mosu bowed with lowered head and said: 'But what have I done?'

Raising his eyes, he saw that none other than his wife, Little Golden Daughter, was standing before him.

Starting with fright, he cried: 'A ghost, a ghost!' But all the servants broke out into loud laughter.

At last Sir Hu and his wife came in, and the former said: 'My dear son-in-law, you may rest assured that my adopted daughter, who came to me while I was on my way to this place, is no ghost.'

Mosu hastily fell to his knees, answering: 'I have sinned and beg for mercy!' And he kowtowed and kowtowed and kowtowed.

'There is nothing more for me to do,' remarked Sir Hu. 'If our little daughter only gets along well with you, then all will be in order.'

But Little Golden Daughter said: 'You heartless scoundrel! In the beginning you were poor and needy. We took you into our family, and let you study so that you might become somebody and make a name for yourself. No sooner had you become a mandarin and a man of standing, than your love turned into enmity, and you forgot your duty as a husband and pushed me into the river. Fortunately, I found my dear adopted parents thereby. They fished me out, and made me their own child, otherwise I would have found a grave in the bellies of the fishes. How can I honourably live again with such a man as you?'

With these words she began to lament loudly, throwing one insult after another.

Mosu lay before her, speechless with shame, and begged her to forgive him.

When Sir Hu saw that Little Golden Daughter had sufficiently relieved herself by her scolding, he helped Mosu up and said to him: 'My dear son-in-law, if you repent of your misdeed, Little Golden Daughter will cease to be angry. Of course you are an old married couple; yet as you have renewed your vows this evening in my house, kindly do me a favour and listen to what I have to say: You, Mosu, are weighed with a heavy burden of guilt, and for that reason you must not resent your wife's indignation, but must have patience. I will call in my wife to make peace between you.'

With these words Sir Hu went out and sent in his wife. Finally, and after a great deal of difficulty, she succeeded in reconciling the two, and they agreed once again to take up life as husband and wife.

They esteemed and loved each other twice as much as they had before, and their life was all happiness and joy. Later, when Sir Hu and his wife died, they mourned for them as if in truth they had been their own parents.

Notes: 'To marry into': as a rule, the wife enters the home of her husband's parents. But when there is no male heir, it is arranged that the son-in-law continues the family of his wife's parents, and lives in their home. The custom is still prevalent in Japan, but it is no longer considered very honourable in China.

As a punishment for disdaining to marry into a family the first time, Mosu is obliged to marry into a second family, Sir Hu's.

'Little Golden Daughter' said: 'You heartless scoundrel!'; despite her faithfulness, she is obliged by custom to show her anger over his faithlessness; this is necessary before the matter can be properly adjusted, allowing her to 'preserve her face'.

# 71

## Giauna the Beautiful

**This story chronicles the eventful life and times of a scholar. At its heart it is about the nature of love and the meaning of friendship, but look out for shape-shifting and major surgery too.**

Once upon a time there was a descendant of Confucius. His father had a friend who held an official position in the South, and he now offered the young man a place as secretary. But when the young man reached town, he found that his father's friend had already died. Then he was much embarrassed, seeing that he did not have the means to return home again. So he was glad to take refuge in the Monastery of Puto, where he copied holy books for the abbot.

About a hundred paces west of the monastery stood a deserted house. One day there had been a great snowfall, and as young Kung accidentally passed by the door of the house, he noticed a well dressed and prepossessing youth standing there, who bowed to him and begged him to approach. Young Kung was a scholar and could appreciate good manners. Finding that the youth and himself had much in common, he took a liking to him, and followed him into the house. It was immaculately clean; silk curtains hung before the doors, and on the walls were pictures of good old masters. On a table lay a book entitled *Tales of the Coral Ring*.

Coral Ring was the name of a cavern. There had once lived a monk at Puto who was exceedingly learned. An aged man had led him into the cave, where he saw a number of volumes on the book stands. The aged man said: 'These are the histories of the various dynasties.' In a second room were the histories of all the peoples on earth. A third was guarded by two dogs. The aged man explained: 'In this room are kept the secret reports of the immortals, describing the arts by which they gained eternal life. The two dogs are two dragons.' The monk turned the pages of the books, and found that they were all works of ancient times, such as he had never seen before. He would gladly have remained in the cave, but the old man said: 'That will not do!' and a boy led him out again. The name of that cave, however, was the Coral Ring, and it was described in the volume lying on the table.

The youth questioned Kung about his name and family, and learned the whole history. Feeling great pity for him, the youth advised him to open a school.

Kung answered with a sigh: 'I am quite unknown in the neighbourhood, and have no one to recommend me!'

Said the youth: 'If you do not consider me altogether too unworthy and stupid, I should like to be your pupil myself.'

Young Kung was overjoyed. 'I should not dare to attempt to teach you,' he replied, 'but together we might dedicate ourselves to the study of science.' He then asked why the house had been standing empty for so long.

The youth answered: 'The owner of the house has gone to the country. We come from Shensi, and have taken the house for a short time. We only moved in a few days ago.'

They chatted and joked together gaily, and the young man invited Kung to remain overnight, ordering a small boy to light a pan of charcoal.

Then he stepped rapidly into the rear room and soon returned, saying: 'My father has come.'

As Kung rose, an aged man with a long, white beard and eyebrows stepped into the room, saying in greeting: 'You have already declared your willingness to instruct my son, and I am grateful for your kindness. But you must be strict with him and not treat him as a friend.'

Then he had garments of silk, a fur cap, and shoes and socks of fur brought in, and begged Kung to change his clothes. Wine and food were served. The cushions and covers of the tables and chairs were made of stuffs unknown to Kung, and their shimmering radiance blinded the eye. The aged man retired after a few beakers of wine, and then the youth showed Kung his essays. They were all written in the style of the old masters and not in the new-fangled eight-section form.

When he was asked about this, the youth said with a smile: 'I am quite indifferent to winning success at the state examinations!' Then he turned to the small boy and said: 'See whether the old gentleman has already fallen asleep. If he has, you may quietly bring in little Hiang-Nu.'

The boy went off, and the youth took a lute from an embroidered case. At once a serving maid entered, dressed in red and surpassingly beautiful. The youth told her to sing 'The Lament of the Beloved,' and her melting tones moved the heart. The third watch of the night had passed before they retired to sleep.

On the following morning, all rose early and study began. The youth was exceptionally gifted. Whatever he had seen but once was graven in his memory, so he made surprising progress in the course of just a few months. The old custom was followed of writing an essay every five days, and celebrating its completion with a little banquet. And at each banquet Hiang-Nu, the beautiful serving maid, was sent for.

One evening Kung could not remove his glance from Hiang-Nu. The youth guessed his thoughts and said to him: 'You are as yet unmarried. Morning and night, I keep thinking how I can provide you with a charming life companion. Hiang-Nu is the serving maid of my father, so I cannot give her to you.'

Said Kung: 'I am grateful to you for your thoughts. But if the girl you have in mind is not just as beautiful as Hiang-Nu, I would rather do without.'

The youth laughed: 'You are indeed inexperienced if you think that Hiang-Nu is beautiful. Your wish is easily fulfilled.'

Half a year went by and the monotonous rainy season had just began. A swelling the size of a peach developed in young Kung's breast, which increased over night until it was as large as a teacup. He lay on his couch groaning with pain, unable to eat or to sleep. The youth was busy day and night nursing him, and even the old gentleman asked how he was getting along.

Then the youth said: 'My little sister Giauna alone is able to cure this illness. Please send to grandmother, and have her brought here!'

The old gentleman agreed, and sent off his boy.

The next day the boy came back with the news that Giauna would come, together with her aunt and her cousin A-Sung.

Not long after, the youth led his sister into the room. She was not more than thirteen or fourteen years of age, enchantingly beautiful, and slender as a willow tree. When the sick man saw her, he forgot all his pain and his spirits rose.

The youth said to his sister Giauna: 'This is my best friend, whom I love as a brother! I beg of you, little sister, to cure him of his illness!'

The maiden blushed with confusion; then she stepped up to the sickbed. While she was feeling his pulse, it seemed to him as though she brought the fragrance of orchards with her.

Said the maiden with a smile: 'No wonder that this illness has befallen him. His heart beats far too stormily. His illness is serious but not incurable. Now the blood which has flowed has already gathered, so we will have to cut to cure.'

With that she took her golden armlet from her arm and laid it on the aching place. She pressed it down very gently, and the swelling rose a full inch above the armlet so that it enclosed the entire swelling. Then she loosed a penknife with a blade as thin as paper from her silken girdle. With one hand she held the armlet, and with the other she took the knife and lightly passed it around the bottom of the ring. Black blood gushed forth and ran over mattress and bed. But young Kung was so enchanted by the beautiful Giauna that he felt no pain, and his one fear was that the whole affair might end too soon and that she would disappear from his sight. In a moment the diseased flesh had been cut away, and Giauna had fresh water brought and cleansed the wound. Then she took a small red pellet from her mouth, and laid it on the wound, and when she turned around in a circle, it seemed to Kung as though she drew out all the inflammation in steam and flames. Once more she turned in a circle, and he felt his wound itch and quiver, and when she turned for the third time, he was completely cured.

The maiden took the pellet into her mouth again and said: 'Now all is well!' She hastened into the inner room, and young Kung leaped up to thank her.

True, he was now cured of his illness, but his thoughts continued to dwell on Giauna's pretty face. He neglected his books and sat lost in daydreams.

His friend had noticed and said to him: 'I have at last succeeded, just this very day, in finding an attractive life companion for you.'

Kung asked who she might be.

'The daughter of my aunt, A-Sung. She is seventeen years of age, and anything but homely.'

'I am sure she is not as beautiful as Giauna,' thought Kung. Then he hummed the lines of a song to himself:

Who once has seen the sea close by,
All rivers shallow streams declares;
Who o'er Wu's hill the clouds watched fly,
Says nothing with that view compares.

The youth smiled. 'My little sister Giauna is still very young. Besides, she is my father's only daughter, and he would not like to see her marry someone from afar. But my cousin A-Sung is not homely either. If you do not believe me, wait until they go walking in the garden, then you may take a look at them without their knowing it.'

Kung posted himself at the open window on the lookout, and sure enough, he saw Giauna come along leading another girl by the hand, a girl so beautiful that there was none other like her. Giauna and she seemed to be sisters, to be told apart only by a slight difference in age.

Young Kung was exceedingly happy and begged his friend to act for him in arranging the marriage. This his friend promised to do, and the next day he came to Kung, offering congratulations and telling him that everything was arranged. A special court was put in order for the young pair, and the wedding was celebrated. Young Kung felt as though he had married a fairy, and the two became very fond of each other.

One day Kung's friend came to him in a state of great excitement and said: 'The owner of this house is coming back, and my father now wishes to return to Shensi. The time for us to part draws near, and I am very sad!'

Kung wanted to accompany them, but his friend advised him to return to his own home.

Kung explained the difficulties in the way, but the youth replied: 'That need not worry you, because I will accompany you.'

After a time the father came, together with A-Sung, and made Kung a present of a hundred ounces of gold. Then the youth took Kung and his wife by the hand and told them to close their eyes. As soon as they did so, off they went through the air like a storm wind. All Kung could sense was the gale roaring about his ears.

When some time had passed, the youth cried: 'Now we have arrived!' Kung opened his eyes and saw his old home, and then he knew that his friend was not of human kind.

Gaily they knocked at the door of his home. His mother opened it and when she saw that he had brought along so charming a wife she was greatly pleased. Then Kung turned around to his friend, but he had already disappeared.

A-Sung served her mother-in-law with great devotion, and her beauty and virtue was celebrated far and near. Soon after, young Kung gained his doctorate and was appointed inspector of prisons in Shensi. He took his wife along with him, but his mother remained at home, since Shensi was too far for her to travel. And heaven gave A-Sung and Kung a little son.

But Kung became involved in a dispute with a travelling censor, who complained and Kung was dismissed from his post.

It so happened that one day he was idling about before the city, when he saw a handsome youth on a black mule. Looking more closely, he saw that it was his old friend. They fell into each others' arms, laughing and weeping, and the youth led him to a village. In the midst of a thick grove of trees that threw a deep shade stood a house whose upper stories rose to the skies. At a glance it was obvious that people of distinction lived there. Kung now inquired after sister Giauna, and was told that she had married. He stayed overnight and then went off to fetch his wife.

In the meantime, Giauna arrived. She took A-Sung's little son in her arms and said: 'Cousin, this is a little stranger in our family!'

Kung greeted her, and again thanked her for the kindness she had shown him in curing his illness.

She answered with a smile: 'Since then you have become a distinguished man, and the wound has long since healed. Have you still not forgotten your pain?'

Then Giauna's husband arrived, and everyone was introduced. After that, they parted.

One day the youth came sadly to Kung and said: 'We are threatened by a great misfortune today. I do not know whether you would be willing to save us!'

Kung did not know what it might be, but he gladly promised his aid. The youth called up the entire family and they bowed down in the outer court.

He began: 'I will tell you the truth just as it is. We are foxes. This day we are threatened by thunder. If you care to save us, we may hope to stay alive; if not, take your child and go, so that you are not involved in our danger.'

But Kung vowed that he would share life and death with them.

The youth begged him to stand in the door with a sword in his hand, and said: 'Now when the thunder begins to roll, you must stand there and never stir.'

Suddenly dark clouds rose in the sky, and the heavens grew gloomy as if night were closing down. Kung looked about him, but the buildings had all disappeared, and behind him he could see only a high barrow, and in it a large cave whose inside was lost in darkness. Already fearful, he was surprised by a thunderbolt. A heavy rain poured down in streams, and a storm wind arose and rooted up the tallest trees. Everything glimmered before his eyes and his ears were deafened. But he held his sword in his hand, and stood as firm as a rock. Suddenly in the midst of black smoke and flashes of lightning, he saw a monster with a pointed beak and long claws, carrying off a human body. When he looked more closely, he recognised by her dress that it was Giauna. Leaping up at the monster, he struck at him with his sword, and at once Giauna fell to the ground. A tremendous crash of thunder shook the earth, and Kung fell down dead.

Then the tempest cleared away and the blue sky appeared once more.

Giauna had regained consciousness, and when she saw Kung lying dead beside her, she cried amid sobs: 'He died for my sake! Why should I continue to live?'

A-Sung also came out, and together they carried him into the cave. Giauna told A-Sung to hold his head while her brother opened his mouth. She herself took hold of his chin and brought out her little red pellet. She pressed it against his lips with her own, and breathed into his lungs. Then the breath came back to his throat with a rattling noise, and in a short time he was himself once more.

So the whole family was reunited again, and none of its members had come to harm. They gradually recovered from their fear, and were relieved when suddenly a small boy brought the news that Giauna's husband and his whole family had been killed by the thunder. Giauna broke down, weeping.

The others tried to comfort her. Finally Kung said: 'It is not well to dwell too long amid the graves of the dead. Will you not come home with me?'

Thereupon they packed up their belongings and went with him. To his friend and his family he assigned a deserted garden, carefully walled off, as a dwelling-place. Only when Kung and A-Sung came to visit them was the bolt drawn. Then Giauna and her brother played chess, drank tea and chatted with them like members of the same family.

But Kung's little son had a somewhat pointed face, like a fox, and when he went along the street, people would turn around and say: 'There goes the fox child!'

*Notes: 'Not in the new-fangled eight-section form': Ba Gu Wen Dschang, i.e., essays in eight-section form, divided according to strict rules, were the customary theses in the governmental examinations in China up to the time of the great educational reform.*

*'The danger of thunder': Three times the foxes must have escaped the mortal danger of thunder.*

# 72

# The Frog Princess

**For better or for worse, when you marry you become part of
your wife's family, but perhaps the young man in this story can
be forgiven for finding his unusual in-laws somewhat trying.**

There where the Yangtze-kiang has come about halfway on
its course to the sea, the Frog King is worshipped with great
devotion. He has a temple there, and frogs by the thousand are
to be found in the neighbourhood, some of them enormous. Those who
incur the wrath of the god are apt to have strange visitations in their
homes. Frogs hop about on tables and beds, and in extreme cases they
even creep up the smooth walls of the room without falling. There
are various kinds of omens, but all indicate that some misfortune
threatens the house in question. Then the people living in it become
terrified, slaughter a cow and offer it as a sacrifice. Thus the god is
mollified and nothing further happens.

In that part of the country there once lived a boy named Sia Kung-
Schong. He was handsome and intelligent, and when he was some
six or seven years of age, a serving maid dressed in green entered his
home. She said that she was a messenger from the Frog King, and
declared that he wished to have his daughter marry young Sia. Old
Sia was an honest man, not very bright, and since this did not suit
him, he declined the offer, pleading that his son was still too young to
marry. Even so, he did not dare look about for another mate for him.

A few years passed and the boy gradually grew up. A marriage was
arranged between him and a certain Mistress Giang.

But the Frog King sent word to Mistress Giang: 'Young Sia is my
son-in-law. How dare you undertake to lay claim to what does not belong
to you!' This frightened Father Giang, who withdrew his promise.

Saddened, Old Sia prepared a sacrifice and went to his temple
to pray. There he explained that he felt unworthy of becoming
the relation of a god. When he had finished praying, a multitude
of enormous maggots appeared in the sacrificial meat and wine,
crawling around. He poured them out, begged forgiveness, and

returned home filled with evil forebodings. He did not know what more he could do, and had to let things take their course.

One day young Sia went out into the street. A messenger stepped up to him and told him that the Frog King urgently requested Sia to come to him. There was nothing for it; he had to follow the messenger, who led him through a red gateway into some magnificent, high-ceilinged rooms. In the great hall sat an ancient man who might have been some eighty years of age. Sia cast himself down on the ground before him in homage. The old man bade him rise, and assigned him a place at the table. Soon a number of girls and women came crowding in to look at him. Then the old man turned to them and said: 'Go to the bride's room and tell her that the bridegroom has arrived!'

Quickly a couple of maids ran away, and shortly after an old woman came from the inner apartments, leading a maiden by the hand. She might have been sixteen years of age and was beautiful beyond compare. The old man pointed to her and said: 'This is my tenth little daughter. It seemed to me that you would make a good pair. But your father has scorned us because of our difference in race. Yet marriage is a matter of lifelong importance. Our parents can determine its outcome only in part. In the end it rests mainly with one's self.'

Sia looked steadily at the girl, and in his heart affection stirred. He sat there in silence. The old man continued: 'I knew very well that the young gentleman would agree. Go on ahead of us, and we will bring you your bride!'

Sia agreed and hurried to inform his father. Seeing his excitement, his father did not know what to do, though he wanted to send Sia back to decline his bride with thanks. But this Sia refused. While they were arguing, the bride's carriage arrived at the door. It was surrounded by a crowd of greencoats, and the lady entered the house, bowing politely to her parents-in-law. They were both pleased, and the wedding was announced for that very evening.

The new couple lived in peace and good understanding. And after they had been married their divine parents-in-law often came to their house. When they appeared dressed in red, it meant that some good fortune was to befall them; when they came dressed in white, it signified that they were sure to make some gain. Thus, in the course of time, the family became wealthy.

But since they had become related to the gods, the rooms, courtyards and all other places were always crowded with frogs. And no one ventured them any harm. Sia Kung-Schong alone showed no consideration; he was young. When he was in good spirits, he did not bother them; but when he got out of sorts, he knew no mercy, and purposely stepped on them and killed them.

In general his young wife was modest and obedient; yet she easily lost her temper. She could not approve her husband's conduct. But Sia would not give up his brutal habit, and was angered by her scolding.

'Do you imagine,' he told her, 'that because your parents can visit human beings with misfortune, a real man would be afraid of a frog?'

His wife was always careful to avoid the word 'frog', so his speech angered her and she said: 'Since I have dwelt in your house, your fields have yielded larger crops and you have obtained the highest prices. And that is quite something. But now, when you are comfortably established, you choose to act like a fledgling owl, who pecks out his own mother's eyes as soon as he is able to fly!'

Sia grew still more angry and answered: 'These gifts have been unwelcome to me for a long time, for I consider them unclean. I could never consent to leave such property to sons and grandsons. It would be better if we parted at once!'

He ordered his wife to leave the house, and before his parents knew anything about it, she was gone. His parents scolded him and told him to go at once and bring her back. But he was filled with rage and would not give in.

That same night, he and his mother fell sick. Both felt weak and could not eat. The father was extremely worried, and went to the temple to beg for pardon. He prayed so earnestly that his wife and son recovered in three days' time. The Frog Princess also returned, and they lived together happily and contented as before.

But the young woman sat in the house all day long, occupied solely with her ornaments and her rouge, and did not concern herself with sewing and stitching. So Sia Kung-Schong's mother still had to look out for her son's clothes.

One day his mother was angry and said: 'My son has a wife, and yet I have to do all the work! In other homes the daughter-in-law serves her mother-in-law. But in our house the mother-in-law must serve the daughter-in-law.'

This the princess accidentally heard. In she came, much excited, and began: 'Have I ever omitted, as is right and proper, to visit you morning and evening? My only fault is that I will not burden myself with all

245

this toil for the sake of saving a trifling sum of money!' The mother answered not a word, but wept bitterly and in silence at this insult.

Her son came along and noticed that his mother had been weeping. He insisted on knowing the reason, and reproached his wife angrily. She argued back, not wishing to admit that she had been in the wrong. Finally Sia said: 'It is better to have no wife at all than one who gives her mother-in-law no pleasure. What can the old frog do to me after all, if I anger him, save call misfortunes upon me and take my life!' So he once more drove his wife out of the house.

The princess left her home and went away. The following day, fire broke out in the house and spread to several other buildings. Tables, beds, everything was burned.

Raging, Sia went to the temple to complain: 'To bring up a daughter in such a way that she does not please her parents-in-law shows that there is no discipline in a house. And now you even encourage her in her faults. It is said that the gods are most just. Are there gods who teach men to fear their wives? Incidentally, the whole quarrel rests on me alone. My parents had nothing to do with it. If I was to be punished by the axe and cord, well and good. You could have carried out the punishment yourself. But this you did not do. So now I will burn your own house in order to satisfy my own sense of justice!'

With these words he began piling up brushwood before the temple, struck sparks and wanted to set it ablaze. The neighbours came streaming up, and pleaded with him. Finally he swallowed his rage and went home.

When his parents heard what had happened, they grew pale with fear. But at night the god appeared to the people of a neighbouring village, and ordered them to rebuild the house of his son-in-law. When day began to dawn, they dragged up building-wood and the workmen all came in throngs to build for Sia. No matter what he said, he could not prevent them. All day long hundreds of workmen were busy. And in the course of a few days all the rooms had been rebuilt, and all the utensils, curtains and furniture were there as before. And when the work had been completed the princess also returned. She climbed the stairs to the great room, and acknowledged her fault with many tender and loving words. Then she turned to Sia Kung-Schong, and smiled at him sideways. Instead of resentment, joy now filled the whole house. And after that time the princess was especially peaceable. Two whole years passed without an angry word being said.

But the princess had a great dislike for snakes. Once, by way of a joke, young Sia put a small snake into a parcel, which he gave her and told her to open. She turned pale and reproached him, and angry words passed.

At last the princess said: 'This time I will not wait for you to turn me out. Now we are finally done with one another!' And with that she walked out of the door.

Alarmed, father Sia beat his son himself with his staff, and begged the god to be kind and forgive. Fortunately there were no evil consequences. All was quiet, and not a sound was heard.

Thus more than a year passed. Sia-Kung-Schong longed for the princess and took himself seriously to task. He would creep in secret to the temple of the god, and lament because he had lost the princess. But no voice answered him. And soon afterward he even heard that the god had betrothed his daughter to another man. Then he lost hope, and thought of finding another wife. Yet no matter how he searched, he could find no one who was her equal. This only increased his longing, and he went to the home of the Yuans, for she had been promised to a member of this family. There they had already painted the walls, and swept the courtyard, and all was in readiness to receive the bridal carriage. Sia was overcome with remorse and discontent. No longer able to eat, he fell ill. His parents were stunned by the anxiety they felt for him, and were incapable of thinking sensibly.

Suddenly while he was lying there only half-conscious, he felt someone stroke him, and heard a voice say: 'And how goes it with our real husband, who insisted on turning out his wife?'

He opened his eyes and there, standing in front of him, was the princess. Full of joy, he leaped up and said: 'How is it you have come back to me?' The princess answered: 'The truth is, I should have followed my father's advice and taken another husband, just as you treat people badly. And, as a matter of fact, the wedding gifts of the Yuan family have been lying in my home for a long time. But I thought and thought and could not bring myself to do so. The wedding was to have been this evening and my father thought it shameful to have the wedding gifts carried back. So I took the things myself and placed them before the Yuans' door. When I went out, my father ran out beside me: "You mad girl," he said. "Will you not listen to me? If you are badly treated by Sia in the future, I wash my hands of it. Even if they kill you, you shall not come home to me again!"'

Sia was moved by her faithfulness, and the tears rolled from his eyes. The servants, full of joy, hurried to the parents to tell them the good news. And when they heard it, they did not wait for the young people to come to them, but hurried themselves to their son's rooms, took the princess by the hand and wept. Young Sia, too, had become more settled by this time, and was no longer so mischievous. So he and his wife grew to love each other more sincerely day by day.

Once the princess said to him: 'Before, when you always treated me so badly, I feared that we would not keep company into our old age. So I never asked heaven to send us a child. But now that all has changed, and I will beg the gods for a son.'

Sure enough, before long Sia's parents-in-law appeared in the house clad in red garments, and shortly after heaven sent the happy pair two sons instead of one.

From that time on their dealings with the Frog King were never interrupted. When someone among the people had angered the god, he first tried to induce young Sia to speak for him, and sent his wife and daughter to the Frog Princess to implore her aid. And if the princess laughed, then all would be well.

The Sia family has many descendants, whom the people call 'the little frog men'. Those nearby them do not dare call them by this name, only those standing further off.

*Notes: 'Little frog men', Wa Dsi, is the derogatory name used by the North Chinese for the Chinese of the South.*

*The frog has accumulated various meanings in Chinese culture, but is most associated with bringing good luck and prosperity.*

# 73

# Rose of Evening

**In this exotic fairy tale, falling in the river and drowning is not the end for Aduan. Rather, it's the beginning of his adventures and his romance with the beautiful Rose of Evening.**

On the fifth day of the fifth month, the festival of the Dragon Junk is held along the Yangtze-kiang. A dragon is hollowed out of wood, painted with an armour of scales, and adorned with gold and bright colours. A carved red railing surrounds this ship, and its sails and are made of silks and brocade. The after part of the vessel is called the dragon's tail. It rises ten feet above the water, and a board floating in the water is tied to it with a cloth. Upon this board sit boys who turn somersaults, stand on their heads and perform all sorts of tricks. Being so close to the water means that their danger is very great. It is the custom, therefore, when a boy is hired for this purpose, to give his parents money before he is trained. Then, if he falls into the water and is drowned, no one has him on their conscience. Further South the custom differs in so much as beautiful girls are chosen instead of boys.

In Dschen-Giang there once lived a widow named Dsiang, who had a son called Aduan. When he was no more than seven years of age he was extraordinarily skilful and no other boy could equal him. With his reputation increasing as he grew, he earned more and more money. So it happened that he was still called upon at the Dragon Junk Festival when he was already sixteen.

But one day he fell into the water below the Gold Island and was drowned. He was the only son of his mother, and she sorrowed over him – and that was the end of it.

Aduan himself did not understand that he had been drowned. He met two men who took him along with them, and he saw a new world in the midst of the waters of the Yellow River. When he looked around, the waves of the river towered steeply about him like walls, and a palace was visible, where sat a man wearing armour and a helmet.

His two companions said to him: 'That is the Prince of the Dragon's Cave!' and ordered him to kneel.

The Prince of the Dragon's Cave seemed to be of a mild and kindly disposition and said: 'We can make use of such a skilful lad. He may take part in the dance of the willow branches!'

So he was brought to a spot surrounded by extensive buildings. Entering, he was greeted by a crowd of boys who were all about fourteen years of age.

An old woman came in and they all called out: 'This is Mother Hia!' And she sat down and had Aduan display his tricks. Then she taught him the dance of the flying thunders of Tsian-Tang River, and the music that calms the winds on the sea of Dung-Ting. When the cymbals and kettledrums re-echoed through all the courts, they deafened the ear. Then, again, all the courts would fall silent. Mother Hia thought that Aduan would not be able to grasp everything the very first time; so she taught him with great patience. But Aduan understood everything from the first, which pleased her. 'This boy,' said she, 'equals our own Rose of Evening!'

The following day the Prince of the Dragon's Cave held a review of his dancers. When they had all assembled, the Dance of the Ogres was performed first. The dancers and musicians all wore devil-masks and garments of scales. They beat upon enormous cymbals, and their kettledrums were so large that four men could just about span them. Their sound was like the sound of a mighty thunder, and the noise was so great that nothing else could be heard. When the dance began, tremendous waves spouted up to the very skies, and then fell down again like star glimmer scattering in the air.

The Prince of the Dragon Cave hastily bade the dance cease, and had the dancers of the Nightingale Round step forth. These were all lovely young girls of sixteen. They made a delicate music with flutes, so that the breeze blew and the roaring of the waves was stilled in a moment. The water gradually became as quiet as a crystal world, transparent to its lowest depths. When the dancers had finished, they withdrew and posted themselves in the western courtyard.

Then came the turn of the Swallow dancers. These were all little girls. One among them, about fifteen years of age, danced the Dance of the Giving of Flowers with flying sleeves and waving locks. And as their garments fluttered, many-coloured flowers dropped from their folds, and were caught up by the wind and whirled about the whole courtyard. When the dance had ended, this dancer also went off with the rest of the girls to the western courtyard. Aduan looked at her from out the corner of his eye and fell deeply in love. He asked his comrades who she might be and they told him she was named Rose of Evening.

The Willow Spray dancers were now called out. The Prince of the Dragon Cave particularly wanted to test Aduan, who danced alone, dancing with joy or defiance according to the music. When he looked up and when he looked down, his glances held the beat. The Dragon Prince, enchanted by his skill, presented him with a garment of five colours, and gave him a garnet set in golden threads of fish-beard for a hair-jewel. Aduan bowed in thanks, and then also hastened to the western courtyard. There all the dancers stood in rank and file. Aduan could only look at Rose of Evening from a distance, but still Rose of Evening returned his glances.

After a time Aduan gradually slipped to the end of his file and Rose of Evening also drew near to him, so that they stood only a few feet away from each other. But strict rules allowed no confusion in the ranks, so they could only gaze and let their souls go out to each other.

Now the Butterfly Dance followed the others. This was danced by the boys and girls together, and the pairs were equal in size, age and the colour of their garments. When all the dances had ended, the dancers marched out, goose-stepping. The Willow Spray dancers followed the Swallow dancers, and Aduan hastened in advance of his company, while Rose of Evening lingered along after hers. She turned her head, and when she spied Aduan she purposely let a coral pin fall from her hair. Aduan hastily hid it in his sleeve.

When he had returned, he was sick with longing, and could neither eat nor sleep. Mother Hia brought him all sorts of dainties, looked after him three or four times a day, and stroked his forehead with loving care. But his illness did not yield. Mother Hia was unhappy, and yet helpless.

'The birthday of the King of the Wu River is at hand,' said she. 'What is to be done?'

In the twilight there came a boy, who sat down on the edge of Aduan's bed and chatted with him. He belonged to the Butterfly dancers, said he, and asked casually: 'Are you sick because of Rose of Evening?' Aduan, frightened, asked him how he came to guess. The other boy said, with a smile: 'Well, because Rose of Evening is as sick as you.'

Disconcerted, Aduan sat up and begged the boy to advise him. 'Are you able to walk?' asked the latter. 'If I make the effort,' said Aduan, 'I think I could manage it.'

So the boy led him to the South. There he opened a gate and they turned the corner, to the West. Once more the doors of the gate flew open, and now Aduan saw a lotus field about twenty acres in size. The lotus flowers were all growing on level earth, and their leaves were as large as mats and their flowers like umbrellas. The fallen blossoms covered the ground beneath the stalks to the depth of a foot or more. The boy led Aduan in and said, 'Now first of all sit down for a little while!' Then he went away.

After a time a beautiful girl thrust aside the lotus flowers and came into the open. It was Rose of Evening. They looked at each other shyly, and each revealed how much they had longed for the other. They also told each other of their former life. Then they weighted the lotus leaves with stones so that they made a cozy retreat, in which they could be together, and promised to meet each other there every evening. Then they parted.

Aduan came back and his illness left him. From that time on he met Rose of Evening every day in the lotus field.

After a few days had passed they had to accompany the Prince of the Dragon Cave to the birthday festival of the King of the Wu River. The festival came to an end, and all the dancers returned home. Only, the King kept back Rose of Evening and one of the Nightingale dancers to teach the girls in his castle.

Months passed and no news came from Rose of Evening, so that Aduan was full of longing and despair. Now Mother Hia went every day to the castle of the god of the Wu River. Aduan told her that Rose of Evening was his cousin, and begged her to take him along with her so that he could at least see her a single time. She did, and let him stay at the lodge of the river god for a few days. But the inhabitants of the castle were so strictly watched that he could not see Rose of Evening even a single time. Sadly Aduan went back again.

Another month passed and Aduan was filled with gloomy thoughts, wishing that death might be his lot.

One day Mother Hia came to him full of pity and sympathising. 'What a shame,' said she, 'that Rose of Evening has cast herself into the river!'

Aduan was extremely frightened, and powerless to stop his tears from flowing. Tearing his beautiful garments, he took his gold and his pearls, and went out with the sole idea of following his beloved into death. Yet the waters of the river stood up before him like walls, and no matter how often he ran against them, head down, they always flung him back.

He did not dare return, since he feared he might be questioned about his festival garments, and severely punished for ruining them. He stood there not knowing what to do, while the sweat ran down to his ankles. Suddenly, at the foot of the water wall he saw a tall tree. Like a monkey he climbed up to its very top, and then, with all his might, he shot into the waves.

And then, without being wet, he found himself suddenly swimming on the surface of the river. Unexpectedly the world of men rose up once more before his dazzled eyes. He swam to the shore, and as he walked along the riverbank, his thoughts went back to his old mother. He took a ship and travelled home.

When he reached the village, it seemed to him as though all the houses in it belonged to another world. The following morning he entered his mother's house, and as he did so, heard a girl's voice beneath the window saying: 'Your son has come back again!' The voice sounded like the voice of Rose of Evening, and when she came to greet him at his mother's side, sure enough, it *was* Rose of Evening.

And in that hour the joy of these two who were so fond of each other overcame all their sorrow. But in the mother's mind sorrow and doubt, terror and joy mingled in constant succession in a thousand different ways.

When Rose of Evening had been in the palace of the river king, and had come to realise that she would never see Aduan again, she determined to die and flung herself into the waters of the stream. But she was carried to the surface, and the waves carried and cradled her till a ship came by and took her aboard. They asked from where she came. Now Rose of Evening had originally been a celebrated singing girl of Wu, who had fallen into the river and whose body had never been found. For this reason, she thought to herself that, after all, she could not return to her old life, and answered: 'Madame Dsiang in Dschen-Giang is my mother-in-law.' Then the travellers took passage for her in a ship, which brought her to the place she had mentioned. The widow Dsiang first said she must be mistaken, but the girl insisted that there was no mistake. She told her whole story to Aduan's mother who, though charmed by the young woman's lovely beauty, feared that Rose of Evening was too young to live a widow's life. But the girl was respectful and industrious, and on seeing that poverty was the ruler in her new home she took her pearls and sold them for a high price. Aduan's old mother was greatly pleased to see how seriously the girl took her duties.

Now that Aduan had returned again, Rose of Evening could not control her joy. And even Aduan's old mother cherished the hope that, after all, perhaps her son had not died. She secretly dug up her son's grave, yet all his bones were still lying in it. So she questioned Aduan – and realised, for the first time, that he was a departed spirit. He feared that Rose of Evening might be disgusted that he was no longer a human being and ordered his mother on no account to speak of it. This his mother promised. Then she spread the report in the village that the body found in the river had not been that of her son at all. Yet she could not rid herself of the fear that heaven might refuse to send him a child.

In spite of her fear, however, she was able to hold a grandson in her arms in course of time. When she looked at him, he was no different from other children, and then her cup of joy was filled to overflowing.

Rose of Evening gradually became aware of the fact that Aduan was not really a human being. 'Why did you not tell me at once?' said she. 'Departed spirits who wear the garments of the dragon castle, surround themselves with a soul casing so heavy in texture that they can no longer be distinguished from the living. And if you can obtain the lime made of dragon-horn from the castle, then the bones may be glued together in such wise that flesh and blood will grow over them again. What a pity that we could not obtain the lime while we were there!'

Aduan sold his pearl, for which a merchant from foreign parts gave him an enormous sum. Thus his family grew very wealthy. Once, on his mother's birthday, he danced with his wife and sang, to please her. The news reached the castle of the Dragon Prince and he thought to carry off Rose of Evening by force. But Aduan, alarmed, went to the Prince, and declared that both he and his wife were departed spirits. They examined him and since he cast no shadow, his word was accepted, and he was not robbed of Rose of Evening.

*Notes: 'Rose of Evening' is one of the most idyllic of Chinese art fairy tales. The idea that the departed spirit throws no shadow has analogies in Norse and other European fairy tales.*

*The fifth lunar month is traditionally the unlucky month, a time when natural disasters and disease are common, and warmer weather brings out poisonous creatures. The Dragon Boat Festival began as a ceremony to ward off bad luck.*

# 74

# The Ape Sun Wu Kung

**A wild and fantastic tale about the trials and tribulations of the charismatic monkey king, featuring his encounters with gods, dragons and characters from other Chinese fairy tales.**

Far, far away to the East, in the midst of the Great Sea, is an island called the Mountain of Flowers and Fruits. And on this mountain is a high rock. Now this rock, from the very beginning of the world, had absorbed all the hidden seed power of heaven and earth and sun and moon, which endowed it with supernatural creative gifts. One day the rock burst, and out came an egg of stone. And out of this stone egg a stone ape was hatched by magic power. When he broke the shell, he bowed to all sides. Then he gradually learned to walk and to leap, and two streams of golden radiance broke from his eyes and shot up to the highest of the castles of heaven, so that the Lord of the Heavens was frightened. He sent out the two gods, Thousandmile Eye and Fine Ear, to find out what had happened. The two gods came back and reported: 'The rays shine from the eyes of the stone ape who was hatched out of the egg that came from the magic rock. There is no reason to be uneasy.'

Little by little the ape grew up, ran and leaped about, drank from the springs in the valleys, ate the flowers and fruits, and time went by in limitless play.

One day, during the summer, when he and the other apes on the island were searching for ways to stay cool, together, they went to the valley to bathe. There they saw a waterfall plunging down a high cliff. Said the apes to each other: 'Whoever can force his way through the waterfall, without suffering injury, shall be our king.' The stone ape at once leaped into the air with joy and cried: 'I will pass through!' Then he closed his eyes, bent down low and leaped through the roar and foam of the waters. Opening his eyes once more, he saw an iron bridge, shut off from the outer world by the waterfall as though by a curtain.

At its entrance stood a tablet of stone carved with the words: 'This is the heavenly cave behind the water curtain on the Blessed Island of Flowers and Fruits.' Filled with joy, the stone ape leaped out again through the waterfall and told the other apes what he had found. They received the news happily, and begged the stone ape to take them there. So the tribe of apes leaped through the water onto the iron bridge, and then crowded into the cave castle where they found a hearth with a profusion of pots, cups and platters – but all made of stone. Then the apes paid homage to the stone ape as their king, and he was given the name of Handsome King of the Apes. He appointed long-tailed, ring-tailed and other monkeys to be his officials and counsellors, servants and retainers, and they led a blissful life on the mountain, sleeping by night in their cave castle, keeping away from birds and beasts, and their king enjoyed untroubled happiness. In this way some three hundred years went by.

One day, when the King of the Apes sat with his subjects at a merry meal, he suddenly began to weep. Frightened, the apes asked him why he so suddenly grew sad amid all his bliss. Said the King: 'It is true that we are not subject to the law and rule of man, that birds and beasts do not dare attack us, yet little by little we grow old and weak, and some day the hour will strike when Death, the Ancient, will drag us off! Then we will be gone in a moment, and no longer able to dwell on Earth!' Hearing these words, the apes hid their faces and sobbed. But an old ape stepped forth from the ranks. In a loud tone of voice he said: 'That you have hit upon this thought, Your Majesty, shows that the desire to search for truth has awakened you! Among all living creatures, there are but three kinds who are exempt from Death's power: the Buddhas, the blessed spirits and the gods. Whoever attains one of these three grades escapes the rod of rebirth, and lives as long as the Heavens themselves.'

The King of the Apes said: 'Where do these three kinds of beings live?' And the old ape replied: 'They live in caves and on holy mountains in the great world of mortals.' Hearing this, the King was pleased and told his apes that he was going to seek out gods and sainted spirits, and learn the road to immortality from them. The apes dragged up peaches and other fruits and sweet wine to celebrate the parting banquet, and all made merry together.

On the following morning the Handsome King of the Apes rose very early, built him a raft of old pine trees and took a bamboo staff for a pole. Then he climbed on the raft, quite alone, and poled his way through the Great Sea. Wind and waves were favourable and he reached Asia.

There he went ashore. On the strand he met a fisherman. Straightaway, he knocked him down, tore off his clothes and put them on himself. Then he wandered around and visited all famous spots, went into the marketplaces, the densely populated cities, learned how to conduct himself properly, and how to speak and act like a well-bred human being. Yet his heart was set on learning the teaching of the Buddhas, the blessed spirits and the holy gods. But the people of the country where he found himself were concerned only with honours and wealth. Not one of them seemed to care for life. Thus he went about until nine years had passed by unnoticed.

Then he came to the strand of the Western Sea and it occurred to him: 'No doubt there are gods and saints on the other side of the sea!' So he built another raft, floated it over the Western Sea and reached the land of the West. There he let his raft drift and went ashore. After he had searched for many days, he suddenly saw a high mountain with deep, quiet valleys. As the Ape King approached, he heard a man singing in the woods, and the song sounded like one the blessed spirits might sing. So he hastily entered the wood to see who might be singing. There he met a logger at work. The Ape King bowed to him and said: 'Venerable, divine master, I fall down and worship at your feet!' Said the logger: 'I am only a workman; why do you call me divine master?' 'Then, if you are no blessed god, how comes it you sing that divine song?' The logger laughed and said: 'You are at home in music. The song I was singing was really taught me by a saint.' 'If you are acquainted with a saint,' said the Ape King, 'he surely cannot live far from here. I beg of you to show me the way to his dwelling.' The logger replied: 'It is not far from here. This mountain is known as the Mountain of the Heart. In it is a cave where dwells a saint called the Discerner. The number of his disciples who have attained blessedness is countless. He still has some thirty to forty disciples gathered about him. You need only follow this path which leads to the South, and you cannot miss his dwelling.'

The Ape King thanked the logger and, sure enough, he came to the cave described. The gate was locked and he did not venture to knock. He leaped up into a pine tree, picked pine cones and devoured the seed. Before long, one of the saint's disciples came and opened the door and said: 'What sort of a beast is it that is making such a noise?' The Ape King leaped down from his tree, bowed, and said: 'I have come in search of truth. I did not venture to knock.' Then the disciple had to laugh and said: 'Our master was seated lost in meditation, when he told me to lead in the seeker after truth who stood without the gate, and here you really are. Well, you may come along with me!' The Ape King smoothed his clothes, put his hat on straight, and stepped in. A long passage led past magnificent buildings and quiet hidden huts to the place where the master was sitting upright on a seat of white marble. At his right and left stood his disciples, ready to serve him. The Ape King flung himself down on the ground and greeted the master humbly. In answer to his questions he told him how he had found his way to him. And when he was asked his name, he said: 'I have no name. I am the ape who came out of the stone.' So the master said: 'Then I will give you a name. I name you Sun Wu Kung.' The Ape King thanked him, full of joy, and thereafter he was called Sun Wu Kung. The master ordered his oldest disciple to instruct Sun Wu Kung in sweeping and cleaning, in going in and out, in good manners, how to labour in the field and how to water the gardens. In the course of time he learned to write, to burn incense and read the sutras. And in this way some six or seven years went by.

One day the master ascended the seat where he taught, and began to speak about the great truth. Understanding the hidden meaning of his words, Sun Wu Kung began jerking about and dancing with joy. The master reproved him: 'Sun Wu Kung, you have still not laid aside your wild nature! What do you mean by carrying on in such an unfitting manner?' Sun Wu Kung bowed and answered: 'I was listening attentively to you when the meaning of your words was disclosed to my heart, and without thinking I began to dance for joy. I was not giving way to my wild nature.' Said the master: 'If your spirit has really awakened, then I will announce the great truth to you. But there are three hundred and sixty ways to reach this truth. Which way shall I teach you?' Said Sun Wu Kung: 'Whichever you will, O Master!' Then the Master asked: 'Shall I teach you the way of magic?' Said Sun Wu Kung: 'What does magic teach one?' The Master replied: 'It teaches one to raise up spirits, to question oracles, and to foretell fortune and misfortune.' 'Will it secure eternal life?' asked Sun Wu Kung. 'No,' was the answer. 'Then I will not learn it.' 'Shall I teach you the sciences?' 'What are the sciences?' 'They are the nine schools of the three faiths. You learn how to read the holy books, pronounce incantations, commune with the gods, and call the saints to you.' 'Will they secure eternal life?' 'No.' 'Then I will not learn them.' 'The way of repose is a very good way.' 'What is the way of repose?' 'It teaches how to live without nourishment, remain quiescent in silent purity and sit lost in meditation.' 'Will it secure eternal life?' 'No.' 'Then I will not learn it.' 'The way of deeds is also a good way.' 'What does that teach?' 'It teaches how to equalise the vital powers, to practise bodily exercise, to prepare the elixir of life and to hold one's breath.' 'Will it secure eternal life?' 'Not so.' 'Then I will not learn it! I will not learn it!' Thereupon the Master, pretending to be angry, leaped down from his stand, took his cane and scolded him: 'What an ape! This he will not learn, and that he will not learn! What are you waiting to learn, then?' With that he gave him three blows across the head, retired to his inner chamber, and closed the great door behind him.

The disciples were greatly agitated, and angrily reproached Sun Wu Kung. He paid no attention and smiled quietly to himself, for he had understood the riddle that the Master had given him to solve. And in his heart he thought: 'His striking me over the head three times meant that I was to be ready at the third watch of the night. His withdrawing to his inner chamber and closing the great door after him meant that I was to go in to him by the back door, and that he would make clear the great truth to me in secret.' Accordingly he waited until evening, and made a pretence of lying down to sleep with the other disciples. But when the third watch of the night had come, he rose softly and crept to the back door. Sure enough it stood ajar. He slipped in and stepped before the Master's bed. The Master was sleeping with his face turned toward the wall, and the ape did not venture to wake him, but knelt down in front of the bed. After a time the Master turned around and hummed a stanza to himself:

A hard, hard grind,
Truth's lesson to expound.
One talks oneself deaf, dumb and blind,
Unless the right man's found.

Then Sun Wu Kung replied: 'I am waiting here with deep respect!'

The Master flung on his clothes, sat up in bed and said harshly: 'Accursed ape! Why are you not asleep? What are you doing here?'

Sun Wu Kung answered: 'You pointed out to me yesterday that I was to come to you at the third watch of the night, by the back door, in order to be instructed in the truth. Therefore I have ventured to come. If you will teach me in the fullness of your grace, I will be eternally grateful to you.'

Thought the Master to himself: 'There is real intelligence in this ape's head, to have made him understand me so well.' Then he replied: 'Sun Wu Kung, it shall be granted you! I will speak freely with you. Come quite close to me, and I will show you the way to eternal life.'

With that he murmured into his ear a divine, magical incantation to further concentrate his vital powers, and explained the hidden knowledge word for word. Sun Wu Kung listened to him eagerly, and in a short time had learned it by heart. Then he thanked his teacher, went out again and lay down to sleep. From that time forward he practised the right mode of breathing, kept guard over his soul and spirit, and tamed the natural instincts of his heart. And while he did so three more years passed by. Then the task was completed.

One day the Master said to him: 'Three great dangers still threaten you. Everyone who wishes to accomplish something out of the ordinary is exposed to them, and pursued by the envy of demons and spirits. And only those who can overcome these three great dangers live as long as the heavens.'

Sun Wu Kung was frightened and asked: 'Is there any means of protection against these dangers?'

Once again the Master murmured a secret incantation into his ear, and Sun Wu Kung gained the power to transform himself in seventy-two ways.

In just the space of a few days, Sun Wu Kung had learned the art.

One day the Master was walking before the cave in the company of his disciples. He called Sun Wu Kung up to him and asked: 'What progress have you made with your art? Can you fly already?'

'Yes, indeed,' said the ape.

'Then let me see you do so.'

The ape leaped into the air to a distance of five or six feet from the ground. Clouds formed beneath his feet, and he was able to walk on them for several hundred yards. Then he was forced to drop down to earth again.

The Master said with a smile: 'I call that crawling around on the clouds, not floating on them like the gods and saints who fly across the whole world in a single day. I will teach you the magic incantation for turning somersaults on the clouds. Turn one of those somersaults, and you advance eighteen thousand miles at a clip.'

Sun Wu Kung thanked him, full of joy, and from that time on he was able to move without limits in any direction.

One day Sun Wu Kung was sitting together with the other disciples under the pine tree by the gate, discussing the secrets of their teachings. Finally they asked him to show them some of his transforming arts. Sun Wu Kung, unable to keep his secret to himself, agreed to do so.

With a smile he said: 'Just set me a task! What do you wish me to change myself into?'

They said: 'Turn yourself into a pine tree.'

So Sun Wu Kung murmured a magic incantation, turned around – and there stood a pine tree before their very eyes. At this they all broke out into raucous laughter. The Master heard the noise and came out of the gate, dragging his cane behind him.

'Why are you making such a noise?' he called out to them harshly.

Said they: 'Sun Wu Kung has turned himself into a pine tree, which made us laugh.'

'Sun Wu Kung, come here!' said the Master. 'What tricks you are up to? Why do you have to turn yourself into a pine tree? All the work you have done means nothing more to you than the chance to make magic for your companions to wonder at. That shows that your heart is not yet under control.'

Humbly Sun Wu Kung begged forgiveness.

But the Master replied: 'I bear you no ill will, but you must go away.'

With tears in his eyes Sun Wu Kung asked him: 'Where shall I go?'

'You must go back where you came from,' said the Master. And when Sun Wu Kung sadly bade him farewell, he threatened him: 'Your savage nature is sure to bring down evil upon you some time. Tell no one that you are my pupil. If you so much as breathe a word about it, I will fetch your soul and lock it up in the depths of hell so that you cannot escape for a thousand eternities.'

Sun Wu Kung replied: 'I will not say a word! I will not say a word!' Once more he thanked him for all the kindness shown him, then turned a somersault and climbed up to the clouds.

Within the hour he had passed the seas, and saw the Mountain of Flowers and Fruits lying before him. Feeling happy and at home again, he let his cloud sink down to Earth and cried: 'Here I am back again, children!' And at once, from the valley, from behind the rocks, from out of the grass and from among the trees came his apes. They came running up by the thousands to surround him and greet him, and ask about his adventures. Sun Wu Kung said: 'I have now found the way to eternal life and need fear Death the Ancient no longer.' All the apes were overjoyed, and fell over each other bringing flowers and fruits, peaches and wine, to welcome him. And again they honoured Sun Wu Kung as the Handsome Ape King.

He now gathered the apes about him and asked them how they had fared during his absence.

Said they: 'It is just as well that you have come back again, great king! Not long ago a devil came here who wanted to take possession of our cave by force. We fought with him, but he dragged away many of your children and will probably soon return.'

Sun Wu Kung grew very angry and said: 'What sort of a devil is this who dares be so impudent?'

The apes answered: 'He is the Devil King of Chaos. He lives in the North, who knows how many miles away. We only saw him come and go amid clouds and mist.'

Sun Wu Kung said: 'Wait, and I will see to him!' With that he turned a somersault and disappeared without a trace.

In the furthest North rises a high mountain, upon whose slope is a cave. Above its entrance is the inscription: 'The Cave of the Kidneys.' Before the door little devils were dancing. Sun Wu Kung called harshly to them: 'Tell your Devil King quickly that he had better give me my children back again!' The little devils were frightened and delivered the message in the cave. The Devil King reached for his sword and came out. He was so large and broad that he could not even see Sun Wu Kung. He was clad from head to foot in black armour, and his face was as black as the bottom of a kettle. Sun Wu Kung shouted at him: 'Accursed devil, where are your eyes, that you cannot see the venerable Sun?' Then the devil looked to the ground and saw a stone ape standing before him, bare-headed, dressed in red, with a yellow girdle and black boots. So the Devil King laughed and said: 'You are not even four feet high, less than thirty years of age, and weaponless, and yet you venture to make such a commotion.' Said Sun Wu Kung: 'I am not too small for you; and I can make myself large at will. You scorn me because I am without a weapon, but my two fists can thresh to the very skies.' With that he stooped, clenched his fists and began to give the devil a beating. The devil was large and clumsy, but Sun Wu Kung leaped about nimbly. He struck him between the ribs and between the wind and his blows fell ever more fast and furious. Desperately the devil raised his great knife and aimed a blow at Sun Wu Kung's head. But the Ape King avoided the blow and fell back on his magic powers of transformation. Pulling out a hair, he put it in his mouth, chewed it, spat it out into the air and said: 'Transform yourself!' And at once it turned into many hundreds of little apes, who began to attack the devil. Sun Wu Kung, be it said, had eighty-four thousand hairs on his body, every single one of which he could transform. The little apes with their sharp eyes leaped around quickly. Surrounding the Devil King on all sides, they tore at his clothes, and pulled at his legs, until finally he was prostrate on the ground. Then Sun Wu Kung stepped up, tore his knife from his hand, and put an end to him. After that he entered the cave and released his captive children, the apes. The transformed hairs he drew to him again and then, making a fire, he burned the evil cave to the ground. He gathered up those he had released, and flew back with them like a storm wind to his cavern on the Mountain of Flowers and Fruits, where he was joyfully greeted by all the apes.

After Sun Wu Kung had taken possession of the Devil King's great knife, he exercised his apes every day. They had wooden swords and lances of bamboo, and played their martial music on reed pipes. He had them build a camp so that they would be prepared for all dangers. Suddenly the thought came to Sun Wu Kung: 'If we go on this way, perhaps we may incite some human or animal king to fight with us, and then we would not be able to withstand him with our wooden swords and bamboo lances!' To his apes he said: 'What is to be done?' Four baboons stepped forward and said: 'In the capital city of the Aulai empire, there are warriors without number. And also coppersmiths and steelsmiths. How would it be if we were to buy steel and iron and have those smiths weld weapons for us?'

A somersault, and Sun Wu Kung was standing before the city moat. Said he to himself: 'To first buy the weapons would take a great deal of time. I would rather make magic and take some.' So he blew on the ground, and a tremendous storm wind arose, driving sand and stones before it, and causing all the soldiers in the city to run away in terror. Then Sun Wu Kung went to the armoury, pulled out one of his hairs, turned it into thousands of little apes, cleared out the whole supply of weapons, and flew back home on a cloud.

He gathered his people about him and counted them. In all they numbered seventy-seven thousand. They held the whole mountain in terror, and all the magic beasts and spirit princes who dwelt on it.

And these came forth from seventy-two caves and honoured Sun Wu Kung as their head.

One day the Ape King said: 'Now you all have weapons; but this knife which I took from the Devil King is too light, and no longer suits me. What is to be done?'

The four baboons stepped forward and said: 'In view of your spirit powers, Your Majesty, you will find no weapon fit for your use on all the earth! Is it possible for you to walk through the water?'

The Ape King answered: 'All the elements are subject to me and there is no place where I cannot go.'

Then the baboons said: 'The water at our cave here flows into the Great Sea, to the castle of the Dragon King of the Eastern Sea. If your magic power makes it possible, you could go to the Dragon King and let him give you a weapon.'

This suited the Ape King. Leaping onto the iron bridge, he murmured an incantation. Then he flung himself into the waves, which parted before him and ran on till he came to the Palace of Water Crystal. There he met a Triton, who asked who he was. Sun Wu King told him his name and added: 'I am the Dragon-King's nearest neighbour, and have come to visit him.' The Triton took the message to the castle, and the Dragon King of the Eastern Sea came out hastily to receive him. He bade him be seated and served him with tea.

Sun Wu Kung said: 'I have learned the hidden knowledge and gained the powers of immortality. I have drilled my apes in the art of warfare to protect our mountain; but I have no weapon I can use, and have therefore come to you to borrow one.'

The Dragon King now had General Flounder bring him a great spear. But Sun Wu Kung was not satisfied with it. Then he ordered Field Marshal Eel to fetch in a nine-tined fork, which weighed three thousand, six hundred pounds. But Sun Wu Kung balanced it in his hand and said: 'Too light! Too light! Too light!'

Then the Dragon King was frightened, and had the heaviest weapon in his armoury brought in. It weighed seven thousand, two hundred pounds. But this was still too light for Sun Wu Kung. The Dragon King assured him that he had nothing heavier, but Sun Wu Kung would not give in and said: 'Just look around!'

Finally the Dragon Queen and her daughter came out, and said to the Dragon King: 'This saint is an unpleasant customer. The great iron bar is still lying here in our sea; and not so long ago it shone with a red glow, which is probably a sign it is time for it to be taken away.'

Said the Dragon King: 'But that is the rod which the Great Yu used when he ordered the waters, and determined the depth of the seas and rivers. It cannot be taken away.'

The Dragon Queen replied: 'Just let him see it! What he does with it is no concern of ours.'

So the Dragon King led Sun Wu Kung to the measuring rod. The golden radiance that came from it could be seen some distance off. It was an enormous iron bar, with golden clamps on either side.

Sun Wu Kung raised it with the exertion of all his strength, and then said: 'It is too heavy, and ought to be somewhat shorter and thinner!'

No sooner had he said this than the iron rod diminished. He tried it again, and then he noticed that it grew larger or smaller at command. It could even be made to shrink to the size of a pin. Overjoyed, Sun Wu Kung beat about in the sea with the rod, which he had let grow large again, till the waves spurted mountain-high and the dragon castle rocked on its foundations. The Dragon King trembled with fright, and all his tortoises, fishes and crabs drew in their heads.

Sun Wu Kung laughed, and said: 'Many thanks for the handsome present!' Then he continued: 'Now I have a weapon, it is true, but as yet I have no armour. Rather than hunt up two or three other households, I think you will be willing to provide me with a suit of mail.'

The Dragon King told him that he had no armour to give him.

Then the ape said: 'I will not leave until you have obtained one for me.' And once more he began to swing his rod.

'Do not harm me!' said the terrified Dragon King, 'I will ask my brothers.'

And he had them beat the iron drum and strike the golden gong, and in a moment's time all the Dragon King's brothers came from all the other seas. The Dragon King talked to them in private and said: 'This is a terrible fellow, and we must not rouse his anger! First he took the rod with the golden clamps from me, and now he also insists on having a suit of armour. The best thing to do would be to satisfy him at once, and complain of him to the Lord of the Heavens later.'

So the brothers brought a magic suit of golden mail, magic boots and a magic helmet.

Sun Wu Kung thanked them and returned to his cave. Radiantly he greeted his children, who had come to meet him, and showed them the rod with the golden clamps. They all crowded up and wished to pick it up from the ground, if only just the once; but it was as though a dragonfly had attempted to overthrow a stone column, or an ant were trying to carry a great mountain. It would not move a hair's breadth. The apes opened their mouths and stuck out their tongues, and said: 'Father, how is it possible for you to carry that heavy thing?' So he told them the secret of the rod and showed them its effects. Then he set his empire in order, appointing the four baboons field marshals; and the seven beast spirits, the ox spirit, the dragon spirit, the bird spirit, the lion spirit and the rest also joined him.

One day he was taking a nap after dinner. He had previously let the bar shrink, and stuck it in his ear. While he was sleeping he saw two men come along in his dream, who had a card on which was written 'Sun Wu Kung.' They would not allow him to resist, but fettered him and led his spirit away. And when they reached a great city the Ape King gradually came to himself. Over the city gate he saw a tablet of iron, and on it was engraved in large letters: 'The Underworld'.

All was suddenly clear to him and he said: 'Why, this must be the dwelling place of Death! But I have long since escaped from his power. How dare he have me dragged here!' The more he reflected, the angrier he grew. He drew out the golden rod from his ear, swung it and let it grow large. Crushing the two constables to mush, then bursting his fetters, he rolled his bar before him into the city. The ten Princes of the Dead were frightened, bowed before him and asked: 'Who are you?'

Sun Wu Kung answered: 'If you do not know me, why did you send for me and have me dragged to this place? I am the heaven-born saint Sun Wu Kung of the Mountain of Flowers and Fruits. And now, who are you? Tell me your names quickly, or I will strike you!'

The ten Princes of the Dead humbly gave him their names.

Sun Wu Kung said: 'I, the Venerable Sun, have gained the power of eternal life! You have nothing to say to me! Quick, let me have the *Book of Life*!'

They did not dare defy him, and had the scribe bring in the book. Sun Wu Kung opened it. Under the heading 'Apes,' No. 1350, he read: 'Sun Wu Kung, the heaven-born stone ape. His years shall be three hundred and twenty-four. Then he shall die without illness.'

Sun Wu Kung took the brush from the table and struck out the whole ape family from the *Book of Life*, threw the book down and said:

'Now we are even! From this day on I will suffer no impertinences from you!'

With that he cleared a way for himself out of the Underworld by means of his rod, and the ten Princes of the Dead did not dare to hold him, but only complained afterwards to the Lord of the Heavens.

After leaving the city, Sun Wu Kung slipped and fell to the ground. This caused him to wake, and he noticed he had been dreaming. He called his four baboons to him and said: 'Splendid, splendid! I was dragged to Death's castle and I caused considerable uproar there. I had them give me the *Book of Life*, and I struck out the mortal hour of all the apes!' And after that time the apes on the mountain no longer died, because their names had been stricken out in the Underworld.

But the Lord of the Heavens sat in his castle, and had all his servants assembled about him. A saint stepped forward and presented the complaint of the Dragon King of the Eastern Sea. And another stepped forward and presented the complaint of the ten Princes of the Dead. The Lord of the Heavens glanced through the two reports, both telling of the wild, unmannerly conduct of Sun Wu Kung. The Lord of the Heavens now ordered a god to descend to Earth and take him prisoner. The Evening Star came forward, however, and said: 'This ape was born of the purest powers of heaven and earth and sun and moon. He has gained the hidden knowledge and has become an immortal. Recall, O Lord, your great love for all that has life, and forgive him his sin! Issue an order that he be called up to the heavens, and be given a charge here, so that he may come to his senses. Then, if he again oversteps your commands, let him be punished without mercy.' The Lord of the Heavens was agreeable, issued the order, and told the Evening Star to take it to Sun Wu Kung. The Evening Star mounted a coloured cloud and descended on the Mountain of Flowers and Fruits.

He greeted Sun Wu Kung and said to him: 'The Lord heard of your actions and meant to punish you. I am the Evening Star of the Western Skies, and I spoke on your behalf. For that reason, he commissioned me to take you to the skies, so that you may be given a charge there.'

Sun Wu Kung was overjoyed and answered: 'I had just been thinking I ought to pay Heaven a visit some time, and sure enough, Old Star, here you have come to fetch me!'

He had his four baboons come and said to them impressively: 'See that you take good care of our mountain! I am going up to the heavens to look around there a little!'

Then he mounted a cloud together with the Evening Star and floated up. But he kept turning his somersaults, and advanced so quickly that the Evening Star on his cloud was left behind. Before he knew it, he had reached the Southern Gate of Heaven and was about to step carelessly through. The gatekeeper did not want to let him enter, but the Ape King did not let this stop him. In the midst of their dispute the Evening Star came up and explained matters, and then he was allowed to enter the heavenly gate. When he came to the castle of the Lord of the Heavens, he stood upright before it, without bowing his head.

The Lord of the Heavens asked: 'This hairy face with the pointed lips is Sun Wu Kung?'

He replied: 'Yes, I am the Venerable Sun!'

All the servants of the Lord of the Heavens were shocked and said: 'This wild ape does not even bow, and goes so far as to call himself the Venerable Sun. He deserves a thousand deaths!'

But the Lord said: 'He has come up from the Earth below, and is not as yet used to our rules. We will forgive him.'

Then he gave orders that a charge be found for him. The marshal of the heavenly court reported: 'There is no charge vacant anywhere, but an official is needed in the heavenly stables.' Thereupon the Lord made him stablemaster of the heavenly steeds. The servants of the Lord of the Heavens told him he should give thanks for the grace bestowed on him. Sun Wu Kung called out aloud: 'Thanks for the command!', took possession of his certificate of appointment, and went to the stables in order to enter upon his new office.

He attended to his duties with great zeal. The heavenly steeds grew sleek and fat, and the stables were filled with young foals. Before he knew it, half a month had gone by. Then his heavenly friends prepared a banquet for him.

While they were at table, Sun Wu Kung asked accidentally: 'Stablemaster? What sort of a title is that?'

'Why, that is an official title,' was the reply.

'What rank has this office?'

'It has no rank at all,' was the answer.

'Ah,' said the ape, 'is it so high that it outranks all other dignities?'

'No, it is not high, it is not high at all,' answered his friends. 'It is not even set down in the official roster, but is quite a subordinate position. All you have to do is to attend to the steeds. If you see to it that they grow fat, you get a good mark; but if they grow thin or ill, or fall down, your punishment will be right at hand.'

Then the Ape King grew angry: 'What, they treat me, the Venerable Sun, in such a shameful way!' and he started up. 'On my mountain I was a king, I was a father! What need was there for him to lure me into his heaven to feed horses? I'll do it no longer! I'll do it no longer!'

With that, he had already overturned the table, drawn the rod with the golden clamps from his ear, let it grow large and beat a way out for himself to the Southern Gate of Heaven. And no one dared stop him.

Already he was back in his island mountain and his people surrounded him, saying: 'You have been gone for more than ten years, great king! How is it you do not return to us until now?'

The Ape King said: 'I did not spend more than about ten days in Heaven. This Lord of the Heavens does not know how to treat his people. He made me his stablemaster, and I had to feed his horses. I am so ashamed that I am ready to die. But I did not put up with it, and now here I am once more!'

His apes eagerly prepared a banquet to comfort him. While they were sitting at table, two horned devil kings came and presented him with a yellow imperial robe. Filled with joy he slipped into it, and appointed the two devil kings leaders of the vanguard. They thanked him and began to flatter him: 'With your power and wisdom, great king, why should you have to serve the Lord of the Heavens? To call you the Great Saint Who Is Heaven's Equal would be quite in order.'

The ape was pleased with this speech and said: 'Good, good!' Then he ordered his four baboons to have a flag made quickly, inscribed with the words: 'The Great Saint Who Is Heaven's Equal.' And from that moment on he insisted on being called by that title.

When the Lord of the Heavens learned of the ape's flight, he ordered Li Dsing, the pagoda-bearing god, and his third son, Notscha, to take the Ape King prisoner. Sallying forth at the head of a heavenly warrior host, they laid out a camp before his cave and sent a brave warrior to challenge him to single combat. But he was easily beaten and obliged to flee, and Sun Wu Kung even shouted after him, laughing: 'What a bag of wind! And he calls himself a heavenly warrior! I'll not slay you. Run along quickly and send me a better man!'

When Notscha saw this, he himself hurried up to do battle.

Said Sun Wu Kung to him: 'To whom do you belong, little one? You must not play around here, for something might happen to you!'

But Notscha cried out in a loud voice: 'Accursed ape! I am Prince Notscha, and have been ordered to take you prisoner!' With that, he swung his sword in the direction of Sun Wu Kung.

'Very well,' said the latter, 'I will stand here and never move.'

Notscha grew very angry, and turned into a three-headed god with six arms, holding six different weapons. He rushed on to the attack.

Sun Wu Kung laughed. 'The little fellow knows the trick of it! But easy, wait a bit! I will change shape, too!'

He also turned himself into a figure with three heads and with six arms, and swung three gold-clamp rods. And so they began to fight. Their blows rained down with such speed that it seemed as though thousands of weapons were flying through the air. After thirty rounds, the combat had not yet been decided. Then Sun Wu Kung hit upon an idea. Secretly pulling out one of his hairs, he turned it into his own shape and let it continue the fight. He himself slipped behind Notscha, and gave him such a blow on the left arm with his rod that his knees gave way beneath him with pain, and he had to withdraw in defeat.

Notscha told his father Li Dsing: 'This devil ape is altogether too powerful! I cannot get the better of him!' There was nothing left to do but to return to the Heavens and admit defeat. The Lord of the Heavens bowed his head, and tried to think of some other hero to send out.

Then the Evening Star once more came forward and said: 'This ape is so strong and so courageous that probably not one of us here is a match for him. He revolted because the office of stablemaster appeared too lowly for him. The best thing would be to temper justice with mercy, let him have his way and appoint him Great Saint Who Is Heaven's Equal. You need only give him the meaningless title, without an accompanying duty, and then the matter would be settled.' The Lord of the Heavens was satisfied with this suggestion, and once more sent the Evening Star to summon the new saint. When Sun Wu Kung heard that he had arrived, he said: 'The old Evening Star is a good fellow!' and he had his army draw up in line to give him a festive reception. He himself donned his ceremonial robes and politely went out to meet him.

Then the Evening Star told him what had taken place in the Heavens, and that he had his appointment as Great Saint Who Is Heaven's Equal with him.

Thereupon the Great Saint laughed and said: 'You also spoke in my behalf before, Old Star! And now you have again taken my part. Many thanks! Many thanks!'

They appeared together in front of the Lord of the Heavens, who said: 'The rank of Great Saint Who Is Heaven's Equal is very high. But now you must not cut any further capers.'

The Great Saint expressed his thanks, and the Lord of the Heavens ordered two skilled architects to build a castle for him east of the peach garden belonging to the Queen Mother of the West. And he was led into it with all possible honours.

Now the Saint was in his element. He had all that heart could wish for, and was untroubled by any work. At ease, he walked about in the Heavens as he chose, and paid visits to the gods. The Three Pure Ones and the Four Rulers he treated with some respect; but the planetary gods and the lords of the twenty-eight houses of the moon, and of the twelve zodiac signs, and the other stars he addressed familiarly with a 'Hey, you!' Thus he idled day by day, without occupation among the clouds of the Heavens. On one occasion one of the wise said to the Lord of the Heavens: 'The holy Sun is idle while day follows day. What if some mischievous thoughts occur to him? It might be better to give him some charge.'

So the Lord of the Heavens summoned the Great Saint and said to him: 'The life-giving peaches in the garden of the Queen Mother will soon be ripe. I give you the charge of watching over them. Do your duty conscientiously!'

This pleased the Saint and he expressed his thanks. Then he went to the garden, where the caretakers and gardeners received him on their knees.

He asked them: 'How many trees in all are there in the garden?'

'Three thousand six hundred,' replied the gardener. 'There are twelve hundred trees in the foremost row. They have red blossoms and bear small fruit, which ripens every three thousand years. Whoever eats it grows bright and healthy. The twelve hundred trees in the middle row have double blossoms and bear sweet fruit, which ripens every six thousand years. Whoever eats of it is able to float in the rose dawn without aging. The twelve hundred trees in the last row bear red-striped fruit with small pits. They ripen every nine thousand years. Whoever eats their fruit lives eternally, as long as the Heavens themselves, and remains untouched for thousands of aeons.'

The Saint heard all this with pleasure. He checked up the lists and from that time on appeared every day or so to see to things. The greater part of the peaches in the last row were already ripe. When he came to the garden, he would send away the caretakers and gardeners on some pretext, then leap up into the trees and gorge himself to his heart's content with the peaches.

At that time the Queen Mother of the West was preparing the great peach banquet to which she was accustomed to invite all the gods of the Heavens. She sent out the fairies in their garments of seven colours with baskets, that they might pick the peaches. The caretaker said to them: 'The garden has now been entrusted to the guardianship of the Great Saint Who is Heaven's Equal, so you will first have to announce yourselves to him.' With that he led the seven fairies into the garden. There they looked everywhere for the Great Saint but could not find him. So the fairies said: 'We have our orders and must not be late. We will begin picking the peaches in the meantime!' So they picked several baskets full from the foremost row. In the second row the peaches were already scarcer. And in the last row there hung only a single half-ripe peach. They bent down the bough and picked it, and then allowed it to fly up again.

Now it happened that the Great Saint, who had turned himself into a peach worm, had just been taking his noonday nap on this bough. When he was so rudely awakened, he appeared in his true form, seized his rod and was about to strike the fairies.

But the fairies said: 'We have been sent here by the Queen Mother. Do not be angry, Great Saint!'

Said the Great Saint: 'And who are all those whom the Queen Mother has invited?'

They answered: 'All the gods and saints in the Heavens, on the earth and under the earth.'

'Has she also invited me?' said the Saint.

'Not that we know of,' said the fairies.

The Saint grew angry, murmured a magic incantation and said: 'Stay! Stay! Stay!'

With that the seven fairies were rooted to the spot. The Saint took a cloud and sailed away on it to the palace of the Queen Mother.

On the way he met the Barefoot God and asked him: 'Where are you going?'

'To the peach banquet,' was the answer.

Then the Saint lied to him, saying: 'I have been commanded by the Lord of the Heavens to tell all the gods and saints that they are first to come to the Hall of Purity, in order to practise the rites, and then go together to the Queen Mother.'

Then the Great Saint changed himself into the semblance of the Barefoot God and sailed to the palace of the Queen Mother. There he let his cloud sink down and entered quite unconcerned. The meal was ready, yet none of the gods had appeared. Suddenly the Great Saint caught the aroma of wine, and saw well-nigh a hundred barrels of the precious nectar standing in a room to one side. His mouth watered. He tore a few hairs out and turned them into sleep-worms. These worms crept into the nostrils of the cup-bearers so that they all fell asleep. Thereupon he enjoyed the delicious viands to the full, opened the barrels and drank until he was nearly stupefied. Then he said to himself: 'This whole affair is beginning to make me feel creepy. I had better go home first of all and sleep a bit.' And he stumbled out of the garden with uncertain steps. Sure enough, he missed his way, and came to the dwelling of Laotzse. There he regained consciousness. Arranging his clothing, he went inside. There was no one to be seen in the place, for at the moment Laotzse was at the God of Light's abode, talking to him, and with him were all his servants, listening. Since he found no one at home the Great Saint went as far as the inner chamber, where Laotzse was in the habit of brewing the elixir of life. Beside the stove stood five gourd containers full of the pills of life which had already been rolled. Said the Great Saint: 'I had long since intended to prepare a couple of these pills. So it suits me very well to find them here.' He poured out the contents of the gourds and ate up all the pills of life. Since he had now had enough to eat and drink, he thought to himself: 'Bad, bad! The mischief I have done cannot well be repaired. If they catch me, my life will be in danger. I think I had better go down to earth again and remain a king!' With that he made himself invisible, went out at the Western Gate of Heaven, and returned to the Mountain of Flowers and Fruits, where he told his people who received him the story of his adventures.

When he spoke of the wine nectar of the peach garden, his apes said: 'Can't you go back once more and steal a few bottles of the wine, so that we too may taste of it and gain eternal life?'

The Ape King was willing, turned a somersault, crept into the garden unobserved, and picked up four more barrels. Two of them he took under his arms and two he held in his hands. Disappearing without a trace, he brought them to his cave, where he enjoyed them together with his apes.

In the meantime the seven fairies, whom the Great Saint had rooted to the spot, had regained their freedom after a night and a day. They picked up their baskets and told the Queen Mother what had happened to them. The cup-bearers also came hurrying up and reported the destruction caused by someone unknown among the eatables and drinkables. The Queen Mother went to the Lord of the Heavens to complain. Shortly afterward, Laotzse also came to him to tell about the theft of the pills of life. And the Barefoot God came along and reported that he had been deceived by the Great Saint Who Is Heaven's Equal; and from the Great Saint's palace the servants came running and said that the Saint had disappeared and was nowhere to be found. Then the Lord of the Heavens was frightened, and said: 'This whole mess is undoubtedly the work of that devilish ape!'

Now the whole host of Heaven, together with all the star gods, the time gods and the mountain gods, was called out in order to catch the ape. Li Dsing once more was its commander-in-chief. He surrounded the entire mountain, and spread out the sky net and the earth net, so that no one could escape. Then he sent his bravest heroes into battle. Courageously the ape withstood all attacks from early morn till sundown. But by that time his most faithful followers had been captured. That was too much for him. He pulled out a hair and turned it into thousands of Ape Kings, who all hewed about them with golden-clamped iron rods. The heavenly host was vanquished, and the ape withdrew to his cave to rest.

Now it happened that Guan Yin had also gone to the peach banquet in the garden, and had found out what Sun Wu Kung had done. When she went to visit the Lord of the Heavens, Li Dsing was just coming in, to report the great defeat suffered on the Mountain of Flowers and Fruits. Then Guan Yin said to the Lord of the Heavens: 'I can recommend a hero to you who will surely get the better of the ape – your grandson Yang Oerlang. He has conquered all the beast and bird spirits, and overthrown the elves in the grass and the brush. He knows what has to be done to get the better of such devils.'

So Yang Oerlang was brought in, and Li Dsing led him to his camp. There he asked him how he would go about getting the better of the ape.

Yang Oerlang laughed and said: 'I think I will have to go him one better when it comes to changing shapes. It would be best for you to take away the sky net so that our combat is not disturbed.' Then he asked that Li Dsing post himself in the upper air with the magic spirit mirror in his hand, so that when the ape made himself invisible, he might be found again by means of the mirror. When all this had been arranged, Yang Oerlang went out in front of the cave with his spirits to give battle.

The ape leaped out, and when he saw the powerful hero with the three-tined sword standing before him he asked: 'And who may you be?'

The other said: 'I am Yang Oerlang, the grandson of the Lord of the Heavens!'

The ape laughed and said: 'Oh yes, I remember! His daughter ran away with a certain Sir Yang, to whom heaven gave a son. You must be that son!'

Yang Oerlang grew furious, and advanced upon him with his spear. Then a hot battle began. For three hundred rounds they fought without decisive results. Then Yang Oerlang turned himself into a giant with a black face and red hair.

'Not bad,' said the ape, 'but I can do that too!'

They continued to fight in that form, but the ape's baboons were sore afraid. The beast and planet spirits of Yang Oerlang pressed the apes hard. They slew most of them and the others hid away. When the ape saw this, his heart grew uneasy. He drew the magic giant-likeness in again, took his rod and fled. But Yang Oerlang followed hard on his heels. Urgently, the ape thrust the rod, now turned into a needle, into his ear, turned into a sparrow, and flew up into the crest of a tree. Yang Oerlang, who was following in his tracks, lost sight of him. But his keen eyes soon recognised that the ape had turned himself into a sparrow. So he flung away spear and crossbow, turned himself into a sparrowhawk, and darted down on the sparrow. But the latter soared high into the air as a cormorant. Yang Oerlang shook his plumage, turned into a great sea crane, and shot up into the clouds to seize the cormorant. The latter dropped, flew into a valley and dived beneath the waters of a brook in the shape of a fish. When Yang Oerlang reached the edge of the valley, and had lost his trail, he said to himself: 'This ape has surely turned himself into a fish or a crab! I will change my form as well in order to catch him.' So he turned into an osprey and floated above the surface of the water. When the ape in the water caught sight of the osprey, he saw that he was Yang Oerlang. He swiftly swung around and fled. Yang Oerlang followed in hot pursuit, and when he was no further away than the length of a beak, the ape turned, crept ashore as a water snake and hid in the grass. Yang Oerlang saw the water snake creep from the water, and turned into an eagle, spreading his claws to seize it. But the water snake sprang up and turned into the lowest of all birds, a speckled buzzard, and perched on the steep edge of a cliff. When Yang Oerlang saw that the ape had turned himself into so contemptible a creature as a buzzard, he would no longer play the game . He reappeared in his original form, took up his crossbow and shot at the bird. The buzzard slipped and fell down the side of the cliff. At its foot the ape turned himself into the chapel of a field god. He opened his mouth for a gate, his teeth became the two wings of the door, his tongue the image of the god, and his eyes the windows. His tail was the only thing he did not know what to do with. So he let it stand up stiffly behind him in the shape of a flagpole. When Yang Oerlang reached the foot of the hill he saw the chapel, whose flagpole stood in the rear. Then he laughed and said: 'That ape is really a devil of an ape! He wants to lure me into the chapel in order to bite me. But I will not go in. First I will break his windows for him, and then I will stamp down the wings of his door!' Hearing this, the ape was terrified. He leaped like a tiger, and disappeared without a trace in the air. With a single somersault, he reached Yang Oerlang's own temple. There he assumed Yang Oerlang's own form and stepped in. The spirits who were on guard were unable to recognise him and received him on their knees. So the ape then seated himself on the god's throne, and had the prayers which had come in submitted to him.

When Yang Oerlang no longer saw the ape, he rose in the air to Li Dsing and said: 'I was vying with the ape in changing shape. Suddenly I could no longer find him. Take a look in the mirror!' Li Dsing took a look in the magic spirit mirror and then he laughed and said: 'The ape has turned himself into your likeness, is sitting in your temple quite at home there, and making mischief.' When Yang Oerlang heard this, he took his three-tined spear and hurried to his temple. The door spirits were frightened and said: 'But father came in only this very minute! How is it that another one comes now?' Without paying attention to them, Yang Oerlang entered the temple and aimed his spear at Sun Wu Kung. The latter resumed his own shape, laughed and said: 'Young sir, you must not be angry! The god of this place is now Sun Wu Kung.' Without uttering a word, Yang Oerlang attacked. Sun Wu Kung took up his rod and returned the blows. Thus they crowded out of the temple together, fighting, and wrapped in mists and clouds once more they gained the Mountain of Flowers and Fruits.

In the meantime Guan Yin was sitting with Laotzse, the Lord of the Heavens and the Queen Mother in the great hall of Heaven, waiting for news. When none came, she said: 'I will go with Laotzse to the

Southern Gate of Heaven and see how matters stand.' And when they saw that the struggle had still not come to an end, she said to Laotzse: 'How would it be if we helped Yang Oerlang a little? I will shut up Sun Wu Kung in my vase.'

But Laotzse said: 'Your vase is made of porcelain. Sun Wu Kung could smash it with his iron rod. But I have a circlet of diamonds which can enclose all living creatures. That we can use!' He flung his circlet through the air from the heavenly gate, and struck Sun Wu Kung on the head with it. The blow on his forehead caused the Ape King to slip. He stood up again and tried to escape, but the heavenly hound of Yang Oerlang bit his leg until he fell to the ground. Then Yang Oerlang and his followers came up and tied him with thongs, and thrust a hook through his collarbone so that he could no longer transform himself. And Laotzse took possession of his diamond circlet again, and returned with Guan Yin to the hall of Heaven. Sun Wu Kung was now brought in in triumph, and condemned to be beheaded. Taken to the place of execution, he was bound to a post. But all efforts to kill him by means of axe and sword, thunder and lightning were vain. Nothing so much as hurt a hair on his head.

Said Laotzse: 'It is not surprising. This ape has eaten the peaches, drunk the nectar and also swallowed the pills of life. Nothing can harm him. The best thing would be for me to take him along and thrust him into my stove in order to melt the elixir of life out of him again. Then he will fall into dust and ashes.'

So Sun Wu Kung's fetters were loosed, and Laotzse took him with him, thrust him into his oven, and ordered the boy to keep up a hot fire.

But along the edge of the oven were carved the signs of the eight elemental forces. And when the ape was thrust into the oven he took refuge beneath the sign of the wind, so that the fire could not injure him; and the smoke only made his eyes smart. He remained in the oven seven times seven days. Then Laotzse had it opened to take a look. As soon as Sun Wu Kung saw the light shine in, he could no longer bear to be shut up, but leaped out and upset the magic oven. The guards and attendants he threw to the ground and Laotzse himself, who tried to seize him, received such a push that he stuck his legs up in the air like an onion turned upside down. Then Sun Wu Kung took his rod out of his ear, and without looking where he struck, hewed everything to bits, so that the star gods closed their doors and the guardians of the Heavens ran away. He came to the castle of the Lord of the Heavens, and the guardian of the gate with his steel whip was only just in time to hold him back. Then the thirty-six thunder gods were set at him, and surrounded him, though they could not seize him.

The Lord of the Heavens said: 'Buddha will know what is to be done. Send for him quickly!'

So Buddha came up out of the West with Ananada and Kashiapa, his disciples. When he saw the turmoil he said: 'First of all, let weapons be laid aside and lead out the Saint. I wish to speak with him!' The gods withdrew. Sun Wu Kung snorted and said: 'Who are you, who dare to speak to me?' Buddha smiled and replied: 'I have come out of the blessed West, Shakiamuni Amitofu. I have heard of the revolt you have raised, and am come to tame you!'

Said Sun Wu Kung: 'I am the stone ape who has gained the hidden knowledge. I am master of seventy-two transformations, and will live as long as Heaven itself. What has the Lord of the Heavens accomplished that entitles him to remain eternally on his throne? Let him make way for me, and I will be satisfied!'

Buddha replied with a smile: 'You are a beast that has gained magic powers. How can you expect to rule here as Lord of the Heavens? Be it known to you that the Lord of the Heavens has toiled for aeons in perfecting his virtues. How many years would you have to pass before you could attain the dignity he has gained? And then I must ask you whether there is anything else you can do, aside from playing your tricks of transformation?'

Said Sun Wu Kung: 'I can turn cloud somersaults. Each one carries me eighteen thousand miles ahead. Surely that is enough to entitle me to be the Lord of the Heavens?'

Buddha answered with a smile: 'Let us make a wager. If you can so much as leave my hand with one of your somersaults, I will beg the Lord of the Heavens to make way for you. But if you are not able to leave my hand, you must yield yourself to my fetters.'

Sun Wu Kung suppressed his laughter, for he thought: 'This Buddha is a crazy fellow! His hand is not a foot long; how could I help but leap out of it?' So he opened his mouth wide and said: 'Agreed!'

Buddha then stretched out his right hand. It resembled a small lotus leaf. Sun Wu Kung leaped up into it with one bound. Then he said: 'Go!' And with that he turned one somersault after another, so that he flew along like a whirlwind. And while he was flying along he saw five tall, reddish columns towering to the skies. Then he thought:

'That is the end of the world! Now I will turn back and become Lord of the Heavens. But first I will write down my name to prove that I was there.' He pulled out a hair, turned it into a brush, and wrote with great letters on the middle column: 'The Great Saint Who Is Heaven's Equal.' Then he turned his somersaults again until he had reached the place from where he had come. He leaped down from the Buddha's hand laughing and cried: 'Now hurry, and see to it that the Lord of the Heavens clears his heavenly castle for me! I have been at the end of the world and have left a sign there!'

Buddha scolded: 'Infamous ape! How dare you claim that you have left my hand? Take a look and see whether or not 'The Great Saint Who Is Heaven's Equal' is written on my middle finger!'

Sun Wu Kung was terribly frightened, for he saw at first glance that this was the truth. Outwardly he pretended that he was not convinced, said he would take another look, and tried to make use of the opportunity to escape. But Buddha covered him with his hand, shoved him out of the gate of Heaven, and formed a mountain of water, fire, wood, earth and metal, which he set down softly on him to hold him fast. A magic incantation pasted on the mountain prevented his escape.

Here the Ape King was obliged to lie for hundreds of years, until he finally reformed and was released, in order to help the Monk of the Yangtze-kiang fetch the holy writings from out of the West. He honoured the Monk as his master, and thenceforward was known as the Wanderer. Guan Yin, who had released him, gave the Monk a golden circlet. Sun Wu Kung was induced to put it on, and it at once grew into his flesh so that he could not remove it. And Guan Yin gave the Monk a magic formula for tightening the ring, should the ape grow disobedient. But from that time on he was always polite and well-mannered.

*Note: Also known as the Monkey King, Sun Wu Kung has his origins in the legends of the White Monkey, from the first millennium BCE. He is an important fi gure in* Journey to the West, *one of the four great classical novels of chinese literature, which inspired the Monkey King Festival held in his name.*